Heed the call of

THE SOVEREIGN SOUL

For yourself take responsibility.

THE SOVEREIGN SOUL

A

STORY OF PERSONAL POWER

CASANDRA HART

CROWN OAK PRESS

The Sovereign Soul-A Story of Personal Power
by Casandra Hart

Printed in the United States of America

ISBN 1-60034-464-X
Registration Number: Txu1-241-909 - May 18, 2005

www.xulonpress.com

Love and blessings
Casandra Hart

DEDICATION

I dedicate this book to my beloved father, who passed away before its completion. His values and wisdom live on with me still, for it was he who taught me, both by word and deed, that to be female was not a liability.

TABLE OF CONTENTS

༄

THEME OF   Each of us comes into this life a sovereign soul,
THE BOOK: gifted with free will and the power to make
choices. In our society, many choose to place
responsibility for their lives outside themselves,
substituting addictions for a true sense of being
alive. This book asks the question, "Why?"

THE ANNIVERSARY WALTZ

Reflecting upon her life, Alexis Alexander
(Lexie), having just ended an abusive twenty-
three-year marriage, asks the haunting question,
"How did it come to this?" So full of life as a
child, so full of her own power, where had she
gone?

THE TAXI STAND

Five years old, feeling abandoned by her father
and fiercely determined to be independent, Lexie

vows that she will never allow herself to feel this pain again.

THE NORTHERN TOWN

Here, Lexie takes her first steps toward abandoning herself. Mistrusting her own insights, she chooses to accept the world as defined by adults.

THE FARM

Our heroine comes face to face with the simultaneous beauty and brutality of nature as life-and-death dramas are played out amidst a farm setting.

THE GAMES CHILDREN PLAY

Dark, destructive sexual energy pulses through this chapter and becomes a theme throughout the novel.

OUT ON A LIMB

While exploring the countryside, Lexie and a friend become the targets of a young man's lust.

THE NEW HOUSE

This chapter brings with it a move and a new friend—Shelley. Awed by the grandness of Shelley's house, Lexie remains ignorant of the nasty family secret lurking within the well-ordered home.

own thoughts and feelings and instead inserts herself into the creations of others.

fill the void inside. Derek's abuse spreads to his children, and Lexie numbs herself with more accomplishment, believing success to be the secret of self esteem.

Foreword

෨

ALL BY MYSELF!

Many times as a child, I was told the story of the great reckoning. It would occur at death when greeted by Saint Peter at the pearly gates. He would want to know how I had spent my time on earth, and, together, we'd have a life review. Of course, I assumed I'd be able to put the best spin on everything I had done or tried to do. It never occurred to me that as I looked over a less than satisfying life, I might be motivated to say, "Saint Peter, I know my life is disappointing and you know what—I did it all by myself! Yep, nobody else had anything to do with it being such a mess! It was all my doing!"

No, somehow, I imagine most of us would offer something that went more like this.

"Saint Peter, I know my life is a bit of a disappointment, but you see my parents didn't support me emotionally, the spouse I picked turned out to be a real jerk, and my kids—what an ungrateful bunch of brats, and that boss of mine—what an idiot! You see, I never had a chance! Nothing went my way. I never got a break! It really wasn't my fault. If only I'd gotten the same advantages as everybody else, my life would have been so much better—blah, blah, blah!"

I pray that when my time comes, I'll have the courage to look at my life and say, "For better or worse, good, bad, beautiful or ugly, this life was mine to create—and I did it all by myself!"

In writing this book, a marriage of fact and fiction, I attempted to heed the call of my soul and take responsibility! I invite you to join me on my journey of self-discovery.

CHAPTER ONE:

THE ANNIVERSARY WALTZ

ॐ

Life is a journey not a destination.
Wade into the stream of being
For in the centre where the current runs deep
There, is the force of life strong and complete.
Not for the timid nor the weak,
For they stand upon the bank
Never to guide the craft of their life,
Only to stand helpless and afraid,
Their inner voices unobeyed.

How had it come to this? she wondered. Sitting there in her night-dress, alone in the backyard gazebo, she allowed the tears to come. The release felt freeing. Startled, she realized she been unable to cry for a long time. Turning her tear-streaked face to the morning sun, she felt its heat. A breeze, like a gentle caress, warmed her, and she felt a quickening inside her.

What had she done? She had finally said the words! Words she had wanted to hurl forth time and time again. Each past wound inflicted had sent her scurrying into her silent self for comfort; yet, there too, a part of her had always raged. Her only consolation a silent promise—

a promise made over and over to one day be free, free from the pain of living a lie. She would never grow old with this!

She did not love him. She never had. Walking down the wedding aisle, at the tender age of twenty, she had known within her this day signalled an ending, not a beginning. His being, his persona, was so powerful, so overwhelming, there had been no room for her. The tentative stirring of her identity snuffed out, she had become a wife, a Mrs., an appendage. From that day on, she had defined herself in terms of another.

Where had she gone? It had been more like a funeral than a wedding—a ritual marking her demise! Handing her power over so sweetly, with just a ripple of uneasiness, the exchange had seemed fair to her. Her identity, her power, traded for protection. Derek would tell her what to do. Derek would take the risks out there in the world. He was male, so of course he was braver, smarter, and more capable, wasn't he?

She remembered. She'd worn the wedding smile as she had posed, danced, eaten, and waited in vain for feelings to come. This was to have been the big day. When was she going to feel? He had pressed his face into hers, kissing her for all to see, and she remembered only wondering how they looked together.

Smiling, nodding, listening as everyone offered congratulations, all the while the panicked question running through her mind. How had it come to this?

Having only taught school for one year, she was just beginning to find independence. Hadn't she painstakingly explained to him just months before she did not want to get married yet? Why had she said, "yet," when she really meant "to you"? Not wanting to hurt his feelings, she had said it as kindly as she could, hoping he had understood, then filed it away under finished business. He obviously had not.

The Christmas before the wedding she remembered well. They'd had a huge fight over money as he demanded she spend less. It was not even his money, and he was telling her what to do with it. Looking back now, there had been so many signs, so many warnings. She had been determined to put an end to it all right after the holidays, not wanting to hurt him at this special time of year. How "nice" she was!

Christmas morning had arrived bright and early, and so had Derek, eager to be included in the ceremony of unwrapping gifts. His family did not make a big thing of Christmas he told her—another clue? Meanwhile, hers had settled in for a morning of laughter, love, and thick rum and eggnog drinks. They did Christmas well!

The gifts were passed out one at a time. Almost all had been given when a large box was presented to her.

Wonderful! she thought, intrigued by its size.

Tearing it open, she found layer after layer of crumpled newspaper inside. Was there nothing in the box? Was this Derek's idea of a joke? No, wait. Her hand fell on a small, blue square, soft and furry to the touch. Derek was giving her jewelry! *How generous,* she thought, *and how unlike him*. Nothing prepared her for what she found. There, twinkling on its velvet cushion, was a ring, not just any ring, but a diamond engagement ring! Her face fell. He hadn't even asked her if she wanted to marry him. She hadn't had the chance to say yes or no and now here THIS was, and in front of all her family! How could he? Suddenly she felt she was suffocating in a sea of silent panic. In that breath caught moment, time seemed to stand still.

"Put it on! Let's see how it looks! Oh, it's gorgeous!" Her younger sisters gushed.

The words crowded out all other thoughts as she sucked in her breath and her protests. On her finger the ring went, and as it did she, as she had so often before, slipped into silent, passive safety beneath the turbulence of her feelings. Remaining outwardly, obediently calm, she hid the storm raging within. Managing only a weak smile as her sisters gathered around her, she looked beseechingly at Derek, her eyes wide like those of a frightened, trapped animal as the question was asked.

"When do you think you'll get married?" They all voiced it together.

Rescue me from myself! Her eyes were pleading as they locked onto his face. She left it for him to decide, as without a whimper she handed herself over, too weak to make a scene in front of her family. She must please everyone. Yes, they all seemed so happy at the prospect of a wedding. The first of the four daughters to marry, that was exciting! How could she ruin it all by saying what she was truly feeling? She wanted to scream, "Stop! Wait! I'm not sure!" But, instead she held out her hand obligingly for all to admire her ring, and, through her frozen smile, she heard her mind's frenzied whisper, *I'll think about this tomorrow.*

But, she didn't think. From then on, Derek did that for both of them. "August is a good month," he said casually. "I get two weeks vacation then."

So there it was. Toasts were drunk and the bargain sealed. Events had washed over her and simply carried her along.

Months later as she gazed into her mirror, a frightened young face with a frozen smile looked blankly back at her. Framed in a cloud of white tulle, her image seemed suspended in time, her hand held in mid-air adjusting her wedding veil, a soft plaintiff whisper rippled through her consciousness, "Why are you doing this? This is not the way it should be. There's so much more!"

A question spoken behind her broke the spell and startled her abruptly into motion. The smile flashed instantly again across her face, the soft furrow of concern disappeared from her brow. She was the bride, and all brides were radiantly happy on this day. That was the way the script was written and that was the way it was to play.

"Yes, I'm ready," she answered softly.

Let the dance begin - the wedding dance, the marriage dance, the dance of life where two move as one. Swirling round and round trying to anticipate moves, desires, and needs, trying at once to lead and to follow. Staring into one another's eyes, revealing and yet not revealing. Swirling round and round like figurines on a music box, the day blurred by her—the hushed church, her vows barely whispered as her voice trembled, the long line of guests to be greeted, the sawdust meal in her mouth, the delivery of the small, wrapped pieces of wedding cake given out with best wishes and wooden smile. She was a puppet pulled by society's strings of expectation—a "radiantly happy bride." Then it came. The climactic moment came when the groom led his bride onto the dance floor for all to witness their happiness. Eyes focused on them as they confirmed the joining of their souls. The two would dance as one.

First came the soft strains of the violins, and Derek nervously took her hand. Always greatly concerned with the correctness of his actions, he did not enjoy being the centre of attention. To do something less than perfectly would be a great embarrassment. He had chosen her as his partner in the dance of life because she was beautiful, and he was envied with her at his side.

His arm encircled her waist, leading her through the steps of the waltz. Self-conscious and awkward at first, she was far more concerned with how she was handling herself than with feeling the emotions of the moment. The tenor's rich voice encircled her and the words slowly penetrated. They had chosen an old tune, a traditional song, "The Anniversary Waltz." As the melodious strains proclaimed enduring love, she knew, and the knowing made her dead inside, this was not truly their song. The dance was wrong. It was all wrong. There was no feeling here. It was never going to happen. There was only absence of feeling, a dullness, an emptiness. The realization hit her in waves as Derek turned her about the room. She danced on. She smiled on, as the skilful puppeteer pulled the strings. Feeling dizzy, ill, and sick of heart, her thoughts raced seeking refuge. She knew what she had to do. It was all she could do! Tomorrow, it would all be different! Tomorrow she would feel!

The dancing ended. Guests continued to eat, drink, and laugh uproariously, not noticing the bride and groom as they left to change. Upstairs in their hotel room alone, Derek watched her undress, not touching her, for that would not have been proper. He could wait. She remembered him remarking on her thinness. He had always been so proud she was slender. As she stood gazing into the mirror, the image looking back was perfect. She matched from head to toe in her "going away outfit."

Downstairs once again, they entered into the large, welcoming circle of wedding guests waiting to bid farewell. Uplifted by the harmony and happiness of the music, the new bride and groom, surrounded and supported by the laughing, loving voices of family and friends, made their way from couple to couple kissing cheek after tear-streaked cheek. Suddenly then, it was over. There was no more happiness to be had. The huge doors of the banquet hall slammed shut behind them, and they stood alone in the void—the sound of the echoing doors to live in her memory for years.

Just the two of them, she could no longer hide in the activity of the day! No longer could she borrow others' aliveness. A deadened, breathy whisper became her epitaph:

"This is all there is.

Freedom foregone, numbness filling every pore.

Long live the marriage, but the bride is no more."

Yes, that's how she'd arrived here exactly twenty-three years ago.

On their anniversary she'd said the words. Softly, tentatively, she'd spoken as he had reached to have his needs met. Firmly, she'd removed his hand from her thigh and it had begun.

"Where do I start, Derek?" Pausing, she drew in a great breath and then plunged in. "I just can't do this any more! It's . . . it's not what . . . I want." Closing her eyes tightly against the pain, she had whispered, "It's over. I don't want to hurt you, but I can't go on living this lie any longer." Then hesitating, her voice quivering, she fought for the courage finally to end it.

"How do I say this?" Sucking in a great breath, she at last sent the words forth in one long anguished cry, "God help me, Derek, I want a divorce!"

He had been oh so silent, not making a sound - only a sharp intake of air into his lungs when she had begun and now, nothing. The momentum of her beginning had pushed her on, words bottled up for so agonizingly long had taken on a life of their own. Their meaning hung now like a palpable presence between them.

Then it was finished. There was nothing more to say. Lifting herself from the bed, she had pulled her robe around her and quietly slipped down the stairs and out into the silent back yard. It was a glorious morning, the sun already shining, the roses in full bloom, and the water of the pool glistening like a jewel. She had worked so hard for all of this and yet she knew it had been in vain. It was like slicing open a plump, perfect piece of fruit only to find the core rotting. She'd lived the dream—two beautiful children, a big house, swimming pool, fur coats, world trips, career, yes, it had all been there, but the centre had been wrong, so wrong. She had built it around the wrong man, the wrong relationship, and, try as hard as she might, she would never be able to make it right. The fruit of her labours left a bitter taste in her mouth.

Surveying her domain again, she wondered, *Could she give all this up? Would she have to?* Somehow, at this point, those questions just didn't seem to matter.

She was free! At least the beginnings of freedom were there, she knew. It would not be easy, for the tentacles of his hold were interwoven with the very essence of her being.

How had that happened she wondered? Why had she abandoned herself to this cold, distant man? How had it all come to pass? She'd been so full of life as a child—so full of her own power. Where had it gone? The question sent an uncomfortable shudder through her body and her mind whispered in its old familiar way, "I'll think about it tomorrow."

Something inside her snapped.

"No," came the quiet response. "Today."

CHAPTER TWO:

THE TAXI STAND

⤳

For in the child there is a power,
To be unfettered and free.
To see what more in the world might be,
For in the passage of our days,
Forgetfulness descends like a haze.

The lonely little figure stood dwarfed by the tall standard that bore the service station logo. At a glance it appeared to be a young boy, but closer inspection revealed a small, pale female form. Her hair the colour of wheat, soft, short, and wispy, it blew about her face as if it had a mind of its own. Cut short and blunt, it framed a small, pale face punctuated by large brown eyes speckled with gold. Her body was slight, clothed in overalls, T-shirt, and jacket. This was her favourite mode of dress, for it allowed her the freedom to roam unencumbered. She looked like a boy and she walked and talked like a boy. The male energy of doing suited her well. Today, though, she was not doing. Stopped in her tracks, she was feeling. Today she was in pain.

The day was grey and bleak. The large metal disc bearing the red and white "Star" emblem creaked and groaned, swaying from its supports high above her head. The dullness of the day and the mournful sounds of the sign matched her mood. She felt grey and she felt buffeted by the events impacting upon her - events over which she had no control, for she was a child, only a child. One who was not consulted about the happenings of her life.

Her father was going away. That's all she knew. She felt chilled by the day, but she did not think to pull her collar up closer around her neck for warmth. Instead she stood and shivered, her eyes wide against the paleness of her skin. The tears stung behind them and her stomach tightened into a deep knot. She felt herself about to cry, to open the floodgates and let the emotion of hurt and anger rush forth. "How could he do this to me!" a voice clamoured inside her head.

Clenching her small fists, she tightened her face in pain. She let the anger wash over her, and she felt a rush of hot, prickly heat engulf her body. Stiffening in response, she thrust her chin bravely skyward, her eyes held tightly closed against the stinging tears. Standing rigid for several moments, she became lost in the strange mix of feelings, fiercely determined not to cry.

Then an unusual thing began to happen. It was as if the sun, missing from the day, had found its way inside her! Gradually a warm glow radiated from the centre of her body. It spread its heat slowly, softly, creeping to her very outer parts. She sensed fluid light behind her eyes, its brightness slowly expanding until it filled her head, as if it were liquid gold being poured gently into her, bathing her in calm safety. She heard two voices, intertwined, gently calling her name, urging her to open her eyes.

Without fear, she knew to obey the voices. Feeling a gentle touch on her shoulder, she turned her head slightly, lifting her chin expectantly upward, and her field of vision took in a large, gentle-looking being with eyes of all-encompassing love. Gradually she became aware there were two beings with her. She did not know how she knew they were friends. She just did. They moved in a soft and gentle way, flowing effortlessly around her and speaking without moving their lips. Yet she knew all they were "saying" to her. They had come from the light inside her head, she knew that, for they glowed just as the light behind her eyes had glowed. They looked like people she saw everyday, towering over her as all adults did, but she did not feel threatened by them. Instead, they stood on either side of her as pillars of support, gently reaching out their hands for her to hold and their touch was soft warmth like slipping one's hand into silk. With them smiling down at her, she felt connected. All of what she was somehow was part of all they were. For a brief instant, a flash of time, their energies moved in and out of her. With the final whispered phrase, "Fear not. We are one," they slipped softly, silently away just as effortlessly as mist is taken up into sun-warmed air.

Somehow, she knew she wasn't to tell anyone about this encounter. This wonderful secret was to be taken deep within her, for to tell of it would diminish it.

Their warmth still around her, her practical little mind wrenched her back to the reality of the present. Clicking in impatiently, annoyed, it said, "Enough of this daydreaming. They are not real! They're not here in this place where pain is everywhere—where you can be happy only in little bits, only long enough for the next bad thing to happen to you!"

Not questioning their visit or their message, she knew she would never be truly alone, but she also understood they could not help her deal with this place. Her quest was to discover why she was here and how to live with pain.

Her body stiffened, her chin thrust itself out, and her fist clenched once again. Yes, it was wonderful to have seen these special beings, but without them here now, she must decide how she was going to be in her world! Her world where those you loved with all your heart went away and left you without telling you what you had done wrong. Her world was a place she needed protection from!

She would NEVER again allow herself to feel this pain! She realized if she could not control the actual events, she could control the way she felt! Even if those she loved abandoned her, she would believe she was special! She was all she needed! No one, NO ONE, would ever get close enough to hurt her this way again! Fierce in her intent, she reasoned if she never needed anyone, she could never again be abandoned!

Digging roughly at the ground with her toe, she sealed her bargain—a pact with herself. Her motto became, "I can do it alone!"

Prodded by pain, her fierce sense of independence had been born.

Two more eyes and ears were opening to this world, becoming aware of their physical separateness and feeling the pain of that knowledge. Small, blonde, boyish Alexis Laird Alexander was this day aware she was no longer a part of someone else. Here, in this earthly place, where special, shimmering friends could not stay, she was waking up to find herself alone—a strange, awake little one in a foreign, sleepy land!

She wandered back to the sturdy old stone building that housed her family—HER family. It had been a wonderful family up to now, she'd thought. She had been the centre around which everything had revolved. Had not her father and mother been put on this earth to meet her needs? Now, for the first time, she was questioning what had seemed so obvious to her before. Her father was going away and she didn't understand what she had done to bring it about. Didn't he love her any more? Oh yes, there had been talk of job opportunities elsewhere now that the business was failing, but none of that made sense to her five-year-old mind. She was the centre of the universe. If anything went wrong in her world, it had to be her fault. That was what she knew. That was the truth she had gleaned from her short years upon this planet.

Gone would be the daylong jaunts in the taxicab with her father. Trips when she had happily accepted the role of "tip gatherer," having had the privileged spot of co-pilot, seated in the front seat, as he skilfully drove his cab and chatted. Inevitably the moment she loved most would come. The customer would make a remark about the adorable, well-behaved little girl. They would always stress what a great help she was and her chest would swell with pride. Yes, he was her father and he was wonderful too, for he shared these trips with her. And the part she liked second best always came at the end of the ride. This was when they would reach into their pockets and find, "a small something for the cute little girl." She well knew the value of this "something." It could be traded for all manner of delicious things at Goodies Grocery. But even better, it was often saved, for there were times when this powerful little being could walk into the concession stand of her father's gas station and, reaching into the cold, icy water of the cooler, pull forth any bottle of soda she wanted—and for nothing! The shelves too were her domain, as long as Mother was not around, that is. Shelves full of chocolate bars, potato chips, licorice whips, and all things a hungry child's dreams were made of.

That was also part of her perfect world. Mother was not around much. She had her father to herself and could do what she wanted most of the time. Mother was busy with a new little intruder. She had heard people refer to this intruder as her sister, but as far as she was concerned, she wanted nothing to do with her—she took up Mother's time. That was bad enough, but at least she didn't interfere with her time with Father and that made the situation tolerable. She had become used to not having her mother around. Recognizing early on the glazed look in her eyes, she knew instinctively that, even though her physical needs were being met, it was as if she were being cared for by a machine. Though fed and clothed, she was not nourished with loving looks and soft touches. Buried somewhere deep in thought, her mother was away wrestling her own demons.

She was a wise little being, this Lexie. That's what everyone said about her and that's what everyone called her when they said it. She supposed that Alexis Laird Alexander was just too long for most people to bother with. Besides, in her family, it was tradition for the firstborn to take their Christian name from their surname. It had been so with her father and with her. She especially liked the fact that, because her father was referred to as "Lex," she had become, "Little Lex" or "Lexie." That really pleased her, for she loved her father so!

He had been away for so long now it was as if he had ceased to exist, appearing only for short visits now and again, and not having much time for her. He was so often locked away with Mother behind a closed bedroom door, Lexie could only hear the soft murmuring of their voices. They had moved to a small house in the northern part of the country. Gone was the family business, and her father now spent his time following whatever work could be found. A new intruder, in the form of a second sister, had arrived, and Mother devoted long hours to the care and feeding of these siblings. Lexie learned early that Mother appreciated her independent and solitary ways.

Young Lexie was to be buffeted by the winds of change once more. Not only was there a new home, but she was about to go to a new place called "school"!

The tall teacher barked out some commands to the children ahead of her. The other students seemed to know what they were doing and that frightened Lexie, for she didn't. It was as if everyone was privy to a special secret and they weren't about to share it with her. Fear gripped the pit of her stomach. Was she the only one who didn't know what to do? What if she did something wrong? What if she was shamed for making a mistake? Her palms were sweaty, her stomach churned. So this was school?

This, she learned, was a place where one did not make errors, for the harsh-looking lady at the front of the class obviously did not appreciate nor reward them. She appeared to be just a voice to Lexie, a voice jolting her harshly out of her reveries. She was so intrusive, always telling, telling, telling, never letting you figure things out for yourself, always instructing you on what to do and how to do it. Was there always just one right way to do things—her way? The wise little one inside of Lexie decided she would do what was required in order to appease this cold, sterile woman, but only that. She gave nothing more of herself. Alone in the world of her head, she was free to think her own thoughts and hold her own opinions. Occasionally, something going on around her would catch her interest and she would join in, but mainly she was content unto herself and her first few months of school passed leaving her landscapes of belief undisturbed enough.

Yet on this particular day, as the class had been settling in after their extended Christmas holiday, the teacher had stepped to the front of the room and wrote the date in large, bold figures across the blackboard—"Welcome back! Today is January 3, 1953"—and that had certainly got Lexie's attention! The numbers literally jumped off the slate at her. 1953! This was new to her, to be aware of the passage of time. This was a brand new year. What was a year? How had it felt? It had seemed like it had been 1952 forever. She had assumed it was a permanent condition, this 1952!

1953 became known in her memory as the "Lifebuoy Soap Year." It was the year she learned that not only did events impact upon her, but she impacted upon events by the way she chose to respond. A lesson in life all neatly wrapped up in a bar of soap.

It was late afternoon and school was letting out. Young Lexie was glad because she had found nothing of interest and besides a far more exciting event awaited her on the long walk home. She lived in a rural community and horses were not an uncommon sight. Horses made her heart skip a beat, for she thought them to be the most magnificent of creatures. This particular day, as she rounded the bend in the driveway leading to the main road, she saw before her a well-muscled team dutifully hauling a hay wagon. Following along behind the wagon was a group of noisy, active boys from her school. Boys who were definitely higher up in the social pecking order, but Lexie, being an isolated and independent soul, was yet unaware of such social convention. All she knew was that she had to get closer to those horses!

She called out to the boys following the wagon. Surely they would make it stop so she could catch up? She was just as important as they were, wasn't she? She deserved an opportunity to pet and stroke those beautiful manes and feel the animals' hot, moist breath as they snorted and blew air in her face, their heads bobbing up and down in response to her welcome touch. Calling out to them again to wait, this time her agitation grew as it began to dawn on her they had no intention of slowing down or even acknowledging her presence. As she saw those majestic creatures moving further and further away, her frustration reached panic level. Didn't anyone know how important this was to her? Couldn't they see it, hear it in her strident little voice?

Then it happened. Her anger bubbled over and tumbling out of her mouth came a string of obscenities which would have made the most hardened backroom boy sit up and take note! The words just felt right. They released her sense of sheer helplessness and a self-satisfied refrain echoed in her mind.

"Well, I guess I let them know how I felt even if I didn't get to pet those horses!"

Even while settling into this sense of smugness, an uncomfortable feeling that all was not well began to come over her. Her chin had been tucked down on her chest and she had been smiling to herself as she swaggered along. Very slowly, she felt her eyes instinctively tugged upward. Also very slowly, as her field of vision expanded, there came into view the figure of a woman, hands firmly placed on her hips, standing on her front porch surveying the situation, a grim look on her face. In that moment of recognition, Lexie felt an ice-cold hand grip her stomach and hold it tight. It was Mother on the porch!

It was then that she first became intimate with a bar of Lifebuoy soap! Literally pulling her daughter by the ear into the bathroom, Mother grimly set about scrubbing her cussing cherub's mouth out with the foul-tasting substance. The tears of humiliation stung Lexie's eyes burning as hot as the physical pain. No matter what, she wouldn't cry, she whispered over and over to herself. What had she done that was so wrong anyway? She had only used words she had heard others use, and they seemed to work so well in letting the energy of those pent-up feelings explode outside of you. The release made you feel so much better! She thought these words were a wonderful invention. Why was mother so upset? Bewildered, she walked down the hall to her bedroom, the realization beginning to take shape. In this adults' world, children were often punished for showing their true feelings. And so Lexie learned to put the first layers of her "mask of politeness" into place. The expressive, exuberant, alive little six-year old had internalized another signpost of her lifelong journey, learning how to "play dead" to her feelings of anger.

1953 continued to unfold uneventfully enough. The small, two-story house they had rented was warm and cosy, even though Mother often descended into the cold and damp basement to do battle with an ancient, coal-eating monster known as a furnace. Worried and distracted, the sound of her laughter did not ring out in the little house often. With Father gone most of the time and Mother tucked away in the back bedroom feeding the baby, the rooms echoed with emptiness for Lexie. Perhaps it was borne of this sense of loneliness that Lexie, the independent one, devised a way to bring fame and glory to herself and her family.

It only seemed logical to her. The story she concocted was a perfect fit. People, in that nosey way they had, were always asking where her father was. She wondered the same thing herself. Picturing him in her mind's eye in his long trench coat, his fedora pulled cockily down over one eye, and with his mysterious comings and goings, it really did seem possible he could be the infamous bank robber, Alonzo Boyd, whose name was splashed all over the newspapers. After all, each time he arrived home he brought them money, didn't he? He was also her father, her protector and her hero, so of course he would have to have a good reason for being away from her so much, wouldn't he? It all seemed so logical that he was out there outsmarting the police, pulling off great feats of bravery in order to provide for his family, especially his tiny, blonde-haired co-pilot.

It was really amazing too that all the other kids understood how it was very possible her dad could be this brave and mysteriously powerful man. All of a sudden her life at school became so much easier! Always included at recess now, everyone was so nice to her. Kids whispered about her as she walked by, and soon the newly-informed classmate would be offering a share of their lunch in order to hear more of the details of her father's exploits—details Lexie had absolutely no difficulty supplying.

All good things must come to an end it has been said, and so too did Lexie's privileged position. Somehow, in ways seemingly mysterious to her, her parents came to know what she was up to. Mother and Father, as well as most of the town, were now aware of her "infamous" father's exploits. It had caused excitement, to say the least, and a great deal of attention had been focused on her! Slowly, however, the realization began to dawn. People expected you to keep your fantasies to your self. It made no difference if your heart ached to make them true. No matter that she had been desperately reaching for something, anything, to make her feel loved and important. Yes, feel important, feel like she mattered, feel the exhilaration of other people's admiration! It had been absolutely wonderful while it lasted. She had been a star!

Somehow, though, the pain of humiliation really wasn't felt. It was as if she had enjoyed the glory, and, when the time came to own up to her dishonesty, any feelings of guilt simply rolled off the shield around her just as water beads up on a protective plastic bubble. She felt no shame at having lied, for to her it wasn't really a lie. She had wanted it so badly that to her it had been her truth—her reality. And now she let that reality slip away as she accepted the truth everyone else seemed to accept. Was it not true then that you could shape your own experiences with your thoughts? The belief you could had echoed somewhere deep inside her. Was this then the lie? Did she not, after all, have the power to impact her life through the energy of wishing and hoping? Desire, then, seemed not to be enough. Sadly, slowly, she let this belief in her power of creation slip away. Perhaps the adults were right. She had to accept life as it came. Not to her, or anyone, was given the ability to change events through wishful thinking alone. Stubbornly, though, a small part of her still suspected that what the adults believed was the lie. In some way she truly did have the power to shape her reality with her thoughts, but she also knew that, for now, she was to take this knowing deep within her, for it would neither be accepted nor appreciated by anyone around her.

Life returned to normal and Lexie retained some of her newly won friends. Ruth and Pia were as unalike as two girls could be. Ruth was small and slight of build, with round, soft eyes, wispy dark hair, and a sweet, endearing way about her. Pia was heavyset, with seeking, searching eyes, blunt, boyish hair, and a rasping, intrusive voice. It was as if they were two sides of a coin. Totally opposite in their way and yet part of the same whole, as if neither was a complete way of being. Perhaps this was why Lexie chose them for friends—their qualities complimented one another. From each one she learned very different lessons in being. Ruth led her to trust others in friendship. In her sweet and gentle way, she touched a part of the tough little independent one, sharing her secret thoughts, laughing with her as if in possession of some special knowledge, and revelling in the ease of being. Their time together was spent in long, lazy days, lying back on soft fuzzy grass, surrounded by golden sunlight.

Pia had a darkness about her with an energy Lexie felt seductively calling to her. There was a "knowingness" about Pia's ways which beckoned, drawing her into its swirling vortex, holding her mesmerized as one troubling revelation after another unfolded in front of her. A strange energy emanated from Pia, and she was so anxious to tell you things—horrible, fascinating things that kept you stuck like a fly on flypaper.

The sand in the sand box was cold and gritty in her hands this day. She was with Pia and she was staring in wide-eyed horror! Her throat and mouth felt as if she had been eating the sand, and her stomach was retching. The wind whipped her hair into her face, stinging her eyes, and she heard her quivering voice ask, "What do you mean he jumps on top of her?"

Pia responded, "Oh, you know. When the father jumps on the mother in bed at night."

No, she didn't know. What was Pia talking about? She listened in wide-eyed fascination and disbelief. More. She felt sickeningly compelled to hear more!

Pia didn't need any prodding, happy to rattle off all the compelling details.

"Oh ya, I hear my folks every night. The bed squeaks like crazy and I think my dad gets up at the top of the bed and then he jumps down on my mom and then they roll around a lot. You know what else? I don't think they have any clothes on either!"

This last bit of information really sent Lexie reeling. No clothes! *Who in their right mind would take their clothes off in front of anyone but their mother?* she thought. Even Mother was expected not to look directly at you when you were getting undressed. That wouldn't be polite. Two naked bodies rolling around on a bed was just too horrendous to believe! And what's more, Pia said they laughed and giggled a lot while they were "doing it." That meant they enjoyed "it"! What "it" was was not elaborated on, for even the all-knowing Pia squirmed a bit when pressed for further explanation.

Lexie had not even had a chance to recover from this incredible revelation when Pia was off and running on a new topic. This grey, bleak sandbox day was obviously earmarked for education!

"And you know what else, Lexie? Your mom and dad are Santa Claus!"

The words went off like a bomb in her head. What! That just couldn't be true! She wanted to stuff something in Pia's mouth to stop the gushing out of all these horrible things. Take it back! Take it back! She wanted her to never have had said them! But, on and on Pia went.

"There's no Easter bunny either, you know. Your parents do it all. And, oh yeah, I saw my mom putting money under my sister's pillow for her tooth!"

My God, thought Lexie. *Is nothing sacred?*

Would it have been too much to hope she could have given it to me in small bits? Lexie thought. Sort of the way she went at eating the liver on her plate? You know, a small bite here, well-chewed, before she got up enough courage to attempt the next piece.

Yet, even as this thought ran through her mind, the sense of horror strangely seemed to be dissipating moment by moment. After all, Pia knew all this "stuff," and she was still walking around alive. No, better still, Pia was literally bouncing off walls most of the time. That was just her way. A child in a hurry to grow up, she believed in meeting life head on, even if it meant a few casualties.

Some of those casualties today had been Lexie's most cherished beliefs. Frozen through and through, she scurried home. It was getting dark and a growing sense of loneliness was engulfing her.

Did adults lie to you on purpose? she wondered. *And what was that strange ritual they went through in the bedroom behind closed doors?*

As she pondered, a growing sense of detachment formed. An understanding came that it just wasn't her time to know.

The wind chilled her even more, and she quickened her pace, clutching her jacket collar tightly up around her neck. Becoming aware of her bare feet frozen in her thin sneakers, tears sprang from a deep sense of feeling sorry for herself. Sorry that she had to walk alone shivering in the cold. Sorry that life itself could often feel like a lonely, cold journey home. Those adults! What could you believe anyway?

Then she sensed it. She was almost there. She could see the glow of soft, warm light from the kitchen where Mother would be busy cooking dinner. Suddenly, she understood what adults were for. Sure, maybe you couldn't trust them all the time on the little things, but somehow the kitchen light glowing through the darkness was a sign for her—a concrete, tangible piece of evidence that someone was waiting for her.

CHAPTER THREE:

THE NORTHERN TOWN

I knew who I was once long ago.
In the distant mists of childhood
I met myself.
Then I saw again what I became,
For in the unfolding midst of power and pain,
I no longer was the same.

It fascinated her that it was illegal to pick flowers! Wasn't that why these glorious things carpeted the forest floor? Her mother had spoken to her in serious hushed tones, that, although she loved the bouquet, she was never, ever to pick them again. This world was a strange place, Lexie thought. You really didn't know what to expect of adults most of the time. She remembered how excited she had been when she'd stumbled upon the carpet of white blooms filling the woods as far as she could see. It was as if they were begging to be picked, offering themselves up so to speak. She gathered her treasure, already in anticipation of her mother's smiles! Instead here she stood, terrified she was to be carted off to jail for picking trilliums, the protected flower of the province! Jail's what happened when you did something "illegal" she'd been told. Mother must have sensed her terror, for she started to speak more softly, telling her that it was all right "this time," but not to do it again. Mothers could be so wonderful at making things turn out right sometimes, Lexie thought. It gave her a lovely, warm feeling to know her parent was wise and powerful enough to keep her from suffering the horrors of jail!

The woods held other surprises that spring. Her family had settled in a small northern tourist town with plenty of fresh water lakes surrounded by thick bush. Consequently, the small rented house, although it fronted on a main road, had dense forest for its back yard. Lexie loved to roam in this still, quiet place full of the scent of pine and filled with comforting, muted light. It was as if the tree boughs formed a canopy overhead, and the stillness beckoned her to stop, sit with her back propped against a sturdy tree trunk, and watch the flickers of sunlight play upon the forest floor. Sometimes though, as daylight was waning, she would sense this could also be an ominous place. Waiting to burst forth were secret, dark energies. So it was one evening.

Their tiny family was seated at the dinner table. From her vantage point, Mother could see through the window in the top of the door and onto the side porch. Her gaze had been transfixed there for a few moments now as Lexie had eagerly been eating her supper— cold, white bread sandwiches. A beanpole of a kid, she was growing rapidly and had a "hollow leg," her mother said. She just shrugged that off as one of those dumb sayings adults said that never made sense. All she knew was she was particularly hungry and looking forward to devouring the rest of her meal when Mother yelled, "Look over there! What's that?"

Lexie of course got up from her chair to look out the door. Was Mom going crazy? There was nothing there. When she sat back down, there was nothing on her plate either! Worse yet, neither her mother nor her three-year-old sister acted as if anything had happened, but she knew she had been tricked. How unfair people could be, even those who loved you! Resigning herself to staying hungry that night, for there was no more to be had, she saw a look of horror cross her mother's face.

Serves her right for eating my sandwich! thought Lexie. *I guess she's feeling really sorry now.*

Slowly, though, the reality of the situation began to penetrate. Her mother's attention was focused on the side door, and she was frantically whispering to herself.

"Oh my God, there's something out there. Why is your father never here at a time like this?"

This was serious Lexie knew, if Mother was calling for God's help! Up out of her chair, manoeuvring quickly around the table, Mother picked the baby up, grasped her under the armpits and yanked the crying infant out of the high chair. Meanwhile, issuing orders over her shoulder, she disappeared down the hallway.

"Don't move! And for God's sake, don't go near the door!"

Against the baby's wailing protests, she laid her in the crib, firmly closing the door behind her. Returning to the kitchen, she appeared somewhat calmer but, eyes still wide with fear, she gathered Lexie and her younger sister close to her and said, "All right, dears. Be real quiet, will you?"

With her head buried in her mother's skirt, Lexie couldn't have answered even if she'd wanted to. Soon jolted from this place of safety by a sudden crashing and scraping sound coming from the side porch, they were thrust aside as Mother threw herself against the door. Did she believe she could stop whatever was out there from invading their small kitchen? What was out there, anyway? It was black as an abyss, and absolutely nothing could be seen. If Mother knew what danger was lurking, she wasn't telling.

"It's the liver! It's got to be the liver!" Mother breathed the words quietly as she stood with her eyes closed. "How could I have been so stupid to put it out there?"

Now, Lexie hated liver as much as the next person, but this seemed to be carrying things to extremes. Besides, liver made you feel sick with horrible growling noises inside your stomach. It did not explain the grunts and growls coming from the side porch!

Mother suddenly leapt away from the door as if it had become alive. It was moving in and out, straining against its hinges.

"Oh my God! It's trying to get in at us! I don't believe it. It's actually trying to get in at us!"

What was? Lexie finally found her voice.

"What is it, Mom?"

Her words barely audible, her mind racing, she tried desperately to make sense of the events swirling about her.

"Lexie, it's all right." Mother seemed to focus on her for the first time now.

"It's a spring bear, honey. You know. They're really hungry out of hibernation, and I guess the liver I put out last night attracted him. I never meant to keep it out so long, but I forgot it today. I was so busy with the baby. Besides, if we could afford a refrigerator we wouldn't have to worry about running out of ice for the icebox and having things spoil. I just wish your father was here!"

The last sentence hadn't really been directed at Lexie. Mother seemed so lost in this train of thought she barely heard her whisper, "Mom, I think it's gone."

"Do you think so?" She looked up hopefully, stopped breathing, and listened intently for a few moments. There was only silence.

"Oh thank God. I think you're right."

Then a strange thing happened. She straightened herself to her full height, smoothed out her skirt, and calmly started clearing away the supper dishes from the table as if nothing had happened.

"I guess you should go upstairs and get ready for bed, Lexie," she said. Just like that. As calm and cool as could be.

Fear had gone as quickly as it had come. The danger passed, they had survived untouched, and little had changed except for two very important things in Lexie's mind. She was still upset about the unfairness of her disappearing food, stung by her mother's trickery, but as she climbed the stairs to her bedroom the second thought caused a smile to slowly creep across her face in the semidarkness.

The liver had disappeared too!

The next day dawned bright, brisk, and sunny. It seemed spring was busy arriving. Mother was up early scrubbing the bloodstains left behind as the hungry spring bear had dragged the pounds of liver, devouring it as he went.

Mother would be busy for some time, so Lexie set about thinking of something she could do. Her younger sister, Tessy, who was three, came stumbling into the kitchen sleepily rubbing her eyes.

"Whatcha doin', Lexie?"

Tessy (she always appeared just too tousled for the formal name of Theresa) was dark of hair and eyes, with permanently rosy cheeks and lips and a plump, round little body that invited squeezing. She was definitely a cuddler and had no trouble at all sliding onto your lap when a hug was needed only to slide off again and go contentedly on about her business. A large part of that business was stubbornly following her older sister around. Lexie really wanted nothing to do with this little person, whom she saw as competition for her parents' affection.

This particular day, though, Lexie had a plan, and the plan required a partner. Mother was busy, the baby was too little, and so that left Tessy. Talking her into it would be easy. The more she ignored Tessy, the harder her sister tried to please her. Like an affectionate puppy, she tagged after her everywhere, convinced her older sister's world was an exciting place to be, even if it meant you had to do what you were told.

It was a perfect day for a tea party Lexie had decided, but not an ordinary tea party. This one was to be held outdoors like the picnic her family had gone on last summer.

There was one thing she knew for sure. This tea party was not going to take place on the ground with all the ants and bugs as uninvited guests! This gathering was going to happen at a proper table with proper chairs, and for that, she needed help.

Up the stairs to her bedroom she bounded. There, by the window, stood the old table and chair set used for many a child's tea party. One glance out the upstairs window to the small figure waiting below confirmed it in her mind. This plan would work! She was sure of it.

Hoisting the window up, she propped a stick under it to hold it open, then turned to eye the size of the table and chairs. They would fit through easily. No need to carry them all the way down when this was so much faster. Besides, Tessy was there waiting to catch it all just as she had told her to. The plan was foolproof!

"Here it comes!" she yelled triumphantly as the first chair sailed through the air hitting the ground with a thud.

"Wow, this is great!" Lexie thought to herself, winding up for the next toss. So fast and easy and what a sense of power she felt! She could get to like this throwing furniture around!

"Bombs away!" Exuberantly, she sent the next chair flying, beginning to feel sorry there were only four in the set. Maybe she could bring them all back up and do it again—even invite the kids next door to try it out! Tessy seemed to be enjoying it too, squealing with delight as each chair hit the dirt and went bouncing down the embankment at the side of the house.

Excitedly, Lexie reached for the third chair, swinging it high over her head to get maximum force. Her body tensed, the muscles in her thin little arms ready to explode forward when she was stopped mid-swing by a sharp, angry sound behind her.

"Alexis Laird Alexander! You put that down right this minute or else!"

Eyes widened in fear, her nostrils flared open, she strained to suck in more air. It seemed as if everything in her system had stopped, freezing her to the spot. Slowly, very slowly, she brought the chair down and placed it on the floor in front of her. Not daring to turn around, she knew what waited for her. It had been Mother's voice thundering behind her and what was more, she had used her full name. When that happened, Lexie knew there was no way she could charm her way out. She had been caught "red handed."

"Where had the plan gone wrong?" she wondered. "Hadn't Mother been too busy to notice?" Unknown to her, Mother had returned to the kitchen, where in the middle of washing dishes, she'd been startled to see a small chair go sailing by the window! It was immediately followed by another and from outside had come the Tessy's gleeful voice.

"Lexie, do it again! Do it again!"

Needless to say, she did not do it again. Nor did she do much else that day as she was restricted to her room and not allowed any visitors. A day begun so promisingly passed slowly and uneventfully. Mother went on about her chores, Tessy soon went for a nap, and Lexie contented herself with the fact that she was still able to sit in comfort for Mother had settled on a scolding this time. Lexie sat quietly in her room basking in the exhilaration generated by putting her bold plan into action. It had been well worth banishment, she thought!

Months passed in this northern town and Lexie's time was marked by the passage of August's summertime picnics; September's discovery of squiggly marks on a page that made the sounds of words; October's trick or treating in snow up to her ankles; December's eagerly awaited visits to local stores for Christmas shopping; January's daily struggles with an unyielding winter snowsuit; through to April's walks home in the soft springtime drizzle. She was content with her life, her surroundings friendly and familiar. From each day she had come to know what to expect. But not this day it turned out!

They were moving.

Mother said the words so matter-of-factly Lexie knew there was nothing she could do. No point in saying anything, for what she felt would make no difference. The pain in her heart would have choked off her words anyway. Her throat closed tightly as the tears started to sting her eyes.

"Are you okay, honey?" Mother asked.

She nodded and went to her room. Her feet felt like lead, her whole body heavier. It was so hard being new. Didn't they understand that? Now she would have to be new somewhere else. Crawling onto her bed, she hugged her knees and cried herself to sleep.

Her own gasping woke her panting and sweating! She felt like retching. It was so black in the room! She couldn't see anything. All she could do was listen to the sound of her own breathing. Where was she? What had happened? Her clothes were stuck to her body, and she felt the air moving around her as cool drafts. Shivering, she realized it had been a dream, a horrible, frightening dream. She had to, could not stop herself from, reliving the images in her mind. As she sat in the darkness panting softly, it all began to come back. What the dream meant she did not know, but it had touched her so deeply it had produced sheer terror!

Ordinarily enough it had begun. In her bed, she had become restless because of a need to go to the bathroom. In her dream she walked through the open doorway into the hall where fear froze her mid-step. There, stretched out before her was a body, but not an ordinary body. A hideous long, spindly, white neck stretched down the hall to its farthest end where it joined a bloated, bobbing head.

Grotesque not only in its deformity, but also in its actions, the head, seemingly divorced from the body, was laughing wildly as if mocking her. As its sounds became even more hysterical, the face lunged up at her, its laughter feverishly escalating, its bloated features filling the room. Would she be swallowed up by the gaping mouth, a mouth slashed with bright red like that of a circus clown?

In the horror-filled split second catapulting her from the dream, she knew a terrible truth! That disjointed, mocking thing was her! Even as a child, she knew that in some way she was fragmented. Becoming separated from other parts of her self had caused her terror. The bloated head had grown at the expense of all other parts of the self. Now she lived only in its logical landscapes. Greedily, her mind had choked off all other aspects of being to ensure its survival. No longer would she experience things spontaneously. All would first be funnelled through the mind, for it would accept no less than total control!

Desperately wanting to seek comfort, her mind whispered, *You don't need to. You're all right by yourself. If you let "them" get too close it will hurt. Don't need anyone, for it only makes you feel empty when they leave you.*

Hugging her knees to her chest, she rocked gently back and forth on the bed, staring into the darkness. Only when the first rays of dawn filled the room did she feel safe enough to close her eyes in sleep.

Through the next week, the terror of the dream stayed with her as they prepared to move. Sneaking up on her, flashing through her mind's eye, came that horrible, mocking face. She would shiver and then quickly shut down the sense of terror it produced. Gradually, as the imprint faded, all feelings faded. As heaviness filled her body, she found no joy in doing. Like a disoriented, weighted deep-sea diver struggling to navigate uncharted, resistant terrain, feeling came to be like walking through water—every step carefully measured, forced, and unnatural.

The day came to say her good-byes. It had been easy enough, but she had left Ruth for last. With leaden feet she stepped up onto her porch and tapped lightly on the door. Her friend's face appeared behind the screen while the fingers of one hand wrapped themselves tentatively around the outside edge of it for support. Looking mournful through the mesh, she then slipped out from behind the door to face Lexie. Ruth moved tentatively, instinctively knowing this encounter was to bring pain. Eyes downcast, she shifted from one foot to another twisting her hands in front of her.

"I'm gonna miss you, Lexie," she said.

The words seemed to explode in Lexie's face! Exactly what she wanted to hear, but inexplicably, the soft, tender sounds seared her with a sense of longing. She must stop this pain! Stiffening her body, she took a step back, away from Ruth. Turning away, her voice came out in gruff little puffs. "Ya . . . Gotta go now . . . bye."

Bolting down the steps, she looked back only once to see Ruth's shocked, bewildered face. With wide eyes and open mouth, her friend stared unbelievingly at her callous departure.

Lexie's body kept her moving faster and faster away from Ruth, away from the pain. Connecting with those loving eyes had produced a searing hot hurt.

"Run!" her body said. "Run from these choking feelings that threaten our very survival! Run!"

Her body propelled her forward to a place where there would be no pain.

Ahead she saw the car, its engine running. Everyone was waiting for her.

Reaching for the door handle, she wrenched it open. Slamming herself down on the back seat, she shot a defiant look around. A look which said she wanted to be alone. Her mother had watched her daughter's grim expression as she had thrown herself into the seat. Her eyes pleading with her daughter to need her, then seeing no softening of the expression on her young face, she had sighed resignedly and returned her gaze to the front.

So tough, this one. So unreachable, she thought sadly.

The excitement of leaving overtook the others in the car, and Lexie was left alone with her feelings.

CHAPTER FOUR:

THE FARM

Robin, robin, straining with your quest,
Of the flickering shadows of time, oblivious.
Living only in complete instinctual trust,
That all unfolds as it must.
Do you see that girl of golden hair
Standing watching there?
What is this world you share?
For of the laws of creation and care
Which of you is more awake and aware?

"I'm sorry, honey, but you're just going to have to walk to school. I know it's three miles each way and you're only seven, but we've been told the buses just don't run all the way up here."

Lexie had no comprehension of three miles, but judging by the concerned look on Mother's face, she had a pretty good idea this was going to be hard. She was new again. A new school, a new teacher awaited her. Not new, though, was the gnawing, twisting feeling inside her stomach when she thought about it.

They had come to live in a rented farmhouse, half of which they shared with a Dutch family. It was a farm in the true sense of the word, for it was isolated on a dusty, country road with pastures full of cows all around. Ending at a large stone house, the long driveway was lined with tall, stately pine trees and a sloping front lawn spread out like an apron before it. The yard overgrown, tall grass and a wild tangle of rose bushes lined the place where it met the road. Anything not essential to the running of the farm was left untended, conserving the efforts of the two immigrant brothers and their wives. Unable, even with their love of farming, to make a full enough living, the men supplemented their income by working at the local manufacturing plant. Consequently, they had little time to be interested in the wanderings of a seven-year-old tomboy.

Mother, too, was busy with the care of Lexie's two sisters, and Father was away following work from one jobsite to another.

It was summertime, so long, lazy days were spent discovering what a farm was all about. There were things Lexie absolutely loved about being there! Wiling away many hours lazily gazing up into a cloud-filled sky watching the white puffy shapes drift by, she wondered what clouds were. If you could magically get yourself there, could you fall asleep on one? To her they looked so soft and inviting. At times like this she'd know a sense of completeness, a deep sense of connection. The boundaries of her body blurring, she became less defined, and she felt that, if she really wanted to, if she really let herself, she could just float into all that was around her. It would be so comforting to let go and become one with everything, to just drift in and out of it with the rhythm of her breathing. At these times, it was as if the whole world was breathing with her. The pulse of the earth rose and fell just as her small chest did with each breath. The green of the grassy fields melded into the soft blue of the skies and the velvet grass beneath supported her as all around expanded and contracted with life. She knew who she was and that what she could experience with her limited senses was not all that was, not all that could be. There was more, so much more! A sense of absolute peace would come over her as she understood intuitively this incredible mystery, as well as her place in it, was a wonderful gift for her to unwrap gradually. Discovered a bit at a time, the process even more precious than the gift. It was the gift.

Such soaring times taught her nature's incredible power to inspire, but she was destined to also learn how it could humble.

Her father had treated her to a wonderful toy. He had hung a rope from the lower branch of one of the sturdy, tall trees lining the driveway and to that he had attached an old tire. It was absolutely heaven on earth to sail through the air, higher and higher with each pumping motion of her sturdy legs, her hands firmly grasping the rope. So engrossed with climbing the fence into the pasture over which the swing hung and so eager to go ever higher, she'd failed to notice something different this day. The wind whistled by her ears, accompanied now by another roaring sound. Looking for the source of this new noise, her eyes widened in terror. On this particular day one of the owners had decided to put an empty pasture to use. With horror, Lexie realized what that was!

There it stood, glaring up at her, head following her movements, becoming more agitated with each swing. Pawing the ground, nostrils flared, it snorted short blasts of air.

Lexie knew this animal was not like the docile females she followed in from the pasture each evening. This fierce and unpredictable animal was a menacing male!

Head lowered, it pawed the ground, tension building in its body as it readied for the charge. The pendulum swing had slowly wound down and was coming to rest, its frightened passenger riveted to the rope running through her hands. Staring in wide-eyed horror, sounds roared past her ears. She couldn't move; she couldn't think; she could only stare transfixed.

"Lexie! Get out of there!"

Startled by a human voice, at the same time she became aware of the rattling sound of the wire fence as the farm owner scrambled over it. All she could see were rubber boots covered in straw and mud planted in front of her as she stared at the ground unable to move. Strong hands dug in under her rib cage and hoisted her roughly up over the fence. Landing with a thud on the other side, dazed and out of breath, unceremoniously dumped on her backside, she watched as the strong man threw himself over the fence, the charging bull coming up just short of them. Stopping inches from the wire, it wildly thrashed its head up and down in violent jerking movements, snorted several times in disgust, and, pawing the ground for the last time, turned abruptly and sauntered away.

Her rescuer's breathing was now coming in short, rasping puffs as he bent over, resting his hands upon his knees. When his gaze finally fell upon the wide, frightened eyes of the little figure whom he had rescued, the lines around his piercing blue eyes deepened and his face broke into a wide grin. He ran his large, gnarled hands through his thick, dark hair. Allowing himself a chuckle, he put out a hand to help her up.

"Are you all right, little one?" he asked. "You sure looked scared. I never thought about you using that swing when I put old Brutus in there."

She wasn't able to get her breath enough yet to answer and besides her mouth felt like it was full of cotton, but she knew she was very grateful to this strong, sun-weathered man. She wanted to learn more about this place called a farm with all its pleasures and frights, and he would be just the one to help her in her discoveries.

Managing to nod her head to let him know she was all right, she gradually picked herself up and began dusting herself off.

"Thanks, Frank," she managed to say. All the while her mind racing, she was now determined to learn all there was about this dangerous, exciting "farm" place.

Wandering the pastures alone, she came upon a short, squat apple tree, which became "her" place. Having one low branch which afforded her a foothold, she could hoist herself up to an excellent vantage point. Custom-made for her bottom, from this spot she could survey the fields for miles around. It was a marvel to her that the farther fields really did look greener, just as the adults were always saying. Somehow though, she knew their brilliant green would fade as one came closer. This, she was discovering, could be true of many things in life. Sadly, this beautiful jewel of a world, glistening with perfection in the distance, often appeared flawed through the lenses of familiarity.

One sun-washed evening, as she followed the cows in from pasture, Lexie was to witness the incredible, glorious gift of life, as well as its dark disappointment. She'd been sending up puffs of dirt with her feet as she walked lazily along behind the milk cows, her head bent, lost in her own world of dreams, soothed by the comforting, rumbling lowing of the cows. Closer to the barn, steadily more insistent to be relieved of their heavy burden of mother's milk, their throaty calls intermixed with the muted, rhythmic clanging of the lead cow's bell, producing a soothing cadence which matched Lexie's contented sense of connection with the ebb and flow of all life. For its part in this idyllic scene, the sky too made its contribution, afire in shades of vermilion and burnished gold, pinks and ivories. As if an artist had taken bold strokes across the sky and then, losing herself in complete abandon, had recklessly splashed bucket upon bucket of paint joyously across the canvas of the horizon.

Lexie, jolted from her reverie by a painfully discordant sound, looked up quickly searching for the source. Just ahead was a single cow standing close to the gate. It appeared she had been there for some time, certainly ahead of the herd. Her neck was stretched out and down, her head close to the ground, tongue hanging out of her mouth, eyes rolled back appearing as huge white bulging disks in her spotted face. Panting for breath, she would, from time to time, extend her neck further, bringing her head up and emitting a long, guttural moan that began in her belly and shuddered its way up into her throat, leaving her body quivering and exhausted. Her head would then collapse back, limply hanging to the ground. When she staggered forward a few steps, it was with horror Lexie saw the cause of her discomfort. She couldn't believe what she saw in the dim light. Yes, there could be no doubt about it. Protruding from the opening under the cow's tail were four tiny, perfectly formed hooves! Glistening with moisture, they had hanging from them long, wet, shiny strings of blood and mucus. Lexie had to be mistaken! How could this creature, attempting to give birth, still be walking around with its infant helplessly trapped inside its body?! This situation was not unfolding as it should!

A shout from Frank, hurriedly shepherding the other cows into the barn, let her know he too was concerned. Both the mother and calf were at risk, and he was silently cursing himself for not being around earlier. Now he feared he may lose both. If she stayed quietly in the background, Lexie hoped she might get to watch an incredible event, one that both fascinated and frightened her.

The barn seemed to be full of men. One large, gruff one had rolled up his shirtsleeve and was standing behind the mother, talking to her in soothing tones. Lexie stood unobtrusively behind a rough wooden pillar. Needing its support, she placed her hands on its cool surface and peered from behind it in wide-eyed fascination. The man continued to talk softly to the cow that was too weak to protest his touch. Putting one hand on her rump to steady himself, he plunged the other hand into the opening from which the young legs protruded, his arm disappearing up to his shoulder. Grunting with the strain of his movements, he then slowly began to withdraw his arm only to return it again, this time cursing and straining. Covered in blood from shoulder to fingertips, his image began to blur in front of Lexie's eyes. The barn became suffocatingly hot, closing in around her, all sounds and lights running together in her head, and she clung desperately to the pillar. Just as she felt her knees weaken under her, firm hands grasped her shoulders and a kind female voice said to her, "Come on, little one. I think you've seen enough for tonight."

With that she was led out of the barn and up the gravel walk to the house. Mary, the plump, rosy-faced wife of Frank, had discovered her and decided it was best she didn't stay to see the final outcome. For, as Lexie learned the next day, the calf had died. Early that next morning, she had seen Frank go to the field closest to the barn, shovel in hand. The tiny perfect creature who had struggled so valiantly had failed. This world, incredibly beautiful and abundantly giving, could also, without reason or explanation, deny. That the young creature had spent many months growing and developing, attempting to fulfil its purpose, did not matter. Its life force had simply been extinguished. Even as the earth magnanimously unfolded its incredible bounty, so, too, could life be choked off, cut short. In her heart, Lexie saluted the young life's valiant attempt; but even heroic effort did not guarantee existence, it seemed.

As the days of summer slid lazily by, she became a sun-bronzed nymph. Her hair, a fine, blonde silk caught by breezes, floated up like a halo around her young face. Thin, sturdy limbs carried her everywhere as she roamed freely, spending her days as she chose. But sadly, her sunny sojourn was about to end. School was about to start.

Having had some experience with the place called school at this point, she felt she could take it or leave it, with the preference being to leave it!

Mother, however, had other ideas and set about stressing the importance of taking a direct route, with no detours. Father would drive her the first few days, but after that, she'd be on her own. Her face lined with deep furrows of concern, her mother expressed frustration at the remoteness of the farmhouse. It was all they could afford she knew. Any extra money was squirreled away in the hope of one day buying a home of their own.

The first day Father dropped her off early in front of the new school, a compact, red brick building, skirted by a large yard that was presided over by a generously spreading oak. A sprawling apple orchard, enclosed by a fence easily scaled by students during apple season, was close enough for temptation.

The schoolhouse boasted two entrances, one for the girls and one for the boys. In case there was doubt, the words were carved in stone above each door. At the clang of the bell, girls and boys would dutifully line up, pass through separate doors and walk silently into one large room.

Lexie was awed by its size. Ceilings seemed to reach to forever. Gazing upward, she could see a row of high windows where sunlight streamed in, dust particles floating lazily on shafts of warm, golden light. A hush fell over the room as the students took their seats. This was a place where silence was revered. The children moved noiselessly to their desks and sat upright, rigidly awaiting a sign from the small, bent woman seated at the desk dominating the front of the room. Instinctively, Lexie knew enough to find a seat and to sit quietly, waiting. The scraping of a chair signalled that the white-haired matriarch of this one-room schoolhouse was about to speak.

Her voice rang out with authority. There was absolutely no doubt—she, and she alone, determined what took place amid these high walls. Lexie shifted uneasily in her chair. Not again, she thought. Another adult to tell, tell, tell.

The children were arranged in neat rows of desks from grades one through eight. Lexie was placed with the other second graders. From her spot in the front, she was able to watch the teacher closely. Mrs. Spearing, as she was called, went efficiently about assigning work to all forty of her students. Even the big boys who had been so noisy, swaggering boastfully in the yard, now became silently docile under the eagle eye of this stern woman.

Not tall, but with chalk-white hair swept severely off her face, she appeared imposing enough. Her wrinkled, weathered hands had a slight tremor to them, but piercing blue eyes which would narrow quickly dispelled any impression of infirmity. Her chin jutting forward, a deep furrow would line her brow at the sign of any unnecessary noise in the classroom. Just this imposing look was enough to bring about the required hush of silence. Rarely leaving her desk, she called her pupils to come forth and present their work.

A pulsing sense of fear pervaded the room as minutes ticked by with hushed tones. All were agonisingly careful not to offend the powerful being at the front of the room. Lexie learned to slip silently in and out of her desk, to control her thirst and bladder functions, and to talk only inside her head for to speak to another would bring an instant reprimand.

Three times a day these incarcerated young beings would burst forth from the doors and explode upon the playground. Recesses were for expressing all that had been denied while within the silent walls. This took the form of heatedly contested baseball matches, rushing games of tag, frantic skipping of rope, and as emotion that has been denied too long will bring forth, ugly name calling and fighting. Often, the boys, pushed to the edge of endurance within the classroom, would explode upon one another with angry taunts and find themselves rolling in the dirt, chests heaving, faces streaked with sweaty soil, and collars and sleeves ripped from their shirts. Nor were the girls exempt; their fear was released by lashing out verbally at others. There was one in every crowd, the weak-willed one, the one who cried easily, who could be teased and taunted and provide the others with a sense of release. All this went on unheeded, for in the playground, the eagle eye of "Witch Spearing" did not see, as she rarely left her desk. When the appointed time came for recess to end, she would appear in the doorway, bell in hand, its clanging sound causing each child's stomach to grip in fear. They instantly stopped what they had been doing and scurried dutifully into line, smoothing hair and clothing, adjusting their faces into that set look of expected angelic obedience.

In this yard, children treated one another as they were treated. The model of domination was played out with the older and stronger ones bullishly exerting power over the weaker, thus alleviating their sense of powerlessness.

Lexie made only one friend. She was new again, and she had become the target of some of this deflected pain. Teased, she had instinctively sought out another who was seen as new and vulnerable, and, in quiet understanding, they formed a bond. This friend stood out even more than Lexie, for her parents had recently emigrated from Denmark. Looking as if she had stepped out of the pages of a European storybook, she introduced herself as Katrin. It was a name that had a strange feel as it rolled off your tongue, Lexie thought. Her hair was blonde with frizzy curls, her body plump, yet with long, straight, thin legs. Her face was as round as a full moon, with fat, full cheeks that looked as though she had squirrelled things away inside them. Around the creases of her nostrils were tiny eruptions of angry red skin. Lexie didn't recognize the early signs of unfolding puberty in her friend, not yet aware of what pimples were.

Katrin was a source of joy and the two became inseparable. Her arrival meant Lexie did not have to stand awkwardly alone wanting very much to disappear when others passed with that haughty "I belong here and you don't" look.

Gradually, though, acceptance came, and Lexie and Katrin became less new. Others joined their games, friendships were formed, and the hours in the playground passed happily enough. It was dealing with Mrs. Spearing that remained a challenge.

The problem, it seemed, was that she could not be pleased. No matter how hard Lexie tried, she just could not get it right. Her arrival time at school, that is. It was a very long walk from the farm to the schoolhouse. The house was a hive of activity in the mornings, with Father rushing off to work and Mother struggling to feed Tessy and the baby. Mother seemed to be more irritable than usual, and Lexie had to be careful not to make too many demands upon her or she might break out in tears or temper. She was moving around more slowly these days and huffed and puffed a great deal when she bent over to help Lexie with her shoes. In no great rush to leave, Lexie herself dawdled, as she much preferred to stay and play with her younger sister or roam the fields rather than face "Witch Spearing."

It was with heavy steps and many long backward glances that Lexie found herself walking daily down the dusty road that led to "learning." She, it seemed, found the learning along the way far more involving.

With breath-caught amazement, Lexie would stand and watch in the bright and still mornings as tiny creatures scurried everywhere. There was this place, just before she reached the school, where the road ran along by the apple orchard. Here was a wide expanse of lawn, before the black iron fence marked the beginning of the acreage of squat, spreading apple trees. On this rich green carpet, the squirrels scampered up the many imposing oak trees, only to perch on a branch and sit upright, jauntily looking about before busily setting to work upon whatever treasure they held between their paws. Here, Lexie saw her first robin straining to pull a worm from the soft, dewy grass. They really do exist, she thought excitedly! In the first grade, she had seen pictures of them in *The Big Book About Birds* and had dutifully coloured in their large outlines, but she'd never really seen one before! This, she was becoming increasingly aware, was happening a great deal of the time. The world she experienced in her schoolbooks did not match what she saw everyday. Was there something different about her she wondered? Everyone else seemed to understand the world of Dick and Jane, Puff the Cat, and Spot the Dog, with Father going off to work in a suit, the mailman and milkman coming everyday to a neat, clean house on a paved street where shiny red fire trucks zoomed along with friendly policemen just waiting to help you. At least they appeared to understand it when they read about it from the first and second grade readers. None of what she read was what she'd experienced. She'd always lived in the country in rented houses, and she doubted her father even owned a suit. Was what she saw in the books real or was what she actually experienced real? She didn't know. All she did know was that it was unsettling.

But now, here it was! A match! How exciting to see this wonderful creature previously existing only in books. She, too, could experience the same reality as others. Stopping to ponder this revelation, she watched the robin with a new sense of wonder. Unaware of how long she stood there, only that now the shadows of light playing on the grass seemed changed, she sensed she would be late! Fear clutched at her heart as she hurriedly turned the corner of the schoolyard and found it completely deserted!

With trepidation, she mounted the stairs and passed through the doorway marked "Girls." Stepping into the classroom, she wished the floor would open up and swallow her. As she ventured forth, a hush fell over the entire room as the teacher, bent over at her desk, raised her eyes sufficiently to glare over the tops of her half-glasses. "Lexie, you're late! See that it never happens again or you'll be severely punished. Here at Orchard Elementary, we begin our day on time. Take your seat!"

It occurred to Lexie that it was a very strange thing to say. Where was she supposed to "take" her seat? However, she also knew this was not the time or the place to question what had been said. Adults just had this strange way of talking. You had to learn to navigate through what you could really believe and what you just had to shrug your shoulders at because it made no sense at all to you. She slid silently into her seat, her red-hot face feeling as if it would burst into flames. The eyes of the others were on her. Some were soft and sympathetic while others were hard and narrowed and secretly pleased another had suffered humiliation. Lexie calmed herself by repeating over and over in her mind, *Tomorrow, I'll be on time! Tomorrow, I'll be on time!*

The next morning, she was awake before dawn. Father questioned her early arrival in the kitchen as he himself prepared to leave for work. Mother was left to cope with the tasks of helping Lexie find what she needed, keeping young Tess from dumping her cereal on her hair, and at the same time attempting to feed a hungry baby. This particular morning, Lexie was determined not to be late, and after much pleading that she absolutely had to be at school early, Mother, against her better judgement, let her young daughter head out into a very early morning mist.

Her walk to school was brisk and determined, with no stops to take in the wonders around her. Yet, when she rounded the last corner—horror of horrors! Looking up, she once again saw the yard completely deserted! How had it happened? She was late again!

They had all gone in, and she would have to suffer horrible humiliation once more. This time she would be punished for her tardiness! She had tried so hard to be good, to be on time. Tears stung from behind her eyes. How unfair this was! Dejectedly, she sat down on the steps of the school, her face in her hands. She just couldn't go in there and face them all. She would wait outside until recess. No, she would walk back home! No, then Mother would be angry with her for not being in school! But if she stayed, all the kids would want to know where she had been, and the horrible secret she had been dumb enough to be late two days in a row would inevitably come spilling out. There seemed to be no way out. But wait, what was Mrs. Spearing doing over there? Why wasn't she in class? She was walking into the yard from the roadway.

Slowly, it all dawned on Lexie. A sense of beautiful relief washed over her. She wasn't late at all! She was early! The teacher hadn't even arrived yet. Settling back down upon the step, her face beamed. She was so pleased with herself. Surely Mrs. Spearing would be happy she'd taken her words to heart.

The teacher stopped short right in front of her. Lexie was aware of thin legs encased in filmy nylon stockings twisted around the ankles and feet placed firmly in dark brown laced up shoes with stout, sturdy thick heels. Expectantly she lifted her face to receive the smile she knew would be forthcoming from the lady belonging to those spindly legs and sensible shoes.

Her ears instead alerted her all was not as she expected.

"Just what do you think you're doing here at this hour! Can't you or your family tell time! I don't want you here this early again. Do you understand me? You'd think your mother would have enough of a brain to . . .".

Her words trailed off and she shook her head. With that, she left young Lexie sitting bewildered on the steps, alone. Again the voice in her head rang out, *Tomorrow, I'll be on time. No matter what, I'll be on time.*

She had learned, in order to please, one had to be EXACTLY right!

CHAPTER FIVE:

THE GAMES CHILDREN PLAY

ᘔ

Sing a song,
Read a picture book,
Chase a ball, help my mother cook.
As a child I claimed
Freedom and sunlight within my domain.
My body belonged to me—a gift.
Swing high, swing free,
I've earned the right to be.
From my mother's womb I came
Vulnerable, soft, struggling and wet,
Fighting for life I won,
My birthright to be
Inviolate and free—
Sacredly sovereign of me!

L exie's friendship with Katrin deepened over the autumn months that followed. They would walk home from school together and linger lazily in the full fall days. The habit of cutting through the apple orchard shortened their walking distance considerably. On the way, they helped themselves to an abundance of ripe, red apples hanging lushly from their heavily laden branches. It made no difference that the orchard manager had warned them repeatedly not to trespass. They didn't take his threats seriously, perhaps because they sensed he really didn't mind sharing the orchard's bounty with two fair-haired young girls who chatted so seriously as they munched their fruit.

After idly walking home together, they often explored the farm and its wonders—especially the barn. There they played hide and seek in and around the steamy bodies of the cows patiently waiting to be milked, chased each other into the loft only to jump gleefully into the sweet smelling hay below. Awestruck, they gazed up the long empty shaft of the silo that reached the sky. Mischievously, they chased the chickens through the yard, imitating their clucking sound and taking great delight in watching their awkward attempts at flight. When weary of all of this, they would find themselves knocking at the door of the Dutch owners' kitchen. Mary would invite them in for she loved children.

It's probably because she doesn't have any. She should talk to my mom, thought Lexie. It seemed to her that having babies only made mothers tired and grumpy.

This thought aside, she knew Mary was always eager to talk and even better than that, she invited you in to sit at the big, wooden table and presented you with the most delicious sandwiches Lexie had ever eaten. They were made on soft white bread, spread with pure farm butter and covered in sweet, white sugar! The outsides were then dusted with brightly coloured, crunchy sugar sprinkles as well. It was a child's dream! Sweet and filling and easy to talk around as you stuffed them greedily into your mouth sharing all the adventures of the day. These hours spent in Mary's kitchen were food to Lexie in more ways than one. Here, she was special. Here, she didn't have to compete with younger, apple-cheeked sisters for attention, and she could easily out talk Katrin. Both Mary and her husband Frank were like gifts of summer sunshine, giving her loving looks of approval.

A different matter were the other brother and his wife. Jerry never looked up from what he was doing, his only acknowledgment a grunt as Lexie passed by. Greta, his wife, always wore a frown, upset with the whole world. If she would happen into the kitchen on these "sugar sandwich" days, the whole feeling of the visit would change. Becoming uneasy, Lexie would feel like leaving. She knew she was not wanted by this grumpy, Dutch lady, and it was as if the glorious, warm sunshine of the visit had suddenly turned into grey, wet rain with Greta's arrival.

It was on just one such grey, dreary November day Lexie rounded the corner to see Greta being helped out of the car and into the house. Barely able to walk, she clung, weeping, to Jerry's arm. His face was ashen grey, and he looked so beaten down! He appeared out of place in his dark suit, with his large, rough, farm hands poking out from its sleeves. Greta also looked strange, Lexie thought. With a large bundle of flowers cradled in her arms, she was dressed in black with a big, broad-brimmed hat partially covering her face from view. Arm-in-arm, the sad figures disappeared from the drizzle of the day through the side door of the farmhouse.

Lexie turned on her heels. She would ask Mother what all this strange behaviour meant. Stomping determinedly up the large stone steps of the front walk, she yanked open the big wooden door that led into the central hallway. From here the house was divided into the two apartments; the rooms to the left occupied by the two Dutch couples and the rooms to the right by Lexie and her family. This hallway had always been a place of reverence for her. Quiet and still, only the large grandfather clock ticked away the silence. Rising from the gleaming wood floors, the smooth oak banister invited her hand to play absently over its finish.

Today there was a hush over the house. Yet, Lexie, straining to listen, sensed this was not the peaceful hush of reverence today. There was pain in the air. Even before she heard the muffled sobs from behind the closed door, she could feel it. Mary's soft, soothing voice reached her ears.

"It's all right, Greta. It's all right. There will be others for you. You have to believe this. You have to try again."

Mary's voice murmured gently on with the cadence of prayer. Lexie could imagine Mary holding Greta and rocking back and forth, as the sound of her voice appeared to ebb and flow. *What was happening*, Lexie wondered? How was it that this woman of steel, this stern-faced, rainy-day lady, was now allowing herself to weep?

Lexie couldn't believe it! Grey, lifeless metal had come to life! She had to find out what had made this happen!

Mother was sitting quietly in the kitchen, gazing out the large window. Lexie placed herself on the generous wooden casement of that window, effectively blocking her mother's view and whispered softly, "Mom, what's wrong with Greta?"

Her mother stirred in her chair and her chest heaved slightly as she drew in her breath, then focused her eyes on her young daughter.

"Lexie, honey, Greta's baby died this week. It died right after it was born. It was only a few hours old, and the doctors told her there was nothing they could do to make it live. They buried the baby today. They've just come home from the funeral, and I guess it's really, really hard for them because they wanted this child so much!"

Mother sighed again, held out her arms, and beckoned Lexie to climb up onto her lap.

"Oh." The word came out of Lexie like a dull thud. She did not want to climb up on her mother's knee. She wanted to be alone to process this new information. Sliding off the smoothly polished window seat, Lexie did not glance back to see her mother's face reflect the sadness that she could not help her daughter understand a world where lives ended before they had even begun.

Feeling drawn to sit again in the sheltering arms of a window seat, Lexie climbed the stairs to her bedroom. She loved the base, polished smooth by the many bottoms which had sat upon it, and the way the window framed her as she sat there, her legs dangling down, crossed at the ankles.

She felt melancholy today. She would not have known the word if you had spoken it to her, but she certainly knew the feel of it. Rivulets of water formed on the windowpane, and drawn one to the other, collected themselves to meander slowly down the glass. Her thoughts flowed with those rivulets and she followed their wanderings.

All this talk of babies being born and then dying. She knew she should feel sad and she did, but there was another force pressing in on her. It was an energy of wondering, wondering how was it that babies got here anyway? They "came out" from that place between the mother's legs. She had heard that much in playground whisperings. That led her to other thoughts. Thoughts that made her shiver in the grey, bleakness of the day. She drew her legs up closer, locking her arms about her knees. She could sense a tingling in "that place" between her legs. What was it Katrin had said on that sunny afternoon they had spent in her bedroom instead of roaming the farm as they usually did? What were the words she had used? A quiver ran over her body as she remembered and instinctively she pressed her thighs tighter together.

"Don't worry! It'll feel great!" Katrin had said as she inched her way down Lexie's body. Lie down. It won't hurt. You'll like it, and then you can do it to me, okay?"

Not even Lexie herself had dared explore there! She allowed Katrin to continue for a moment, but became overwhelmed by the feeling that this was terribly wrong; yet she felt immobilized, as if in a trance.

"No! No more!" she heard herself say. "I don't want to do this any more, Katrin!"

Reaching down, she shoved her friend's head roughly away, at the same time pulling at her dress to cover herself. She knew she didn't like doing this, sensing it was not what young girls should be doing on a sunny afternoon—or any afternoon for that matter!

Katrin's voice came at her.

"You liked it. I know you did! Don't try to pretend you didn't. My brother and I do this all the time together, and I know he likes it! We do other things, too. I got my period a few months ago, so I guess I could get pregnant if we aren't careful. That's what my brother told me anyway."

What was she saying? Lexie's mind was reeling! What did what they were doing have to do with getting pregnant anyway? How did you get pregnant? She didn't know, and, what's more, at this point, she didn't really want to know.

What on earth was a period anyway? All she knew was that it was a dark mark put at certain places on the page to make the teacher happy! Her seven-year-old mind was racing to make sense of what was happening. Was this what you did with your Saturday afternoons when you became a nine-year old like Katrin?

61

Well, forget this, she thought. She'd rather be out playing Tarzan, swinging from the ropes hung in the hayloft, or chasing the chickens! At least those games made you feel full of energy. This game made her feel strangely frozen, immobilized, trapped. It was something that was happening to her; something she had no control over; something that made her feel uncomfortable.

In the flick of an eye, she had decided. This was not for her! Not now, anyway. She just didn't want to invite this knowledge into her world. Katrin would have to put these activities aside, no longer would they be part of their Saturday afternoons. Lexie may not have consciously known this decision had been made within her, but her body certainly did. Her resolve translated into movement as it force-fully lifted her up from under Katrin's weight. What's more, her startled friend also recognized the decision. The suggestion to "play bedroom" was never made again. Tacitly, they both understood Lexie had decided no longer to be a participant in the games children play.

"Do ya wanna play school, Lexie?"

The question jolted her back to the present as she looked up to see the round, chubby face of her sister Tessie hopefully awaiting a yes. She did not often say no to this request, because she loved the role of teacher. There was a special corner in the upstairs hall where they felt tucked away from view and where the wallpaper was a great substitute blackboard. As Lexie slid down off the window casement, she thought to herself, *I'd rather play school than those dumb games of Katrin's that make you feel all squirmy inside.*

"C'mon Tess, I'll teach you how to do take-aways today."

With that statement, the memory of Katrin's games became tucked away in Lexie's mind. A place, however, not locked securely away from the energy of the memory, and it lingered, seeping subtly into the fabric of who she was. Lexie had entered into a part of herself not experienced before, and, in doing so, had lost forever her way back to innocence.

CHAPTER SIX:

OUT ON A LIMB

༄

Sun bronzed wood nymph
Dark energies around you swirl
Eye of the storm,
Centre of calm,
Innocent girl.
Others watch and wait,
For in this whirling dance of lust
You are the bait!

Some say there is a law afoot in the universe that decrees that what you send out from yourself, you receive back in kind; and as a corollary—thoughts shape internal realities and those realities draw events from the outer world to mirror them.

As young Lexie grew, roaming unfettered on the farm, she began to ripen into a woman. Approaching maturity announced its arrival in her long sun-browned legs; plump, round bottom; curving hips; slender waist; and the protuberance of two tiny pink and perky nipples on a flat, white chest. Yet all the while, the secret of secret places lay dormant on her body, the energy of that Saturday afternoon experience locked away. They never spoke if it again, her and Katrin, yet raw, sexual energy lived as a brooding force in her friend.

On this hot August afternoon, did the unspoken draw darkness just as a beacon beckons?

Katrin was taller than Lexie. Their two blonde heads bobbed like pistons in a car engine as they walked excitedly along the deserted country road. Their adventure having animated them today, broad smiles spread across their faces. Their bronzed, browned skin crinkled around their squinting sun-filled eyes and then spread itself tightly over noses dotted with pale, brown freckles. Occasionally, laughing, one of them would throw back her head, revealing a flash of white teeth and eyes fringed with soft dark lashes.

Like two nymphs, they were off to partake of nature's wonders. Exhilarated by being on their own, they had exuberantly decided to head for the stream two miles from the farm. The sun warmed them, and tiny beads of perspiration formed on their faces as they walked intently along.

The water gurgling under the bridge annnounced itself before they could see it, calling them to partake of its coolness. To go for a swim seemed the most logical thing to do!

It was Lexie who suggested it first.

Katrin's wide-eyed response was, "But we don't have any bathing suits, Lexie!"

"Well, we'll just go in our underpants then," Lexie said matter-of-factly.

"We don't have to really swim, anyway. We can just wade in it. I don't think it's deep enough to swim. Look, you can see the bottom."

"But what if somebody sees us? Our mothers would kill us!"

"Whose gonna tell 'em? You? 'Cause I'm not. C'mon, you're not chicken, are ya?" Lexie taunted.

For all her swagger in some areas, Katrin could be extremely proper in others. She looked again at the water and then at the excited face of her friend. Caught up in the adventure of doing something she was not supposed to do, she blurted out, "Okay, I'll do it if you will!"

Removing her shirt as she went, Lexie started down the bank of the stream. She plopped down at the edge of the water to remove her shoes. Surveying the situation from this vantage point, she realized the water was moving along faster than she had first thought. With only her panties on, she ventured into the gurgling stream. Shockingly, it was colder than it looked also! Her enthusiasm for dunking herself was waning, and as she carefully inched her feet along the bottom, her nose wrinkled up in disgust for it was covered in slimy, slippery stones that caused her to lose her footing. Her feet hurting, she nearly lost her balance and went splashing into the water. On closer inspection she saw that the bottom was covered with long trailing pieces of algae clinging to the rocks with tiny fish darting in and out. When her gaze settled upon a bottom crawling creature with huge, bulging eyes, feelers, and claw like appendages, it was enough to make her scramble for the side!

Meanwhile, Katrin, who had been observing this, had wisely decided to content herself with dunking her feet while safely seated on the bank.

Then it caught Lexie's eye! It was the absolutely ideal spot to sun herself while still being cooled by the stream! Just a little further down was a fallen tree, its limbs spread out over the water. One was large and sturdy and would afford the perfect place to sit while putting on her shoes. Her feet had had enough of bare-footing for one day.

With an easy scramble along the fallen branch, she was soon perched above Katrin and surveying her domain.

It was a movement in the bushes that caught her eye first. Her head shot up to look, only aware of the branch as it snapped back into place. She saw no one, but a chill of fear crept over her. She sensed someone was there. Suddenly, aware of her semi-nakedness, she scrambled to pull the T-shirt over her head. She had carried her clothing in a crumpled ball with her up onto the fallen tree and now panic and frustration set in as the shirt stuck unmoving to her wet back. She tugged at it frantically, while scrambling down from the tree limb. As she came alongside Katrin, her words came in little puffs, "I think...we should...leave here..., Katrin."

"Why?" Katrin asked, somewhat annoyed. "I like it here."

"I thought I saw someone watching us from those bushes over there." She pointed in the direction of the movement she had seen, and, as she spoke, her body gave an involuntary shudder. Katrin looked up to see Lexie's face was not beaming as it had been earlier, but, instead, was drained of colour. She also was shivering, even though the air still warmed them.

"Okay." Katrin did not argue, sensing fear in her friend.

Silently, hurriedly putting on the rest of their clothing, they moved away from the stream, following the road back to the farm. As they walked and talked, their young minds put behind them what Lexie thought she had seen. When no one appeared to be following them, they soon returned to their carefree ways—especially when a tangle of wild raspberry bushes beckoned them from the side of the road.

Berries grew unattended between the fence and the dusty edge. Lexie plunged into their midst, loving the sweet taste, calling Katrin to join her. Excitedly, she reached out to cull a clump of them, shifting her weight to avoid tumbling head first in her hot pursuit of the delicious treasure. She felt her ankle wrench as her foot, instead of finding firm, even ground, lurched down into a hole. She was completely off-balance and heading for a fall.

A dark streak lashed out at her and only when it fastened itself like a vice grip around her wrist, steadying her, did she recognize what it was. It was the brown, muscled arm of a young boy. He stood transfixed, staring at her, his breath coming in bursts. Lexie watched his chest rise and fall rapidly, only slowly raising her gaze to look into her captor's face. It was broad, with wide, staring eyes, flared nostrils, and a mouth set in grim determination. His strength was apparent as he roughly pushed her down into a sitting position on the grass. Transfixed, she could not take her eyes from him. Everything felt as if it was happening while moving through a thick fluid, slowing down all responses, all movements.

As her body descended, her eyes came into line with his lower half. Crouched in front of her, a dark hole in the front of his pants gaped open. Horrified and fascinated at the same time, her mouth hung open in incredulity.

She was held, not able to move or speak, attracted and repelled at the same time. He spoke and with his words the spell was broken. She looked up and wondered where Katrin had been while all this was going on.

She, too, was mesmerized by what was transpiring. It had been Katrin to whom her captor had spoken. Katrin, who had stood rooted to her spot this whole time.

The young boy did not have his hands on her. He did not have to. It had become obvious Katrin intended to stay and experience. In a flick of an eye, Lexie understood! She watched Katrin and the young man. The pull of energy between them was palpable. He spoke softly, seductively to Katrin.

"Come on now, girlie. I'm not gonta hurt ya. I just never seen what a girl looks like down there before. You're gonna show me now aren't cha?"

Katrin inched closer. He shifted his weight and spread his legs wider, exposing himself more fully to her view. She came closer and closer, slowly, as if in a daze, her eyes never leaving the source of searing energy.

Lexie understood. Slowly, the realization dawned. Sickened, she realized Katrin had no intention of getting away from this! She wanted to stay! She liked it!

As the draw intensified, Lexie's captor strained forward to grasp Katrin, and, in so doing, had loosened his hold on her. She was like a rocket going off. Exploding out of the bushes, she ran screaming hysterically, "You can't make me! You can't make me! I'm going to tell my mom on you!"

The words went off like a bomb! They shocked Katrin into rapid motion. Experienced in these matters, she knew this was something to be kept from moms! The fear of having this most secret activity exposed caused her to scurry after Lexie, with only a quick backward look of regret directed at the bewildered boy.

"Slow down, Lexie," Katrin called out irritably after a few minutes of sustained running.

"He's not even following us! Whatcha gonna do when we get home anyways?" she whined.

"Mom will know what to do," Lexie said tersely.

She did not want to be around Katrin. Straining her muscles, she pulled ahead of her friend and finished the walk home with only her thoughts for company.

CHAPTER SEVEN:

THE NEW HOUSE

ॐ

Life oft feels like a circus to you and me,
Random events under the big top canopy.
Like awed children we look amazed
Seeking, searching endlessly through life's maze.
For at its centre we're convinced,
Is life's mysterious Source of Sense.
For what child could ever believe,
The Ringmaster has taken leave?

Mother did know what to do. Silently, she listened to Lexie's grim tale while Katrin remained strangely still. The police were called, a description given, and then a man with a small, black bag took Katrin into the upstairs bedroom to examine her. Lexie did not question her mother or Katrin about this event. She'd had enough of "examinations" to last her for a very long time. The thought was never expressed, but she'd had enough of Katrin, too. There was a difference now between them. As time passed, Katrin's visits to the farm became less frequent.

Mother did not offer, nor did Lexie seek, further explanation of what had transpired that day among the raspberry bushes. Unnoticed by Lexie, Mother was distracted by other impending events.

Not her usual bustling self, Mother had seemed weary of late. Lexie was not prepared, however, to hear what she had to say that hot August afternoon.

"You'll be staying with your Aunt Millicent for about a week, Lexie. I'll be going into the hospital any day now, and your dad has to work so he can't look after you. Your aunt can't take all three of you because she's got three kids of her own, but I know you'll have a good time there with your cousins, even if your sisters aren't with you."

Mother was looking somewhat anxious that Lexie accept what she was being told.

What was all this about going away and what did the hospital have to do with anything? Lexie must have look puzzled for Mother went on.

"Lexie, you do know I'm having another baby, don't you? I just thought you had figured it out with me getting so big and all. That's why I have to go away to the hospital for a few days, and just think, when I get back, I'll have a brand new baby sister or brother for you. You'll like that I bet!"

Oh, no, not again! Lexie thought. *Another brat to bother me, tag after me, and get into my things.* She sighed resignedly, having learned that if mother insisted on bringing home babies, there was nothing she could do about it but ignore the whole situation. She really didn't understand it anyway. Things had seemed perfectly fine to her without any sisters at all!

She brightened a little at the thought of her Aunt Millicent's. She actually did enjoy going there. Her aunt made the most delicious lunches! Hot, steaming tomato soup (Campbell's, of course) served with slices of soft, white bread spread with thick creamery butter, not the margarine they always had at home. She could taste it right now, and it made her mouth water.

"Sure, Mom. I'll be fine. I like Aunt Millicent's cooking." And then she remembered to ask, "Will Quinn be home too?"

She adored her cousin. He was thirteen, five years older than she was, and he knew absolutely everything! At least in Lexie's eyes he did. Following him around like a little puppy dog, she was willing to do whatever he told her to. That was unusual, for very few people had that effect on her.

Much of the week at Aunt Millicent's was spent in Quinn's company, so it seemed to fly by. There were afternoons spent roaming creeks and woods, walks along long, dusty roads doing "boy" things, or at least things that were considered to be within the domain of boys. Lexie enjoyed the swaggering bold self-assurance of Quinn and his gang. They appeared to be masters of their world. What was this seemingly innate drive to manipulate and control their physical environment, she wondered?

As young boys, they were consumed with changing and rearranging the natural elements. They loved to build miniature landscapes, move the soil, diverting the flow of rivulets from pools of water they made, and then put themselves into their created environments, lying face- and belly-down in the dirt, as larger-than-life tyrants controlling all they surveyed. Lexie had enjoyed partaking in almost all of this.

The day of the slingshot adventure still lingered in her memory. On this particular day, the boys had been exerting their power over all they came across, taking aim at telephone poles, trees, fence posts, and anything else that came into view on the deserted country road.

Quinn discovered the young bird first. Its wing crumpled, it lay on its side, eyes staring unblinkingly, its beak opening and closing in its attempt to breathe. Without so much as a second thought, he acted. Raising his slingshot, he sent a stone hurling into the defence-less creature. It hit with a thud, sending the feathered body spinning. Without a word and in silent agreement, the other boys raised their weapons, and one by one pumped shots into the body only stopping when it lay pulverized and lifeless.

In horror Lexie watched. She had wanted to take the bird and nurse it back to health! Instead, her male companions had acted on an unspoken code. Weakness was never to be tolerated. Only the strong survive and then dominate. Power was the ultimate prize!

An instinct, born of centuries of developing power to ensure survival, drove them to manipulate and control their surroundings. It upset Lexie to witness what she did not understand. For her, power took the form of responsibility. She had wanted to help the poor, weak creature. To use power to cause suffering left her feeling deflated, empty.

Turning sadly from the bloody, feathered carcass, she started to walk on ahead of the boys. Silently they followed, heads lowered, the rush of adrenaline draining, leaving a small, but fleeting sense of remorse.

Eventually, their chatter resumed and Lexie forgave them their brutality, choosing to quickly forget the incident. She was willing to overlook her momentary uncomfortable feelings because most of the time she felt more alive, more connected, in the company of these rough and ready fellows.

She detested playing with dolls. Girls who did had to sit still and stay clean! Playing with the boys was far more exciting, for they made things happen! Girls were only allowed to watch things happen! Adults did not cluck their tongues nearly as often at the antics of boys. It was as if they, the masculine gender, were expected to be wild and adventurous, even verging on outrageous. Parents' reactions ranged from a mild shrug of the shoulders accompanied by, "Oh, well, he's a boy. What do you expect?" all the way to a father's puffed up chest exclaiming, "That's my boy! He's just like I was as a kid!"

Lexie chaffed against the dictum: "Boys will be boys and girls will be nice!"

And it was another girl! A noisy one at that! In spite of herself, Lexie was interested in the new arrival. In the past, she had always looked upon her sisters as inconveniences, usurpers of parental attention, and, only at best, someone who could come in handy when there was no one else to play with. Yet, she felt strangely attracted to this squirming, gurgling, chubby bundle laid out on the bath table. She watched the baby Mother had called Millicent, after her aunt, begin to thrash her arms and legs wildly into the frightening space around her as the security of the tightly bound blanket was removed. Lexie tentatively edged forward, fascinated, and wondering if she might help hold her. Mother looked on encouragingly as Lexie reached out her hand and enfolded the baby's tiny clenched fist in hers. The skin was smooth and soft, and, thus encouraged, Lexie moved ever closer, venturing finally to look directly into the baby's face. She leaned over her tiny, new sister, smilingly, hopefully, for now she, Lexie, was ready to be interested in this new world of babies.

It was as if she had pulled the handle of a fire alarm! This tiny creature wound up and let go with such an incredible wail that Lexie dropped her arm in fright. Startled, she looked up at her mother questionly. Mother, too, was surprised by baby Millicent's reaction.

It was decided then. Lexie turned on her heel uttering the words, "If she doesn't like me, then I guess I won't like her either!"

The world of babies would just have to get along without her for a little longer!

They were a family of six now: Mother, Father, Lexie, Theresa (Tessie), Celine, and Millicent. This day, as they were all packed into their black 1953 Ford, the air was filled with tense expectancy. They were going somewhere important, somewhere that was going to dramatically affect their future. Even Lexie, who was not privy to her parents' dreams and plans, knew this was a big event.

The children were left to wait in the car. Mother had taken new baby Millicent in with her, and Lexie had been put in charge of her other siblings. Siblings who now were contenting themselves with bouncing exuberantly up and down on the back seat of the car, making the tired grey cloth upholstery give up puffs of stale smelling dust. Disdainfully, she looked back from the front seat. Didn't they know how important this was? How could they play at a time like this? Sitting on the edge of the seat, her eyes straining to look out the front windshield, she was staring at the building into which her parents had disappeared. On the way, she had heard enough of her their conversation to understand that the answer they received from the man they were meeting today was of vital importance to all their futures. She just wished those two noisy, bouncing bodies in the back seat were not there. They distracted her from focusing on what she wanted to do most—worry. Worry without distraction, that is. Of course she would not have recognized it as worry, but it was a pattern of feeling that was becoming her companion more and more—a gnawing in the pit of the stomach that said, in effect, if things did not go the way you expected them to, your world would come crashing down. No ifs, ands, or buts, things had to go as prescribed or it would be disaster! The belief that this world was not a particularly friendly place also was growing. She had seen the frown of disappointment crease her father's brow far too often to believe things always worked out the way you hoped they would. With this budding belief system in place, she sat, straining every part of her small being, waiting for some powerful human being, who, with a word, would direct her family's entire future!

She knew! She knew the minute they came out of the building and approached the car! Beaming and talking excitedly, they slid in on either side of her. Now, Lexie could relax. Her parents were confident and in control of the situation again. Gone were the worried, concerned looks. She let her body settle back onto the seat, revelling in her parents' excited chatter. Things were more than all right! Things were going to be brand new. They were about to join a certain elite group in post-war society. The powerful man, the bank manager, had said yes, and her poor, working-class family was about to become owners of their very own home!

They moved into bare wooden floors and walls you could walk through! At least that's what Lexie and her sister did as they explored the new house, slipping easily between the studding. There was an air of excitement, for it was larger than their rented house and it was all one level. Lexie did not understand the talk about a furnace for heating instead of the pot-bellied stove she had shivered around for many winter mornings, but she did know her parents were thrilled with all the conveniences this new dwelling would afford them when it was finished. They had been able to borrow enough money to get the house built, as long as Father did much of the finishing work himself. In order to save rent, they had decided to move in as soon as the basic shell had been erected. The wiring had all been done, but the siding was yet to be put on the outside, and the plumbing work was not yet finished. Even with all this, the tiny bungalow seemed like a mansion to them! They had their privacy again and with two girls in each bedroom, it meant that Mother and Father no longer had a crib and its occupant in with them as they'd had since the beginning of their marriage.

Lexie was also pleased because the new house was much closer to her school. It would be a quick ten-minute walk for her now. That meant more friends, as this house was not located on a lonely country road, but was in what was called a "subdivision." They had neighbours so close you could see their houses! Not only did subdivision living afford her with new friends, it also supplied the most amazing places to play. Many of the newly started homes consisted only of a large gaping hole, its sides lined with concrete blocks and wooden planks placed from wall to wall spanning the opening. A great test of courage for the neighbourhood kids became "walking the plank." As well, the unfinished basements provided great places to play hide and seek. Often Mother had to come looking for her charges in order to feed them, this new environment filling them with such excitement that they often forgot their bellies.

Lexie had turned nine that winter, and they had moved into the new house the following spring. The months passed quickly as Father busied himself with the work of completing the house. Mother shepherded her flock of four offspring through piles of diapers, laundry, endless meal preparation, while still finding time to sew all their clothing. Tess waited impatiently for September's big event to arrive. She was to start first grade! Celine, who was now three, was a busy streak of blonde-headed curls, who seemed to be everywhere at once. Small and wiry and full of nervous energy, she was always on the go. Millicent, or Millie as she was called, was now a year and as different from Celine as day from night. Dark of hair and skin, she was placid and slow moving. Content to lie in her crib, she would sleep and eat and explore the world of her toes. Not walking yet, Mother carried her everywhere, even though she was a large baby. Whereas Celine was outgoing and anxious to explore everything new, Millie clung to Mother and wailed unmercifully if anyone tried to remove her from her side. Even though they were so different, because they were close in age, they were lumped together and referred to as "the babies"—a term that would stay with them well into their teen years.

Lexie introduced Tess that September to the doors marked "Girls" and "Boys," and to the ways of Mrs. Spearing. It was really quite simple. Keep your mouth shut in class, listen when she talked, and don't ever, ever let on that you don't understand! If you dared ask her to explain something again to you, it would unleash a tirade of frustrated and angry statements such as, "What's wrong with you? Weren't you listening? Stop daydreaming and pay attention!"

Lexie had learned it did no good to defend yourself by saying you had been paying attention. The fault of course was yours if you weren't learning. You just had to try harder or give up as some others did. All these insights she shared with Tess, and her little, affable, dark-haired pixie of a sister, it appeared to Lexie, managed her transition into school life with relatively few bumps. Hadn't she already taught her sums and take-aways on the walls of the farmhouse? Tess had enjoyed a head start.

Lexie was good at her arithmetic, and this particular day when she had been called up to Mrs. Spearing's desk to have her homework checked, as the teacher went over row after row of answers placing bright red check marks after each question, her spirits soared! She was going to get it all right. She knew she was! Finally the teacher put a huge check mark at the top of the page that looked like a big smile. Lexie knew that meant she had done it perfectly! Beaming as she walked back to her seat, she sat down at her desk, basking in the glow of her accomplishment. Her pride was literally about to make her burst if she didn't share with someone. Turning around to the student behind her, she waved her arithmetic paper with its big smiling check mark, and said out loud, "Look what I got! I got them all right!"

She heard her name boom out from the direction of Mrs. Spearing's desk.

"Alexis! Were you talking? You know I just told the class there would be no talking allowed during this work period!"

Not waiting for Lexie to respond, she said curtly, "Come up here right now, young lady!"

Lexie obeyed, a sick feeling growing in the pit of her stomach. Not knowing exactly what to expect, she sensed it would not be pleasant. Mrs. Spearing stood up, walked from behind her desk and positioned herself at the front of the room, legs planted slightly apart and hands held behind her back. Looking sternly down at Lexie, she said gruffly, "Do you know what the punishment is for talking out of turn, young lady?"

Lexie stammered that she did not, and she was being truthful. She had paid little attention to the punishments previously given out to others because it had frightened her and she wanted to know nothing of them.

Growing impatient at her stammerings, the teacher barked, "Hold out your hand then!"

Lexie did as she was told, still not knowing what to expect. Tentatively, she reached out her right hand, palm down. The teacher grasped it impatiently and roughly turned it over, forcing her fingers out flat. Where the leather strap came from, Lexie did not know, but all of a sudden she realized that this black, solid chunk of material was about to come crashing down on the flesh of her right palm! Instinctively, she shot her hand back behind her to a place of safety, unable to believe she was going to be hit in such a manner! Inconceivable to Lexie, who always tried to please, who was so careful to obey the rules of the classroom, who adored learning new things, she was about to be punished this way and in front of everyone! Her faced burned with humiliation. She would not allow the teacher to strap her!

Her hands firmly locked behind her, her resistance only inflamed the teacher's wrath! The tiny, terrible teacher lunged at Lexie and pried her right arm free from behind her back. Holding it firmly in her own hand, she raised the strap to strike.

Lexie knew there was nothing she could do to prevent this. The teacher was in control. Submitting, she steeled herself to take the blows. And blows they were. Angered by the tenacity of a young girl who had dared to thwart her, the teacher spent out her wrath, striking with force while muttering under her breath that students just never learned—they just never learned!

When she was done, she turned her back on Lexie and said as she walked away, "You can spend the rest of the morning in the corner thinking about what you did!"

Not daring to look at the class, she turned and stood staring at the walls. After awhile she did dare to look down at her hand. It was swollen and red in places, and it stung. Unobtrusively she rubbed at it with her other hand, dreading the teacher's wrath, which might again befall her if she were caught.

Standing, humiliated, the minutes ticked endlessly by. Finally, Mrs. Spearing's gruff voice announced it was time for recess and all, including Lexie, filed dutifully out the door. In shock, her young mind was still trying to make sense of the events that had just transpired. What had she done wrong, she wondered? Even when she had been right, she had been wrong. Her mind had to make sense of this. The teacher could not possibly be at fault, for she was the teacher. She was an adult, and adults always knew what to do. So, if the teacher was not wrong in what she had done, then Lexie's troubled mind settled on the only other available conclusion. She, Lexie, had somehow been wrong! This began to sink into her mind, and she went searching for where she had made her mistake. It wasn't the arithmetic. That she knew had been done correctly. It wasn't the talking out of turn either, she reasoned, for she had done that before and only been given a stern look as a reprimand.

Then she understood. She had it! It was because she had been so proud of what she had done and because she had shown it off to someone else! Her young brain, struggling to make sense of her world, formed a conclusion.

Too much pride in what you have achieved would lead to pain! It was better to remain silent about abilities!

Finally digesting this, she raised her head to come face to face with Tessie's huge, dark eyes. Filled with liquid concern and empathy, she whispered, "You okay, Lexie?"

When she could only shrug, unable to form her words because of a huge, tight lump of self-pity closing her throat, Tessie went on bravely, trying instinctively to relieve her older sister's pain. She was like that. She hated to see anyone suffer.

"Boy, that old Mrs. Spearing is really a witch, eh, Lexie? You sure didn't deserve the strap for that! Ya gonna tell Mom and Dad, though? I betcha they'd tell her off!" Her voice trailed off while she watched and waited for some kind of a response from her older sister.

Her words struck Lexie like a thunderbolt! Her parents! She hadn't thought of them before now. There had been stories of the times when someone in their families had been strapped at school. They didn't dare tell because they knew they'd get it again at home. They always added that part! The teacher was always right. Then and there it was settled in her mind!

She found her voice. "I'm okay, Tessie. You know that old lady Spearing doesn't bother me. She could strap me all she wants. It didn't really even hurt either," she boasted.

As Lexie lied her way through this litany, she began to feel better. With each denial, she came to believe what she was saying, feeling braver by the moment, but not brave enough to tell Mom and Dad.

"Tessie, let's keep this a secret. Just you and me, okay? Mom and Dad don't need to know. It's just not that important. Holy cow, you know, Mrs. Spearing straps kids all the time! Okay, you promise, okay?"

Honoured to be sharing a secret with her big sister, Tessie agreed. Besides, Lexie wanted to put the humiliating event behind her as fast as she could.

Forgotten, but nevertheless fitted into place in the building of Lexie's being, in that terrifying, humiliating moment suffered at Orchard Elementary, pride and pain had become wound inextricably one with the other.

Walking home by herself that day, her hand didn't sting any more, only her heart did. She was sure Tessie wouldn't tell. She was loyal, that kid, and besides she wasn't that worried if her Mom and Dad did find out. They weren't the type to punish you without good reason. Lexie had known this all along and had just used that story about getting strapped again at home as an excuse. She just didn't want her parents to know her shame.

Her downcast eyes matched her mood, and, as she turned into the driveway, she did not notice the long, white vehicle until she was upon it. As she passed slowly, questionly beside it, her eyes took in the large red letters, "AMBULANCE." Her breath caught in her throat. Ambulances took people to hospitals, didn't they? Hospitals were where you went when you were really sick or hurt, she knew that.

Her own pain forgotten, she ran around to the back door, yanked it open, and raced up the steps into the kitchen. She was looking for Mother. Mother would explain. Instead, she encountered two men in white, starched coats, carrying satchels, with funny black and chrome instruments dangling from their necks.

They called over their shoulders as they went out the door, "We'll be back in for him in a minute."

"Him!" There was only one "him" in this family and that was her dad! What was going on, she wondered? Her father had come home early yesterday and had gone directly to bed, complaining of a throbbing pain in his left eye. This must be serious, for he never missed work!

The men rolled the stretcher into her parents' bedroom. Mother was there, white-faced, and holding Father's hand. Soft moaning sounds came from the bed, and Lexie could see her father's eye was covered by a cloth. A look of fear was etched into the muscles of his pasty white face. His body tensed rigidly, expectantly, waiting for the next wave of pain.

Small, wide-eyed faces at the door now moved aside, and the two uniformed men wheeled their father out of the room and down the hall.

"Will you be coming with us, Mrs. Alexander?" the driver of the ambulance asked.

With a worried look at her oldest child, she asked, "Lexie, can you look after your sisters? I know you haven't done much babysitting, but I'm sure you can do it. It will be just for a little while until I can get a neighbour to come and take over. Your Daddy really needs me to come with him now. You'll be all right won't you?"

Lexie knew her mother needed her to say yes, she'd be fine. She did, all the while wanting the horrible scene to disappear, leaving her father sitting in the living room reading his paper just as he did every evening. It terrified her to see him helplessly carried out by two strange men to a strange place: a place, from which, she had heard, people did not always come back.

As she watched the long, white vehicle back out of the driveway, a sense of responsibility came over her. With purpose, she switched on the television set and got Tessie and Celine settled in front of it. Having had television for just a few months, it was still a very exciting to watch. In a few minutes, The Lone Ranger would come riding across the screen, his beautiful horse Silver rearing upon his powerful hind haunches, only then to go galloping off to right the wrongs of the world. You just had to feel safer knowing that wonderful team was out there assuring good would triumph over evil!

Lexie and her little charges needed to feel safe now. Their own hero, the one in the family who was strong and bold and fighting for their good, was now helpless and far away from them. They needed to know there was still someone "out there" who could protect them all—even the fathers of the world!

In front of the flickering light of the television, the three of them huddled together, a blanket wrapped around them for warmth. After a time, a ghostly little whisper came from the space where Tessie's frightened little face was pressed against Lexie's side.

"Is Daddy going to come back soon, Lexie?" Her eyes appeared huge and dark against the paleness of her skin. She tilted her chin upwards to look at Lexie, whose face stared expressionlessly straight ahead.

Nuzzling herself in closer to Lexie's warm body, she awaited a reassuring answer.

"Of course he is. He's our Dad isn't he?" Lexie replied flatly.

Father returned, but only after six long, difficult weeks - weeks with meals supplied by concerned neighbours and credit from the local store. Weeks when their new home echoed the silence of idle tools and work left undone. Weeks filled with nights of bowed heads and knees bent in prayer.

It had happened at work. Welding without safety glasses, in a hurry to get the job finished, their father had left his eyes vulnerable, and one had literally been torn to shreds by an errant piece of flying steel. After the operation, the eye began inexplicably to swell, the pressure compelling her father to tear at his bandages to the point of being restrained. Searching for the cause of the swelling, the doctors realized an allergy to the dressing was the cause. The eye had swollen so much it ruptured the sutures inside and another surgery was necessary. With this came the potential for another disaster. When one eye has been severally traumatized, as this one had, the other eye can shut down in sympathy! Their father could go blind!

For many of those same six weeks, their father spent his evenings in his bed, surrounded by darkness, the healing eye bandaged and the other staring up at the ceiling. He was acutely aware of the soft green glow cast by the lighted dial on the portable radio beside his bed. Deep in the middle of one black, lonely night, the light had flickered. Lexie's wounded hero stopped in mid-breath. Was this it? Would the light flicker and fail?

He squeezed his eye tightly shut and opened a dialogue. He unashamedly bargained with God! He would acknowledge God's existence in exchange for his deliverance now! For the first time in his life, he asked for help from a power greater than himself. He prayed.

How long he remained that way, his eye squeezed shut against fear, he never knew. At last, finding courage, he opened it to the light of the radio dial, shining like a beacon.

Ever after, he referred to himself as a "tea-bag Christian"—only praying when he was in hot water. Even while saying it, the smile would spread across his face, for it was evident to all that his faith was strong. A bargain had been struck that fateful night. He would allow God to work through him, as long as He didn't make a big deal about it. Mr. Alexander became one of those rare individuals who lived his beliefs, walking his talk.

And he needed his God, for there was another, even more sinister threat now to face. Because multiple surgeries had brought excruciating pain, the strongest known painkiller of the time, morphine, had been prescribed. The inevitable happened. Lexie's father became addicted. Mercifully, a third surgery was successful, the torment of withdrawal was endured, and the healing finally took place. Her father had travelled a long and arduous road of recovery.

Their savings depleted by Father's illness and the building costs, the family was now virtually penniless.

As each day dawned, their dream of a new home became less and less bright. The rosy hue of expectation now became a grey film threatening to envelop them all—hope-filled technicolour now black and white. They lived holding their breath, not daring to think what the future might bring, content to just get through the present moment. The days followed one upon the other this way as Lexie and her sisters went about their childhood explorings, an undercurrent of energy always present that made them feel slightly off-balance, a sense that all was not right with Mother, therefore, all was not right with their world.

This particular Saturday morning, though, it was as if someone had put the colour back! Lexie awoke to bright sunshine and a beehive of activity! Peering out her bedroom window, her eyes surveying the scene, her jaw dropped in wonder. Who were all these men and why were they here?

A large piece of roaring equipment was burrowing into the ground, spitting up great bits of soil. Men, with their hard hats and work boots, were carrying long white planks of shiny aluminum siding. More were arriving in the driveway, noisily banging truck doors closed and calling to one another while they grabbed picks, shovels, and tool boxes from the back of their vehicles. It appeared to Lexie they had simply descended from nowhere and now, like bees in a hive, were overrunning the place, intent upon their task.

Wandering bewildered into the midst of all this, she found her mother directing traffic in the back yard.

"What's going on, Mom?" she asked with a sense of awe.

"Isn't it wonderful, Lexie?" her mother gushed. "These are men who work with your dad. They heard about our situation, and they've arranged to have the well and the siding finished, and they're doing it out of the goodness of their hearts! It's like a gift from God! I just can't believe it, Lexie! It's wonderful to know there are people like this still left in the world."

Satisfied she had given explanation enough, she went off in the direction of a waving workman, who had been trying to get her attention.

This is pretty neat, thought Lexie as she went inside the house to pour herself a bowl of cereal. She snapped on the television set. It was Saturday morning, and *Under the Big Top* was a favourite. She sincerely hoped the "circus" going on outside would not interfere with the one she wanted to watch unfold on the screen.

One by one, as her sleepy sisters joined her and asked the same bewildered questions she had, she impatiently shushed them and told them to ask their mother. The drama on TV seemed far more captivating than the one in her backyard. She had always felt that somehow the house would get finished. What had Mother been so worried about? Adults always found a way to solve problems, didn't they?

CHAPTER EIGHT:

TWICE ON SUNDAY

❧

FOR SHELLEY

Daddy, do you see me?
I see you
As I sit, small and curled, on the stair.
The three of you below,
Fill my world.

What horror locks you in its grip?
Brutal man,
For you is fit, the lash of a righteous whip!

From your sons, innocence you took.
And me, oh Daddy, from me,
You did not see.
You wrested more.
My world, you made a place of terror to be!

Lexie had never seen anyone so thin! Standing before her was a girl about her age, blonde hair tied tightly back, her hands pressed demurely against her primly starched dress. Her legs were like two thin poles, almost entirely without shape, and they ended in neatly turned down white socks and black, patent leather shoes. She appeared as if she had just stepped out of the pages of the Sears catalogue, wearing all the latest fashions. Fashions Lexie would have ordered if she could. But, she's so thin, thought Lexie. I wonder how she manages to stand up?

The skinny girl broke the silence, revealing a mouth full of large white teeth—definitely oversized for her tiny, thin face.

Her face is so skinny, any teeth would be too big, Lexie thought to herself.

"Hi," she said shyly. "My name is Shelley. What's yours?"

"Alexis, but everyone calls me Lexie. My mom says I should walk you to school because you're new. That okay with you, Shelley?"

Lexie tried out her new friend's name. It then dawned on her that if Shelley was new, it meant she must have come from somewhere else.

"Where'd ya go to school before, Shelley?" she asked.

The girls had been standing on the grassy strip separating their two houses, and, as Shelley began to tell how she had come from a big city and had gone to a large, two-story school with a cafeteria, Lexie, for the first time, became aware of Shelley's house, never really noticing it before. Focusing her attention on it now, it dawned on her that it was quite a bit larger than her own, and it had a brick exterior, while hers was siding. Now she knew enough to know brick cost more. As she continued to listen to Shelley tell about her school, it began to sound more and more like what she'd read in her *Dick and Jane* readers at school. Here was someone who really had lived on paved streets with mailmen, milkmen, and firemen zooming along in shiny trucks. Because Shelley was obviously a city kid, Lexie was all ears. To her the city experience was better than her country existence. Everyone knew people who lived in the big, exciting cities were richer, happier, and smarter! They did more, saw more, and had more, didn't they? At least that was what Lexie had been led to believe. She'd be happy to escort this shiny new friend to school, even if she was too skinny.

Two surprises waited for Lexie that day. Having filled Shelley in on the rules of school survival, and thus being somewhat late, it was with trepidation they slipped noiselessly into seats at the rear of the classroom. All the students were listening intently to the voice at the front. Lexie was too busy thinking about her new friend to pay much attention until a collective intake of breath brought her to awareness. *What had been said to cause such a reaction"?* she wondered. Looking around for a clue, she saw students beaming, nodding in approval, broad smiles spreading across their faces. *What was going on?* thought Lexie.

The only thing Old Lady Spearing could say that would make me that happy is that she's quitting or planning to drop dead tomorrow! Lexie thought to herself.

Then the word hit her brain. That's it! Finally it sunk in. No, she wasn't planning to die, but she had said a word almost as good. She was planning to RETIRE!

Lexie sat up and listened. This she had to hear. It got even better. Not only was Mrs. Spearing going to teach just until Christmas, but a new, four-room school would be opening for the start of the second term. They would be free of "Witch Spearing," and have a big, shiny new school to boot! This was absolutely amazing news!

The children erupted out into the playground at recess, exhilarated by what they'd heard. They were soon to be free—free of the fear gripping at their insides every time they had passed through those doors marked "Girls" and "Boys"!

The second surprise came as they settled back into the classroom to begin their arithmetic lesson. Mrs. Spearing had found Shelley a desk close to Lexie's, then she had filled the blackboard with questions for the fourth graders, left them, and gone on to teach the smaller children their spelling words. Looking over at her new friend, Lexie sensed something was terribly wrong! Shelley's face was as white as the sheet of paper in front of her, the pencil shaking in her hand as she stared straight ahead, transfixed. Feeling Lexie's gaze upon her, she turned to face her friend and, as their eyes connected, a ripple of fear ran through Lexie. In that moment of recognition, she knew Shelley was terrified! Like a trapped and frightened creature, Shelley only wanted to explode out of her desk and escape from this room—a room that now held humiliation for her. Somehow Lexie knew those questions on the blackboard had elicited the same response from Shelley in other classrooms.

Suddenly, there SHE was, looming over Shelley! Mrs. Spearing had also sensed panic and was circling in.

"What's wrong child?" she asked irritably. These are grade four questions, and you were in grade four in your other school, weren't you?"

"Yes, ma'am." Shelley's whispered response was barely audible, her head lowered in shame.

"Well then, what's the problem?" the teacher asked sharply. "Get on with it!" she barked.

"I can't." Shelley's words could hardly be heard.

"What do you mean you can't do it!" Mrs. Spearing's amplified answer was blurted out for the entire class to hear. Putting down their pencils, they prepared to silently watch the humiliation of yet another classmate. This one hadn't even made it safely through her first day!

"Stand up when I'm speaking to you, child!" The teacher was growing more agitated, working herself into the frenzy the class knew so well.

Shelley stood up slowly, her hand holding the edge of the desk for support. As she opened her dry mouth in a vain attempt to speak, it was as if a signal had been given to her body. It folded up just like an accordion! Thin legs buckled under her, her head rolled back and she became a pile of rumpled cloth on the floor. The teacher stood dumbfounded for a moment—a child had literally fainted in fear at her feet! Shelley had indeed escaped the situation.

"Someone help her up!" Mrs. Spearing spluttered when she regained her composure.

Then, turning abruptly on her heel, she walked back to the second graders she had been working with. The entire class stood immobilized, staring, their mouths open. Finally a few who were closest to Shelley ventured over to her and propped her into her seat. All knew Shelley would now be safe from Mrs. Spearing's "teaching." She would leave her alone now.

Lexie had watched the scene unfold, too fascinated to move, and a new conclusion began to formulate in her young brain. This shiny new city friend may have appeared more exciting, may have done more, and may have lived in a more expensive house, but one thing she was not was also for sure. Even though it seemed she had stepped out of the pages of *Dick and Jane,* Lexie realized with a jolt—Shelley was not smarter than she was! Perfection was not a package deal. Because all the externals had been there, Lexie had been willing to feel less than this new friend. Up to that point, Shelley had fulfilled expectations that anything different was somehow better. Rather than reject the idea that perfection was not attained if one just did the "right" things, wore the "right" clothes, and came from the "right" neighbourhood, Lexie chose instead to believe that somehow Shelley herself was the problem. Shelley obviously didn't understand how it all worked. Why would anyone who had all the things she had faint over something as simple as arithmetic questions? Schoolwork was easy, wasn't it?

On the walk home together, Lexie, less in awe of her new friend, was more willing to share her secret self with her. She learned Shelley fainted when she was frightened, which, it turned out, was quite often. When they reached their driveways, Lexie, eager to continue the discovery of one another, suggested Shelley come over to her house.

"Oh, no. I couldn't. I have to be home right after school to help my mom. My dad gets home from work soon and he wants his dinner right away!"

At the mention of her dad, Lexie thought she saw fear flit across Shelley's face.

"Okay," Lexie said easily. "I'll call on you in the morning for school then."

"Oh, no, don't do that!" Shelley sucked in her breath. My dad doesn't like it when people ring the doorbell. I'll call on you, okay?"

With that, she hurried off, calling over her shoulder, "Remember, I'll call on you, okay?"

"Sure," Lexie called back, but Shelley's words played over in her mind, for they struck her as strange, very strange.

"My dad doesn't like it when people ring the doorbell."

Lexie muttered out loud to herself, "What on earth does he think they're for then?!"

She soon discovered he knew what doors were for! Later that evening, after supper, she had decided to call on her new friend anyway. Standing on their front step, she rang the doorbell, impressed with the mellow sound it made. At her house they had to put up with the loud bang, bang, bang of knuckles on wood.

A very disgruntled man answered, asking abruptly, "What do you want?"

Taken aback by his rudeness, Lexie managed to stammer, "Can Shelley come out?"

"No." The word slammed her in the face at the same time as the door. That was it, no explanation, nothing. She walked down the steps wondering what she had done to make him so mad. It never occurred to her young mind that Shelley's father was angry at a lot of things, the least of which was her.

A tall and sinister looking man was this Mr. Marcus Dehavilland. It was a strange and formal name to Lexie, and he appeared that way to her as well. As she came to know him, she came not to want to know him. Cruel and stern, he never used his face to smile, only snarling out orders to his children, of which there were four, three girls and a boy. Shelley was the second oldest of his brood, and it was apparent she lived in fear of him. On the rare occasions Lexie was allowed to enter their silent, perfect house, she kept out of his way, learning quickly the rules of this strange family. Their austere silence contrasted with the bubbling boisterousness of her home, where children tumbled over one another in good-natured romping and where one had to fight to be heard amid the chorus of happy voices around the dinner table. In the house of Dehavilland, however, it was another matter.

She sat at the table expecting the family to erupt in smiling conversation as hers did. She watched, she waited, she grew uncomfortable. Sitting, with only the tense silence to nourish her, she gave up expecting. She too dropped her head, put the tasteless food into her mouth, and mechanically chewed it. The others did the same, watching from the corner of their eyes. The smallest child, still in her highchair, had already learned the rules and ate silently. Not a word was said. The food was eaten, the table cleared. Each child asked politely to be excused and then slipped away quietly, their request to leave acknowledged by a grunt from the dark, brooding man seated at the head of the table. Once during the meal, when the baby had begun to protest what she had been given to eat, he had looked up sharply, and there had been a collective intake of breath Even at this young age, Lexie recognized their fear. They were terrified of this man! *What was it he did to them?* she wondered.

Never was she allowed to stay overnight. Mrs. Dehavilland, who rarely spoke out strongly about anything, stood firm on this. No one was ever allowed to sleep over at the Dehavilland house.

Especially if it was a request for a Saturday night, the excuse would always be that the family had to get up early to go to church the next day. This frightened family that went to church twice on Sundays was quite amazing to Lexie, her family being what could be called "hit and miss" Christians. If all six of the Alexanders came trooping into service, it was definitely a hit, as they filled an entire pew. If they failed to show up, they were rarely missed, for the youngest of them often wailed in impatience at the length of the minister's sermon!

Sunday mornings she would watch all the Dehavillands march out, dressed in their best, and pile into their latest model car, a car Lexie's father was always marvelling over how they could afford. Still dressed in her pyjamas, she sat down to her Sunday morning breakfast of pancakes, and wondered why a family who was so "good and perfect" always looked so unhappy.

Years later, when Lexie was a grown woman with a child of her own, she would often return home to the small bungalow her father had built. Even though it seemed so much tinier now, it was still much the same with its perky white siding, the well under the willow tree in the huge back yard, and, of course, the kitchen table, complete with mother and the bottomless teapot. Over cups of tea, problems were discussed, opinions given, and, of course, gossip swapped. Never would they have admitted to this judgmental indulgence, for they felt they were above it, but their habit attracted others like bees to honey, and their teapot was often in use, their table a gathering place where friends shared stories, laughter, and tears. Perhaps it was because Lexie's mom was now a trained psychiatric nurse, and living under the benevolent illusion she could "fix" just about anyone, that they came to tell their tales of woe.

Lexie had maintained her friendship with Shelley sporadically through the teen and marriage years, as had her sister Tess with Shelley's younger sister Bonnie. Bonnie had been the baby of the Dehavilland family when the Alexanders had moved in, but since then, several years later a "menopausal" baby had come along to the Dehavillands and had been called Paul. Lexie had always looked up to the oldest Dehavilland girl Marnie, who had then been a very pretty teenager and was their babysitter until Lexie had been old enough. There had been another son in the family, whom Lexie and her sisters had steered clear of. His name was Larry and he was a brutish bully who took great pleasure in terrorizing the neighbourhood girls.

They had lived side by side with this family while Lexie went from prepubescence to marriage. Years later, around the kitchen table, over what seemed like gallons of tea drunk into the wee hours of the morning, when the liquid of choice would become a bottle of truth serum labelled "Product of France," the saga of the family who went to church twice on Sunday began to be told.

Like a cancer growing beside them all those years, there had been a sickness eating away all that was trusting in that silent, perfectly dusted, and ordered hellhole. He had been ill for a long time, their father. When he had returned from the war and taken his bride to live in the East, he had severed all ties with their prairie families. He would make it on his own. And he did, functioning five days a week as a normal working man. Only on the weekends did he allow his sickness to control.

Refusing to dress, he would instead lounge naked under a loose-fitting robe—a garment to be dropped whenever the urge took him. His illness was one of the flesh, consuming him with the need to feed upon the pleasures of sexual excess. His new bride darted about him like a frightened bird, wanting to please, yet her eyes widening in horror at the frequent requests made of her body. She knew no different, for she had suffered the same powerlessness at the hands of her own father. As sick in her way as her mate, she acquiesced, she submitted, she cried silently inside herself and plotted her escape.

But escape never came. Babies did. They arrived rapidly, one on the heels of another. If he kept her pregnant and thus dependent, he knew she would never be able leave him. Four children, one right after the other, and life settled into a routine resembling normalcy. Working hard as a supervisor in a manufacturing plant, he progressed and was able to provide well for his growing family. Their house was grander than all the neighbours'. His car was the newest, and the only one on the street to have a garage to park in. The hardwood floors in "his" house shone and gleamed because his daughters gave up every one of their Saturdays to see that they sparkled. Image was everything. Never was a cigarette lit within the walls of their immaculate palace; never was a case of beer allowed through its doors, because these things were of the devil and would corrupt and destroy. Their living room was also the only one in the neighbourhood devoid of the now omnipresent blue flicker of a television screen. Entertainment, if not sanctioned by their church, was forbidden. He had beautiful, willowy daughters growing up under his roof who never knew what it was to be guided around a dance floor, their beau's arm encircling their slim waists. Dancing would lead to sex and was to be avoided at all costs. Years later, through her tears, Shelley was to confess how she had snuck into her first dance at the age of sixteen, only to pass out from the sheer terror of being there. Surely, she believed, all those bodies writhing to music and wrapped around one another in the semidarkness belonged in the devil's domain! This was only one of many gut-wrenching revelations to come forth, for there was more horror to be told.

Every Sunday morning, Marcus Dehavilland left his spotless house, dressed in a crisp dark suit, his hatted wife following behind with the children, their heads down, faces glum, obediently completing the parade as they all primly seated themselves in the polished and gleaming new car and sped off to church. Every Sunday afternoon, Marcus Dehavilland's two sons would stand outside in the weather of the day, their backs against the rear wall of the house, staring blankly out over the gardens. There they stood, with their hands crossed at the small of their back, not speaking to one another, for it was as if words could not express what their bodies revealed. Many times Mrs.Alexander had looked out her kitchen window to see them there, so silent, so bewildered looking, and she herself had wondered at it. Never had she acknowledged them, her Sunday afternoons hectic enough, and, besides, she felt little closeness to these two boys, one of whom bullied the world and the other who hid from it.

They stood until they were called in for a silent dinner and then once again were taken to church. Year after year, their Sundays passed this way, and no one ever asked why it was that two young boys would often endure blustery, inhospitable weather to stand outside, backs to a wall, staring off into space.

If only the roof of that house could have been pealed back as the crusted top of a wound, revealed would have been the oozing emotional infection, the sickening, scarring stench caused by the powerlessness of the young inmates of the Dehavilland "prison."

Shelley saw and Shelley knew, slipping noiselessly from room to room, undetected, pale and unobtrusive. Suppressed memory built like a volcano over the years, finally erupting in a flood of tears and choking words. Shelley remembered and finally told.

On those Sundays, her mother had sat diligently working in her sewing room. An expert seamstress, Mrs. Dehavilland, as her machine hummed noisily and productively away, could escape for a few hours the oppressiveness of her life.

Further down the hallway, past the sewing room, was the large bedroom housing Shelley and her two sisters. A large dormitory with beds, dressers, and desks, here the girls would read or do schoolwork, as it was the father's decree that on Sunday afternoons no one could venture out. It was expected that young women, being fragile creatures, needed their rest. Their door was tightly closed through tacit mutual agreement, for this too was a rare time of peace for them.

Further down the hallway, the door to the boys' bedroom would be wide open and the room empty, the two single beds along each wall undisturbed. The room at the very end of the hall, the parents' bedroom, was also empty. The floors here gleamed under the woven scattered rugs placed on either side of the large double bed. Directly across from it stood a huge dresser with a large mirror tilted on an angle to give a full view of the bed. The room was austere, silent, and cold, but on Sundays, strange muffled sounds could be heard drifting up from the basement below. Sounds resembling sobs and moans.

Under the master bedroom was a workroom where Mr. Dehavilland spent his hours. Here, too, it was expected that his two young sons would join him every Sunday afternoon because, he said, there were many skills a young man needed to know about carpentry and such things. Their empty bedrooms were an accepted norm after returning from church—accepted and never questioned by Mrs. Dehavilland. Unbelievably, the horror of what went on in that hellhole did not just erupt of its own putridity and flow into her awareness.

The hand that held the young boy's mouth stuffed closed with a cleaning rag was strong and powerful. It whispered curt commands of "Be quiet! Don't let anyone hear you! This is my right as your father! You must honour your father!"

The other son stood terrified, eyes wide at first, but after many times, learning to remain submissively silent, he then squeezed them tight against the horror of it all, waiting his turn. It was a scene never to be forgotten. His ordinarily stern face now a mask of wanton desire, eyes glazed over, all that was decent and human suppressed to allow the feeding of his insatiable appetite for sensual things. His speech was guttural and his words came out in animalistic grunts. He was rough in the handling of his son.

"Let me die from this. Please, God, let me die!" Marcus's son would say.

Each had been present for this scene many times before, waiting their turn, shutting their eyes against it, only to have their ears and noses forever filled with the sounds and smells. Struggling not to retch and vomit, barely audible would be the pathetic whimpering of the brother under siege before being roughly muffled by the wad of rag.

"Please, Daddy, don't. It hurts me! You're hurting me! Please, Daddy. I don't like it. Stop it, please. Stop it!"

Always the beginning had been the same—desperate words that seemed only to inflame their father's desire. Somehow, they had to survive until the last moan left their father's lips, and the blessed silence told them, finally, it was over. When the assault had at last subsided, two bewildered boys made their way outside, to stand, backs against the wall, hands behind them, staring silently, blankly out over their world.

If anyone had wiped the tears from their cheek, they would not have responded. In their fevered minds, they were struggling not to be there. Several hours would pass before they could process the terrifying event that happened to them again and again. It had to fit. It had to be made to fit! It was their father who was doing this thing to them; the father who was supposed to love and protect them from the evils of the world, the father who was always right, who was looked up to by the other young people at their church, the father who could speak words of Scripture with authority and passionate belief. How then could this possibly fit? Their tortured minds went in circles, always arriving at the same conclusion. If their father was always right, always respected by others, then there was only one place to lay this horrific shame. Somehow, someway, the blame was theirs! It was the only thing that made it all fit! He was right to command them not to speak of this, for the fault was theirs! They must endure. They must submit. To do otherwise would lead into uncharted thoughts, which were far more threatening. If their father was weak, then they were not safe in this world, because he was their protector. The pain and shame was endured, for they believed their very survival depended upon it!

They knelt with him each Sunday evening in prayer, begging forgiveness, shamefully submissive, while he, unrepentant, revelled in his power.

Unchallenged, he practised his religion twice on Sundays.

CHAPTER NINE:

SUGAR AND SPICE
(That's What Little Girls Are Made Of)

⤳

Ribbon of fear,
Pearls of tears,
Decorate the top of the bottomless box
Into which is dropped
Memories and secrets of childhood
Best forgot.

Sweet, innocent youth,
In your world exists a bitter truth.
Not for you was song and rhyme the design.
Nurtured by your passive trust,
Adult power lusted and preyed
In the innocent, sacred place
Where childhood laughed and played.

Shelley continued to faint her way through grade school, it having become her way of escaping frightening situations. Lexie still could not comprehend how anyone could become so terrified by schoolwork, which came so easily to her. The fact that Lexie progressed effortlessly through the grades became a problem for her and Shelley.

It began to surface in Mrs. Givner's grade five class. By this time they were in their new four-room school with four teachers, three female and one male. The male teacher, of course, was also the principal. In the 1950s, the possession of a Y chromosome was a guarantee of advancement in a predominantly female profession.

Lexie and her friends were not even vaguely aware of this imbalance. No one, it seemed, was. It was just accepted as the natural course of events. Men ruled. But, when each classroom door banged shut to begin the day's lessons, it became evident that if men ruled women, women ruled children. Room one, down the hall from Lexie and Shelley's classroom, was Mrs. Farlow's domain. She was married to the principal, who taught the grade seven and eight class in room four. A matched set it seemed — both believed in teaching through tyranny. Mr. Farlow, a quiet man, would not yell, but would simply take the offending parties into the back office adjoining his classroom and swiftly administer the required lashes of leather. The students left sitting frozen in the classroom had no choice but to see through the frosted upper glass of a closed door the rippled figure move through the motion of raising the strap high above his head, only to bring it down full force. Their ears were then assaulted by the horrible smacking sound of leather meeting flesh, accompanied by the whimpering of the punished student. Mr. Farlow would return to class, wipe his brow with his handkerchief, look around, and be startled to see a class not working. Then he would simply grunt, "You all have work to do, don't you? Well, then. Get at it!" He would then seat himself at his desk as if nothing had happened.

Students in his wife's domain were not quite as fortunate. Sometimes they'd be sent to Mr. Farlow to be strapped as a last resort, but, as well as that potential threat, they had to endure, on a daily basis, the great power of Mrs. Farlow's vocal chords. She fancied herself to be a singer as well as a music teacher. Daily she would round up her charges in the hope of adding to their musical proficiency. As her students came in from afternoon recess, they would troop to the front of the room and form a motley crew she liked to call a choir.

There the boys would shuffle and stand, brows and hair still damp with perspiration, faces streaked with dirt, clothing dishevelled, and more often than not, sniffling and wiping their dripping noses across the backs of their sleeves. Intense arguments about who had "really" won at recess and whether or not the outcome had been "fair" often would erupt. Meanwhile, the girls dressed primly in skirts and dresses, would busily be pulling up errant ankle socks shaken loose while skipping. Being wiser, or perhaps just more caring about the ways of school, they would be casting furtive glances at the door, watching for Mrs. Farlow's arrival, and at the same time desperately shushing everyone in an attempt to bring order to chaos.

Certain predictable boys never learned, or wanted to learn, the rule of school silence and would carry their argument on just a little too long only to come face to face with the teacher's scowling look and a five-minute lecture on how to come in properly from recess.

And then it would begin—another predictable event. Mrs. Farlow, though she fancied herself a singer, was not. What she was, however, was a spitter, and every time she gave these face-to-face lectures, she'd become so impassioned that several white droplets of frothy foam would come flying out of her mouth and land on the face of the accused. The more the offending student tried to ignore its presence, resisting the temptation to wipe it off, the more he would squirm and grimace. The more he squirmed and grimaced, the more the class wanted to howl with laughter. Finally the torture would be over, and the embarrassed student would be allowed to take his place in the choir, only to be assaulted with a situation that again produced the most compelling urges to burst out in hysterics. Mrs. Farlow couldn't have carried a tune even if it had been strapped to her back, but what she did have was musical eyebrows! Or so it seemed anyway. It appeared that these bushy tufts of salt and pepper hair had a life of their own as they moved up and down in time with the music! Seated at her piano, banging out the notes, she would be entirely off-key, and her eyebrows would be having a concert all their own! They swooped up and around, hanging suspended and quivering when a high note was held, only to descend rapidly when it was over and then dart side to side in time to the next few bars. It was altogether too much to bear! The greatest challenge in Mrs.

Farlow's music class was not to learn the new songs, but to keep the explosive force of your laughter bottled up inside!

It almost always happened. The giggle would start out small, like a tiny ripple of sound, become infectious, contaminating the student next to its source. There would be a quick exchange of glances, a smile, a nudge and then it would escape. It was impossible to hold it back, for the woman was unintentionally excruciatingly funny!

Those not yet infected would look worriedly around, for they knew the giggling would grow louder until even Mrs. Farlow could hear it over the pounding of her piano. Fortunately, it could go undetected for some time, as Mrs. Farlow was also slightly deaf. This caused her to sing not only off-key, but incredibly loudly, often entirely blotting out the sound of her choir.

Eventually, almost as if she had a sixth sense, she would stop mid-note, focus her eagle eyes on the group, aware something was different. There was, unfortunately, nothing wrong with her eyesight. In an instant she would know someone had been laughing at her! Like a thundercloud, her face would darken under her billowy grey hair. Pulling her lips tersely together, she would spit acidly,

"All right, who thinks music is so funny?"

Coming closer to the group, she would give each one the eye, waiting for someone to break under the strain, and someone always did. Even though they knew full well that to laugh would mean disaster, somehow the picture of those dancing eyebrows would mischievously float back over their mind's eye, and it would happen. First putting their hand to their mouth to stem the tide of giggles, they would find this tactic rarely worked and their laughter would come bursting inevitably out, only to then react in wide-eyed horror at what they had done. But sadly, then, it was too late. The escaped giggle would be hanging in midair between them and the stern face of Mrs. Farlow. There was just no taking it back. It was done and they might as well accept punishment, the only compensation to be the merriment that the memory of those incredible dancing eyebrows would forever bring to mind.

Often the price of that memory would be high, for Mrs. Farlow was known to lose her patience completely with repeat offenders and drag them off by the ear to the principal's office for strapping.

She also was known to have incredibly good aim. It went with her good eyesight. When she became truly frustrated with an offending student during class, she would stand behind her desk, and not only hurl a stream of angry words accompanied by saliva, but also anything else she could lay her hands on. The caretakers became almost as good at sweeping up pencils and erasers strewn on the floor at day's end as the students became adept at ducking them during class hours.

In contrast, Lexie's classroom, where Mrs. Givner ruled, exhibited a different type of tyranny. She heard the stories of Mrs. Farlow's idiosyncrasies from her sisters Celine and Millie, who were just one grade apart and consequently together in her primary class. Lexie herself was subjected to the "dancing eyebrows," but only at recital and Christmas concert time, when a whole school choir was formed. She could only shake her head in disbelief at the stories her sisters told, while at the same time accepting their truth, for she well knew how terrifying teachers could appear to young, powerless children.

On the other hand she thought her teacher, Mrs. Givner, was absolutely perfect, idolizing her. It helped that Mrs. Givner was young and very beautiful, or so Lexie thought. Fascinated, she would watch as she moved effortlessly up and down the aisles of working students, checking their assignments. When she'd stop at Lexie's desk, she would become aware of the lovely, soft fragrance the teacher always seemed to exude. Totally mesmerizing were the long, slender fingers ending in perfectly manicured and brightly polished red nails, which she ran carefully over the columns of her students' work, checking for accuracy. The woman was tall and slender, her words came sliding silkily out of her perfectly formed and lipsticked lips, and, to Lexie, she was the most perfect female on earth. It was decided right then and there in this fifth-grade classroom what Lexie would be! She would grow up to be a teacher just like Mrs. Givner!

Many of the others felt about Mrs. Givner just as she did. The woman had impeccable control over her band of students, never needing to even raise her voice. Always she spoke with calm assurance, expecting, of course, that which she asked to be done. The students adored this lovely woman so much they would do anything to please her. This incredible desire to please was what allowed tyranny to take hold in this smoothly running little mini-society called a classroom.

It began with a seemingly innocent idea, an idea even sanctioned by the other teachers and heralded by the principal as a fine motivational method. In fact it was one he felt all teachers should be encouraged to institute. And so it was that, as the students entered the school this particular spring day, they saw displayed on the side blackboard a list of names with numbers beside them. Not all the students' names were on the list. In fact, only five were listed. In big, bold letters written in chalk above the names were the words, "STUDENTS OF THE WEEK." Beside each of the five names on the left were numbers indicating the placement from first to fifth, and numbers on the right-hand side indicated their total score on the various tests of the previous week. Mrs. Givner proudly announced this scoreboard was to be updated each Monday after she'd had time on the weekend to grade papers and tabulate results.

Lexie's breath caught as she looked over the scoreboard. The name at the top of the list was—Alexis Alexander! Her eyes quickly scanned the rest of the list. Next came Billy Wells. This could pose a problem, because she had been romantically intrigued with Billy's blonde head and athletic abilities of late. Next came Rita Matisco. No problem, thought Lexie. I can easily beat her at tests, even though she's better at playing baseball than I am. Mental not physical muscle was what counted inside the classroom. As she scanned the last two names she realized they were no threat either. The contest would clearly be between her and Billy. What she didn't count on was the fact that the arena for the competition would not be confined to the classroom alone. It was to spill over into the area of Shelley's domain. In playground politics, her friend Shelley would play a critical part in the life lesson she was about to learn.

So now the tyranny had a name. It was called competition, and it was believed by the educators of the time to "bring out the best" in their students. Designed to make them stretch themselves, they would then work their hardest and produce their best results. This was often achieved, and many students were helped to feel better about themselves, but it seemed no one was concerning themselves with the fallout—the broken sense of self-esteem, the sense of failure, experienced by the majority of the students. For each winner there were many losers. It was the way the system was structured. The winner was glorified while the potential of the loser often went unexplored and unexpressed.

Even the winners didn't go unscathed. Week after week Lexie managed to keep her name at the top of the list. At first she did so to please Mrs. Givner, enjoying the teacher's approving smiles, her recognition and praise in front of the other students. After a while, however, Lexie began to realize this whole process just did not make her feel the way she had imagined it would. It was wonderful to be praised in front of your peers, but gradually, as she was receiving the recognition, she began to hear the little mutters and grumbles of, "That Lexie. She always thinks she's so great."

The downcast looks of those whose names would be bumped off the list by others began to haunt her, and she also became aware of the expressions of total despair or even disgust on the students' faces whose names never appeared on the list! Gradually it became less and less fun, and Lexie began to wish it would all go away. She felt caught, trapped. Mrs. Givner and everyone else in the class expected hers to be the top name week after week. Learning, easy and effortless for her in the past, now became more like a chore. Studying for tests and rewriting assignments until they were perfect became a "have to" not a "want to" activity. Sometimes, walking into the classroom on a Monday morning, fear would knot in her stomach. What if today I'm not number one? She knew the price exacted if she failed to maintain her status, for being human, Lexie had succumbed to the temptation of lording her special status over others. At first, she had truly enjoyed the attention she had received. Not yet knowing how these things worked, she had made no attempt to hide her light under a bushel. In fact she had blinded some people with it! Her friend Shelley had been one to whom she had gone on and on about how wonderful Mrs. Givner was and how much she enjoyed being in her class and how she was going to be a teacher just like her. She had been a little nauseating and obsessive about it all. Part of her knew she had then and there allied herself with the teacher and her methods and had somehow set herself apart from the other students. There was a name for what Lexie had become. It was "teacher's pet"!

Because she was so busy trying to please this wonderful woman, it only slowly began to dawn on her that, the way things were going, this wonderful teacher would soon be her only friend. Gradually, it became apparent there was a reason why, when she emerged from the washroom at recess, all her classmates had taken off without her to the baseball diamond. When she arrived, all the positions were taken and she was left to watch from the sidelines. The other students in her class often formed tight, little groups in the play-ground and would move away from her as she approached them. Huddled together whispering, they would cast furtive glances her way. Lexie could feel they were talking about her. Achievement, poorly handled, can set one apart, as the group defensively rejects the achiever. If Lexie chose to be a winner inside the classroom, then she would have to accept the designation of loser outside the classroom. Her peers refused to bestow both titles upon her.

Shelley, the undisputed queen of the playground, made sure of this. She may have been weak and ineffective when it came to school-work, but she was a master at playground politics, knowing exactly what to say and, more importantly, what not to say. Everyone's friend and no one's friend, her loyalty was as fleeting as whatever new gossip she had just concocted. She was driven in her campaign against Lexie by an intense jealousy. Not only did her friend effort-lessly outstrip her in academics, she also, maddeningly, seemed to be in possession of something Shelley desperately desired—a sense of calm self-assurance, an inner knowing that no matter what came, she would be all right. Shelley had no such feeling about her world.

Shelley's world was a place of night terrors. A place where she felt stuck like a beautiful, exotic specimen on a display board, there to be poked, prodded and examined. Unable to get away, held in horrendous fascination by what unfolded in front of her eyes as the hushed quiet of the late evening hours descended upon her home.

It was then that he would prowl the hall. She would hear the floor squeak under his slippered feet, her breath would stop, for she knew what was coming next. Squirming her way further down under the covers of the bed she shared with her older sister, Marnie, she would all the while be thanking God that she, Shelley, slept on the inside of the bed against the wall. Safe, she would stop and listen, the room deathly quiet. Not even the sound of her sisters' breathing could be heard, but she knew. She knew they lay rigidly awake just as she did. They too knew the script.

It did not happen every week, but they always saw it coming. It would start at dinner. Their usually uncommunicative father would bitterly scold one of them for something trivial, and they would wonder why he was so angry about something they had done before without reproach. Later, after dinner, he would make a point of approaching the disciplined daughter and, in a sickeningly sweet tone, tell her he had only reprimanded her for her own good and that he would let her know later what her punishment was. As he would turn to leave, he'd lay his hand on her shoulder and run it slowly down the length of her arm, and she would know.

They would hear the soft click as their bedroom door was opened, and there he'd be, a dark figure outlined in the doorway. Softly closing the door behind him, he would move noiselessly into the room, coming to the side of one of the beds. Over the years, the role of the disciplined daughter was played by both sisters in turn. Standing there, breathing heavily, huskily, one hand would always be jammed inside his pyjama pants through the open slash in the material. With his other hand, he would reach down and slowly, ever so slowly, pull back the bedcovers from his intended victim. He seemed to enjoy the painstaking slowness of the process as the material slid away, revealing his daughter's nightgown. It was then that the pace would quicken, his breathing becoming more rapid. He would now take both hands to roll up his daughter's nightgown.

Shelley would hear her sister's sobs, aware of the rhythmic movement of the bed beneath her as it matched the movements of her father's hand inside his pyjamas. The movements would build to a frenzy and then subside. A few moments more, her father would stand there by the bed, swaying slightly, then turn abruptly and leave the room. Water would run gently in the bathroom and then there would be silence. Her sister would rearrange her bedclothes, turn over on her side, bring her knees up under her chin, wrapping her arms tightly around them, and rock herself gently back to sleep. Marnie never attempted to talk to Shelley about what was happening to her then or ever afterwards.

Shelley was not destined to escape knowing. The summer Marnie was away at church camp, her turn came. Mrs. Dehavilland had allowed Bonnie to go as well, only because it was a camp sponsored by the church and that left Shelley as the only girl at home. It was felt that she was too "delicate" for camp life, as she still suffered from regular fainting spells. Each night, as she prepared for bed, a sickening feeling of dread would wash over her. Would it be tonight? Would she awaken from her fitful sleep to see that silent, sinister figure bending over her bed? As the nights passed and he didn't come she began to hope she might be spared.

Her father knew her well. She would faint dead away if he came near enough to touch her, and he did not want her unconscious. No, he wanted her fully awake and aware of what was happening, believing in his twisted, tormented mind that she was consenting to this ritual. Because he'd wanted a willing participant, he'd had to write a new script for Shelley.

The drama began as Shelley was awakened late one summer evening by the sounds of soft moaning. At first she couldn't make out what was being said, but as she strained her ears to listen, she heard her name repeated over and over. It was her father's voice and it was coming from the bathroom down the hall. At first she tried to ignore the sounds but they came steadily, insistently.

It sounds as if he's sick, Shelley thought to herself. *Where's Mother? Why doesn't she come to help him? Where is she?!*

Panic-stricken, yet horribly torn, a part of her felt loyalty to her parent. *What if he is hurt and needs help?* she kept asking herself. *I should go and see.* Yet the other part of her was frozen in dread, rooted to the spot. *What if I go and he wants to do to me what he does to Marnie and Bonnie?* She was not sure exactly what it was he did, but she knew it left them sobbing afterwards, and she did not want whatever it was to happen to her.

The insistent calling of her name drew her, trance-like, out of bed. She could not help but answer his call. After all, it was her own father. How could she fail to do his bidding?

Sliding out of her bed, she padded softly, tenuously down the hallway to the bathroom. The door was slightly ajar, and she could see a shaft of light through the opening. Holding her breath, she stood at the threshold and her fingers slowly curled around the door handle. The moans came faster now, closer together, her name being called out more insistently. She must find out what he wanted! Sucking in a great breath, she shoved the door open!

What greeted her made her knees buckle! Retching, she wanted to vomit on the spot! Her head swimming, the room began to spin wildly. She knew she was going to faint. She had felt these sensations many times before. But, she couldn't faint this time! She knew she couldn't! She had to get away from the sight!

As she fought for the strength to leave, his depraved image burned itself into her brain, destined to haunt her for the rest of her life. Always it was there, lurking just behind her closed eyelids, forever present, thinly disguised by the sheer veil of denial. What she had seen just couldn't be! It was not possible a father could be doing such a thing while calling out the name of his own daughter!

As she turned and fled, he did not appear to notice, by this time in his own hazy world of sensual medication. Sex—the substance he lived for—was like an opiate to this man. The sweet innocence of the tender young females in his house pure intoxication, he was drunk with the satiation of his sexual power.

His power left unchecked, undisclosed year after year, a fortress of silent denial walled in the whole Dehavilland clan. The children, as they grew, ceased hoping for deliverance. They submitted silently, their enslavement never spoken of. Believing they would not be listened to, they did not talk. Because they could not speak about the reality of their lives, the abuse became unreal, invalid, a part of their existence hidden away. Their truth lived in a secret place entered into only when the brutal acts of their father's appetite opened up the unhealed wounds.

It seemed like eons later, another life almost, when Shelley received the phone call that blustery fall day. A mom herself now, married to a man who drank too much, struggling to make sense of her own existence, the voice on the phone had simply said, "You had better come. It's your sister Marnie and we don't know what to do with her. She's hysterical. She needs someone from her family and you were the closest one. Can you come?"

As she put on her coat, she mechanically checked her watch to see how much time she had before her children came home from school while her mind worked to assimilate the pieces of information she had been given over the telephone.

It had been some time since she had driven the route out to their old house, not having been back for the many years since her mom had died. Her father lived there alone now, and Shelley had no desire to visit. It had been an old neighbour who had called, one of the few original families left. The Alexanders had moved away after all their children had married and moved on. Shelley thought of Lexie as she turned down the street to her old house. She knew she was also married now with two children and had moved into the big city to pursue her teaching career.

Funny, thought Shelley. *Lexie always believed I was the big shot city kid, and now I'm still stuck in this small town and she's off to bigger and better things. Life is strange, very strange.*

She felt disconnected—as if she was floating through this event. She was here, but she wasn't feeling it. It was safe to think back and reminisce, but only about certain things. She pulled into the driveway two doors down from her father's house on that grey, bleak afternoon. She would sit here a moment and collect her thoughts before going in to get her sister.

Had it finally happened? Had another of them finally broken the unspoken vow of silence? Shelley had told, but privately, only hinting at some of the horrors as she had sat around the Alexander's kitchen table. But this! Marnie had decided to tell the whole world! She had been found, coatless, shoeless, crying uncontrollably, running down her father's street screaming at the top of her lungs, "My father abused me! He abused me! My God, the things he's done to me!"

Shelley knew what had happened. The secret had become too big to hold.

Marnie had gone that day to see her father about a loan. She needed money. She always needed money since separating from her husband. She was desperate, had sought out all other sources and out of this desperation had gone to the one person in her family with money—her father. Her denial had been such she had chosen to remember him in her hour of need as a father, as one who cared for and provided for his children. Numbed to the truth by her need, the grim reality of the situation she had pushed aside. In her child-like heart there was hope he would redeem himself. Children see themselves as a part of their parent. Surely that parent must love as they love, loyally, unquestioningly?

And so his damaged daughter clung to this hope, this illusion, believing her father would be there in her time of trouble. Had she not been silently, obediently there for his need, never questioning his right to even ask?

When he had coldly refused, something had snapped inside of her. The last tie had been ruptured. No longer did she feel she owed this man anything, not her loyalty, not her silence.

When Shelley arrived to pick her up, Marnie had sat unmoving. Without a word passing between them, she was loaded into the car and dropped off at her apartment. Both women knew what had happened, yet, how could they speak the horror of it out loud? It was easier to deny its existence, to pretend it was a huge piece of life that both had surgically, systematically, cut from memory. Shelley instinctively knew Marnie did not wish to speak of it. She had gone only this far with her admissions and could not, would not, go further. The lid had been slammed firmly back on Pandora's box. It was the way it must be, both knew that. To continue the unveiling of truth would bring them more hurt than they could bear. The pain of staying silent was less punishing than the pain of exposing the ugly truth. A tacit understanding was reached between these two sisters, a bond forged out of mutual shame and experience. They would not speak of this day again, going on with their lives as if this event had never occurred.

"You all right?" Shelley asked weakly as Marnie got out of the car.

"I'll be fine," she answered flatly. "We've managed up to now haven't we, Shelley? Thanks for being there. See ya."

Shelley watched Marnie slowly walk into her apartment building before she drove away, the events of that day destined to be dropped in to the bottomless box of forgotten childhood memories.

CHAPTER TEN:

TAKE TWO ASPIRINS

❧

The pain of knowing and growing is intense
As youth stretches into itself.
To be clothed in the full flesh of womanhood
The body inevitably intends.
Yet, girlhood clutches still,
At anything affording momentary content,
The process of growth being bewildered torment.
The body, day by day,
Becoming more foreign and strange,
And all the while, watching its unstoppable unfoldment,
Youth seeks the existence of a magic, soothing pill,
The void of fear inside to fill.

The making of such memories went unmentioned. Side by side the two families lived year after year as passing acquaintances; fear was the wedge that kept them from intimacy. With dark secrets lurking, how could there be honest connection? Emotional pain, with its constant presence in the Dehavilland children's lives, came to feel normal. "Better the devil you know than the one you don't" was their unspoken credo. Only much later did some of the Dehavillands dare to dismantle the facade.

Totally self-absorbed, Lexie, as an emerging young adult, was oblivious to even the possibility of what was occurring in the house next to hers. She was only aware of Shelley's pain when it affected her. Perhaps this was as it should be.

Inevitably, clashes between the two drove Shelley and Lexie further apart. In this power struggle, Lexie lost more often than not because she did not understand what motivated Shelley. Wisely, she decided this was a war she could never win and simply withdrew, spending less time in Shelley's company, until by high school, when they were streamed into different classes, they rarely saw one another.

A final betrayal in the last year of grade school had sealed the fate of the friendship for Lexie. A loyal friend, tolerant of the behaviour of others, she most often gave the other person the benefit of the doubt. But this particular act had been so blatant even she could not find a reason to absolve her friend.

It all started on a Sunday morning when Lexie woke up feeling very ill. This was unusual because she enjoyed robust health. True, she was a touch on the scrawny side, but that was because she was so active, not sitting at home mooning over the boys, but out climbing trees and playing ice hockey on the local ponds with them. In her mind, boys led a more interesting existence, making things happen, instead of sitting around waiting for life to come to them as so many of her girlfriends seemed to.

To be doubled over with sharp pains in her abdomen then was a shock to her twelve-year-old body. Totally bewildered by the pain, she lay in bed trying to convince herself it was nothing serious. Surely, it would soon go away she thought as she rolled over and attempted to go back to sleep, but it was no use. As the pain increased in intensity, her abdomen felt as if it were on fire, becoming distended and bloated with a sharp, searing sensation running down its centre. At last, unable to stand it any longer, she did something unusual for her—she asked for help. Staggering into her parents' bedroom, leaning over their bed, she described her excruciating pain.

Lexie's mother was a nurse, and she was not easily rattled by her children's many physical complaints. As any mother will tell you, young children are always aching somewhere, and it is usually chronic around exam time. Lexie's mom had become very aware that tests caused more "illnesses" than the most virulent of germs. Consequently, she always answered any request to stay home ill with a single response, "Get the thermometer. No fever, no day off."

It may have seemed like a callous reply, but with four children who were not entirely sold on the merits of school when their time could be spent lounging in pyjamas, being served meals in bed, tucked in with a favourite book while the cold winds blew outside, she had to be sure. If you did qualify by proving you really were sick, Mother's training would go into high gear. You were so well looked after that long afterward, the memory of her care made you wish again for that special sense of snug security, even if you did have to put up with a few sniffles and a scratchy throat in order to enjoy a pampered day—a day where all you had to do was be sick. You were let off the achievement merry-go-round and you could just be.

Lexie, burning up, knew she would easily pass the thermometer test this day. Mother raised herself up on her elbow to squint at the long sliver of mercury.

"Lexie, honey, you do have a fever. The first thing we better do is get it down. Go into the bathroom and get the aspirins. You know which ones they are don't you? Just take two aspirins, and I'm sure you'll start to feel better. There's a lot of flu going around that makes you feel sick to your stomach and gives you terrible cramps. That's probably what you've got."

Obediently, she shuffled her way into the bathroom, holding one hand protectively over her stomach. Weak and dizzy, she really did feel like retching, and these pains in her abdomen just weren't going away.

Swaying back and forth, she stood in front of the bathroom cabinet staring at her image in the mirror. She looked awful. A pale face with dark circles etched under her eyes looked back at her. She reached one hand up to search out the bottle of aspirins, and as the mirrored cabinet door swung open, her own image slid by her eyes. Going, going, gone—her knees buckled under her, and her body folded up like a crumpled heap on the tile as everything went black. From a far away place she heard the thud as her body bounced off the hard porcelain bathtub on its way to the cool floor below. How comforting that smooth, chilled surface felt. When she absently watched the drool from her mouth form a small puddle in front of her face, she knew she must be awake again. Staring at it, unable to move, she wanted only to go back to sleep. Gratefully, she noted the pain in her stomach had eased.

It's going away, and I didn't even have to take the aspirins! she thought to herself with amazement.

Suddenly Mother burst through the door. "Lexie, are you all right! Oh my God, what on earth happened?"

"I guess . . . I fainted, Mom. Gee, that's kind of neat. I never fainted before! Shelley would be proud of me." Her voice trailed off, and she closed her eyes again, content to sleep on the cool floor.

"Honey, we've got to get you back into bed. C'mon now. Help me get you up."

"Mom, can't I just lie here? I just want to go to sleep. I feel a lot better now. The pain's gone away. I'll be okay here, please."

Something in her mother's voice made Lexie obey. An urgency in her tone and movements communicated on some level that it was very important she stay awake. As she was tucked into bed, she heard her mother whisper to her father that he should get the doctor on the phone right away!

Mother sat there talking to her, not allowing her to drift off to sleep, but keeping her involved. This began to annoy Lexie. Why wouldn't her mother stop bugging her and just let her sleep? A sense of incredible drowsiness overcame her as the oblivion of unconsciousness beckoned. She revelled for in the delicious thought of how wonderful it would be to drift off and never have to worry about anything again. How dare her mother annoy her at a time like this! She was being so intrusive!

Suddenly, as if out of nowhere, there was another being poking and prodding her.

"Who is this guy, and why is he pulling down my pyjama bottoms?"she wondered.

Groggily she rallied enough to struggle up onto her elbow and stare him in the face. The recognition hit at about the same time as Mother's voice said, "Lexie, you remember Dr. Wright, don't you? He just wants to look at your tummy. It's okay, honey, really. I'm right here."

Lexie plopped back down onto the bed, relieved she didn't have to defend the sanctity of her body when all she wanted to do was slip into sleep. She soon jolted awake however, when he pressed down on her hot, bloated abdomen!

"That hurt!" she blurted out indignantly.

She heard him respond with a typical, "Hmm."

He hovered over her a little longer, still poking and prodding and then came the flat statement. "We have to get her to the hospital right away."

Neat! thought Lexie. *This will be great. If I'm in the hospital, that means I'm not at school! I get to just lie around all day with nothing to worry about.*

Worry about. The words hit her like bricks. With spring finals coming up in just two weeks, she had to start studying! It was expected she would top the class, but how could she study in the hospital? She needed all her books, and they were in school. How could she get them? What about all the material she would miss while she was away? Her conscientious young mind began to work itself into a frenzy.

Lifting herself up from the pillow, she protested, "Mom, I can't go to the hospital now. What about school? Exams...."

She didn't get a chance to finish as her mother pushed her gently back down onto the bed.

"Lexie, honey. Listen carefully to me. You have to go to the hospital. You're very, very sick. Do you understand? You need an operation, and you need it right away. School will be there waiting for you when you come home. Don't worry. We'll talk to Mr. Farlow for you and explain everything. Come on now, can you help me lift you up? The doctor's gone on ahead, and we're going to take you in the car to the hospital. It's faster than waiting for an ambulance to come all the way out to get you. Can you stand, honey?"

Her legs like licorice whips as they bent and swayed under her weight, her head a big empty sphere sitting on her shoulders with sounds echoing inside it, Lexie felt as if everything were unfolding in slow motion. They bundled her in cosy blankets, and she snuggled inside them. So wonderfully welcoming was sleep, she really didn't care where she was or why.

A change in motion under her jarred her awake. The energy around her felt different too - more urgent, rushed. She opened her eyes to the blur of white ceilings punctuated by rows of hanging florescent lights whizzing by overhead. *This must be the hospital,* she thought. She looked down at her body wrapped around with crisp white sheets securely tucked in under the thin mattress of the stretcher and saw her arms held tightly captive under the sheets.

I feel like a stupid mummy, she thought to herself. *Where are they taking me anyway?*

It was then she noticed her mother walking quickly beside the stretcher. *She looks so worried,* thought Lexie.

"Mom, what's happening to me?" Seeing her mother's tense expression scared her. This was the woman who always made things right, who always had the answers, who could always fix things. To see her frightened made Lexie wonder if this could not be fixed.

"Doctor Wright's going to operate on you, Lexie. Your appendix burst and the poison is spreading all through your system. That's what is making you feel so sleepy, honey. Don't worry. You'll be fine. They'll put you out, and you won't feel a thing. In a week or so, you'll be climbing trees with the boys again. You'll see. I've got to leave you now, okay? Your dad and I will be here when you wake up. We love you, you know."

With that, the stretcher was pushed through the big double doors marked, "NO ADMITTANCE," and Mother's assuring voice was left behind.

A kindly nurse took over, speaking softly to her. Lexie watched as she removed her left arm from under the covers and swabbed it with a cold, clear fluid. She turned her head away as she saw the approach of the needle. The scent of the fluid was still in her nostrils when she felt the sharp prick of the needle penetrate her skin.

As the room swirled around her, the last thought to drift through her mind concerned Dr. Wright.

I really hope he studied for his exams when he was in school, she thought. *I'd hate to have a doctor who graduated at the bottom of his class. I wonder how you can tell? Do doctor's get report cards?*

She'd heard her father say doctors buried their mistakes.

As she gave up her hold on consciousness, her mind was going round and round with the phrase, *I hope he's smart. I hope he's smart!*

She wasn't a mistake, and she didn't get buried. Lexie woke up with a dry, cracked mouth and a sore stomach. When she finally had enough nerve to peek down at the area of discomfort, she saw the skin of her abdomen streaked with a orangish-yellow liquid extending out beyond the bandages. Lifting the edge of the gauze just a bit revealed, to her horror, little black tufts of thread poking out of her skin. They really did "sew" you back together! She was amazed.

Having enough information to process for the moment, she let her head flop back down on the pillow. *Now what?* she wondered.

She didn't have to wait long for answers. Her parents soon arrived and were so pleased to see her awake and functioning that they chatted on about how she had come through the operation with such flying colours, how the doctor had been positively amazed by the thick layers of muscle in her abdominal wall, and how the appendix had definitely ruptured. Yes, and now it was safe to tell her that she could have died if she had simply been left to drift off to sleep on her own.

Which was the more startling revelation? Was it the fact she had nearly died or the fact that the doctor had been impressed with her great stomach muscles? Her mind skipped over the first for it had never occurred to her she might die. Living to a ripe old age was something she just took for granted. In some part of her, Lexie knew she was not destined to leave this planet until she was much older and had learned far more. Now, as for the other revelation…that fascinated her. Why would she have such abnormally strong stomach muscles? Then a shudder of shame and a sense of foolishness swept over her. Could it possibly be that the hours she had spent as a young child rocking herself back and forth on all available sofas had exercised them into top form?

A habit that had been with since her earliest childhood, she would only do it in the privacy of her own family settings, having a sense it wasn't quite "normal" behaviour. All she knew was whenever she felt agitated or restless, it helped her to plunk herself down on a couch and literally throw herself backwards against it continuing this back and forth rocking until she was exhausted enough to have a sense of calm. Her parents seemed to accept this behaviour as something she did that relieved her stress and took it as a sign of a precocious child. It was behaviour, however, that she secretly worried about.

She did not have too long to worry about the doctor figuring this behaviour out and exposing her, for soon she wearied of the talk and drifted off into the haze again.

When she next awoke, it was to a large basket of fruit staring her in the face. The nurse had left it on the tray which was now pulled across her bed. Groggily, she struggled up to have a closer look. It was glorious—a large wicker basket brimming with all manner of delicacies—bananas, apples, pears, and yes . . . even grapes! With three siblings to compete for the weekly bunch of bananas bought on shopping day, all fruits other than apples, which grew in abundance close by, were a treat. Consequently, Lexie was in heaven over this exotic gift. So pleased was she with its contents, she had overlooked who it was from. Curiosity finally got to her, and she went searching for the card, further overwhelmed by what she read. It had been sent by the kids at school! That must mean they had taken up a collection for her! This thought sobered Lexie for she truly believed she would not be missed. Her fierce independence had already made her some-what of a loner, and now, because of classroom competition, she had felt even more set apart. As she turned the card over in her hand, the thought came to her that perhaps she should not take everything quite so personally. Perhaps some of the kids did not feel as threat-ened as she about measuring themselves against another, even using the measuring process as a way to test or stretch themselves. Maybe they were able to learn from their failures and shortcomings rather than feeling destroyed by them. Perhaps, not everyone felt they had to be perfect, that they had to be the best in order to be accepted. Some of the others in the class it appeared could accept being "less than" as a natural part of life. Up to this point Lexie had tended to see life as win or lose, all or nothing. Maybe, just maybe, one could realize their own strengths and abilities and not be shunned by others. It began to dawn on her that her aloneness had been her own doing as well as the result of her classmates' actions. In order to feel alone, one had to see herself as separate. In her feeling "more than" another, she had separated herself. In choosing to see herself as superior, she had set up the consequence that others were perceived as less. This perception, even if consciously hidden from others, always trickled its way out into the relationship. It was as if others had radar for this sense of superior self-containment and responding to it, they withdrew.

While her young mind was still grappling with thoughts stirred by being cared for, her mother arrived with an armload of books. From her experience as a nurse, she knew the boredom that often set in with recovering patients and had seen this as an excellent opportunity to get her tree-climbing daughter to read. When she had heard Lexie was to be hospitalized for eleven to twelve days, she had made a trip to the library and pulled out all the books considered to be classics and as such, necessary reading for all refined young minds.

So began Lexie's lifelong love affair with books. The eleven days sped by as she sailed the seas, lived in tree houses on distant deserted islands, worked in sweat shops in eighteenth century England, and fell in love with the handsome young French officer who led the charge on the Plains of Abraham amidst the shaping of her country's history. It was all there between the pages. She could effortlessly experience all the elements of life by simply turning a page. The world truly was there at her bidding, the universe contained within the bounds of her own mind. In her imagination she could go anywhere, be anyone, do anything. Her books became an incredible, heady drug expanding all that she could conceive of being.

Thus, a different girl was wheeled down the hall on discharge day. Hospital policy demanded all patients be escorted to their cars in wheelchairs. Lexie was glad of this because she was still pretty shaky, not trusting her own legs completely as yet. When she had slipped on her own clothes to go home, she had noticed how the material hung loosely on her. Her legs were white and thin; as she did up the buttons on her slacks, she noted her hip bones were protruding and her abdomen was caved in. She was thin; there was no doubt about that. Better thin than fat she said to herself. It had not escaped her young mind that society did not glorify fat women. In the case of weight, to have more was definitely to be less.

Her body may have shrunk, but her mind had definitely expanded. The world would never again be made up of simply her own experiences. Through books, she could become one with someone else, privy to their thoughts and dreams, her perceptions altered by what she read. In the form of the written word, she had rediscovered the potent creative power of imagination. It was with some trepidation and regret then that she returned to the demanding world of school. On her return she was to learn of Shelley's betrayal.

Discharged on a Friday, her exams were to start on the Monday. Mother had already spoken to Mr. Farlow, and he had agreed to excuse her from writing. When this news had reached Shelley, she had gone into action stirring up the other students about how unfair this was, her position being that if Lexie was out of the hospital, she should not get special treatment. If everyone else had to suffer the torment of Mr. Farlow's difficult cross-examination, why shouldn't Lexie?

"What's she afraid of?" went Shelley's litany. "Is she afraid she won't be number one this time?"

Shelley's taunts gained support from the playground league. Even some parents joined in, and one mother went so far as to complain to Mr. Farlow about the "special treatment." Her argument was that since there had been time for Lexie to prepare while in the hospital, she should have to work just as hard as all the other students in order to be promoted. "What was education coming to, that diplomas could be handed out without being earned?" she argued.

Even though Lexie did not write her exams, there had been a test. One her friend Shelley had failed. From then on each had an invisible wall around her. Each felt too insecure to deal with the situation directly. They tried to appear as if nothing had changed. Their spoke as if things were the same, but being together brought out old hurts, no matter where they turned. Lexie's pain of being rejected for being what she was kept bumping up against Shelley's brittle, hollow shell of not being enough. As the pain of being without each other's friendship became less than the pain of being together in a dysfunctional one, they simply drifted apart. They became friends on a surface level, both tacitly understanding what topics were safe and neither one courageous enough to venture into that dangerously painful realm called true feelings.

Although Lexie lost a close friend because of her hospital experience, she had also observed something new about relationships.

Passion! In books she had read about romantic love, and a whole new world had opened up to her. Up to that point, she had found the opposite sex interesting and strangely compelling, but she had never imagined they could evoke such strong feelings of longing!

These powerful feelings also coincided with dramatic changes beginning to take place in her body! She didn't really notice the changes much at first. All she knew was the consuming of food had now taken on a new significance. She began to be the first one at the dinner table where before she'd had to be called repeatedly. Mother also looked askance at the heaped mounds of food she was consuming each meal. The money she now earned babysitting found its way to the local store, plopped down on the counter in exchange for Coca-colas and chocolate bars.

Changes began to become apparent to Lexie when she could no longer fit into her clothes. New skirts had to be ordered. Still the trips to the store continued as well as the exploration of the owner's refrigerators when she babysat. She also became familiar with some-thing else at one of these homes. It was an instrument she'd heard a lot of the women talking about. They all seemed to regard it as an enemy with which they did battle on a regular basis. It was called a bathroom scale.

When Lexie had started out on this voyage of self-discovery, she had been pleased her weight was under one hundred pounds. In her mind, that seemed like a good place for it to stay, indefi-nitely. She had a regular Friday night babysitting job at the house of the bathroom scale, and every Friday night she weighed in. She would hold her breath in anticipation as she stepped on it, for as they did not have a scale at her house, each week was a revelation. And what a revelation! In horror she watched as she easily broke the one hundred mark and still her weight kept on climbing! It didn't seem to take any effort at all, like her body was out of control! Bigger and bigger, she was now getting these lumps of flesh on her chest that flopped around and hurt when she ran. They had to be bound up in thing called a brassiere. Of course nobody said the full name. It was cool to talk about your "bra." Lexie was really secretly pleased, for she knew it was a mark of desirability to have them. The thing that worried her was the lump of flesh that was collecting on her tummy and the fact that some of the male population had of late been making comments on the size and spread of the part of her anatomy that she could not easily see—the part referred to politely as her backside. It seems one young gentleman felt it resembled a "barn door." All this bewildered Lexie. How could this be happening to her body? Would it ever stop or would she just keep exploding? It was absolutely terrifying to step on the scales week after week and see the numbers go up. And no matter how she resolved to stop them, they just kept climbing! It could very well be that the reason she had no control over her runaway weight was due in part to the changes brought on by puberty. But Lexie also had no control over her runaway appetite. She simply couldn't get enough to eat! Eating, never a pleasure for her before, had simply been a necessary function in order to live. Now, it took on a whole new dimension. She noticed it made her feel good to munch on snacks, and soon she was eating even when she felt full just to enjoy the sensation!

For the first time she could not take for granted that her body size and shape was acceptable to others. Her peer group, especially the boys, were making cruel comments. This was doubly hurtful, because for the first time she had become aware that what they thought of her was beginning to matter.

Even the discovery of a highly touted slimming device wasn't much help. This item of torture was known as a panty girdle and was purported to turn all women back into the svelte siren depicted in the magazine ads. What it did for Lexie was simply make her ample rear ooze up over her clothing waistband giving her a roll of extra flesh around her middle. Even more distressing was the fact that the girdle flattened her backside, making it appear like a block of solid granite, carved in one piece, unyielding and huge! This device also made it difficult to bend over as it cut off any oxygen that was supposed to find its way through thus leaving the wearer gasping.

Through her first year of high school, Lexie's body continued to change. One such change caused her to discover what those dispensing machines mounted on the walls of the girls' washrooms were for. Her femininity now made itself known once each month. This was something she had eagerly looked forward to. There had been one false alarm when she was about eleven and a half. A time when, instead of rushing outside at recess, it became much more intriguing to hide out in the washroom, stuffing your new, triple-size-A bra with Kleenex and listening to the discussions of the older girls who already had "it". These experiences created in Lexie a desire to be the same as her peers. If they had "it" she also wanted to have "it." She had no comprehension of what having "it" entailed. All she knew was the expectancy built excitement within her.

With a heady sense of having arrived, she came sailing over the vacant lots separating her house from the neighbours' in search of her mother. Rapping excitedly on the door of the house where mother was visiting, Lexie blurted out in a semi-secretive whisper, "Mom, I need you. I think I've got 'it'!"

Intuitively, Mother realized what her daughter meant. Calmly, she told Lexie to go on home, and she would come and help. It was a grave disappointment when the required blood did not continue to flow. After talking with Mother the mystery of the disappearing period was eventually solved.

The source of Lexie's phantom period was not the workings of nature at all, but rather the result of physics. Specifically the law which states, "for every action there is an equal and opposite reaction."

Lexie had been "doubled" on the back of a friend's bicycle. The friend, none other than baseball's star player Rita Matisco, also happened to be a rather reckless thrill seeker. So much so, she had played chicken with the corner of a building, intending to veer off at the last minute. Unfortunately, she misjudged and hit the wall with such force that the resulting jolt sent Lexie flying first forward, then back, her teeth rattling in her head as the blunt, rounded point of the leather seat made contact with the soft unprotected area between her legs. She was aware of a brief burst of searing pain, a sharp expulsion of breath and an explosion of light points behind her eyelids. She now knew what people meant when they referred to, "seeing stars"!

Not wanting to appear like a sissy to Rita, she slid off the bicycle into a heap on the ground, ignoring her discomfort, acting as if she was just fine. Rita, having come through apparently unscathed, was surveying Lexie critically to see how tough she was. Lexie knew that to admit pain would result in teasing. Instead, feigning hunger, she suggested they head home for a snack. Once inside the house she felt safer. At least here Rita couldn't invent any other daring activities.

It was then, when she visited the washroom, that she was greeted by the long-awaited smear of blood which sent her exploding excitedly out of the house and across the field in search of Mother.

Mother had been skeptical from the beginning, she confessed, because of the bright-red nature of the stain. Disappointedly, Lexie put the Kotex pads back into the cupboard, accepting she was not yet to join the ranks of mature young women. What was not explained, however, was what had truly caused the blood. Much later, when the realization came that technically she was no longer a virgin because it had been the membrane at the opening of the vagina which had ruptured and caused the bleeding, she thought, "Great! How do I explain to my husband-to-be that I lost my virginity to a bicycle?!"

These were the days when prevalent values decreed that a woman was to remain a virgin until her wedding day. To be anything else was to be, "damaged goods." The fact that she didn't have the right to ask her prospective husband about his sexual history, or have the same expectation of his virginity, never occurred to her. She could just imagine pleading with her bridegroom, "It was a bicycle! Honest!"

"A bicycle, eh? Now, that's a good one! Original, too!"

She blushed at the thought of it all. Hers would be the shame. She never stopped to wonder, *If it was a man's right to sow his wild oats, did he only sow in nonvirginal fields?*

Those thoughts far in her future, now she was struggling with the transformations puberty continued to foist upon her. All through grade nine, her body just kept exploding until finally the Christmas of her grade-ten year, she looked and felt like the stuffed holiday turkey! Her five-foot-seven frame was amply covered with 145 pounds of flesh. Bursting out of her skirts, her bust size had escalated to the point where the home economics teacher, while taking her measurements for a blouse, was heard to remark, "My, you're a healthy one aren't you?"

As if this wasn't enough in itself to bear, nature had another dirty trick up its sleeve! Not only did her face resemble a round, full moon, it was now working on craters too! Red, angry bumps were appearing on every available inch of her face. It pained her to look in the mirror. She became a regular customer at the local pharmacy, spending her babysitting revenue on the latest zit-zapper creams or lotions.

Needless to say with all this going for her, there was not exactly a stampede of young men wanting to take her out. Grade nine was a definite dry spell. Perhaps, drought might be more accurate. There had been occasional respites where some awkward young male creature had shown an interest, but Lexie sadly observed the ones who noticed her were never the ones she noticed! What was this? Was it some kind of dastardly plot which destined young girls to fall in love with someone who had no interest in returning the sentiment? She did discover from these interludes, however, that she had a very hard time saying no to male attention. Even if she was not remotely attracted to them, one of two things would keep her responding. Loathe to hurt their feelings, she unwittingly led them on by being friendly and more importantly, on a deeper level, using them to convince herself she was not a complete write-off because someone was showing an interest!

Boys replaced food as her focal point. Winning their approval became more important; however, she was still very naive about what boys really wanted from girls. She knew she experienced a sense of excitement in their presence, but sexual contact with them had a feeling of unreality.

She'd had a brief fling with real dating when she had just turned thirteen, just before weight cultivation and zit farming had caused her dating drought. At that time, she was perky, petite, and confident she knew it all. Having nagged her parents until they had allowed her to wear nylon stockings and high heels, she really thought she had arrived as a woman as she wobbled her way to church each Sunday. Church had become more attractive to her when she had realized it provided an opportunity for social interaction with, yes, boys! It was at one of these functions she met Gary.

Gary was sixteen and the only reason he darkened the door of a church was, of course, girls! Tall and attractive, always with money in his pocket and the proud owner of a great car, he was a real "catch"! It did not occur to Lexie that it was very unusual for a young man Gary's age to be in possession of such wealth and independence. It did, however, occur to her parents. They were less than pleased when she came home with the news that Gary wanted to take her out on a date. This was to be Lexie's first official date. (Her last for a while it also turned out.)

She was ecstatic! After days of negotiating and assurances that she would be careful, behave herself, go straight to the movie, and come straight home, they relented and let their firstborn sail out on the sea of dating.

The date started out calmly enough, with Gary coming in to meet her parents when he picked her up. He was polite, calling her father "Sir" and her mother, "Ma'am." Lexie—nylons, short skirt, heels, lipstick and all—bounced out the door and slid into the front seat of his car. *This was really living*, she thought. *Just like the shows on television.*

She didn't resist when Gary asked her to sit close. She just slid across the seat. What harm could there be? She also didn't react when his hand casually went from resting on the gearshift knob to resting on the smooth, slippery material of her nyloned knee. She only stared down at his hand in bewilderment. Why would he possibly want to put his hand there she wondered?

I guess the knee is okay as long as he doesn't go any higher, she thought as she continued to chat animatedly to him. It was very important to her that she please him as she was excited to be on a real date and to be doing one of her most favourite things in the world—going to see a movie.

He didn't go farther up her leg. He waited until they were in the movie to make his next move. That consisted of stretching his arms up into the air as he non-chalantly yawned, bringing one arm down to rest around her shoulders. This did not go unnoticed. Her body tensed a little for she sensed what was coming next. The next yawn and stretch left his hand planted firmly over her breast.

Lexie interrupted her popcorn eating to swiftly remove his hand! So swift had her reaction been, she instinctively knew he would not try that again.

It was a heck of a lot less complicated to watch a movie when I was a kid! she thought.

Distracted from enjoying the action on screen by the action off screen, she wondered warily what would come next. What possible fun could he be getting out of pawing her like this? Not sharing the same stirrings he obviously had, she felt ambivalent—frightened, yet flattered by his attentions. For her there was not yet a connection between what she occasionally felt in her genitals and the activities to which Gary was attempting to introduce her. Not yet ready for that level of involvement with a boy, she simply sought validation of her worth in the fact that she was doing what all females her age seemed to care about most—dating. As far as all this groping in the dark went, she could take it or leave it. She decided she'd rather leave it.

Just as she made this decision and started to get up to seek some respite in the ladies' room, Gary made another move. Tugging her back down into her seat, when she turned her head to protest, he aggressively planted a kiss right on her lips! She had put on so many layers of thick, pink lipstick (what had she been preparing for?) that he nearly slid right off! Before she could react, he had realigned his mouth with hers and seemed to be grinding his lips around on hers. As Lexie experienced the greasy sensation of her lipstick being smeared all over her face, she detached from it all. It was as if she were looking down on the scene thinking, *And they say this is fun! Yuck! Let's get back to the movie!*

The date ended early with Lexie demanding that she be taken directly home. Once in her driveway she escaped Gary's attempts at fondling her by quickly grasping the door handle, wrenching it open, and sliding out with only a quick, "Thanks. See ya."

She didn't. See him, that is. That was her first and last date with Gary. Attracted by her innocence, he later realized it would be the very thing that would block his progress. He would look elsewhere for what he wanted. As for Lexie, she filed the experience away under the heading "Think About Later." She would think about what compelled boys to touch you in those ways later. For now she was content to dream about being with boys, accepting their attention without filling in any of the details.

The details, wanted or not, came one Saturday afternoon shortly after her experience with Gary. The prospect of a dating daughter had put Mother in high gear, and she had been searching for a way to have a talk with her firstborn. Mother had been raised in the era when you just didn't speak about these things and had been expected to pick up knowledge of the sexual processes by osmosis or some other strange and mysterious means. She herself, at the tender age of twelve, had attributed her own bloodstained underwear to an over indulgence in ripe tomatoes the day before. Her own mother, Lexie's grandmother, had been unable to comfortably explain what was happening and had turned that job over to another daughter who was older. Only through her subsequent nurse's training had Mrs. Alexander become aware of the bodily functions related to reproduction.

Lexie was sprawled out on her bed reading when her mother entered holding an innocent-looking magazine. Telling her to read a certain article, she then turned and walked out of the room with the words, "I think it's time you knew about the things that are in there, Lexie. I think you're old enough to handle it."

That piqued her interest. If she needed to be "old enough," that meant something formerly forbidden was now accessible. Mother had left the magazine folded back at the designated article, and it was with anticipation that her eyes roamed over the print looking for the title. There it was, staring back at her from the pages of *Parent Magazine*.

"What Your Teenager Needs to Know About Reproduction." How bold and daring it seemed, considering the non-communicative era of the fifties was only just over. This was a new decade, and with it came the subtle beginnings of a new way of thinking concerning that most primitive and compelling force — sex!

Oh, this stuff, thought Lexie. Boy, Mom was really hot on her knowing about all this. Just a month or so ago, she had asked her to watch a show on television. It had been about reproduction too. She had felt a little squirmy watching it with her father in the same room, but it had all seemed straightforward enough. What was all the fuss about? What did all the older girls whisper about, and why did the boys nudge each other when a good-looking girl walked by only to exchange comments and then erupt in laughter? *What was going on?* she wondered. One thing was certain after watching the programme. She was never going to kiss any male on the mouth ever again!

So that's how you make babies! She watched fascinated as the outlined figures of a man and a woman were shown kissing each other and a little white dot floated from the man's mouth into the woman's and then progressed down into her uterus (through her stomach?) to grow into a baby. Lexie by now knew all about the role the womb played as the site of the baby's growth and development. She also knew that a child resulted from the union of a sperm cell with an ovum. The only missing link had been the information of how that sperm cell got transported from one body into the other, and now the announcer's voice booming over the action on screen explained it all for her. He was saying that as the man and woman kiss, the "seed" travelled from the father's body into the mother's body, and then they joined together to form one cell from which the baby began to grow. She had seen her mother and father kissing, and they'd had babies. In her young mind it made sense enough. Her next realization had been, as long as I don't kiss any boys, I won't have a baby. Dad's a boy, so I guess no more kissing him! Oh well, she had already stopped kissing her dad on the mouth a long time ago. He seemed content with a peck on the cheek, so Lexie figured that wasn't going to be a problem. Besides, he was watching this with her, *So he knows too*, she reasoned.

Then the image of Gary's face flashed through her mind! With sudden panic, she wondered if that kiss counted. She squinted her eyes in order to focus more closely on the diagram on the TV screen. Thank goodness! She breathed out a sigh of relief. The man and woman had to have their mouths open for the seed to travel through! She thanked her lucky stars that she had kept her mouth clamped firmly shut as Gary had ground away on her lips. Saved!

It did not dawn on her that a great deal more kissing went on than babies were born. Furthermore, she did not stop to question that she was already very fascinated with the opposite sex, and perhaps her desire to experience her first open-mouthed kiss might not coincide with her desire to become a mother. Logistics were not her concern that night. She simply took at face value what had been presented to her, not only by adults who should know, but through the medium of television under the guise of public education. Therefore, it must be true!

Because of this, when she saw the article was again about reproduction, her enthusiasm waned. *I know all about that, already*, she thought.

Nevertheless, she began. She had told her mom she would read it, and read it she would.

Comfortable on her tummy, the rolled magazine in her hands, her legs bent up over her backside, she moved them back and forth at a leisurely pace in time with her reading. The words flowed along, the concepts fit what she already knew to be true. She nodded her head from time to time indicating her acceptance of the information being presented. Everything fit. The world was a sensible and safe place. The facts presented matched what she had already come to accept as truth.

While reading the paragraph explaining how the sperm was deposited into the mother's body, she began to sense a new truth. Her body alerted her first. As her eyes gobbled up each new revealing sentence, they expanded in a wide-eyed desire to negate what she was reading, to go back to a place of ignorant innocence. The muscles of her body began to tense, and she stopped breathing momentarily. It was as if her body was preparing to be hurled off a steep precipice, to take a leap after which it would forever be different.

Her eyes were like runaway freight trains! She could not have stopped them gobbling up the printed words even if she had wanted to. On and on they went, charging forward, pulling her, preparing her for that one explosive sentence which was to come. Her eyes, her mind, her heart, and her soul took in the group of words. She was left reeling in disbelief!

It had begun innocently enough. There was talk about how a man and a woman love one another and desire to be close. This also meant close in a physical way as they enjoyed touching one another by hugging, kissing, and often by sleeping together. *So far so good*, she thought. *If they're kissing already this should be it*. The words, however, went relentlessly on.

Man and woman, the article stated, in wishing to be even closer, often pressed their full bodies together. Lexie did not like where this was leading. Like a sleepwalker, entranced, she read helplessly on. Then it happened. The next sentence took hold and hurled her into the adult world of carnal knowledge. She landed in breath-caught horror, innocence forever gone, called to acknowledge her place in the sexual scheme of things.

If it was there in bold, black print it must be true! Her mind reasoned; her emotions rebelled. She read it again and again. The sentence mocked her from the page. She kept hoping she had misread it, but it stubbornly refused to be different. The bold, black defiant words read: "Because the man and woman love one another, they desire to be close, as close as any humans can be. They lie so close together that the father places his penis inside the mother's vagina."

That was it. Blunt, straightforward, no nonsense, no apology. Was it too much to ask that there be an apology for destroying the innocent belief that a woman's body was just for her own use? Here it was all at once. Not only would Lexie one day be expected to turn her body over for nine months to an invader called a fetus, she would first have to endure the thrusting entry of something entirely foreign. That something would be attached to another human being—a male! A creature she had very little understanding of and the presence of which now made her feel very uneasy.

Do they ask you first? she wondered. *Or do they just do it to you when they decided to?* The article had said the two people did this when they loved each other. Well, she loved people, and yet there was no way she was going to let any of them stick their parts inside her! No way!

Just as she was about to trounce her way indignantly off the bed to tell her mother what she could do with this dumb article and to set her straight that no way could people make babies this way, she was stopped dead in her tracks! The thought paralysed her as the information hit home and became personalized. She couldn't go to Mother with this. The man and woman they were talking about in the article were no longer distant, unreal beings.

Oh my God! thought Lexie. *My mom and my dad do THAT!*

Unbelieving at first, she struggled repeatedly to push this new knowledge out of her thoughts, but it kept coming persistently back. *They do THAT! My dad really does that to mom and she LETS him!*

To Lexie it seemed like such an invasion of the self, she could not yet comprehend how a female might allow it. Beyond her realm of belief was the fact that a female might not only allow it, but even actively participate.

She lay back down on the bed, knowing that she wasn't going anywhere. She wasn't going to seek Mother out, for in so doing she might run the risk of having this horrific discovery confirmed.

But as she rolled over and buried her head in her pillow, a little voice inside her head prodded her into acceptance as it whispered compassionately, *You know it's true don't you, Lexie?*

And so this new knowledge found acceptance in her psyche. In the past, like a sleeping nymph not yet ready to face its metamorphosis, Lexie had repeatedly and patiently stored away each bit of troubling truth in her chest of memories labelled "Think About Later." Yet this new knowledge undeniably fit with other bits and pieces she had gathered over time and now emerged whole in her understanding.

She got up to seek out two aspirins, her body and mind reeling from the changes brought about by growth. She would have the rest of her days to think about the mystery of men and women creating life together.

For now that was enough.

CHAPTER ELEVEN:

GATHERING THE THREADS TOGETHER

ـﻰ

Pretty, dark-eyed, sparkling girl,
What is that smoky haze around you curled?
Drug of acceptance, ticket to partake
In a ritual for which you mistake
The sleep of denial for the
Living act of being awake.

With its sensual commands
Your body demands
And like a sleepwalker you obey.

Choosing not to understand,
Feeling not the terror of aloneness,
Looking to others for truth
Desperately seeking answers outside the self
Convinced in the existence of
The Ultimate, Universal Information Booth!

The head and body ache went away, but the new knowledge did not. When she ceased to think obsessively about it, Lexie knew she had accepted it as truth.

There was one immediate benefit in possessing this new knowledge. If that was how you made babies, it meant kissing was safe! This pleased her greatly because to her kissing had been the most exciting and glamorous part in all those twenty-five cent Saturday movie matinees she had sat in the dark watching over and over again. The rest of what went on may have been unappealing, but being held gently in a man's arms and kissed softly while romantic music played in the background appeared absolutely wonderful to Lexie! As the lovers stared into one another's eyes, the warm glow of candlelight flickering across their beautiful, larger-than-life faces, Lexie would melt inside. In the world of movies what came after the kissing was a crescendo of music and a slow, lingering fade-out of the images from the screen. That was just fine with her because she was content to experience everything only up to the point of fade-out anyway. It was a good plan for now. Girl meets boy. Boy asks girl out on a date. They fall in love. They kiss and then, FADE-OUT.

When she wasn't at the movies, she was fighting for acceptance in the rigidly stratified society of Gibson High. Named after one of the most prominent members of the small town of Whitfield, Dr.Gibson had been an adamant proponent of the small-town way of life, as long as it was synonymous with the White Anglo-Saxon way of life. The upper strata of Whitfield society clung tenaciously to their privileged positions, their code dictating that if you came from a "good" town family of long standing, or if you were a distinguished professional and thus a valuable addition to the town's prestige, you were accepted. Those in the privileged inner circle had memberships in the country club and pews in the right churches. They received invitations to join service organizations and sponsored sports teams meant to build young heirs into men and provide young daughters an opportunity to cheer them on.

In the hallowed halls of this microcosm of society, Lexie learned the power of labels. Labels on people, labels on jobs, labels on conduct, labels on locations, all the way to yes, labels on the very clothes one wore. It was here she was labelled "outsider." Oh, the labels weren't distinct enough to actually be spoken of out loud, but it didn't matter. Everyone already knew the rules without verbalizing them. If you lived in town and you came from one of the accepted families you of course were "in." If you had the misfortune to have located outside of town (which was tacitly accepted to mean that your family could not afford to live in town), you were definitely "out." It's not that these divisions were so much consciously practised as they were a result of the dynamics of familiarity. The children of the long-established town families had played and schooled together since infancy. They liked many of the same activities, and they shared the same values and experiences. To them, a family who had to scrape to afford the necessities of life was like a family from another world. They had no comprehension that life could be lived so precariously close to financial ruin or as Lexie's father liked to put it, "One step away from the poorhouse."

She became respected by her teachers for her academic abilities, but was never accepted by the "in" crowd. She took this rejection personally, not yet worldly enough to know it had very little to do with who she was and everything to do with what she was—a poor kid from outside of town.

There were others like her. They hung around on the fringes of the "in" crowd hoping no one would notice they weren't really a part of anything that was going on. Who ruled was clearly understood and the unspoken code acknowledged a definite hierarchy of power. Your first year of high school attendance was basically considered to be a write-off socially. Even the town kids had to pay their dues that year. Considered a "minor niner," all were inconsequential in the scheme of things and were expected to be unobtrusive or worse, to be the willing butt of jokes. A young boy who was a star athlete, or a girl who was exceptionally pretty could get noticed by the power brokers and be accorded special status, but this was rare. Another ticket of acceptance, not able to be used by many because it required a special talent, was the route of musician. Being able to project the tortured and aloof image of the rock star, sound and persona, was an automatic ticket of acceptance. However, most had to content themselves that grade nine was the "suck up" year. The year where you tried to attach yourself to the older, more sophisticated members of the "in" crowd by emulating their behaviours and espousing their values.

There were some exceptions of course—mavericks who went their own way, some of whom were actually in the institution to get an education and whose primary source of validation was not social acceptance. Anyone who was anyone socially considered them to be inconsequential, labelled them "eggheads" or "goofs" and never considered them as a threat to the established social order. It was rare that they ever crossed over into the "in" circles.

That left the accepted "in" crowd and those who *wanted* to be the "in" crowd. Grades ten and eleven were the years when you established your group, gathering around you other students with similar standing in the social order. It truly helped if you had a legacy membership. That consisted of an older brother or sister who had previously passed through these hallowed halls as a member of the privileged populace. Such siblings guaranteed automatic acceptance. Even individuals who did not perfectly fit the mould would be tolerated because of their bloodlines. By grade twelve if you had done it right, you had arrived. The remaining two years were left to enjoy the rewards of power and influence. By then it was widely accepted who the leaders of the school were. They went unchallenged, and they ran the student council, organized the prom, planned the after-game parties, terrorized the minor niners on initiation day, and even sometimes were seen having serious, in-depth conversations with the other power brokers of the school—the teachers. These students became a select group, dating one another, for who else could the star quarterback of the senior football team be seen with other than the head cheerleader? And so it went down the line. Not only did they stake their claim in the social order, they chose a partner known as a "steady" with whom to consolidate their position. Here, too, was another important exception to otherwise rigid, if unspoken, acceptance codes. Female beauty was often a ticket in. It was accepted that a reigning senior male could have a female of lower social status as a "steady" if she was beautiful. It was also understood by these reigning senior males and their cohorts that occasional "slips" with girls of lesser status were known to happen when raging hormones took over. There were girls who believed their bodies would provide them with the acceptance they sought. What they did not know was that word went out like the beat of a primal jungle drum that they were an "easy lay." Consequently, they were suddenly much sought after, not realizing their ticket of acceptance was stamped, "temporary only," for these senior boys knew the code: "Good enough to screw, but not good enough for you!"

It was the chant they used to remind one another that this girl was not the one to be taken home to Mother.

Lexie kept bumping up against these unspoken rules, coming away feeling raw and bewildered. She had always been taught to believe that if she worked hard and was honest and nice, she would be successful. Successful, at that time in her life, was translated "accepted." Acceptance was what she wanted more than anything else. She worked exceptionally hard at her studies, she was honest in that she did not pretend to be someone she wasn't, and she was so-o-o nice. She smiled, she laughed, she talked animatedly to everyone. She bubbled up and down the halls, and then she sat home alone and dejected on Friday and Saturday nights wondering why it didn't all work. Was there something she was doing wrong? She would resolve to simply try harder, do better, be more. What she didn't know, was that what she sought was not in her power to gain for herself. She did not understand enough to rail against the unfairness of expecting herself to succeed in the game of life when she didn't even know the rules much less that they were stacked against her!

It was precisely because she didn't know these rules that she, unwittingly could break them. Had she truly understood, that knowledge could have paralysed her. Her innocent belief in the world as a fair place, with the only requirement for happiness being a willingness to embrace it fully, led her to test the adage that love can conquer all.

His tall frame slouched. With his hands jammed into the pockets of his jeans, the boy looked as if he didn't care who won the basketball game. He was tall—over six feet—lean, dressed in tight, faded jeans and a denim jacket suggesting a contempt for the school dress code which still saw young men attending class in crisp slacks and thin, dark ties. There was no doubt he was a town kid, part of the "in" crowd. He wore his air of superiority like a mantle. An accepted leader, this fact was so much a part of his persona it simply was taken for granted that others would step aside so that he, Geoff Courtland, could be given a better view of the ongoing game. Life always met him on his terms. He had grown used to that.

Lexie watched him intently from across the room, filled with a strange longing. He had something she wanted—a sense of being effortlessly connected—a feeling of total acceptance.

It didn't occur to her to remember she'd had that feeling at one time. When and where had she begun depending upon the validation of others?

Was that what Geoff had? Others who mirrored back a reflection which said he was of value? That's what she wanted—more mirrors - shinier, more brilliant mirrors. The more they reflected acceptance, then by merely being with others she could feel all right. If they, the brilliant ones, liked her, then by definition she had to be likable.

The more this limited loop of thought played in her mind, the more determined Lexie became to place herself in the picture beside Geoff Courtland.

She was startled back to reality when a pretty, pert young woman, whom she recognized as having been on the other end of a set of pom-poms at last fall's football games, slid in to take her place at Geoff's side. He looked down at her and then returned to watching the game. Even from a distance, Lexie could see there was tension between them. The attractive cheerleader was unknown to Lexie except for hearsay and what she herself had assumed that pert, pretty cheerleaders were like.

Today, as the girl stood beside Geoff, she did not fit the image. Her face was clouded with concern. Melody was her name, but because she was so tiny and because she was the other half of someone called Geoff, she was referred to affectionately as, "Mutt, as in "Mutt and Geoff." They definitely were an odd-looking couple. Melody was barely five feet tall, standing beside Geoff, and the top of her head only reached his chest.

"I wonder how they manage to do it?" Lexie thought to herself, and then felt totally shocked for thinking such a thing. *Where had that come from?* she wondered. She had heard the whispered rumours. After all Melody and Geoff had been "steadies" for over a year now and that seemed to be about the length of time it took a persistent, hormonal young male to wear down the resistance of an equally persistent, virginal female. Word was out that Geoff had scored with Melody some time ago, but was now looking for a way to move on to other conquests without hurting her too much. It wasn't that he didn't like her, because he still did. It was just that he was a restless male, and there were so many other beautiful young women.

A few more weeks of asking questions and observing Geoff confirmed it. The relationship between Geoff and Melody was over. Lexie made her move. She invited Geoff to a party a friend of hers was having. It was a fringe-group party and no one from Geoff's crowd would be there. In retrospect Lexie came to understand that was why he had agreed to go with her.

He arrived promptly on time, pulling into her driveway in a car which, just as he had, stunned her. It was often parked outside the school where it gathered crowds of admirers. The car technically belonged to Geoff's father, a man who had an appreciation for enduring good lines in cars and who felt passionately about the statement a 1957 Ford Thunderbird sport coupé made. It was sleek and white, with wide whitewalls and a small round porthole on each side of the roof. As she slid into it, Lexie became aware of the smell and feel of leather.

She was feeling increasingly awkward reflecting on Geoff's distant air of politeness as he had said hello to her parents, his eyes taking in their small, cramped bungalow.

God, I hope he likes my friends! They're not going to be what he's used to, she thought.

When they arrived at the party, Geoff remained distantly polite. He headed for the punch bowl and reaching into his jacket pocket, pulled out a metal flask and poured something into his drink.

That bad, thought Lexie. *This date is going so horribly, he needs alchol to face it!*

It did not occur to her that Geoff needed a drink to face a lot of life.

It just wasn't fair! She had worked so hard to prepare for this date, and she was proud of the way she looked!

Since noticing Geoff for the first time, she had lost her interest in food. Beginning to recover from the reeling, overbalancing effects of having been thrown headlong into womanhood, her body was finding its equilibrium, and as the fat melted away from the round full-moon face, there began to emerge the promise of beauty.

But Geoff had no eyes to see. Only painfully aware of the awkward outcome of a yes said too quickly, a response prompted by the misconception that, because Lexie Alexander was an out-of-town girl striving for popularity, she might be persuaded to share the wealth of her abundantly proportioned chest as well as other sexual favours. It had not taken him long, however, to discern the disappointing fact that he was not going to score.

They drove home in silence. There seemed to be nothing to say to each other. Geoff had spent the evening shrouded in cigarette smoke, distantly apart as Lexie had tried to cover her hurt by bubbling away to her friends. She thanked him politely as they arrived in her driveway, told him not to bother walking her to her door, and slipped quietly into her small house. She knew she would never again be transported by her dream man in his cherished chariot.

The hurt and shame ate away at her for months. Hurt that she had not been good enough for Geoff and shame because she had foolishly hoped she could be. She avoided him at school and dreamt about him at home. She spent hours in her bedroom sprawled across her bed, getting up only to change the stack of 45 rpm records on her new record player. Listening over and over to the same sad songs, she lost herself in them. They transported her to a world of bittersweet longing where to be a jilted lover had a noble air of suffering. The pain sustained her, nourished her, allowed her to feel connected to life. She no longer had to stuff herself with food to feel. As she lived through her first true brush with unrequited love, not only did Geoff melt from her life but so too did the pounds! Her mother had jokingly suggested she was living on love and so it had been. There came the day when she awoke from her lovesick slumber to find a slender young woman, staring back at her from the mirror! Geoff never knew it, but from then on he held a special place in Lexie's heart, for he had shown her the incredible power of romantic love to sustain the body if not the soul.

Lexie's new body had arrived just in time for summer! When she tried on her new bikini for Jayne's approval, her friend's face had darkened. Her expression confirmed what Lexie had seen, but been too afraid to believe. Reflected in the mirror was a body boys fantasized about. To Jayne it meant only one thing—competition. Up to now she had enjoyed the position of superiority her lean body had afforded her. Things were about to change.

The summer after grade nine a newcomer had walked onto the ballfield, bluntly informed the coach she was a pitcher, and proceeded to prove it. Built like a boy, Jayne moved like one when on the mound, concentrating her energy and delivering blistering, bullet-like pitches. She didn't waste words either. When introduced to Lexie, she blurted out, "I hear you're pretty good in school. I could use some help with a summer school assignment. You busy after practice?"

The friendship began with Lexie tutoring Jayne and falling in love with her handsome twin brother, Tim. Jayne never knew if her girlfriends were truly hers or just using her to meet her brother. Lexie proved herself to be a true friend. Even after Tim made it quite clear that, although he found Lexie cute, she was entirely too young (two years younger than Jayne), she still continued to seek out Jayne's company.

The two became inseparable, spending the summer of Lexie's fifteenth year together. It was a magic time of freedom; summer jobs began the year you were sixteen. Jayne was off at noon after summer school classes, and they spent their time together biking down to the lake to lie on the beaches with Tim and his friends. Tim worked mostly evenings as a bus boy, so he was around enough to keep Lexie in a constant state of infatuation. Their evenings were spent at the ball diamond playing or cheering on other teams and taking long walks to the local overpass where they would stand on the high bridge over the four-lane highway below and wave at the cars zooming by below them. Sometimes they would wave more than their arms, pulling up their blouses to flash the passing motorists and give themselves a thrill.

There was also another attraction at the "bridge" as it was known by the local kids. When you scrambled down the grassy sides of the hill and climbed in under the arch of the concrete structure, you found the section of the hill that supported the bridge was smoothly paved with rounded stones. There was also a concrete slab forming a perfect bench. When you sat there you could not be seen from the road above. This anonymity afforded an opportunity to indulge in a secret and forbidden pastime.

Under the cover of darkness, with her bum firmly seated on the cool slab of stone, knees up under her chin, arms firmly wrapped around them to warm herself in the chill of the summer night, Lexie first participated in a ritual of acceptance. She learned to smoke.

Jayne, more accomplished in these things, deftly pulled the pack from her jacket, unsheathed the book of penny matches stored inside the cigarette package for easy transport, pulled out a long filtered cigarette and while still explaining to Lexie that there was absolutely nothing to it, lit it, sucked in the smoke, and finished her sentence with a long, jet stream of smoke carrying the words.

God, she looked so sophisticated the way she did that! thought Lexie. She took a cigarette, holding it between trembling fingers. If Jayne could do it, so could she. Besides, a lot of the kids she considered worth hanging out with smoked. Her mother smoked, and she knew that her dad had smoked when he was young, so why not?

She put the cigarette between her lips. It felt dry and smooth. She touched the tip of her tongue against the end of the filter. Not much taste. She felt Jayne shift her weight and come closer to her. Her face was right next to hers and all of a sudden it exploded in a burst of light. She sat there looking at Jayne's face framed in the glow of the match.

"Ready?" she asked.

"Sure," came Lexie's reply.

Jayne touched the glowing end of the match to the cigarette clamped between her teeth. Her nostrils flared as the stench of sulphur from the ignited match reached them. *This was not terrific so far,* she thought. It got worse.

"Puff on it, dummy!" Jayne instructed her. "You've got to breathe in the smoke. Not just into your mouth. That's how sissies do it. You've got to inhale!"

Lexie puffed as instructed and soon a cloud of acrid smoke surrounded her. Her mouth and nostrils smarted and her eyes were watering.

"No, no," Jayne instructed again. "You're not going to get any good out of it unless you inhale!"

"How can you tell if you're inhaling?" Lexie removed the cigarette from her mouth long enough to ask. She certainly wasn't enjoying smoking so far. She felt like she wanted to brush her teeth already.

"You can tell you're inhaling when the smoke comes back out in a long, steady stream like this."

As she demonstrated, Lexie watched amazed because the smoke truly did not drift up lazily around the face as it had done for her, but left Jayne's body as if propelled forward aggressively and forcefully. Jayne controlled and directed the smoke's path. Jayne projected an image of power and sophistication that was irresistible. Lexie would master this activity of smoking no matter how awful it smelled or tasted.

She tried again. This time she sucked. She held the smoke in her mouth for a second and then it happened. She breathed in and as she did she felt the smoke rush in to fill her waiting lungs. It seared its way down, and she could gauge its progress by the burning sensation. Her body wanted to explode in a cough, but she held on, she resisted, taking the smoke all the way into her lungs and then the reversal of air as she began the exhale. Holding her chest muscles rigidly, tightly, so as not to explode in a coughing fit, she felt the searing smoke again in her throat, mouth, and nostrils as her lips instinctively formed a channel for its passage. Her nostrils flared sending two other streams of smoke downwards to join with it.

"All right! You've got it!" Jayne exclaimed excitedly. "You look like a real pro, now!"

Great, thought Lexie. *I wonder how pros look when they puke?*

She didn't puke; she persisted. She persisted even though every part of her body rattled and shook in its attempt to expel the intruding toxins. Her stomach retched and turned over. She ignored that and puffed onwards. Her head felt as if it had expanded to the size of a hot air balloon and hung suspended somewhere above her body, totally unconnected. Still she persisted for the rewards were perceived to be great. If her body felt disconnected, being initiated into the ritual of smoking made her feel emotionally connected. Smoking with others allowed a bonding to take place as all other activities stopped. The drug created the illusion of a shared experience of inner peace and outward strength. Lexie liked this "high" enough to endure a retching stomach and swirling head.

She learned to smoke, persisting in her lessons under the worst conditions. Her parents of course had made it clear that none of their children would be foolish enough to indulge. It was a case of do as I say and not as I do or did. Smoking openly in front of her parents was out of the question, and this posed challenges for Lexie and Jayne as Jayne had a similar situation at home.

A terse and stern Englishman, the single parent of a brood of five rebellious youngsters, ruled the house. Jayne and her twin brother Tim were third in the birth order with one older sister who chose not to live at home and boarded elsewhere, another older sister who was training for a nursing career and still lived at home when not seeing her numerous boyfriends, and then a much younger brother who unhappily played the dual roles of father's favourite and siblings' scapegoat. Lexie couldn't believe Jayne's family history. Completely beyond her comprehension was the fact that Jaynes's mother had left her husband and five young children because she had fallen in love with another man! She had simply given them up! A bewildered father had bundled his brood up and headed for Canada in an attempt to rebuild his shattered life. Consequently, he appeared to be angry most of the time, his task such a formidable one that he lay awake nights, struggling with the panic he dare not reveal during the daylight hours. Anger was easier.

With both houses unavailable to them, the girls spent many hours tucked under their bridge, strengthening both their addiction and their friendship. When they would come into the house reeking like smokehouse meat, Mother's nostrils would flare, and she would tartly ask them, "Have you girls been smoking?" True to their bonds of friendship, they would promptly lie for one another stating with wide-eyed innocence, "You know that we don't smoke, Mom!"

"I don't know any such thing!" she'd retort but she also knew it was useless to pursue the topic and would leave the two of them to nudge and wink at each other behind her back as she walked away with a resigned shrug.

They thought they were so smart, so grown up. Funny how "smart" people don't give others credit for having brains as well. They all played the game of we know that they know, but let's deny it and pretend. So it went; from cigarettes hidden in the lingerie drawer, often soaking up the taste and smell of perfume sachets, resulting in true dedication to the art of smoking in order to puff away at tobacco cured with sickeningly sweet, cheap perfume; to filling the house with air freshener; to opening the windows wide allowing the temperature in the house to drop to subzero after smoking up a storm when Mom and Dad were out; to younger sisters living on an expense account furnished by bribe money that kept them from snitching; to cruising cooly by your parents after being out deeming that to kiss them hello was too babyish to consider, when really you needed to remove any evidence first by a trip to the bathroom sink and a date with your toothbrush. So the game of denial was played.

Testing the limits, Jayne and Lexie eventually became so emboldened and addicted that they dared to smoke in Lexie's bedroom. (They may also have been encouraged by the subzero weather outside.) There they would lie sprawled across the bed on their stomachs, ashtray conveniently ready to be shoved quickly under the bed out of sight, window open wide to allow the billows of blue-grey smoke to escape and one ear always cocked for the sound of parental footsteps outside the bedroom door. After Jayne would leave, Lexie's mom would often poke her head through the door and ask, "You girls been smokin' in here?"

Why did she bother to ask? Lexie wondered. She knew and Lexie knew she knew, but it was part of the game parent and child played called: Do what you do, but don't tell me what you do, so that I won't have to react to what you do, and therefore I'll let you do what you do even though I'm frightened and upset by it.

Lexie discovered that in raising parents, sometimes what they didn't know didn't hurt them or you! It was so much easier to play the game of denial, or so she thought.

Denial, denial, not a river in Egypt, but a profoundly efficient coping strategy. It let things go on that were going to go on, but relieved you of the pain and anxiety of really feeling it. Denial allowed Lexie to indulge in the smoky drug of peer acceptance and lessened the pain of her parents' disapproval. It also served as a very effective coping mechanism in allowing her to explore another area of growth. An area she believed to be riddled with sinkholes that could suck the very nobility from the soul and drag it down into muddied, depraved energies. Denial provided her with a life raft as she explored the sexual swamp.

How had it started, this tingling awareness that came over her and short-circuited all other thoughts? It held her in a trance and left her breathless, wondering what had just shuddered through her body. It often had come upon her when she lay on her bed, daydreaming about being with a boy. Lately it had started to come to her as she lay naked in her bath, the water lapping gently around her full and rounded female body. She was aware of her large, firm breasts, the contours of which rounded down to a rib cage definable under the thin layer of smooth flesh, on down over her slightly rounded tummy and ending between her thighs where it still amazed her to see dark, thick hair. The source of the short circuit was here. Here in this area between her thighs. It would begin as a warm, pulsing energy and spread, warming its way up through her belly and branch off to her breasts making them heave and their nipples tingle. As the water lapped sensuously around her, her breath would begin to come in shorter bursts, and her brain ceased to think about anything else except the sensations flooding her body. There was a compelling energy radiating from between her long, sturdy legs - an energy that demanded to be touched and explored. Lexie could not bring herself to accept that she desired to touch herself in this way. It seemed unthinkable to her. She had been taught that "nice girls" touched there only to clean themselves. This was done in a quick and detached way. To touch oneself deliberately and for the purpose of pleasure seemed abhorrent to her. Nowhere in the romance novels or movies did anything prepare her for this overwhelming urge to explore, touch, and experience a part of the body that held captured and caged so much explosive, sensual energy.

It was absolutely unthinkable she should move her hands to that area of her body, but as she lay suspended in her sensual trance, feeling the water lapping gently against her skin, it became acceptable that the water should caress her. To allow the water from the tap to trickle over her vagina in a steady stream was somehow acceptable; it placed the responsibility for what she was experiencing outside herself. That she could accept. She wasn't actively doing this; she was simply allowing it to happen. In her mind, to passively allow freed her from responsibility. She experienced in a detached, unconnected way. To do otherwise would be like taking in an abandoned child, accepting the responsibility of integrating her sexual self. That, she still could not do. Her sexuality was explored only when chemicals coursing through her system demanded release. Once satisfied, she stuffed the act away in a dark part of her psyche labelled, "Danger! Handled with shame!"

Her fifteenth summer continued to unfold. The family, true to tradition, planned its annual summer vacation. There were two things Lexie's mother always insisted on celebrating no matter how poor they were—Christmas and summer holidays. It was a familiar scene to see a beleaguered Mr. Alexander rubbing his furrowed brow and bemoaning the fact they simply could not afford these extravagances while his equally determined wife expressed adamantly that these were not luxuries but necessities to nurture the soul. The issue simply was not negotiable in her mind. So every year he worried and every year they went anyway.

This particular year the family had discovered the cost-efficient benefits of camping. Even Mrs. Alexander had to concede that with four children on one workingman's salary, they simply could not afford anything more elaborate. So it was that the family's tiny compact car (Mr. Alexander was ahead of his time in recognizing the value of a fuel-efficient vehicle and shunning the large gas-guzzling, expensive models) was loaded to its limit with the required gear. Not only was it crammed full with the six bodies, the family pet, a dog called Gyp (they had paid five dollars to get him out of the pound and Mr. Alexander had said even that was too much), but also the roof of the car was piled with equipment almost as high again as the vehicle itself! When they rolled into the provincial park grounds, it was with stunned disbelief and total respect for a packing job well done, that park officials watched as the bodies, pet, and equipment just kept spilling out. Needless to say it took a few hours for the family to establish themselves and set up a well-ordered camp. Each member of the family had assigned duties and Mother supervised much like an army sergeant overseeing a foray into enemy territory.

When she was satisfied all was safe and secure and the camp operable, it was tacitly understood that the holiday had officially begun and all were free to pursue their favourite activities. Mom and Dad enjoyed sitting peacefully under the shade of a tree and escaping into a good book or the newspaper. Lexie's youngest sisters Celine and Millicent spent hours on the beach, burying ants in the sand. And Tessie consoled herself with her fashion dolls after Lexie had bluntly told her that she didn't want her kid sister tagging along.

Tagging along on what, Lexie wasn't quite sure. She felt compelled to slip a leash around Gyp's neck and set out to explore her surroundings. She followed the camp road until it ended in a fine, white sand beach. As she surveyed the long crescent of shoreline, she noticed a clump of young teens standing around down near the boat launch. Coming closer, she realized they were all girls except for the tall figure in the middle. At the prospect of new people to investigate, Gyp began to strain expectantly on his leash, bounding around excitedly as they came closer to the group. Lexie hurried her steps to keep up with him, her eyes down, concentrating on not getting tangled in his leash as the excited animal darted back and forth around her legs. Impatient, Gyp had suddenly taken off heading straight for the group, Lexie's head snapping upwards with the jolt. By the time she had gained control of the dog, she found her eyes had come to rest on the most incredible creature she had ever seen. Her jaw dropped slightly as, in a snapshot moment, she took in his features. He was tall and slender with hair the colour of pale wheat, framing a face with aristocratic, high cheek bones, soft parted lips over straight, even teeth, and a smile gracing his beautiful, sea blue eyes as well as his slightly amused face.

She looked away quickly. She knew if she stared too long, she would become entranced, and she dared not even hope. What was the point of attempting to be with this beautiful one? She knew the hurt of failure.

She reigned Gyp in, wound the leash tightly around her hand to gain control and, lowering her head, walked past silently. She steeled herself with the thoughts, *Don't even think about it. He's got every girl on the beach already. Why would he bother with you?*

She filed the possibility away under the heading: "Hopeless Causes."

The next day dawned hot, bright, and sunny. After breakfast and camp chores, Lexie packed herself up and headed for the beach—alone. She didn't want to be seen associating with her family. It wasn't that she was ashamed of them, for she loved them all. It's just that they were so noisy and boisterous and would draw too much attention. She didn't feel like being noticed that way today. She walked onto the beach, so self-conscious in her body-hugging bathing suit, that she didn't raise her eyes from sand level, but spread her blanket and settled herself without so much as a glance around. She lay back, eyes closed, body drinking in the warmth of the sun.

She sensed him before she saw him. She knew someone was standing over her, surveying her. She struggled up onto her elbows and shielding her eyes from the sun with her hand, her field of vision took in a long pair of bronzed legs covered in soft blonde hair. Her eyes travelled upward, resulting in a sharp intake of breath when they reached his face. She could not fully discern his features as he stood blocking the sun, his face in semishade, blonde hair floating about it like a halo, but she knew who it was.

"Oh, it's you!" she blurted out in surprise.

"Hello," he said in a formal clipped way. There was a hint of an accent in his way of speaking. "I noticed you and your dog on the beach last night. Uh, do you mind if I sit and talk to you a minute?"

He didn't wait for an answer but rushed on into his next question. "By the way, where is your dog today?"

Did she mind if he sat and talked to her!!? My God, it was more than she had dared hope for!

Then in a split second she realized two important things. One: walking dogs was a great way to meet boys because it gave you something to talk about besides each other. And two: the rapid way he asked questions meant he was nervous. Would wonders never cease! *He* was nervous talking to *her*!

So that's what they did - talk about the dog - at least at first. The day ended with them knowing a great deal about one another. His name was John Andersen, and he was Danish. That explained the blonde hair and the slight accent. He now lived in Georgetown, which Lexie discovered to her dismay was quite a distance from Whitfield. He loved dogs, he hated his younger sister, he loved sports, and he hated being dragged along on family vacations. A year older than Lexie, he felt keenly that he should have been able to stay back home alone with his many friends.

They laughed. They talked. Lexie fell in love. She knew exactly the moment it happened. They had been standing knee deep with the clear Georgian Bay, water lapping around their knees, when he had looked directly into her face and had said so sweetly, "They're very pretty." He hesitated and then added, "Your eyes, you know. They're pretty."

He then reached down and intertwined his thin fingers with hers, and they walked up onto the beach. Lexie could not respond. She was still processing the incredible fact that he thought her eyes were pretty. It was like a scene out of a movie - all that she could ever hope for. How could she, Lexie Alexander, have the most-sought-after young male on the beach intertwining his hand in hers?

Later, as she was pondering this same question, her image staring back at her from the round camping mirror nailed to the tree, she was startled when a woman passing on the road nearby yelled back over her shoulder to a young man, "John, why don't you ask the pretty girl to join us for a walk?"

Lexie looked around her. She was the only young girl in sight. She must mean me, she thought incredulously to herself! This deserved a closer look in the mirror. Was she really pretty? How had that happened? She had never really worried about it during her tomboy days. And when it had started to matter, cruel comments about her exploding size and zit-filled face had dashed all hopes that she might someday be considered attractive. But here it was. That woman had said she was pretty. Maybe, it was true! How could you tell? She wasn't quite sure yet.

For the next two weeks the sun, and John's presence, warmed and coloured her skin and her days. Just being with him made her glow all over. They walked and talked, swam and ate together, raced along the beach, and sat with arms enfolding each other staring silently at the water as it lapped gently against the rocks.

He even tipped her face up gently to his and softly brushed her lips with his own. He was so gentle, so shy. He made no attempt to invade her body with his. Lexie, boldly, on their last evening together, her body wanting more, took charge. They were sitting on a large rock which jutted out over the bay. He had his arm around her and was kissing her softly, when, not knowing where the knowledge came from, but following instinct only, she tentatively probed his soft, supple mouth with her tongue. He shot back from her, startled.

"No, no," he said to her.

She felt puzzled and ashamed. She was thankful for the darkness as she could feel the flaming of her face. It had seemed a natural enough progression for her, but he obviously had felt it was not. She had been wrong. In this game of love perhaps it was best to let the male take the lead. Judging from John's response, she assumed males did not like an aggressive female. Lesson learned and filed.

It was never spoken of again. They went back to kissing in that soft, gentle way as they spent their last day together. John asked her for her address and promised to write to her. She did not ask for his for was it not the boy's prerogative to decide if the romance would continue? Lexie could not conceive of chasing a boy who might not be interested in her. She would do what females do in relation-ships—wait for the male to make contact.

It was with an aching heart that she did as Mother instructed, "Say good-bye to the nice boy and get into the car."

She travelled home feeling empty, as if something very impor-tant had been left behind. She had felt so complete, so accepted, so important at the side of her beautiful, gentle boyfriend. So much so that it left an ache in her heart intense enough to be a physical hurt. Even years afterwards, the memory could cause pain.

He never wrote. Her many hopeful trips to the mailbox were not enough to produce the desired letter. Wishing and wanting it with every bone in her body just wasn't enough to make it happen.

It took her many years before the mention of his name failed to produce a shiver of remembrance. It took as many years to figure out that he hadn't written because their summer romance had obviously meant more to her than it had to him. Or perhaps, as she preferred to believe, he — in his older and wiser way — had understood that a long-distance romance was doomed. For whatever reason, their connection in this life eventually mellowed into a warm and wonderful memory for Lexie and a conviction she would ever be grateful for the gift John Andersen had given her — the beginnings of a belief in her own attractiveness — pretty eyes and all.

As John's presence receded from her life, it left a vacuum for another energy, as different from his as day is to night, to flow into Lexie's experience. In all her excitement over her summer love, she had forgotten her promise to Jayne. She tried every way that she could to get out of it, but Jayne stubbornly insisted. They had planned that she would accompany Jayne, her father, her youngest brother, and his friend on a camping holiday as soon as she returned from her family vacation. Lexie had absolutely no interest in going. She had every intention of babysitting the mailbox, but Jayne simply would not take no for an answer.

Lexie resigned herself. She supposed she could be just as miserable at Algonquin Park as she could be at home. She made Mother promise absolutely not to open any of her mail, and she started repacking her things.

The trip started out innocently enough with Jayne and Lexie breaking the rules no more than to smoke secretly in their tent at night. It was here that she learned that filters do not burn well as she tried, in the blackness of a northern Ontario night, to light the wrong end of a cigarette. She persisted, though. She was determined to get this smoking thing right!

It was on the third day that they met them, and Lexie came to know the tall, dark man who was to have such an impact upon her life.

She didn't like him at first. Two sites away, he was camped with a shorter, swarthy-faced friend. Jayne had her radar tuned for the opposite sex and had noticed them soon after arriving. She dragged Lexie out on numerous walks which just happened to go right by their campsite. The next thing Lexie knew, they found themselves flanked by these two strange boys while they were sunning themselves on the beach. They had some tired line, such as, "Where you girls from?" and the conversation went from there. Lexie was really not interested, but quick, beseeching glances from Jayne informed her that her friend certainly was! She played along.

They had agreed to go for a hike later that afternoon. After they left, Jayne wasted no time, staking her claim on the shorter, heavier-set one called Danny. He had soft, warm brown eyes and Lexie, if she had been interested, would have chosen him over his tall, dark, brooding friend as well.

Their hike began with Jayne jockeying for position behind Danny, and Lexie clustered close as well because she had little desire to spend time with the silent, uncommunicative friend. Something about his energy rattled her. There was an underlying air of arrogance about him. He did not rush to present himself to others but waited silently, patiently, as if he knew, that given time, he could influence whomever he chose.

Hiking, however, was different. Here, he aggressively took the lead, leaving absolutely no doubt as to who was in charge of this mini-expedition. This was not, by his definition, to be a leisurely walk, but a test of strength and stamina. He pushed them to fight through heavy bush, disdaining to travel the well-worn paths. He insisted they climb steep and rocky cliffs, their feet sliding precariously backwards on the loose shale. With every complaint, he reassured them the view they sought would be well worth their effort. They pushed on, exhilarated by it all in spite of themselves, and every time Lexie looked up, there he would be, well out in front of them, meeting challenges head on, leading, controlling, his presence growing with each step, becoming larger than life for Lexie. Such was his power, to take charge, to shape events, his energy becoming like a beacon to the lost, a "more than" magnet that drew the "less than" shavings of society.

Compelled by all that he appeared to be, Lexie was drawn like a moth to a flame. She manoeuvred herself closer to him and struggled to keep up in order to impress him, convinced he effortlessly possessed what eluded her.

She looked up to him in more ways than one. He was tall, exceptionally tall, with his thin frame sparsely covered with flesh. His hair was black, swept severely off his face, exposing a high, wide forehead. Nestled under softly feathered brows, his eyes were small, grey-green almond shapes with his sharply defined, high cheekbones rising up to meet them. His nose was ordinary enough, fitting his face in proportion, but it was his mouth which arrested the observer's gaze! A wide gash across his face, two thin strips of lip rested on an incredible set of teeth. Perfectly straight and even, all thirty-two of them filled his mouth. Incredibly strong, successive layers of enamel gave them their most distinguishing quality. They were distinctly yellow!

This and the fact that his bathing-suited body appeared like a skeleton with skin repulsed Lexie physically. Yet, he mesmerized her! His confidence transformed into an energy which drew her ever nearer, seducing her with its promise of powerful secrets - secrets of self-mastery and control.

She began to see him as a man of the world. The more she learned about him, the more his influence grew. He was so much older and more sophisticated than she. He made a point of letting her know she should feel extremely flattered to be the recipient of the attentions of a twenty-one-year-old male. He also owned his own car, lived in the big city, had a full-time job, and hinted that he had dated many, many women. That was his justification for taking her on as his pupil. He knew how women should be. They spent many hours seated on the rocks overlooking the northern waters with him instructing her on how to behave. It appeared that he considered her raw material to be shaped and moulded.

Jayne and Danny were fast becoming inseparable, and Lexie was left struggling to meet the expectations of her inscrutable new mentor. The attraction of these new male companions was so compelling that Lexie and Jayne blatantly flaunted all the camp rules. So much so that upon arriving home Jayne's disgruntled father unceremoniously dumped Lexie's belongings in her driveway vowing never, never to take two teenage girls camping again! They had spent many hours late into the night in the company of these young men leaving Jayne's father to surmise the worst. Lexie, however, returned home still in possession of her female virtue and had even earned herself a new name.

He wrote letter after letter to her after they returned home. Letters in which he instructed her on how she should conduct herself and how she should express her sexuality. There were suggestions on what to wear, how to move her body, what to say, what not to say - pages and pages of critical analysis of all that she was. He would always begin each letter with the name he had invented for her. To him she was "The Ice Queen."

John had warmed her, building within her the desire to unfold slowly, sensually, a flower opening to the sun. This cold one, forced, rushed, demanded, took from her. He would kiss her roughly, his tongue probing, forcing her open, his large mouth seeming to devour her. His hands roamed her body in ownership and when she objected, he would ridicule her for being so naive, so unsophisticated. Pinning her against a tree, he had once sucked upon her neck until the blood rose to the surface leaving a large bruise. He called it a "hickey" and said that it was a mark of affection. To Lexie it was a blight to be hidden from everyone. Then, as always, he left her in a state of agitation.

This was the source of his power over her, and he knew it. He witheld his approval, and because he could not be pleased, he became irresistible. With each new hurt, Lexie only vowed to try harder, be more beautiful, more capable and to earn his love. If he was not loving, she must give more of herself. The fault must be hers.

They dated sporadically for six months, when he could fit her in. He stood her up regularly; she cried over it regularly. Always afterwards were the letters, long and critical, never with an apology. Always, she was the one who needed to change, to grow and mature. Every letter carried the same message and every letter was signed simply, dispassionately, coldly, with only his name—Derek.

Time and distance weakened his hold. September came and with it grade eleven. She was busy with school, the workload demanding. It was well known as the watershed year—only serious students bound for universities stuck it out through the Maths and Sciences required. Derek's letters and visits became less frequent. After another ruined weekend when she had waited by the window until late into the evening, she decided she would put an end to a relationship that always left her feeling like imperfect goods. The decision was made in a moment of determined anger. When the anger receded, she was left wondering just how she would bring it all about.

While she had no difficulty talking to others, Derek left her mute. He silenced her with accusations that she was too talkative in social gatherings. Yet at times he could stand back, admiring her naive and innocent brashness, her bold confidence with others. It was his unpredictability, his ability to jealously stomp that very confidence out of her with cruel, critical words that left Lexie struggling to know how to be. The very qualities he criticized were the ones which attracted him.

When contrasted with the wellspring of innocent happiness that bubbled up naturally inside of her, he came face to face with the hollow void inside himself. A vortex of churning pain, it greedily sucked the joy from his being. The spontaneity of simply being alive had long been sacrificed on the altar called control. He had learned as a young child never to trust the world around him. He would control all he experienced. Whatever price that exacted, he would pay. The tense, fearful energy that consequently coursed through him, leaving him humourless and constantly vigilant, was little enough price to pay for the illusion of safety control provided.

When she reminded him with her tinkling laughter and sparkling eyes of his own innocence lost, his sense of self-betrayal crushed her smile with cruel words.

There was no smile this night, as with halting words, after an evening spent watching a drive-in movie in tense silence, she told him she could not see him again. Because of the age difference, her mother had decreed she could no longer date him, Lexie lied. She held her breath after the words had left her lips, wondering if Derek would erupt in anger. He nodded his head silently in acquiescence and as she moved to get out of the car he had only one request. In soft, hushed words he asked that she kiss him good-bye. It was a small price to pay for freedom. She leaned over to comply and saw this man of stone unashamedly let a single tear slide down his face.

Derek was crying! Why now? Why had he not let her see this vulnerability sooner? There was that split second of hesitation and then wise, experience-worn words ran through her mind. It was just too little, and it was just too late. With determination she planted a quick kiss on his thin, hard lips and removed herself from his car and his life. Determinedly, she walked up the driveway to her house, not looking back, only hearing tires scrape against gravel as he shot the car back onto the road. Immense relief washed over her! She was free! She had been strong enough to stand up to him and to express, finally, what she wanted, even if she had hidden behind the pretense of her mother's wishes.

"I guess Mother was wrong," she mused as she let herself into the darkened house. She remembered her lively, French-Canadian mother's edict when she had first met Derek. He had arrived formally clad in a suit to escort her daughter to a movie. Mother had taken him in from head to toe, and had decided then and there, this was the man her first-born daughter was to marry! She believed in such things as precognition of events and other psychic phenomena. They had been accepted parts of her cultural conditioning. She had cheerfully informed Lexie of her insight, perhaps only half-believing it herself, but nevertheless enjoying the concept of a daughter happily married with a family of her own. Never did she imagine the impact such predictions could have on a young, impressionable daughter. No different than most youths, Lexie was always looking for clues to reveal her future, giving it more credence than even she herself would have liked to admit for she had seen her mother's insights come true often enough.

She filed the whole experience away under "In the Past" and believed she was never to see Derek again.

Her grade eleven year was uneventful enough. She did well in school. She always did well in school. She was getting better grades in dating too. Her sisters now incredulously handed over the phone with the announcement, "Lexie, it's for you and—it's a boy!"

Her friendship with Jayne had also deepened, so much so that, even though Jayne had left school to attend business college, their relationship provided leads for lots of new men in Lexie's life. Jayne, it seemed, had absolutely no difficulty attracting the male species into her life, and Lexie put it down to the fact that she was two years older and more sophisticated, whatever that meant. Having by now been told often enough by people other than her parents, for they didn't count, that she was pretty, she knew that Jayne was not better looking than she was and that only made what was happening even more puzzling to her. The boys they met would start out being attracted to Lexie and then, after a few dates where she jealously guarded her reputation as the "Ice Queen," they would lose interest and stop calling. She would hear a few weeks later, through the grapevine, that some of these boys were now dating Jayne. This happened several times and each time Jayne would approach her sheepishly, protesting she just didn't understand it, but somehow she just couldn't help what had happened. They had fallen for each other she would say, and oh well, there were lots of fish in the sea for Lexie weren't there? And Lexie would wonder, *If Jayne isn't prettier, then what's wrong with me that they like her better? What's she got that I haven't got?*

To Lexie being pretty and nice should be all that was required of a girl in a dating relationship. It really never occurred to her that while the rumour went around that Lexie Alexander was great to take on a picnic because she could keep the beer cans cold between her legs, her friend Jayne could provide so much sizzle that a barbeque wasn't even necessary!

Lexie did not yet understand the incredible sex drive of the young male and how it so often blinded them to any other attributes a young woman might have. In their eyes, girls were categorized. Phones rang accordingly.

It gradually began to dawn on her that she had something the opposite sex wanted. Her first experiences with boys had been hurtful and left her very tentative about her attractiveness. Now she heard the word "pretty" and her name often used together in the same sentence, but it wasn't until many years later, as she caught a glimpse of herself in a store window one fall day, that the realization struck. "I AM a beautiful woman! Wow!"

Sadly, the realization had come far too late.

As she headed into her sixteenth summer knowing that in the battle of the sexes she was better equipped and eager to participate, Jayne, again, provided another lesson in the ways of the heart.

Lexie had been babysitting. Boys or no boys, money still had to be earned. Jayne had gone to a dance where many older boys hung out. Of course, true to form, she had caught the eye of a charismatic young male, and also true to form, she wanted to show him off to her best friend.

They pulled into the driveway of the house where she had been babysitting just as she was pocketing her earnings and preparing to leave. Jayne's voice called out to her in the dark, offering her a ride home. A stormy night, high winds having knocked down power lines, the entire neighbourhood was in complete blackness. Lexie could barely make out the kind of car it was, as it too was black. She felt around for the back door handle. There wasn't one. Suddenly the front door swung open, Jayne leaned forward allowing her to slip behind her into the back seat. Her face flaming with embarrassment, Lexie hadn't seen that it was only a two-door car. She got in, head down, not even glancing at the young man behind the wheel. The door slammed shut and there they were, two young women in a total stranger's car, cocooned in blackness, unable to see each others' faces.

His name was Eddie, and he was French Canadian. He was here from Quebec because of the work at the car assembly plant in Oshawa. He was twenty-one, had come up here with his cousin Gilles, and was living with an aunt and uncle.

Lexie pieced the information together as they talked. They were now parked in her driveway and as he put the car into park he also reached down and pushed in the cigarette lighter. So, he smokes too, she thought. She watched intently as he drew the glowing lighter close to his face. She liked what she saw. The more she listened to him talk, the more she liked what she heard, and as her eyes took in her surroundings, she began to be impressed. She had noticed an unusual odour when she had slid into the back seat, but because she had been under the stress of meeting someone for the first time, the churnings of her own internal programmes had completely blocked out any sensory input. She was so self-aware at those times that she became unaware of anything else. Now, however, it clicked in that the odour was one of canvas. This was a convertible!

Jayne had really scored tonight! Not only was he good looking from what Lexie could see, but he drove a great car! This added up to fun! Her interest in him was growing stronger, minute by minute.

She was startled by his sudden request for a match. Why did he need a match when he had the cigarette lighter? As it flamed in a burst of light in front of her face, she knew why.

"I just wanted to see what you looked like, Lexie", he explained. "You sound really nice."

So, she had made an impression on him as well. She was secretly pleased.

Later, as she got ready for bed, the image of his strong profile, illumined in the soft red wash of the lighter's glow, burned into her brain.

Over the course of the next few weeks, the sight of his beautiful face became a source of pain. It became evident he was Jayne's, and she was not about to give him up. She had dated him first and in the unwritten rules of the game, if she was not yet ready to let him go, Lexie would have to back off and keep her feelings a secret. You did not make a move on your best friend's boyfriend, no matter how attracted you were to him. Instead, she did the only thing she felt she could legitimately do. She prayed like crazy that they would break up, and she dressed to kill every time they went out together as a foursome. Eddie had been so impressed that he had introduced her to his cousin Gilles and they had all become constant companions.

Gilles was tall, thin, affable, and a true romantic. He pursued Lexie like a lovesick puppy while she pined away after Eddie. Jayne remained in the dark about all of it, and Eddie continued to set up more and more dates as foursomes.

Did Eddie like her? That became the question that tortured Lexie each and every time they were together. She became like a detective in search of clues, analysing everything he said to her, going over and over it in her mind after she left him. Meanwhile the weeks ticked by. Gilles continued to greet her with, "Hi, Beautiful!" each time he saw her. Jayne continued to date Eddie, and Lexie continued to feel like she would burst if she kept her feelings for Eddie bottled up any longer! And Eddie? He continued to play his cards close to his chest, never openly suggesting to Lexie how he felt, but dropping hint after ambiguous hint. It was driving her crazy. So much so that she jumped at the opportunity to get away from the situation for a while.

Jayne had been working on a plan for weeks. Some months before, she had left school and taken a job in an office. Here she had met a whole group of new friends. She had introduced Lexie to them, and even though they were older they seemed to accept her. The plan was this. A group of girls from Jayne's office were renting a cottage for a week in late August. Jayne had asked Lexie if she wanted to come along.

Now she realized this would take monumental effort on her part to convince her parents to let her go. She was, however, determined to get her way on this. Perhaps her parents sensed her determination or perhaps they felt she deserved a reward after a long, hot summer spent scrubbing pots and ironing shirts in a nursing home. For whatever reason, they said she could quit her summer job a week early and go.

Lexie was ecstatic! Eddie and Gilles were less than thrilled. Perhaps they sensed that, at this stage in her life, Lexie—somewhat unconsciously, but nevertheless wholeheartedly—felt that boys were like streetcars. If you missed one, there was always another one coming along to take its place! To her dating was still somewhat of a buffet experience. You sampled a little of this and a little of that. Some left a sweeter taste than others.

Besides, Gilles and Eddie had promised to drive up at least once to visit them, so it was with a clear conscience that she packed her bikini and shorts and headed for the adventure of a lifetime.

She didn't think to ask why the car trunk was full of suitcases jammed with clothes but without a single grocery bag. They stopped for supplies at the local liquor store before heading out and were content they had everything they needed for the week. They sure didn't pack like Mom!

When they arrived, they checked out the cottage, learned the numbers of all the fast food delivery joints, and set up the bar! This was holidaying, teenage style!

The girls quickly established a routine: sleep until noon, have coffee, toast, and peanut butter for breakfast, walk down to the beach to bake the body for a few hours, come back to shower, shave the legs, paint the nails, curl the hair, layer on the makeup, and run around the cottage in your bathrobe, hair in rollers, cigarette dangling lit from the mouth, waiting for the nails to dry, and discussing the pros and cons of all the outfits displayed on the bed waiting for a decision to be made as to which was the best for the evening's activities! All the while, the bar was open. As each bottle was consumed, it gained a place of honour upon the open studding which formed a ledge where the wall and ceiling of the cottage met. As the week progressed, the girls were surrounded by "dead soldiers"—empty glass sentries looking down upon them. Their cottage had become a gathering place for other teens on the beach. The newcomers soon joined in the spirit of things and realized that liquor bottles thrown in the trash bins could arouse suspicion, so they too added theirs to the collection.

It was here Lexie learned to drink and experienced her first bar.

The legal drinking age was then twenty-one. In the wide-open tourist town of Wasaga beach, however, it was not strictly enforced. Even with that, Lexie and her friends knew it would take some stretching of the imagination, along with some clever work with make-up and clothes, to get a sixteen year old past the bouncers at Jake's Bar.

It was midweek, but even so this local hangout was jammed with sun-bronzed youths and seasoned drinkers standing around small, round tables. The tops of the tables were littered with jugs of beer, half-filled glasses, heaped ashtrays, empty matchbooks, crumpled wads of dollar bills, and carelessly tossed coins - all evidence of the exchange of money for a few hours of heady experiences where one could feel the rush of being alive.

The air was a blue-clouded haze, and the smell of beer was everywhere as Lexie shouldered her way through the crowd. She navigated by sight only for it was impossible to hear anything above the loud thumping of the amateurish band. No one paid any attention to the music anyway. People moved and laughed and talked in the semidarkness. So THIS was a bar!

As they cut their way through the crush of bodies, Lexie was exhilarated. She had made it past the sentries at the door. They had looked at her somewhat askance, knowing full well that she was blatantly underaged, but played the game called, "She knows that we know, but it's too much trouble to bother. Besides she's a looker so we'll let her in."

She didn't give them long enough to change their minds, slipping quickly by them, and following close on Jayne's heels to a table well at the back of the dark room.

As the music thumped in the background, she faced another challenge. She had to convince the waiter she knew what she wanted to drink. Feeling very insecure about the whole ritual of drinking, she had held back at the cottage, only occasionally splashing a minimal amount of liquor into the odd soda. No one had seemed to notice or care. So, now the question? What to order?!

She liked to drink Coke, and she had noticed that all the other girls had been pouring rum into it this week. Rum! That was it. She'd ask for a rum and Coke!

Just as she decided this, she lifted her head to find herself staring into the eyes of the waiter. As she ordered her drink his look definitely communicated that, in his experienced opinion, she was in over her head. Nevertheless, he brought her drink and later that night he brought himself to their table.

She learned that he was a man exactly twice her age as they talked after closing time. He was tall and muscular with dark, wavy hair, and he moved with a definite sense of purpose. He may have been only a waiter, but the way he moved and worked his tables said that he knew absolutely everything there was to know about being a good waiter. It was this sense of definiteness about his place in the scheme of things that was more intoxicating to Lexie than the rum.

Lexie flirted outrageously with him and it was no surprise when, at the end of the evening, he invited her and her friends to continue the party at his beach house. Why end such a great party, Lexie remembered thinking?

That was about all she remembered. The evening had begun to blur after her second drink. She did not know how it all came about, but she found herself lying with this man, stretched out on his couch, with none of her friends around. They had talked away the night, holding one another as they spoke of love and sex. He had confessed to her how he still ached for the warm, close body of his wife beside him at night; how they had been so impassioned for one another that at times their love making had bordered on causing physical pain — so intense was their desire to stir feeling in one another. Then had come the ultimate betrayal—the emptiness he had felt when he discovered her gone one day. Without words, she had left. He spent his next years trying to make her actions fit into what he had perceived their love experience to have been. How could he have not seen it coming? Rather than striving to deepen his understanding, he instead sought solace in the arms of the many whose smiling faces looked up at him through the smoke-filled haze of Jake's Bar.

Lexie listened. She comforted him as he again wept out his story. She knew she had nothing to fear from this older, more experienced man. He wanted only to be touched by a woman's hand, to be surrounded by the scent and softness of her, nestling himself into the curves of warm, yielding female flesh.

They talked and touched and dozed and awakened to the pale, pink streaks in the morning sky. He took her to breakfast. He watched tenderly, protectively as she wolfed down coffee, bacon, and eggs. She could not understand it, but she was ravenous! She felt strong and in control. Entrancing a desirable man twice her age had given her a sense of incredible power!

They talked some more. He lied. He told her he would come by to see her that day on the beach. He took her back to the cottage. She waited all that afternoon. Wisely, he never came. She returned to the cottage to face the downcast glances of her companions. They did not speak to her. Their sidelong looks showed the disgust they felt. She had become an outcast. She had dared to do openly what each of them did only secretly. They had assumed she had slept that night with the friendly, persistent waiter from Jake's, and they had judged accordingly. Such was her naivete; she believed one was innocent until proven guilty. She also assumed, incorrectly, she would be measured by her own standards. Standards that said she would never commit that most intimate of sexual acts with a total stranger. No one would, would they? To her it was natural to believe they had spent the entire night only talking.

What Lexie did not know, could not yet know, was that each of us sees others through our own filter of experience. Each of the young women there with her had, on other occasions, done things very similar to what they now condemned. Did it make them uncomfortable to look into her eyes, their contempt a contempt they felt for themselves but suppressed? Was to look upon what Lexie had done like prodding, with the sharpened stick of memory, a coiled shame that lay within themselves? Roused, did it strike out at the one who triggered the recognition?

She felt their rejection, their judgement of her, but she could not find the words to defend herself. What good would it do? They wanted to believe the worst of her, and any argument she could produce would be weak at best. What could she say? That she had known, and her waiter had sensed, she was only flirting with that experience of experiences. She was not yet ready. She knew it, and he had honoured that knowing. Her companions had taken a moment of human connection and defined it within the limits of the sexual.

Because she had done it openly, feeling no shame, they further labelled what she had done as cheap and vulgar. It never occurred to them that she was shameless because she felt blameless.

Lexie withdrew into herself for protection. Jayne still spent time with her. Perhaps she felt responsible.

If Lexie went unnoticed within the cottage, she certainly did not go unnoticed on the beach. She was astounded when one young man, standing by a car parked on the beach, yelled out to his buddies to hold him back as she walked by! It seemed to be in direct proportion that as she became more and more sought after by the male population, she became less and less liked by their female counterparts. Did you have to choose, she wondered? If you pursued the attention of men, did that mean forever setting yourself apart from closeness with women? It all seemed so unfair and so confusing. Why were other women so angry with her? Was it a cruel trick of life that the more you were given, the more you were made to pay? She had been bestowed with beauty and intelligence, but those attributes set her apart and made her a vulnerable target for those who wished to test their own strength by tearing down the substance of another.

Gilles and Eddie arrived and provided some relief. They spent time with her and Jayne, checking out all the local attractions. They roared up and down the open stretches of beach in Eddie's convertible. They rode the Ferris wheel. They ate greasy hot dogs and guzzled cokes purchased from the street vendors, and they hit Jake's for happy hour. She searched faces looking for her waiter, but he never appeared.

They partied and drank late into the evening—so late that it was decided Eddie and Gilles should stay overnight at the cottage. They arrived back to another party going on there. By this time, she'd had enough of parties and said her good nights. She plopped herself, clothes and all, on one of the double beds and dozed off. She awoke to find Gilles curled around her. She was cold so she struggled to get under the covers. In doing so, she woke him. He nuzzled in closer to her and gently began kissing her all over. She responded sleepily. It felt pleasant to be held, touched and kissed softly while still in the haze of half-sleep.

His kisses began to come faster and more urgently. He swung his body around so that he now lay on top of her. She was virtually pinned under his weight. He began to rub his body back and forth against her, kissing and moaning softly.

At that point, she detached. She became like a clinician, cooly observing what was happening from a vantage point outside of herself. She felt curious about what he was doing, nothing more. She did not understand yet about male orgasms. Suddenly the moaning stopped, he rolled off her and without uttering a word, pulled the covers up around himself and went to sleep. She lay there dumbfounded. What on earth had just happened? Why had he suddenly stopped?

A joke she had heard months before surfaced in her memory. She had not understood it at the time, but had sensed that it held a secret she should understand. Now as she remembered it and put it together with all the other bits of information from her sexual file it clicked. Gilles had just "come" in his pants!

She had first heard the word "come" in that joke. It had gone like this: a man and woman were making love on the train tracks. The train was roaring down on them. Someone who happened along and saw the situation tried to warn them by yelling out, "The train's coming!"

The punch line was the response, "So what! I'm comin' and she's comin' too!"

What did it mean to come? she had wondered. And was it so compelling a happening that it was worth dying for as the joke suggested?

She remembered now what she had read about the male depositing sperm in the woman's body, and the act being a release for them. She had heard rumours, mostly spread by boys she was sure, about how painful it could be for a male to have an erection and not ejaculate his sperm.

My God, Lexie sucked in her breath as the 'aha' moment struck! Boys experienced the same incredible, compelling sensations that had led her to explore her own body. They too were seduced by sensation to press it further and further—to reach finally its waves of completion. They didn't just deposit sperm as the clinical articles said! They rejoiced in doing it! They revelled in it! So great was the drive to complete the act of love that they felt they would die for it! That was what made the joke funny! It held a grain of truth. Everyone saw themselves in the joke!

She smiled inside herself. So that was coming. Boys were sure messier about it than girls. *I wonder how Gilles will feel waking up with all of that in his underwear? Yuck,* she thought. *Glad I'm not a boy.*

She drifted back into innocent sleep, not knowing that the events of this week had conspired to prepare a new identity, a new label, for the "Ice Queen."

"Slut! You're acting like a slut, Lexie!"

The words slapped her in the face as Jayne spat them out at her. With stunned silence she reacted. What had she done that was so horrible?! How could she defend herself when she really didn't even comprehend the charge? Why did other people always label and judge what you did?

The ride home was spent in silence. There was no desire for words. Each in the car was lost in their own swirl of feelings. Lexie was being punished by the others' silence because she had broken the rules. She had openly pursued sexual experiences, flaunting the fact she was sampling the sensual stew.

She had only to look at them to know what they were thinking. She could read the sad disappointment in Eddie's, eyes and she knew he believed Gilles had scored with her last night. She felt his pain, and she felt shame for she was unable to explain herself. She could only continue in silence, to endure the long trip home knowing that now

Gilles also felt uncomfortable with her. He felt shame, struggling to accept that his desire for gratification had been so overwhelming it had driven him to act while in a cottage filled with his peers. Peers, who although silent about it, nevertheless made it known they had few doubts about what had happened on that double bed.

And then there was Jayne. Her silence was born of anger. Lexie had been her guest, her protégé. She had vouched for her and now the youngest of them all had dared to be more outrageous than any of them! Lexie had turned into a man magnet and what infuriated Jayne most was that she didn't even have to work at it! In fact, she was blissfully unaware of what she had! Jayne knew that if Lexie had now entered the sexual arena, as she incorrectly supposed she had, there was to be a definite shift in the friendship's power balance. Jayne would no longer be in possession of secret, powerful knowing that had left Lexie disadvantaged in competition. Jayne did not like that prospect at all!

That fall Jayne sought out Lexie's company less and less as she returned to school and Jayne to her job. Their lives seemed to go in different directions. Jayne had a new steady boyfriend. She had moved on from Eddie, and Lexie noticed she was different with this new love. She seemed consumed by him. She had very little time for anyone or anything else. Lexie also moved on to others, but she missed the incredible closeness she'd had with Jayne. Now she had been replaced by a male. It seemed they both only knew this one way of relating. You were either totally and obsessively involved, or you rarely saw one another as you moved on to the next object of desire. Lexie, too, was ready to move on.

CHAPTER TWELVE:

THE TAPESTRY REVEALED

ॐ

Artists are we all,
Weavers of yesteryarns.
Yet, mysterious still to us remain
The very fibres of our mien.
All once were taught our landscapes to shape
In our birthplace amongst the stars,
The right to create bestowed as ours.

To grasp fully our coloured threads,
To be empowered as we know each one,
For even those of darker, denser dreads,
Though painful to embrace and endure,
Give texture and hue
Allowing me to know you.

For I am you; you are me,
All entwined, yet free.
And our artistry, if honestly done,
Through trust teaches us,
The human race is to be
An interwoven tapestry!

"You're not afraid of anyone are you?" The words startled her. She looked up into his soft, liquid eyes. He knew. He had articulated something that had been a part of her for as long as she could remember, and yet it now startled her to have it put into words.

"You weren't even afraid of your parents when you were growing up, were you?" he went on.

"You have hands like a man - strong. You're a doer - always going, going. You meet life head-on." His eyes sparked and his face crinkled in a warm smile as he let her hand fall gently from his loose grasp.

"You'll live a long, full life."

With that he turned his attention from her to the children clamouring around him in the crowded schoolyard.

Lexie put her gloves back on her bare hands, cupped both of them around her warm coffee cup, and continued to patrol the yard. Now forty-three and a schoolteacher, Lexie pondered the aged Shri-Lankan's words.

"Not afraid of anyone. What a joke! Now, I'm afraid of everything!"

She had seen him in the yard, surrounded by clamouring children, when she had stepped out into the grey November day to take her turn at yard guard—professional jargon for supervision duty. In these days of custody battles, it was her business to know what he was doing there, for parental abductions of children were not uncommon.

As she moved closer to him, and he raised his turbaned head in greeting, she recognized him as the school's part-time crossing guard. He was surrounded by densely packed children all eagerly wanting his attention.

Lexie moved to the outside of the circle to observe. At her arrival he flashed a gold-toothed smile and went back to what he had been doing. It was then that she realized with a start that he was reading the children's palms! Come to think about it, she had heard the kids in her class discussing him a few days ago. They had been amazed by the things he had told them.

Suddenly when one of the young ones turned to her and trilled out, "Mrs. G., why don't you let him do it to you?!"

She instinctively responded.

Mrs. Derek Gaust, teacher, wife, and mother of two, had removed her glove and placed her hand, palm up, into his, allowing the penetrating dark eyes of a soothsaying stranger to see her old fearlessness now dormant, bound, sacrificed for safety, buried beneath layers of accumulated identities. Where had she gone, this Alexis Alexander?

Standing in the yard, looking out over her many busy young charges, their laughter and voices swirling around her, she drifted in and out of her memories. Had she truly ever been fearless?

What she had done would certainly be labelled by many as more foolish than fearless. She could have been killed, just as her mother had said.

She had been out for a walk alone one foggy, fall evening. The bridge and a cigarette had seemed to suit her mood for she was tense and restless. She had returned for her grade twelve year without the comfort of a boyfriend.

Standing at the crest of the bridge, she saw a figure looming in the dark distance. She turned to face the form, squinting to better discern who was approaching through the fog.

It was a male. She could tell by the confident way he strolled towards her, never slowing his pace to see who she was. She stood her ground.

Details began to emerge. He was wearing a long trench coat, carelessly open down the front. The rhythmic swing of his arm as he raised his lit cigarette to his lips, its end flaring as he dragged on it, left a trailing glow of warm, red light.

He walked directly at her, stood facing her and said simply, "Hi."

He then turned to look down on the traffic below, leaned casually on the bridge, and took a long, deep pull on his cigarette.

Spellbound, Lexie could only stare in silence. This stranger who had just swirled forth from the fog fascinated her. He was young, perhaps just a bit older than she, and he wore his hair slicked back off a lean chiselled face. In the soft red glow of his cigarette, the outline of his jaw seemed set, even defiant. He waited for her response.

"Hi," she answered, casually turning her attention to the cars passing beneath them.

That simple response had given him the permission he sought. He took charge of the conversation, appearing eager to talk. He asked what she was doing in the dark alone, where she lived, if she came here often, how old she was. Then he moved on to more philosophical issues.

All the while, he revealed little, testing her trust, waiting to share who he was.

When she showed no fear, her dark stranger began to tell his story.

She was right about his age. He was just twenty. He had hitch-hiked his way here. He was now on his way north to the highway where a bus would take him home to relatives who would help him.

At this point in his story, he hesitated and turned to look at her.

"You're not afraid of me, are you?" he stated with a twinge of incredulity. "I could have hurt you, you know." He paused and then looking her in the face said, "I have a knife. I used it to break out of jail this morning."Lexie's eyes widened, but she spoke softly, her head lowered.

"I knew you wouldn't hurt me," she whispered.

There was a long pause and then he said, "Walk me to the highway, will you?"

She nodded.

In silence they walked the quarter mile to the crossroads where the bus would pass. He then turned to her, and taking her shoulders in his hands, stared down into her eyes. In the glow of the street lamp, Lexie saw sadness in his face as he said softly, "I'll never get the chance to know you because you'll never see me again, but can I ask you something?"

Again she nodded.

"You helped me a lot just because you listened to me. You didn't run away from me when I told you what I was." He hesitated there for a moment, and then with an intake of breath he asked his question.

"Can I kiss you good-bye?"

As a response, she simply tilted her face up to his. She closed her eyes and felt his lips brush hers ever so lightly, then briefly press harder. For an instant she felt the warm, moist, fleshiness of him pressing down on her. As his lips left hers he grabbed her into him, hugging her close, his chin resting upon the top of her head. For the briefest of moments, he clutched her desperately to him as a drowning man might grasp anything to keep himself afloat.

Out of the blackness came sounds of gushing air brakes and the thud of the closing bus door, and he was gone.

Walking home alone in the dark, she wondered why she hadn't been afraid. Did her fearlessness come from a fatalistic attitude or despair about life? Did it matter if she lived or died for weren't both just different ways of existing? What she was, her essence, her energy, would always be, wouldn't it? Wasn't dying really the easy part? The true challenge was living each day. Maybe it was because she sensed her time to die was a long way off. There was to be a lot of the hard parts yet.

The sun streamed in through the tall windows of the chemistry lab. The grade twelve class was busy getting itself organized as the teacher droned on calling out the attendance roster. Books were dropped with a thud on desktops and the metal of the stool legs scraped against the floor as students settled themselves. It was a room Lexie was not particularly fond of. It was full of strange smells and equipment she was sure was deliberately uncooperative. They never turned out. Her experiments, that is. Her anxiety in this particular class was compounded by the watchful eyes of a droll, dull teacher who never smiled and seemed not to enjoy what he was doing.

As she struggled to set up her bunsen burner yet again, she heard it. In answer to the teacher's query the voice rumbled out a reply with a definite air of carelessness and just a hint of disrespect. She had never heard the voice before but it quite obviously belonged to someone who was not intimidated by the stern, white-coated teacher. Lexie looked through the forest of her fellow students to see the source of the voice standing tall, straight, and alone at the far side of the room. Her breath caught in her throat. Who was HE? She knew she had never seen HIM before!

As all around her appeared to stop, her awareness of everything but him fell away. Her breath held captive in her throat, her eyes moved over him. Suddenly she was pierced with the suffocating pain of longing, knowing he was for her. She must find out everything about him.

His name was Mark Shepherd, and he was a year ahead of her in school, in her grade twelve chemistry class because he had failed the subject the year before. Disdainfully, he had not shown up for the first several weeks of classes as he had decided the introductory stuff would be a waste of his time. In a school of well over five hundred students, Lexie had somehow managed to be unaware of one handsome, blonde senior. She was about to fix that!

As she began asking questions about him, she unfortunately was not encouraged by what she found. It seemed that failing chemistry was not the only challenge facing Mark Shepherd these days.

What she discovered explained the tense scene she had witnessed. Lexie had watched as Mark and a girl stood talking to one another. She was obviously upset, and Mark's face was pulled tight in an expression of concern. He had reached out and touched her shoulder. She had sadly nodded her head and turned to leave. As she walked quickly past, Lexie knew she was fighting back tears.

The girl's name was Penny. She was tiny, just five feet tall, plump and rather plain, and she had been Mark's steady since they had been in grade eight together. It made sense then as to why Lexie had not been aware of him before. Because he did not date other girls, he had chosen not to take part in much of the social scene at Gibson High.

He was, however, a town kid, son of a professional, well accepted by his peers, a star player on the football team, and now, it seemed, about to take on a new role—that of a father!

Rumour had it Penny was pregnant!

Obviously this posed a problem for Lexie. How was she to stop liking him? Especially when it seemed fate continually put him in her very path.

After school one day Lexie had spent an hour over sodas and gossip and now was saying her good-byes. She was walking backwards, still talking to her friend who was headed off in the opposite direction.

Her body thudded into his. She turned around to look up into his grinning face, and she knew! *He knows I like him. Damn!*

Flustered, she walked around him as he jostled his buddy.

"Better watch what you're walking into! You might just get picked up that way!"

He laughed good-naturedly and sauntered on in the direction of her friend.

God, I like the way he moves! thought Lexie.

Thoughts of Mark Shepherd's strong, masculine body and soft, warm smile filled her all the way home.

It happened again! She didn't see him coming. She had gone without a date to the dance hoping Mark would be there. It was now official. Penny was not pregnant, nor was she any longer Mark's steady. Mark was available, and Lexie was determined to make him notice her.

But why did it have to be like this? Having circled the gymnasium many times in vain, she decided he just wasn't there, and she headed upstairs to her locker. Lost in disappointment, she was climbing the stairs head down, when, thud. Her shoulder collided with his torso. He and his buddy had been coming down the stairs, had seen her coming up unaware, and had put themselves directly in her path. Again the smirk and that knowing look. Her face flamed. In awkward silence she heard him throw the words laughingly over his shoulder as he continued down the stairs.

"Do you make a habit of meeting boys this way? You could be dangerous!"

Why did she always look like such an idiot when he was around?

That's why she felt she had nothing more to lose. It was the week of the Sadie Hawkins dance, and the school was abuzz with rumours about girls asking boys. It was the one dance of the school year where the girls could usurp the strictly male prerogative of asking for a date.

They had just finished chemistry, the last class of the day, and there was a mad crush to get out to their lockers. Mark's locker was directly across the hall from this particular class, and as Lexie made her way out through the classroom door, she saw him busily spinning his combination lock, getting ready to make a quick exit. He had a part-time job at the local grocery after school, and so he was not one to linger long after classes.

She hesitated in the doorway, staring at him. The dialogue went round and round in her head.

What will I say to him? What if he laughs at me? What if he doesn't even know who I am? It concluded with, *I can't do it. I just can't do it!*

As she turned to walk the other way down the hall, she saw him shucking on his jacket, first covering his broad shoulders, then zipping it up over his muscled torso. He had the confident stance of an athlete and every movement appeared effortless.

God, I know it's a cliché, but what a gorgeous hunk of man! Lexie felt herself go weak in the knees at the thought.

He's leaving, Lexie! the voice inside her head urged her on. *You'll not get another chance this good! Just DO IT and do it NOW!*

She wasn't quite sure how it happened. Like a sleepwalker, she put one foot in front of the other and then found herself standing in front of him.

"Hi," she stammered, then stalled wondering what came next.

Ask him, you idiot! the voice in her head said!

"You going to the Sadie this week?" She wanted the floor to open up and swallow her as she waited for his words.

"I might. It depends."

She could hear the smile in his answer.

Encouraged, she looked into his slightly amused face and asked, "Would you... do you think... you'd like to... go with me?"

His face warmed into a big grin as he formed a single word with his lips. It was the last word she really heard even though they continued to talk.

She hugged the word to her, feeling its warmth. Over and over in her mind the realization kept intruding into all her other thoughts.

He'd said yes.

They met at the dance because Mark had to work late at the grocery store that Friday night. He arrived still wearing the store's uniform—a white butcher's apron—under his leather jacket with his jeans tucked into heavy work boots. Because Lexie had been in the cafeteria talking to friends, she had not seen him arrive. One of them nudged her and said, "Mark just got here."

She pushed her way through the big double doors of the gym, her eyes blinded for a moment as she was met by its dark interior. She stood looking out over the undulating crowd. Where was he? She caught sight of him standing with a buddy and still wearing his work clothes like a badge of honour.

So....He's determined to act casual about this date! Not like it was important enough to get off work early to go home and change! Well, we'll see about this.

Again she put one foot ahead of the other and found herself standing in front of him.

"Hi," she said.

"Hi, there." He picked her hands up in his and looked directly into her eyes. As he began to steer her towards the dance floor, he casually threw the words over his shoulder at his buddy, "See ya, Barry."

They danced awkwardly at first. He apologized for stepping on her feet. She assured him it didn't matter. They talked and touched the evening away.

Just before the last dance, he abruptly pulled back his sleeve to look at his watch.

"Ho-ly! I forgot! You've got a bus to catch! Can't have you getting home late on our first date. Your folks wouldn't let you go out with me again!" With that he looked smilingly, teasingly down at her. "Wouldn't want that now, would we?"

She felt protected as Mark slid his arm around the back of her waist and guided her through the crowded dance floor to the door.

There was a light drizzle falling outside as they began the walk to the bus stop. Mark didn't yet have a car of his own and obviously felt meeting her at the dance and putting her on a bus home was enough commitment for a first date. Lexie also was content with this limited amount of involvement for, at times, a boy's car could be a bedroom on wheels or a moving prison depending on your point of view!

They walked along in the light rain, holding hands, talking little. He took his leather jacket and wrapped it around her shoulders insisting he didn't need it. The way he touched her, guided her, was so considerate of her, made Lexie feel safe and special. They stood at the side of the road waiting for her bus, simply smiling into one another's eyes, watching as the water ran in tiny rivulets down each of their faces. He saw the bus first and aggressively, in that protective way he had, stepped out onto the road to hail it for her.

She didn't know if everyone on the bus watched nor did she care. It stood there with its door open and waiting. Mark, taking her wet face in both of his hands, gently tipped it down and softly, sweetly placed his lips on her forehead.

As Lexie turned to make her way up the steps and into the bus, she knew his gentle caress held more power than a hundred other boys' sexually urgent, passionately needy kisses. It had softly said, "I care about YOU."

She heard the words, "I'll call you!" as the door slammed shut, and the bus lurched forward. She shyly made her way down the aisle, aware that some smiling passengers had been watching. She found herself a seat, and—unaware she was shivering—felt wrapped in Mark's warmth.

He called. She called. They talked every day on the phone after classes. They smiled and nodded at one another when they passed in the hallways and the rumours began to circulate that they were an item. Still, he did not ask her out.

Their friendship grew through their long phone conversations. They came to know more and more about one another. One evening when she phoned him at the usual time, his younger brother answered. He was nine and the proverbial pain-in-the-neck type of kid. As he lay the phone down, Lexie could hear him yell at the top of his lungs, "Mark, it's that girl! You know, the one you want to ask out, but are scared to!"

So, Mark did like her! That's all she needed to hear. She put away her shyness just as she had put away last year's fashions. Mark, too, must have recognized the time for openness had come. When he came to the phone he simply asked, "Hey, Lexie. How about a movie or something on Saturday night?"

When she hung up the phone, she danced around the kitchen like a crazy woman! Courageously she had gone after what she wanted! Sometimes dreams did come true!

Why did life so often disappoint? Lexie had often wondered. No one came into this world wanting to be a failure. Becoming one took effort. Not all at once, but bit by bit, after each unsuccessful attempt at success, a little piece of hope died until there was no hope left. To learn to meet life head-on, literally shaking it tenaciously until it yielded what was desired—that was the beginning of a potent belief system. Would Lexie remember her success, when faced with her next inevitable defeat?

Her audacity would also yield two other important life lessons. One: even when we get what we want, there can still be pain. Two: life lessons once learned are not always applied or even remembered.

Mark and Lexie became inseparable that fall and winter. They spent every available minute talking and touching. She had never been with anyone like Mark before. He loved to touch. It was his way of expressing his affection. He always reached for her hand when they walked together. His favourite way of announcing his presence was to sneak up behind her and, gently lifting her hair, place an affectionate kiss on her warm neck—a move that always left her weak in the knees. Like a desert flower new to the rain, her senses responded slowly, tenuously. Mark coaxed and cultivated her responses like a gardener in love with his work. He was a worshipper of women, adoring the look of them, their movement, swaying in that seductive way they had, their smell and taste when he nuzzled his face against their soft, sweet flesh.

He saw his role as one of protector and provider for the source of his passion—women. He would do all he was asked in order to be enfolded in those silken, scented arms, cradled against the firm, rounded breasts as he listened to the soft beating of the female heart. A heart, that to him beat out the very rhythms of life itself, for to imagine a world without their gentler, sweet presence would be a world in which his very own heart would not wish to beat. He recognized that his own being was only half complete. He was a young man who unashamedly accepted the fact that his maleness was brought into sharper focus when contrasted with the female essence.

Mark had loved before. Because of this, he understood the ambivalent nature of a young woman's psyche. He sensed her growing willingness to consummate their passion, but he also knew its counterbalancing force—fear!

Fear formed from the ingrained restrictions of a society which had made woman the keeper of the flames of passion. Society, whether fairly or not, entrusted the female with the decision to fan them into fullness or leave them banked and smouldering. She was the one to decide because she was the one who would be judged and possibly destroyed by passions run amuck. She alone would be blamed for the fall from virtue and any unwanted pregnancies. It would be her lack of control that would set tongues wagging. All accepted that the male of the species had little or no control over his urges. It was expected he should attempt to spill his sperm at every opportunity! Men celebrated this fact, joked about it, measured their self-worth by it. It was likened to other revered physical activities, and they even referred to it as "scoring." On the football field, the basketball court or the bedroom, men faced certain expectations: there would be no fumble, the pass would be completed, the shot would hit the mark, and the exhilaration of a task completed would be experienced.

It was Lexie, not Mark, who was called into Miss Prim's office. The tiny, immaculately groomed, white-haired history teacher was highly respected by both staff and students alike. Unmarried, she was affectionately referred to as the "Little Lady." Precisely because of her fine sense of decorum, the unpleasant task of talking with Lexie had fallen to her. So unpleasant, it stunned Lexie, leaving her bewildered and hurt.

Ramrod straight she stood, her face fixed in a serious expression, as Lexie, fresh from nuzzling Mark good-bye and still aglow, waltzed into her office.

Miss Prim attempted to be kind, but there was no kind way to say what she had to say. Put simply, the teachers felt that Lexie was making a spectacle of herself with Mark in the hallways between classes. They felt she should know that everyone in the school was talking about her and assumptions, whether they were true or not, were being made about her virtue or lack thereof.

No mention was made of Mark's role in all of this and what stunned Lexie even more, when years later she could finally look back on this scene without cringing, she too, had abandoned herself, accepting total responsibility. It had not even occurred to her that Mark, also, was responsible for the displays that were offending the sensibilities of so many.

Stunned, she walked silently from the office, her face flaming. Not accustomed to hearing criticism from the lips of a teacher, she felt a deep sense of shame.

Feelings of love and tenderness were not for public viewing; they made others uncomfortable. Could it be that evolution had implanted a sense of impropriety as a safeguard? Did we fear loss of control and see ourselves becoming drawn into frenzied public consummations? Was sexual energy such a powerful force it must be kept hidden? Whatever the reason, Lexie would accept the responsibility for their behaviour as a couple in public as well as in private. She would suppress her feelings while with others, but alone with Mark, she edged ever closer to consummation of the sex act.

As Mark's hands explored more and more of her body, she was haunted always by the same thoughts. Nice girls didn't let boys have what they wanted. Boys would lose respect for the object of their desire and more often than not toss her aside afterwards, bragging that they had scored! Raised on these stereotypes, she did not yet see Mark had no intention of tossing her aside, nor did he have the need to strut his ego before his friends. What he did very much need and what he was patiently grooming her for was an ongoing sexual affair.

She made him work for it. It took months of patient talking and touching with Lexie growing used to his soft, gentle caressing of her breasts. But when Mark's hands attempted to travel below the waist, she froze! She knew what sensations could spring forth from there!

She remembered the night well. Leaving a note for her mother, she had gone crying to Jayne's some time after midnight! She had to tell someone and even though she had been judged by Jayne's friends, Jayne herself had seemed to accept Lexie's behaviour.

As she crawled into Jayne's warm bed, emboldened by the dark anonymity of the room, she confessed and waited for absolution from her friend.

She had let Mark touch her "down there." He had caressed her only briefly, then kissed her face gently and said, "Don't be scared, Lexie. I'll never hurt you. I promise."

With that he rolled off the couch, pulled on his jacket, and sat talking gently to her before he left.

Feeling terrified and violated, she barely heard his words. She said nothing. Instead she chose to work out her feelings while haltingly telling her story to Jayne. By the time her friend's response came, it mirrored the conclusion she herself had formed.

"Lexie," Jayne whispered softly, "if you love him, that's what you do. It's what we all do. Don't feel so bad. You're not the only one that's let a boy touch her there. Most of us have done even more than that! I thought YOU had done more than that!"

Lexie lay silent in the dark, staring into the nothingness, listening to her friend's breathing, and she felt a surge of love for her. In sharing her intimate self, Jayne had lessened Lexie's painful sense of being freakish or different. For that she was grateful. She also felt tremendous relief that Jayne's misconceptions about the wild week at the cottage had been cleared up.

Reaching out to squeeze her friend's hand, she arrived at two conclusions. The first being that it was Jayne, not "sluttish" Lexie who was obviously no longer a virgin. She savoured this knowledge for there was great comfort in knowing her one-time heroine and mentor was not infallible. The second landed with a thud in her consciousness. Even if she didn't want to have sex, if she stayed with Mark, it would be inevitable.

Mark's patient and persistent passion wore away her resistance. His need was great enough for both of them. Because she loved him, she passively acquiesced. Her own sensual gratification played no part, for as Mark's passion built, hers became detached, brutally and abruptly shutting itself down! She simply ceased to be there!

It happened simply enough. Each time she had been with Mark he had pushed a little closer to completion. One night, surrounded in darkness, Mark had rolled his weight on top of her. He had already been caressing her gently. She now felt the hardness of him pushing against her. He had gone this far with her before as he had rubbed his hard penis against her. This time, however, he did not pull away. This time, she realized with a shock, he was moving inside of her, pushing his way in, going in further with each thrust!

My God! What had she let him do? There was no going back now. It was done. No longer a virgin, she couldn't believe she had felt so little. She had heard stories about how painful the first time could be. Surprised, she thought, "That was it? That was all there was?! What was all the fuss about? The sensations of her bathtub encounters had promised so much more! Where were the shuddering waves of pleasure?!"

Mark was whispering something over and over in her ear, his hot breath coming in bursts as he thrust his body back and forth on hers.

"Don't worry, Lexie. It'll be all right, you'll see. I won't hurt you, and I'll take care of everything."

What was he talking about? she wondered. *Take care of what?*

His rapid thrusting ended with a shudder, and he abruptly fell away from her. She felt a warm trickle of fluid spill down her inner thigh.

At least I won't get pregnant, she thought. *I guess Mark doesn't want another scare.*

She had handed over access to her body, trusting completely that Mark would protect her from any negative consequences. Not even in this, did she participate.

Easier to hide behind someone else's need rather than admit to herself she was a fully active sexual being, she did the only thing she could to deal with a fact that was still abhorrent to her. She would think about it later; she would feel it much later. For now she would sleepwalk through the experience. There, but not there.

What had become of the sexual stirring she had felt? Why had she detached, focusing instead on the needs of another? Sadly, she did not even think to ask that startling question. She had abandoned herself. Rather than discover what it was she wanted, she looked to what others wanted of her. She did not have the courage to even expect others to respect her desires. The transformation from self-directed to other-directed was becoming a familiar way of dealing with her world. Her recent lesson of empowerment forgotten, she handed herself over to another.

They became as one, inseparable, blurred together.

Mark's wild, unfettered energy led them all through that spring and summer. He lived life with abandon and together they flaunted all the rules. Roaring recklessly down dusty country roads in his father's Chevy, he taught an inexperienced, thrill-seeking Lexie to drive. Other times, seated on his powerful new motorcycle, with its wheels flashing as scenes blurred by them, she entwined her arms about Mark's strong waist, her hair flying in the wind, the rushing air robbing the sound of laughter from her throat.

He thrived on risk. Speed and excitement were his drugs. Like liquid adrenaline they allowed him to feel connected to life. To drink fully, deeply, and often of the sweet, sexual nectars was an infusion of life for him, bringing with it a sense of total completeness. Like a true addict, he mistook these sensations for life itself and frantically sought always to experience them, for not to do so left him feeling empty, a great gaping hole of nothingness.

His great need for sex and Lexie's great need to please led them to risk the shame of exposure time after time.

They had their place. As darkness was descending, they would leave her house under the pretence of taking a walk. No one saw the blanket tucked under a jacket. Once far enough from watchful eyes, Mark would fling it over his shoulder, and then they would climb the fence into the acres of deserted farm fields near "Lexie's bridge." In the middle of one such field stood a lone and imposing oak tree. Its canopy of branches was witness as always as the same scene unfolded. It never varied from their first experience, always leaving Lexie in bewilderment, asking herself, if there was more. There under the tree, in the midst of an open field, she would watch amused as Mark would thump his chest with his fists afterwards, his throat thrown back emitting a Tarzan-like whoop in celebration of his sexual prowess, while she, in a self-conscious attempt to silence his rowdy celebration of life, would laughingly pull him down against her again, burying his head in her breast, all the while wondering why this act did not unleash such powerful feelings in her.

They had always had the cover of darkness on those nights under their oak tree, but as Mark's appetite grew, so too did his willingness to flaunt the danger of discovery. Opportunities were few as both their houses bustled with the coming and goings of parents, sisters, and brothers. There was no car as Mark relied solely on his motorcycle for transportation now. Even if there had been, the police regularly patrolled all the deserted places where hormonal teens went to experience one another, boldly shining their flashlights into faces and ordering the youthful participants to go home. Many such adults made it their crusade to protect all youths from the rampage of their own hormones.

Even though the act itself left her feeling incomplete, she was drawn to it nonetheless. Passions thwarted by lack of privacy only increased the intensity. So on one warm summer day, as they lay atop a hill dotted by groups of sunbathers, Lexie consented to commit an act which left her shuddering in shame at its memory.

They lay seminude in their swim suits, bodies lightly touching as Lexie's gaze travelled over Mark. She loved his warm, blue eyes, his golden sun-washed hair, and the well-defined, rounded muscles under his bronzed skin. He teasingly traced over her rounded breasts with a soft stalk of budding grass. He moved with the rhythms of her breathing, as her body rose and fell, bringing the soft tickle to her tightened abdomen and then allowing it to linger between her tense thighs. She felt her body tighten, her breath catch in anticipation. It was without protest then, that Mark pulled the blanket over them, exposed his own desire and slowly slipped over her. He parted her legs with his and thrust himself into the moist recesses of her body. Like the slow rhythm of waves rolling onto shore, the blanket undulated with the rhythm of Mark's gentle entries. The end came quietly, with only Mark's quiet moan to signal it. Lexie, lay silent, still suspended in anticipation, but it was over. Unable to express her feeling of frustration, she pulled her awareness free of it, becoming suddenly focused on the people on the hillside. Had they been watching? Intense shame washed over her, blotting out all other emotions.

She abruptly stood up, her face flaming, and shook out the blanket in staccato like snaps. She was angry, angry that Mark had gone this far in this place and furious with herself because she had let him. Had she no boundaries? Did she always have to say yes to him even when it made her feel ashamed afterwards? Why had she not stopped him? Why had he insisted on completing the act in front of others? Did he value her that little? Did she value herself that little? She could easily have shut down her desire. Did she not already do that each time Mark penetrated her?

She shrugged her shoulders as the thought took hold that it had been what Mark had wanted, and therefore, she had simply fulfilled her role as acquiescing woman. It was easier to lay the blame at the feet of the male libido than to accept the fact that she had wanted what she got, that she too had been shameless in her conduct. To displace her feelings of guilt, justifying them as meeting the needs of another, freed her and even allowed a sense of smugness. She was a female, nurturing the inferior male. She, not controlled by her primal urges as he was, had chosen only to met his needs. It was a comfortable, soothing lie she told herself.

As the leaves coloured for fall, Lexie's feelings for Mark also began to change, subtly at first. She became aware of a vague sense that Mark lacked a key ingredient. Oh, he loved her well, showering her with gifts and caresses. That was not the problem. As she entered her final year of high school, her future began to looming up in front of her, and she began to look at Mark in new light. He was her reckless, fearless blonde god of love, who, quivering at the thought of writing exams he had not bothered to prepare for, had asked his grocery store buddy to smash his writing hand under a case of canned goods! Sadly, she began to realize she wanted more in life than a man who ran recklessly from responsibility could ever provide. His values, his signposts, were not hers. They would lead him down paths she would not want to travel.

There would be pain. She knew this. The fibres of her being reached into his, intertwined with what he was. They had drawn from one another, neither feeling safe without the other's affection. To rip free would be a shredding of the whole they formed, leaving each with raw wounds, as with separation they pulled away emotional chunks from one another.

The catalytic event came the night Mark's sexual feeding compromised Lexie in front of another male—her own father.

She had been home ill that day, and Mark had come to see her after class. As they stood together saying their good-byes in the back hall landing, Mark's hands had begun to roam under her floor-length housecoat. He deftly undid the buttons down its front and as she was standing a step above him, he positioned himself so that his erection aligned with her now exposed triangle of dark pubic hair. When he reached down to unzip his jeans, she protested, pushing him away from her.

"Mark, no! My dad's due home any time now! He'll catch us!"

"Lexie, please! I need it! It'll only take a few minutes. Ple-as-e!" He looked pleadingly up at her.

She could not say no. She could not risk his being angry with her. As long as he adored her, she knew she was lovable. She submitted.

The rattling sound of a door being pulled open riveted them both to the spot. They froze.

It would be a matter of a heartbeat before someone came through the door to stand face to face with them! There was nowhere to go, no time to hide, and for Mark to withdraw now would leave him with an exposed body part and absolutely no time to stow it away again inside his pants. They were trapped in mid act.

They did the only thing they could do. They pressed their bodies closer together, pulling the material of the housecoat in around them to cover their union.

And there they stood as Lexie's weary father came through the door after his day of work, his lined face darkened with grime, his lunch box in hand. Miraculously for Lexie and Mark, he was also deliberately unobservant. He had enough sensibility to recognize he had stumbled upon a private moment. Thus, with downcast eyes, and a passing, polite hello he made his way by them and up the stairs.

That night Lexie lay in her bed alone with her thoughts, her face hot, praying fervently that her father had seen only what she wanted desperately for him to have seen—his daughter hugging her boyfriend good-bye.

God, don't let him know what I was doing! I couldn't bear the shame of it if he knew! She cried herself to sleep that night knowing this all had to come to an end. In pleasing one man she loved, she had risked losing the respect of another. She would avoid feeling more shame by stepping back into the safe world of celibacy. She would end her relationship with Mark!

They began to fight often now. The more she tried to pull away, the harder Mark clung. She had made her decision to go and now his constant touches, his cloying demands on her body annoyed her. His incessant need to touch, once the very thing she had loved about him, now suffocated, smothered her.

When she finally made him see the relationship was over, he cared enough to let her go. For weeks she cried over it. It was as if she had amputated an unhealthy part of herself. She knew she would grow stronger without the relationship, but still she mourned its loss. She couldn't eat. She pined away in her room, and she could not bring herself to open her textbooks. She made excuses not to go to school - for to be there would be to see Mark. Her parents were at a loss as to how to help her heal.

Once when her soft-spoken father slipped into her darkened bedroom to comfort his sobbing daughter, she thought, *Why is he doing this now? He's never done this before.* It was always her mother she went to with problems. Her father's gesture of concern made her uncomfortable. What did he know about feelings? He never talked about them. His world was one only of tangibles. He hid behind his newspaper night after night, content to let his wife deal with the emotional uproar of a household of four growing daughters.

She closed down. She could not talk to him about this. She wished he would just go away. He left the room with a sigh. Years later when she was to understand parental pain, the memory of that night evoked only a sense of compassion for her work-weary and emotionally distant father. He had loved enough to reach out.

Exam week arrived and Lexie came apart. She could not face writing them unprepared. In her all or nothing way of thinking, she believed that if she had not studied her hardest, she of course would fail. In actual fact, she was probably conversant enough with the material to maintain a pass, but that was not her habitual way of thinking. Her models had not taught her to see the middle range in anything. Her household thought in extremes. Everything was either good or bad, right or wrong, proper or improper. That was the way it was. To hide behind maybes and what ifs was regarded as vacillating in a grey area of weakness. To judge swiftly, to label and to categorize people and their actions was to have control. That was seen as strength. It allowed one to squeeze a messy world into a neat checkerboard way of thinking - black and white compartments of the mind into which all was filed.

To her take-charge mother it was simple. A phone call was made to the school principal stating that her daughter was unable to write her exams because of health reasons. She simply neglected to put the word *mental* in front of the word *health*. Lies designed to protect the family integrity obviously fit into the "white" category of the checkerboard.

She rallied. She did not like being at home each day with only a coward for company. She picked up her books and went to school to write her last exams.

She saw them as soon as she stepped off the bus. She couldn't believe her eyes! People bumped into her as she stood, mouth open, staring at the two figures talking and touching. Her stomach felt ripped from her, ready to spill its contents there on the sidewalk. How could he do this? It was only short weeks ago he had touched and talked with her that way!

She had to get away before he saw her reaction. Her mind reeling, she took refuge inside the building. She tried desperately to make sense of the swirl of gut-souring feelings inside of her. She had ended it. It was what she had wanted, but she had not counted on this! She wanted to jealously rip this new girl from his grasp. Even though she no longer wanted him, she still wanted his love!

Seeing how quickly Mark had healed opened new wounds. Yet, his actions had far more to do with masking pain than healing. Desperate, he had begun cultivating a new source of the opiate he so needed.

Lexie threw herself into her schoolwork. She lived the celibate life. With whispered rumours that yet another student was leaving because she was pregnant, Lexie would experience a tremendous sense of relief knowing it was more good luck than good management that she had escaped such a fate. She watched the prospective father as he laughed in the halls with his friends. He would not be asked to leave school. His career would not be derailed nor would he even most likely be expected to help raise the child. That was assuming, of course, he even admitted to being the child's father! Pregnancy and subsequent abandonment by society was a reality ritual faced each month by so many girls. She, for now, was no longer one of those girls.

Christmas holidays arrived and with them came a delicious sense of freedom. The days were hers to do as she pleased, and one of the things she pleased was to go shopping. She found herself in the middle of a shoe store. To her, the epitome of female glamour was a pair of long, shapely legs covered in silky nylon and ending in a pair of shiny, sleek, high-heeled pumps! The stiletto heel symbolized not only glamour but power - power on the move. For what male did not stop to notice a beautiful woman as she walked in them? Whether slinking seductively or striding purposefully, a woman in the right shoes got attention. To get others to notice you was to have power!

She picked up just such a pair, turning one over to see the price, when she became aware of a short, somewhat-stocky young man pushing his way past the female salesclerk who was on her way to serve her. She smiled to herself when she overheard him say, "I'll take care of this one."

Men! Were they all the same? This one might as well have approached her wearing a sign flashing, "Score! Score!"

No wait; he's a salesman too, Lexie thought. *Better revise that sign. It's probably flashing, "Sell, then score!"*

Did all men think with their crotches? She was beginning to believe so.

A true salesman, he sold her the shoes and then himself. He bull-dozed away her negative first impression and went on to package himself as something she absolutely had to have.

David Siggler knew this one thing well. People buy the image you project if you project it with conviction. They look to categorize you within seconds of meeting you. Whatever unified, congruent image is convincingly presented is accepted. It saves them doing the research on you themselves. They can feel smug that you fit into a familiar stereotype they carry around. Understanding this dynamic of human nature, David had perfected the projection that said, "Up and coming young success!"

Most bought his image AND his shoes.

Lexie was no exception. His rapid talk dazzled her! He had an opinion on everything, and he knew exactly where he was going. He had the plan and the panache to pull it off. At least that's what he told her.

He talked her into one date, then another. He took her to visit his home in the wealthy suburban area of town. True to the success stereotype, his father was away on business and his mother, away on pleasure. Photos were plastered everywhere of his older brother, star athlete, university graduate, successful entrepreneur. This was a whole new world for working-class Lexie. She had not known it existed outside of movies. They really had their own pool in the back-yard, and the house seemed to ramble on forever! It did not occur to ask why the extremely well-stocked bar seemed to be the focal point of the house or why David smoked as rapidly as he talked or why HE was not in university. No, instead she accepted only the input that plugged into the success scenario, and she blamed the nagging bits that did not fit on her own misperceptions.

He began to talk of marriage. That really made her head spin. He moved so fast. Then it came, the guilt. She was used merchandise. All young men expected to marry a virgin, didn't they? She could not let him go on under a misconception. Did she want to marry him? She never faced herself with that question. What was important here was to deal with what David's expectations were.

She sat facing him from the other side of his desk. They were in the back room of the shoe store he managed. With her hands in her lap and her eyes downcast Lexie tearfully, painfully confessed her shame. She could not meet his gaze. He listened without comment. Then he did the strangest thing. He got up abruptly out of his chair, came around and handed her a tissue, and suggested she go upstairs to his apartment to rest. He would join her as soon as he could get away from the store. He moved with a sense of purpose, hustling her out the door and up the stairs.

Lexie did as she was told. She lay down on the bed wondering what would come next. For a bright young woman, she at times was incredibly naive.

As soon as he walked through the door, she understood. Now, in his eyes she was merchandise that wore a huge red sticker marked, "Reduced for Quick Sale."

He climbed on top of her. He began to kiss her passionately, touching her where he had not dared to before. He did not speak to her, his eyes closed, lost in his own lust. He pulled away briefly to unzip his pants, impatiently tugging them off, then he came at her again. This time it was her undergarments he wrested off. He moaned as he slipped into her.

She closed her eyes to shut out what was happening. She did not want this! How dare he just assume it was now his right!

She escaped the only way she knew how. She removed herself. The body lay there buffeted still by each thrusting assault. Her energy no longer filled her body with light, but huddled as a tiny, frightened flicker in the deep dark within her.

It stopped. The thrusting abruptly stopped. Her eyes flew open. He was above her, his pupils wide, his body stopped in mid-stroke. She focused a questioning look at him. He collapsed in on her. He crumpled up like a wad of used paper. Burying his face in the soft recesses of her stomach, he sobbed openly, shudders of recognition rippling over his body. He knew where she had gone. It was where he lived everyday. He knew she would never be his. How can one give away that which one does not possess for himself?

She never saw David again.

Her pattern of relating had emerged. Lexie had pulled together all the threads of her tapestry of being, weaving them into images of female and male energy intertwined - each facing the other, reaching out for the other, knowing rich, vibrant completeness with the other. Ancient, primitive images, she had carried them within her, and her years of awakening had only been to rediscover their shimmering richness and promised vibrancy. All her soul needed was there in the ancient patterns.

And Lexie looked upon the tapestry she had unveiled, and she did not believe in it. She could not accept the dual threads of her sexual energies, taking power from both her male and female sources. Nor could she go within to look upon the vibrant portrait of their possibilities. Instead, she chose only to live in the grey passiveness of the incomplete female self. She hung her rich tapestry of experience outside herself, turned her back on all it was, and went searching to believe in the tapestries of others.

CHAPTER THIRTEEN:

CALIFORNIA DREAMIN'

Youth, still unformed, still unaware,
Yet to discover the force of life
To be impartial and fair.
It gives no more than one can accept,
The fullness the self declares.
For like new wineskins, unprepared,
Our human vessel cannot receive,
More than we ourselves
Our measure of worth believe.

Youth, on your threshold of power,
Approaches rapidly your hour
To deny or accept
The elixir of self-empowerment.
Distilled through each act of living,
Drop by precious drop
It bears life in a drought of passivity.
The secret recipe known to each of thee,
The directions simply be—
For thyself—
Take responsibility!

It was a typical Thursday evening in the Alexander household, bursting with noise and confusion. Mother was working evenings at her nursing job, and Lexie's dad was reading his evening paper, wishing everything else would disappear. Lexie and Tessie were arguing over whose turn it was to cook dinner while Celine and Millicent were arguing over everything else. Newspaper comics were strewn over the living room rug. Homework was stacked carelessly on the hall table, jackets and shoes covered the floor, forming a minefield only the determined could navigate. Bodies lounged on the carpet, flat on their bellies, faces propped in their hands, eyes glued to a flickering TV screen, looking away only to toss some grumpy comment at one another. All were hungry, but the person who prepared the food had deserted them. Mother had displayed true audacity by getting a job when her youngest had started school.

Gone were the days when the aroma of hot soups and homemade cakes wafted from a waxed and polished home. Now, they were greeted by toast crumbs and dirty dishes! What had once had structure and order was now chaotic.

This particular night, even the family dog had taken refuge under a bed. Many families with newly working mothers came to call this time "The Arsenic Hour" for whoever was left in charge was tempted to feed all their hungry, whiny family a good dose of it instead of dinner.

In the middle of yelling at her sister, Lexie felt compelled to deal with one more source of irritation. The most persistent invader of privacy, everyone seemed to feel it had to be responded to whether you wanted to or not, even if you were in the middle of a fight.

She yanked the telephone receiver off the hook and barked, "Hello!"

There was something very familiar about the clipped, formal tones of the voice asking to speak to her.

The style was familiar too. The speaker gave only clues to his identity.

Then it slowly sunk in. "My God, it's Derek!"

He was in town taking a course and wondered if he could stop by to see how she had "turned out." He chuckled at his wit.

Lexie's curiosity got the better of her.

"Sure, why not?" she heard herself say into the phone.

Turned out, indeed! I wonder if he's "turned in" his license to criticize the world,? she thought wryly as she hung up.

He arrived formally dressed in suit and tie. He hadn't changed she noted. Just like him to dress like a banker to take a mechanics course. He flashed her a quick smile.

Same teeth. She shivered.

He sat amongst her family and held court, proceeding to tell them what was wrong with the world and how he would fix it.

License still in operation! Lexie thought. *There's nothing here I'm interested in. Hope he soon leaves.*

What happened next baffled her for years to come. Only after some painful honesty, did she realize Derek knew her better than she knew herself. Skilfully, he had played her just as a musician plays a favourite instrument.

"Lexie, come and see this!" Excitedly, her sisters called her in from the kitchen where she had been busy making tea.

Derek was showing pictures.

Lexie slid onto the couch beside him, taking the photos he offered. Silently, he waited for her reaction, then smiled at her expression.

"Wow, you've got a convertible! It looks great! Well, you know what I mean…It doesn't look great now, but it will when it's fixed!" His car was being repaired. That's why he'd arrived in an unexciting old sedan.

Almost more than anything, Lexie loved the excitement of riding in an open car, the countryside blurring by, her hair flying in the wind, the music blasting in her ears. To her, it was as close to pure freedom as you could get.

Later when he asked her out, she of course said yes.

In the flickering light of the movie theatre, she found it impossible to follow the plot of the picture. Instead she stared at Derek's profile. As her eyes roved over his face, he became increasingly more appealing. Suddenly, she had the most startling thought.

When he asked what she wanted to do next as they filed out of the theatre, she boldly, without a heartbeat of hesitation said, "I know this place we can go to park."

His startled expression clued her in to the forwardness of her statement and she backpedaled hastily.

"I mean, you know, we could just go and, well, talk. We haven't really had a chance to catch up just you and me, you know."

Laughing at her boldness, he took her by the elbow and steered her out of the brightly lit lobby into the darkness of the night.

She took him parking, and they did talk. Lexie informed him she had been accepted at Teacher's College. The guidance counsellor had called her parents expressing disappointment that she had chosen not to go on to university. She laughed while telling this for it seemed so obvious to her. It wasn't a matter of choice. She had wanted to be a teacher from the time she had been in the fifth grade, not to mention the fact that her parents just couldn't afford to send her to university. This way she would be earning her own money that much sooner. University, with its heavy financial burden for her parents, was not even considered by Lexie to be within the realm of possibility.

Derek listened. He then went on to tell her that he, of course, had a job. He was completing the mechanics apprenticeship programme and was soon to write the final exams required for his license. Lexie had no doubt he was good at what he did for she had observed he could fix almost anything.

He went on to tell her he was still living at home and was busy saving his money. He did not say for what and she did not ask. He then magnanimously offered to bring her into the big city on their next date and show her around.

As Lexie had rarely been to Toronto, this prospect pleased her greatly. Here was someone from whom she could learn the ways of sophisticated city life—or so she believed.

Her foray into the big city turned out to be disastrous. Derek had decided they would go for dinner, on to a movie, and then home to meet his parents. She spent all that day worrying about what to wear. Not that she had many choices—that was the problem. She finally settled on a pale, powder-blue sheath dress and a pair of high spiked heels.

Derek offered no opinion of how she looked when he arrived to pick her up. That made her even more unsure of herself. The dress was not one of her favourites—her mother had sewn it for her—and she did not feel attractive in it, but it had seemed the most appropriate. She knew Derek would appear formally dressed in a suit and she had been right.

She never questioned that they were overdressed for Derek's choice of restaurant as the gum-chewing waitress led them to their booth. She was just thrilled to be eating out. Rarely had the Alexander family darkened the door of any restaurant. Derek seemed to be tense and out of place in the restaurant, so Lexie gave up trying to talk and instead contented herself with another of her most favourite things—people watching.

When her meal finally arrived, she opened her jaw wide to take her first bite. She knew something was wrong immediately! She felt, more than heard, the snap and pop. It was with great difficulty that she closed her jaw again. She had dislocated something and it hurt! Derek was watching her. She smiled weakly. She just could not tell him what she was feeling. She went on nibbling at her meal, the tears of disappointment stinging her eyes. She had looked forward to this outing. It seemed unfair to be so uncomfortable.

It only got worse. In the movie theatre they were cramped into seats high up in the rear balcony with their feet up under their chins. It was hot and stuffy and the movie was long and complex. Lexie was highly uncomfortable, but dared not complain.

The next event of the evening was to meet Derek's parents.

From the street led a series of steep, stone steps up to the house perched high on a hill. The building itself looked odd because one side was painted with blue trim and the other with brown. Lexie later learned this type of housing, where two different families each owned half, was referred to as semidetached.

"C'mon, Mother's expecting us," Derek said as he pushed her ahead of him up the many steps to his front door.

Lexie, in her vanity, hated to wear glasses and would only pop them on her face when she desperately needed to see her surroundings. This was one of those times, but with Derek propelling her from behind, she did not have a chance to reach into her purse for them.

Gravity too was working against her. She was trying to thrust her one hundred and twenty pounds up a steep incline while at the same time being supported by two tiny pinpoints at the base of three-inch-high stiletto heels. To say that her centre of balance was off would have been an understatement.

It was dark. The concrete steps were unfamiliar and uneven. Her knees, however, were about to become intimately connected with some of them! She felt the shredding of skin and nylon as her knee skidded and scraped over the step's gravelly surface. The next thing she knew, she was picking herself up, brushing her dress and feeling the cool, liquid trickle of blood running down her leg.

They arrived at the Gaust's front door with Lexie bleeding, and Derek silent and self-contained.

Mrs. Maria Gaust, veteran of two world conflicts that had raged over her European homeland, was herself a short, compact and determined war machine. She surveyed Lexie's bedraggled form, grunted a welcome, and as was her way, proceeded to take charge of the situation. Bandages and hot cloths appeared. Tea and cakes were served and rapid-fire questions asked. It felt like a job interview. She wanted to know all about Lexie and her future plans. Never once did she smile. Never once did Mr. Gaust appear. Mrs. Gaust simply stated that he had been tired and gone to bed.

During the course of the meeting, Lexie learned Derek had an older sister named Inga who had married and moved to California with her husband and young daughter. Derek had never talked of her before and even now very little was said about her. That seemed to be the way of this family — very little was said. There was a feeling in that half-house, a sense that the house itself was not only thing that was incomplete. Lexie felt so unsettled there. True, she hadn't started off on the right foot, so to speak, but it was more than that. As she looked about her, taking in the tiny immaculate rooms, she noted nothing out of place. Everything in this house was under the iron-fisted control of the matriarch. Not for sitting were the plump seats of the chairs, nor for walking upon was the gleaming polish of the waxed floors. Perfection did not welcome people with their messiness. The ripple of their presence might disturb the precious possessions this material matriarch had assembled as her fortress of identity. She lived and defined herself through what she owned. In her frame of reference, things, and the attainment of them, always came first.

Her eyes, in that first meeting had coldly said, "For my son, perhaps you'll do. You're not perfect yet, but you can be changed and with work..."

Strangely bewildered by the new set of values she had scraped against, Lexie left feeling she had just earned a D+ on her report card. More had been penetrated by the rough places of this home than just her skin. In this household no one was loved just for being who one was. All were evaluated by what they had achieved or possessed. Here, having was being.

As she descended the steps, bruised in both heart and body, she could not know she had just been taken on as a pupil. Derek and his mother were to be her self-appointed teachers, guiding her to explore her own potential for "havingness," promoting the enticing belief that having more, she would feel more and thus be more. All that was required was to put Derek in charge and let him lead the way.

Continuing to date Derek all through her graduating year, Lexie missed her senior prom because he did not want to go. What Derek wanted now controlled more and more of what she experienced. He shaped her reality, told her what she should think and what she should do. So often her language included the phrase, "Derek says . . . "

She quoted him as though he were an expert on everything.

Derek may have made demands on her behaviour in many ways, but his sexual demands were rare. He prided himself on his control, holding himself up as a young man who honoured the tradition that girls should be virgins when they married. He proudly informed Lexie that his previous girlfriend of four years had retained her virginity. It did not escape Lexie that, although Derek was telling her this to gain her admiration, he was also informing her indirectly that he had been unfaithful to his former love, having been her "steady" when he had dated Lexie the first time. He had neglected to clarify that detail and she did not ask. It was beginning to appear Derek had a selective memory.

Derek's lack of urgency about sex suited her well. She still did not feel attracted by his physical appearance, even though many others thought him handsome, nor was she compelled to touch him. His hold on her was not physical; it came from an unspoken promise of protection. His relentless and total control of everything around him allowed him to appear all powerful. After being buffeted by events in a family whose male leader often projected the image of being helpless and hopeless, Lexie found Derek's appearance of mastery to be an exhilarating elixir. Derek, she believed, would introduce her to the ways of the world and teach her how to manipulate and control what went on. He would keep her safe from the unexpected nastiness of life. Foolishly, she believed mastery of the self could be achieved through mastery of others.

When he did approach her physically, their touching always stopped short of sexual union. Derek believed her to be a virgin and after her experience with David, Lexie was not about to risk a repeat performance. Twice before she had explored her sexuality, only to discover she always left part of herself behind. Derek was not to be much of a guide here either, for he was more lost than even she. In this, she was different with Derek than she had been with Mark. She dampened her desire, taking on Derek's values. Sex, with this man, was to be a dull thread in her life's tapestry.

She moved to the big city. The busy first weeks of Teacher's College passed. She dated Derek, and a gnawing feeling of emptiness continued to grow inside her. She had wanted to be a teacher for so long, why wasn't she happy now the process had begun? There were so many people here. So many teachers too, and none of them bothered to learn your name. At home in Whitfield she'd a sense of identity through a host of labels. She had been known as "the smart girl," or "big sister," or "Mark's steady," or "Jayne's best friend."

In Toronto, attached to no one, she couldn't define herself. She felt invisible, becoming day by day sick at heart for her home, never realizing before just how much her family and friends had supported her. She yearned for the warm, safe haven where she had known it was all right just to be. She had been a big frog in a small puddle. The puddle had now grown substantially. The question she faced was, would she?

Swamped with emotion, drowning in waves of doubt and self-pity, the fear of separation immobilized her. She stopped attending her classes, preferring to stay in bed, giving in to her sense of helpless hopelessness. The umbilical cord cut, she was being called to grow up and the prospect terrified her.

Her first teaching experiences had not lived up to her expectations. She had envisioned herself standing in front of a group of admiring young minds receiving their adoration as they responded to her every word. Instead, as she ventured out on her first assignments, she discovered the label of "teacher" did not automatically confer respect. That was often hard won. Consequently, she became disillusioned with the whole process. Again in her black-and-white, all-or-nothing way of thinking, Lexie was ready to reject teaching because it was different from what she had imagined. She was beginning to see that her chosen profession would demand a great deal from her. In love with a dream, her concept of teaching had existed for only one purpose. Desiring only the rewards, she had not seen the dedication demanded by the craft. Her thinking was also skewed now by isolation from her family; she was overwhelmed by the task of building her dream. Homesick, alone, and isolated, Lexie needed the support of a loving friend.

She had never seen shoes like these before. The young woman who stood in front of her had brazenly come to class with browned, bare legs comfortably placed in flat, soft leather slippers. Not for her was the formal attire of nylon stockings and high-heeled pumps. She looked Lexie over and informed her they would be sharing lockers.

Lexie was never quite sure how it happened, but from that point on it was as if the conversation never stopped. They simply went from topic to topic discovering more and more about one another and rapidly beginning to feel as if they had been friends for a lifetime. From that very first afternoon, they became inseparable.

Her name was Lynn, and she was from Phoenix, Arizona. Her parents, who every summer vacationed in Canada, had enrolled her in college here as a last desperate attempt to get her graduated from somewhere or something. Lynn confessed that her passions were for the horses she rode in various competitions and for the young, attractive men she subsequently met, rather than for her studies. Exasperated by the fact that their attractive, yet rebellious young daughter had failed to complete her academic courses, they had shipped her off to Toronto with dire warnings that this was her last kick at the educational can, so to speak.

If they knew they had been manipulated, they never acknowledged it. Toronto was exactly where Lynn wanted to be. The summer before, while staying at the family cottage on Georgian Bay, she had happened to meet a young handsome, blonde, up-and-coming stockbroker named Taylor. He was six feet tall, broad shouldered, the strong silent type, and he came from a distinguished, wealthy family. He had gone to all the right schools and was now working to build himself a reputation on Bay Street. Because he was young, he would have to prove himself he knew, but he also understood he was well connected enough that doors would open for him. Like his father before him, Taylor believed he too could build a family fortune.

Lynn had decided he was husband material from their very first meeting. He was exactly what her family would expect. She, herself, came from a wealthy Bostonian family, and her father had also succeeded in adding substantially to family assets through his business ventures. Taylor would fit her family like a hand in a glove. To marry well had been programmed into Lynn since she had been a child. Marriage seemed the next logical step for a young woman of twenty-one who cared little for the world of school or employment.

Taylor, on the other hand, saw marriage as the lowest of his priorities. It was something to do one day, but there certainly was no rush. He did not count on the persistence of the light-haired, blue-eyed American girl who drove her boat so skilfully through the channels near the island where his mother had her cottage.

By summer's end they were sleeping together. In September, when Lynn returned to Arizona, Taylor wrote her off as a summer fling. It appeared to be coincidence that she also took her Christmas break skiing in Colorado. After several passionate encounters, Taylor was not sure he could write her off quite so easily. He was beginning to like her more than he wanted to.

She persisted, seeing him again through that winter and then arriving in his home city to attend school. Another coincidence? She had counted on Taylor enjoying their sexual trysts enough to continue seeing her. It was just a matter of time, she believed, before he would see the wisdom of putting a Mrs. in front of her name. That was the degree she was after.

Lexie, fascinated by all of this, became an avid pupil as her sophisticated new friend introduced her to so many experiences she had only dared dream about. Lynn casually took for granted all the things Lexie would have been thrilled to have. Just as books had opened up a whole new world for her years before, Lexie found Lynn to be a walking encyclopaedia, teaching her the ways of a previously closed strata of society. Through Lynn she learned there were other ways to look at the world. The rich were different. They had different perspectives on just about everything. It was fascinating to be with someone who did not worry or care about what things cost. Money was not a yardstick for measuring experience. It was just assumed there would always be more than enough to do whatever was desired. Lynn was unfamiliar with the gut-wrenching worry, the ever-present fear that there would not be enough money for even the necessities of life. Lynn and others like her had not grown up with a legacy of longing the way Lexie had.

Lynn had one goal in mind. Fixated upon it, she was determined to graduate from Teacher's College, get the car and money her parents had promised her, and thus be able to stay in Toronto and marry Taylor. That was it, and if she had to drag her new best friend along to graduation, so be it. She needed Lexie's help on assignments, and she needed her friendship. There was a bond between them. The long, boring days of classes were made tolerable when they could sneak over to the local greasy spoon to sip Cokes, eat french fries covered in gravy, and share a smoke together.

When day after day, Lexie didn't show for classes, Lynn just wouldn't accept her excuses. Lynn began calling Lexie every morning to get her out of bed, accusing her of being a coward, of not facing up to her life, of feeling sorry for herself. Lexie knew it was all true, yet it didn't stop her from being furious that her friend could be so cruelly blunt. Indignant at her perceived interference and determined to prove her wrong, she went to class again. Truthful words were just what she had needed.

She had not dared to share the agony of her homesickness with Derek; she knew she would receive only angry criticism. He had never shown tenderness or compassion, considering them weaknesses. To Lexie it appeared to be the price he paid for his strength. People like Derek never felt fear at the threshold of their adulthood for they had everything under control, didn't they? They never went searching late at night through medicine cabinets looking for a way to end it all, or wondered if ingesting a whole bottle of aspirins, the only drug she could find, was enough to kill, did they? To share with Derek her feelings of panicked inadequacy would only give him another opportunity to parade his superiority. She did not need that.

It was not Derek's affection, but that of her new friend that kept Lexie going forward until, startled, she found herself graduating and applying for jobs with local school boards.

She sat across from the balding head and abundant abdomen of the elementary school principal conducting the hiring interview. His school was under the jurisdiction of the most prestigious board in the province, and Lexie had heard they were hiring only the cream of the crop. So elated by the fact she had graduated as well placed as she had, Lexie had decided to go for it. Nothing ventured, nothing gained, she reasoned. It seemed she could at times suspend her fear of failure and naively go for the top. This was one of those times.

Having answered the questions on curricula and discipline procedures quite well up to now she thought, the next question really floored her.

"Do you play baseball?" the principal asked.

"Yes," came tumbling out of her mouth. Yes, was always a good answer at a job interview wasn't it?

Yes, I'll eat chalk dust. Yes, I'll be nice to bratty kids. Yes, I'll kiss your bald head. Yes, I'll coach a girls' softball team all the way to the regional championships, just give me the job! All this ran through her head.

My God, what had she said? As she watched him scrawl across her application in large letters, "I want this teacher placed at my school," she began to realize what she had done. She hadn't really verbalized that she would do all of those things, but she had embellished upon her baseball career to the point of convincing him that, not only was he getting an enthusiastic and capable grade three teacher, but also a star baseball coach. Had she gone too far? Could her undistinguished performance as a right fielder be enough to help her really pull it off? Where was Jayne when she needed her? Lexie had done a terrific job of selling herself, but, unfortunately, the only one who wasn't buying was her.

Her worries were soon forgotten, however, in the heady moments of rejoicing that followed. She met Lynn and the two of them whooped and hollered together celebrating that two less-than-dedicated students had each landed jobs with prestigious school boards in a day when being placed as a rookie teacher was getting tougher and tougher.

"Do you think being young, good looking, and female had anything to do with it?" Lexie asked, tongue in cheek. She needed to make light of the growing feeling of inadequacy building inside of her. So often, it seemed, she was ready to doubt her own abilities and to fall into a way of thinking which assumed if something good happened to her, it was just dumb luck, but that if good things happened to others, it was because they were smarter, more skilled, or knew something she didn't.

"Nah," answered Lynn. She laughed as she snorted, "We're just good!"

Maybe you are, Lexie thought to herself, *but right now I wish I'd gone to more classes.*

Finding herself in front of thirty-nine rambunctious eight year olds, she rapidly learned to teach on her feet. Lord knows, she was on them long enough that first year. They were crammed in so tightly, it was almost impossible to navigate between the rows of desks to her chair. Everywhere she turned, she tripped over a student. No one had told her eight year olds could be smelly, noisy, disobedient, practically illiterate, unable to multiply or divide, and possesed attention spans about as long as a three minute TV commercial.

It came as quite a surprise to her that they didn't sit all day in their desks without moving or talking the way students had when she was in school. This was a new breed of pupil. Student liberation had arrived while she had been busy preparing to enjoy the perks of a teacher's power and position. How had they changed the rules without her noticing?

Not having been educated properly in child psychology, she resorted to what she had learned from her own childhood. Her mother had used the two polar powers of sweet, patient charm and swift, unquestioned punishment. If the sugar didn't work by the time her patience ran out, she poured on the vinegar, the force of her temper erupting in a final, unchallengeable ultimatum! The trouble with this method was there were no warning signs, no half-way points. She became a benevolent dictator, making the rules and meting out punishments. Thankfully, she loved to teach and her students loved her in return, innocently accepting that it was her role to tell, tell, tell.

She maintained control, but, as she matured into her calling, she discovered the price for this absolute teacher-centred method was the stunting of the spontaneous development of her student's self-discipline. Her persona had been so large it had given others little room to grow.

She taught the way she had been taught, integrating some of the very practices she had abhorred as a child. Increasingly often her conscience was pricked by the unhappy, or angry expression of a student who chaffed under her rules. It was natural for children to act out at times, she told herself. They were lucky the strap was no longer used as it had been in her day, she rationalized. Forgotten was the sense of sheer powerlessness she had felt as a child at the hands of a teacher. The mantle of authority rested easily on her young shoulders as she stood amid her small charges. She had yet to grasp fully the other face of power—responsibility—insulated as she was from that knowledge by her lack of readiness for it. For now, she accepted with little anxiety the fact that her actions could profoundly affect the lives of those young individuals smiling so trustingly at her each day. In turn, they accepted without question her version of the way the world worked.

That version came from heavily bound documents labelled "Curricula," and although not sinisterly designed to do so, succeeded very well in perpetuating the mores of the society. A society that still saw power as a force to be laid hold of and used to further or maintain status.

At times Lexie caught glimpses of the whispered promise of a new kind of power in the wishful eyes of her students. *What if?... What if?...*she began to think. What if these children could be motivated from within to love, to rejoice in, learning; to co-operate for the sheer joy of it? No longer would she as teacher need to control, to threaten, to punish. Like sleeping seeds in winter, these thoughts lay dormant under the furrowed brow of her increasingly concerned countenance.

But we've come ahead of our story. Before Lexie was to stand in front of her first group of students as a full-fledged teacher, she was to be exposed to the classroom of world travel.

It was an absolutely amazing idea! All she had to do was sell it to her parents. Even as a young woman of twenty, soon to be out on her own, earning her own way, she still felt this was something she could not do without their approval.

Derek was driving to California a week or so after her graduation, planning to stay there for four or five weeks, and he had asked her to come with him. He had gone the summer before to visit his sister, and she had spent the entire time dateless because she was his steady and that was what was expected. Because she had been lonely then, she did not care to repeat the experience. Also, the prospect of spending her summer in a place so hallowed in the culture of the day was like a dream come true. She thought Derek was absolutely wonderful for bringing her this opportunity.

Her parents gave their approval only after they learned Derek's mother, Maria, would be joining them on the drive down and back and that they all would be staying at Derek's sister's home. If they knew Derek and Lexie were now intimate, they were not open about it and played the role of protective and concerned parents. It was what was expected in this time of denial known as the sixties. Nice girls still didn't.

The miles flew by them as Derek drove hour after hour. He never seemed to get tired, hungry, thirsty, or need to go to the bathroom. As they whizzed by restaurant after restaurant without even slowing down, Lexie began to realize this was to be a trip on a tight budget. She had already learned on their many dates that Derek intensely disliked being parted from his money. They munched on sandwiches his mother had packed; they changed drivers while still moving at sixty miles an hour with Lexie sliding in under him to take the wheel, and the two of them slept in sleeping bags under the car for shelter while his mother slept in the back seat—when they did pull over to catch a few hours' rest. They made it across the entire country to California in two and a half days and arrived at his sister's doorstep tired, disgruntled, and smelly but very, very happy to be there. That was Derek's travel style—get there in the fastest, cheapest way possible no matter how unpleasant. This style reflected his way of looking at life. To him, life was a series of destinations - one goal on the heels of another, with Derek never learning to savour the process of getting there.

She would never forget that first night in his sister's home. The house itself was charming, one of its occupants was not.

Derek's sister, Inga, warm and responsive, beamed at her brother and it was obvious that she, being older, felt protective towards him. Graciously she gave a tour of their sturdy, stuccoed, Spanish-style home, sparsely furnished in the European style, but with expensive, well-crafted pieces. It was obvious someone cared a great deal about the statement the home made for it possessed a sense of meticulous order and design. Nowhere, however, were there mementos of people and their lives - no wedding photograph, no child's toys, no souvenirs of family outings—the home had a formal sterility about it with as much warmth as a furniture showroom.

There was a sense of unease about the place. Even though Inga's face was smiling and Derek's niece Heidi's tousled, curly head peaked out shyly from behind her mother's skirts, there seemed to be a forced brittleness to the whole scene. As if both had been shattered many times and were now holding themselves valiantly together for the sake of others.

The cause of the uneasiness revealed itself that evening. Walking in at dinnertime, he brought tension with him. Everywhere he went in that house, his energy disturbed. He had to control, to order the events, to monopolize the conversation. With him, even Derek was silent. His name was Eric, and he was Inga's husband. He was blunt, arrogant, and self-centred, and Lexie disliked him immediately.

Dinner that night was deliciously prepared, but served in meagre portions, with Inga uncomfortable all the while that there would not be enough to go around. She only revealed much later in the visit that Eric had decreed her family could come to visit, but that he would not give her one penny more for their food! She now had to feed six individuals on a budget intended for three.

Later, they retired to the living room, and Eric made a great show of serving some expensive, rare sherry from his private stock.

He was generous only when it suited him. The sweet liquid still on lips, he spoke the cruellest of words.

"You know I only married Inga because she was pregnant," he laughed arrogantly.

Noting the stunned silence, he settled back in his chair, satisfied he had made it obvious a fallen woman such as Inga should be grateful for a man's presence, even if it meant he was the undisputed master of the home.

Observing the humiliation Inga lived with, Lexie came to dislike this cruel man. He was a lecherous creature as well, always arranging to retire to the garden for his evening cigar just as Lexie was undressing for bed. Looking out her window one evening, she had discovered him looking up. It made her flesh crawl. *Why would any woman stay with such a boor of a man?* she wondered.

The answer was simple. A second child was on the way, and Inga, believing herself unable to make her way in the world, stayed, stuffed her feelings, and escaped into her many books whenever she could.

Escape. Derek also had a plan. A plan he had worked on since leaving Toronto. One evening he simply announced they were going to spend a week, just the two of them, in Los Angeles. It meant they would drive down from San Francisco where his sister lived, rent a motel, and spend the time taking in the sights. Lexie was thrilled, but apprehensive. How would this look to his family? They had kept up the pretence of being celibate while staying with them, sneaking away only once to have sex while parked on a cliff overlooking the beach. This, then, would be a blatant admission that they were lovers, or from her point of view, that she was giving Derek what he needed.

But this chance to get away and to see Los Angeles was just too tempting. She would risk raised eyebrows if she must.

The coastal highway was breathtaking with its twists and turns as it hugged cliffs plummeting hundreds of feet and ending in foamy white surf beating against black-grey rocks jutting out from emerald-green waters. Derek drove well and Lexie never asked nor expected to drive. Derek assumed that his skills were superior. This had become the pattern of their relating. Passively, Lexie contented herself with drinking in the most incredibly beautiful scenery her inexperienced eyes had ever seen, while Derek drove and decided their every move.

The sprawling city of Los Angeles stretched on forever, its palm-lined boulevards reaching out like long fingers to consume all the land of the desert basin. Without much difficulty they found a respectable motel. How would they register? Checking into the same room would be met with questions unless they lied. Derek left her sitting in the car. When he came back out, he had a silly grin on his face and said to her, "Well, how does it feel to be Mrs. Gaust?"

Good question, she thought to herself.

It haunted her all that week. Everywhere they went she found herself looking at Derek in a new way, trying on the persona of his wife. She really began to focus on him—on his mannerisms, on what he said and did. Like a new husband, he approached her frequently for sex, and Lexie became aware of her growing indifference. Not only was she left unsatisfied by it all, now she found herself becoming impatient, only wishing his passion would quickly spend itself leaving her free to focus on other things besides meeting his needs.

She also began to listen, really listen to him, and she did not like what she heard. Derek was critical of everyone and everything, and his stinging words were often directed at her. As she struggled to defend herself, he would laugh cruelly at her trembling voice, cooing mockingly at her, "But, Lexie don't take it so seriously. You know I was only teasing you. You always tease the one you love."

Derek could give new meaning to the phrase "love hurts," she thought bitterly. When she really looked, listened, and paid attention to what she was feeling, Lexie came to a startling conclusion.

Fingering the book of specially printed matches with the dark green background and gold lettering that said, "Congratulations, Mr. and Mrs. Gaust," it hit her. She did not want to be his wife. She did not really even like this man she was with.

Had she ever really been with him?

She had always held back, never letting him in, not trusting enough for that. How could she blame him for seeing her as a possession when she had never shown him who she truly was. Instead, she had always passively acquiesced, deferring to him as smarter and more capable. She had been so willing to sell herself short, willing to hand her power over to a man in return for his protection.

On that last day, she made up her mind as the scenery flashed by them, their radio blaring, speeding along the coastal highway back to San Francisco. Her resolve grew with each mile, fed by the energy of the blasting beat and echoed in the black-souled, prayerful words of a musical messiah who sang of the empty generation whose fires of passion could only be lit by another.

This is wrong, wrong, wrong. Her heart beat out a pounding rhythm inside her silent, still body. *There is no sense of aliveness within this man. He knows only suppression and control. I will surely shrivel and die with him. How can he nourish another, when he cannot even nourish himself?*

These inner whisperings swirled in a great, steamy emotional cauldron. Out of the turmoil came the moment of transformation. In that white-hot flash of intuition, when at last, breaking free from the bubbling, boiling mass, there came forth a distilled essence of pure knowing.

As the energy of the moment of truth seared her, Lexie had an overwhelming compulsion to fling open the door beside her and escape from him, the car, the whole reality of her life with him.

I want out! her mind and body screamed. *I do not want to marry you, ever!* the voice inside her head screamed.

The emotions were rolling like thunder inside of her. She was seething with feeling, yet to look at her no one would ever know. Derek didn't. Her words went unspoken. He never knew the resentment raging under her calm, composed face. She simply had turned away from him and appeared to be looking out at the scenery. If he controlled, she let him. She hid her feelings so well even she had lost touch with them. And so she sat, saying nothing, giving no clue of what went on in the recesses of her mind, but knowing at that point in time, she never wanted to be Mrs. Gaust.

She would, somehow, at the right time, talk to Derek about this marriage thing and make him understand.

It is a truism that for effective communication, it takes two, both a sender and a receiver. She did talk. Derek chose not to hear.

They had been back from California for many weeks now, and Lexie had settled into a one-bedroom apartment with a roommate. She had her first month of teaching and two pay cheques under her belt. Perhaps it was a heady sense of financial independence that gave her the courage to make her wishes known.

They had been talking on the phone, and Derek had hinted at the idea of marriage. Lexie took a deep breath and plunged in. This was it. She felt somewhat more at ease with it over the phone than in person. She said the words. Words she thought were in plain English and therefore easy to understand. She stated simply she was not interested in marriage. Where she made her mistake was in softening the blow by saying "yet" instead of "to you." She wanted to let him down easy.

For the time being. She would wait and hope a solution would present itself. There was no risk in being passive she thought. She did not understand that in not deciding, she had decided.

Perhaps it was because she needed Derek — because he made her feel safe at a time when so many new and frightening events were taking place in her life — that she kept seeing him. He helped her find a place to live, find a roommate, and get moved in. In short, he worked hard at making himself indispensable. She did not want commitment, yet she did not want to let go of the safety net he afforded her. She decided to try to have it both ways, not understanding that what she perceived as a net of security was really bonds of dependency. Ties that were becoming so entwined around her they were weaving a web that would choke off and constrict the very things she needed most — safety and security. Belief in herself, not another, held the power to dissolve those unhealthy ties. Truly, where was the terror? It lived and breathed within her. Even enmeshed as she was in this web of dependency, it was there inside with her. Wherever she went, she was there. What she feared most, to step out into the world alone, to face its terrors without another, could be no worse, for the fear was always within. It must, sooner or later, be faced. But this day, Lexie decided to postpone the pain. She hung up the phone choosing to believe her weak words had been enough to settle the marriage thing once and for all.

Marriage was never spoken of again.

As she ventured forth, with tentative steps, believing she was taking ownership of her own life, she began to enjoy a heady sense of freedom. True, Derek was always in the background, giving unsolicited advice, but for the most part she was enjoying taking care of herself. She was paying her rent, holding down a good job, cooking and cleaning, and even buying some new clothes. Being on your own could be frightening, but she was beginning to discover that it was also extremely rewarding. For example, she could act on her first spontaneous impulses without checking in with anyone else. There was also a sense of pride which came with self–management, and most satisfying of all, there was the love of what she was doing. She was having so much fun with teaching.

One particular day the secretary had come into her classroom and handed her a brown envelop. Lexie, startled, asked her what it was for. The secretary informed her it was her pay cheque. She remembered thinking, *That's right, they pay me for doing this! I think I would do this even if they didn't!*

The fall months rolled busily by. She was content with her new life, full of dreams for her future. One day, she would marry Mr. Right, have 2.2 kids, drive a station wagon, and live in the suburbs while baking cookies and attending PTA meetings, but for now her life held out such a promise of more. She could travel to exotic places or perhaps buy her own car and know the heady freedom of driving out on the open road of adventure. There was so much ahead of her. So much to learn and do. With wide-eyed wonder she saw the choices spread out before her in the giant buffet called life.

Packing up the things on her desk one December day, she heard the voice of a friend call from the hallway, "You goin' home to your family for the Christmas holidays, Lexie?"

"You bet! Wouldn't miss that for anything!" she chirped back in reply, smiling silently inside herself. She had a sense that, for some reason, this particular family Christmas was going to be an event!

CHAPTER FOURTEEN:

THE RABBIT DIED

Mommy, Mommy, can you see
Here in your life I was meant to be?
Written on our souls in heavenly decree
Stretching out in front of you and me
Age-old lessons to be learned
Setting both our souls free.
The door slams and we are alone,
A child within a child.
We both cry and long for home
Stranded here amid the cruelty.
Our only hope, our only joy to be
Growing up together
You and me!

"YOU'RE marrying a mechanic?!" the woman sitting beside her blurted out. Lexie looked into the incredulous face of her coworker who hadn't bothered to hide her opinion that Lexie could and should do much better.

What a strange thing to say. I wonder why she thinks that? mused Lexie.

The remark was added to a collection of other troublesome observations. Phrases such as, "You'll outgrow him, you know," and "Does he always tell you what to do?" She would stuff these annoying insights down with the thought, *What does anyone else know anyway?!*

It seemed they knew more than she did, at least on that eventful family Christmas. When her hand had come up with the little blue-velvet box, everyone but Lexie had known what was inside.

It had been done the old-fashioned way. Deciding the time was right, Derek had approached Lexie's parents to ask for her hand in marriage. Flabbergasted by the entire procedure, but assuming their daughter had made up her mind, they gave their blessing.

One very important person had not been consulted. Derek, in his egotism, had assumed Lexie would be thrilled at having landed such a good catch. It did not matter what Lexie wanted, Derek wanted it enough for both of them.

Nothing had been said about marriage in the weeks before Christmas. Her family assumed Derek had proposed, and she had accepted, but the presentation of the engagement ring was to be kept a secret surprise. Derek was adamant about that. Everyone obeyed Derek's wishes. Derek always got what he wanted.

He got what he wanted and more. After an uneventful honeymoon, they had moved into Lexie's one-bedroom apartment and life had settled into a routine. They each went to work, and then Lexie came home to work again. Determined to be the perfect wife, she cooked, cleaned, shopped for food, and tried to turn their tiny, meagrely furnished apartment into a home. Derek had decreed they would spend no money on new furniture, so cast offs had to do. It frustrated Lexie that their small rooms had a worn, dingy appearance, but her tears of frustration did not move Derek to change his mind.

Something else bothered her too. The same summer another young teacher on her staff had also married. Jan was a petite, energetic blonde, and she came back in September absolutely aglow. She talked on and on about her husband and how wonderful he made her feel. Often she would come roaring in at the last minute, give a wink and mention that everyone knew the trouble newlyweds had getting out of bed.

Did they? Lexie wondered. *She* was always on time. A heavy lump formed in her stomach. What was wrong that she didn't feel that way?

Wanting with all her heart to believe her marriage was normal, she went so far one morning as to insist that Derek make love to her. She needed the illusion that yes, they too acted like newlyweds.

In those early years when she would snuggle up against Derek's back, he would grumpily inform her he did not want to be touched. He never wanted to be touched as he slept. He insisted she sleep on her side of the bed and he on his and if by accident she happened to roll over against him, he would react to her touch with a violent kick or poke of his elbow. He explained his behaviour by saying he had hair-trigger reflexes, and he simply reacted without regard for the person beside him. Lexie contented herself with sleeping alone even though he was in the bed.

A vague sense of dread became her sleeping companion. Marriage had not changed them, her and Derek. They had brought all that they were into this union. To admit the marriage was less than it could be was then to admit that Lexie herself was somehow lacking. Unable to accept this as truth, she coped with the gnawing emptiness as she always had done in the past. She filled it with frenetic activity. She would do, do, do her way to happiness. She would be the perfect wife and housekeeper, the best teacher, the most beautiful woman. Her flurry of busyness kept her spinning so fast, she had no time to think or feel. Six months of her marriage flew by this way.

"Are you using any kind of birth control?" her mother asked out of the blue one day.

Lexie stammered a reply. "No. Well, yes, sort of."

"What do you mean, 'sort of' using birth control?! That's like being 'a little bit' pregnant. Are you or aren't you?" Her mother seemed relentless in her questions. Why didn't she just drop the whole thing?

"I decided not to use the pill you know, Mom. I worry about all its side effects. I just don't think something that unnatural can be good for women. So Derek and I are using the foam instead."

Lexie finished her speech with a heave of relief. There, that should end the discussion. It was embarrassing talking about such intimate details with her mother. That's what girlfriends were for, weren't they? No one wanted their own mother to know they were doing "it"! Even if you were married!

It wasn't enough. Mother kept right at it like a bull terrier with a mailman's pant leg. She obviously felt it was now her duty to inform her daughter how to avoid unwanted pregnancy.

Why now? thought Lexie to herself. *I've done allright for years!*

She blushed at the thought. Thank goodness parents couldn't read minds!

"Well, the foam doesn't work in the drawer you know!" her mother rattled on. You have to make sure you take it out and use it. It only takes once, and if you and Derek aren't ready to have a baby, you need to be careful."

"Don't worry, Mom. I'll be careful. Derek and I have no intention of starting a family." The words kept on flowing in her mind. Words that wanted to say, "I'm not even sure I'll stay with him, let alone have his child."

She didn't say them, though. She knew her mother didn't want to deal with her ambivalent feelings about marriage. She had her hands full with her own life.

Her mind drifted back to the time late one night when she had come to her mother for advice. She had been in so much pain, so much turmoil. The invitations had been sent, everything was arranged, and the wedding was rapidly approaching. She was so scared. She knew she didn't want to do this, and she wanted to call it all off, but what would people think? What would they say? She would look like a complete idiot! She went to her mother for guidance. She would know what to do.

She talked. Her mother listened, her face sad. The words and the tears flowed. She felt so vulnerable, so wounded, like an innocent child who had been tricked into giving something up before knowing its full value. She wanted so desperately to go back, to negate all she had agreed to.

Her mother cradled her head in her lap, stroking her hair as she spoke in soothing tones.

"Lexie, honey, it's only bridal jitters. All brides have second thoughts before their weddings, you know. I did before I married your father and Lord knows, look how much I love him. It's normal.

Don't worry. Derek's a good man. He's a hard worker, you know, and he'll always provide well for you. That's important. I don't want to see you struggle the way your dad and I did. Come on now, dry your tears. You'll be fine. You'll see. Things will look different in the morning. It's late and you need your rest. How about a nice cup of tea together, and then we'll both turn in?"

In Mrs. Alexander's mind, a good cup of tea sipped with a sympathetic friend could soothe away any troubled feelings.

As Lexie sat up, drying her tears and nodding her head in agreement, she knew what she had to do. She would be a good girl. She would do what was expected and marry Derek. The critical moment with its possibility of escape had passed. Had her mother given her any encouragement, even one small word to validate her feelings, it would have been enough to carry her forward into action. Without it, she simply could not move to save herself, passively letting events carry her along. She did not value herself enough to act in her own best interests. The defining of her own worth still came, for Lexie, from others.

She did not blame her mother for failing to rescue her. She, Lexie knew, had sincerely done what she thought was best for her daughter. Derek was a good catch by many standards. Mrs. Alexander knew her daughter would be provided for. As for being happy, how many marriages were truly happy? Could one realistically expect that from marriage? You simply made the best of it. That's what Mrs. Alexander had seen around her. That's what the women of her time had done. Marriage, at its best, gave a woman security, a sense of purpose and an identity. Love, if it continued to thrive throughout the marriage, was a bonus.

"You'll be pregnant in six months, mark my words!" Her mother's voice jolted her back to the present.

"What did you say, Mom?" Lexie asked bewildered.

"You'll be pregnant in six months if you don't get on the pill! I can't tell you how many babies have been brought into the world because the birth control got left in the drawer. The pill's the only sure way, you know."

"Don't worry, Mom. We'll be careful." Lexie answered absentmindedly. Having a baby was the farthest thing from her mind.

Her palms were sweaty, her knees were weak, and her stomach was churning as she picked up the phone in the staff room to make her call.

"That's right, Mrs. Gaust. The test came back negative. Yes, we're sure."

Slowly she sat down in the chair, shaking with relief. Thank God. She wasn't pregnant after all! She felt sorry for the rabbit giving up its life so she could know, but ever since she had been a few days late with her period she had been in constant turmoil. Long hours had been spent soaking in scalding hot tubs, looking down at her stomach, praying the hot water would relax her and start the long awaited menstrual flow. To no avail. So as soon as she could, she had gone off to a doctor, a sample had been taken and shipped to the lab. Then the agonizing wait began. Those three days had been the longest in her life. The relief at now finally knowing swept over her in waves. She wasn't pregnant! The words played over and over in her brain, and she was ecstatic with her reprieve!

She rolled over in bed and threw up! It was the Saturday morning two weeks after receiving the test result. Derek was already up and off to work. Mechanics were expected to work half days on Saturday.

So there it was. She knew. She was normally never sick to her stomach and she still had not started her period. All the evidence pointed to one conclusion. That damned rabbit had been wrong; she was pregnant after all!

She spent that morning with herself. Sitting wrapped in her bathrobe, rocking herself gently back and forth, a cup of tea in one hand, the other resting gently on her stomach as she began to get acquainted with the new life within her.

She told no one about the morning sickness. Strangely, it never occurred again. Instead, she made another appointment to see her doctor. She had to be sure.

Like a mad woman, she ran down the main street in the frigid winter air, hatless, her coat wide open, her steamy, panting breath surrounding her in a cloud of vapour, her eyes wide and wild, all the while talking rapidly, hysterically into the emptiness ahead of her.

The doctor's painful, probing hand had left no doubt. She was, after all, pregnant. She was laughing. She was crying. She was doing both at once. She was ecstatic; she was terrified, her emotions wildly out of control. Unprepared, she didn't know what to feel. Having made no conscious decision to have a child, it seemed as if this thing had just happened to her. She had just drifted into this pregnancy. By not making a strong enough commitment to not becoming pregnant, she now found herself more dependent, more enmeshed in a situation that left her completely trapped. Had she once again, by not actively deciding, actually decided? For is not to decide, to decide?

As she unlocked the door of their tiny apartment, her mind went over how to tell Derek. They had not even discussed whether they would have children. She had just assumed they would—someday. God knows what Derek had assumed. She had no idea what to expect from him as she picked up the telephone and dialled his work number.

Haltingly through her tears, she spoke the words. When she had finished, there was only silence. Then, to her surprise and great relief, his voice came through soothingly, gently, telling her not to worry. He assured her they would manage somehow and that everything would be all right. She relaxed. If Derek believed they could handle it, then she could believe too. She had not known how much her reaction had depended on him. Now that he had seemed to accept the pregnancy, she began to relax into the idea. By that evening she was actually beginning to get excited about becoming a mother.

Whether Derek had been self-conscious about being overheard at work or whether he had now had time to think through all the ramifications, Lexie never knew, but he hardened his heart against the new life growing within his wife.

The very next morning, after a fight about moving to a larger apartment, he had slammed out the door. He knew she would be required to resign her teaching position that June, and he was furious that the arrival of this child would interrupt his financial timetable - a timetable that up to now he had not seen necessary to discuss with Lexie. Apparently he had already set their course well into the future based on two uninterrupted incomes. A baby definitely was not part of his plan.

"Get rid of it!" he hurled the words over his shoulder as he stormed out in a rage. She stood leaning against the door, shaking, shivering, the tears rolling down her face. So, she was to be alone in all of this after all. There was to be no loving support. She had no intention of giving up the life within her. That was unthinkable for her, but obviously not for Derek, the 'good Catholic'.

She felt herself straighten. Determination filled her, strengthening her. Derek would just have to get used to the idea whether he liked it or not! He could rant and rave all he wanted. Her mind was made up. She was having this baby!

Acceptance of any event out of his control came hard for Derek. When he realized she was not about to change her mind, he tried another approach. If he could not get Lexie to be sensible, perhaps her mother could. Alone with Mrs. Alexander one Sunday as he drove her to work, Derek brought up the subject of Lexie's pregnancy.

"Mother, I don't think Lexie is ready to have a baby. She's too young and besides I don't think we can handle it financially with just me working. Talk some sense into her, will you? She'll do what you tell her to. If you tell her an abortion is the only sensible solution right now, she'll listen. I've tried to talk to her, but she's being really stubborn on this one. Talk to her for me, will you?"

Disbelieving what she was hearing, Mrs. Alexander's jaw clenched as her son-in-law spoke. How could she have so badly misjudged this man? A father wanting to abort his own child! It was foreign to her French-Canadian mind where large families were seen as God's blessing.

She stiffened indignantly in her seat. Waiting until he finished speaking, she then carefully chose her words of reply.

"There's never a convenient time to have a baby, Derek. You'd better get used to the idea. The faster you accept it, the better for you and for Lexie. I have no intention of speaking to my daughter. If she was old enough to be your bride, well then, I guess she's old enough to be the mother of your child. I give you both my blessing, and I'll choose to believe you didn't mean what you asked of me. As far as I'm concerned, this conversation never took place."

With that, she pulled on the door handle and let herself out of the parked car.

True to her word, she never spoke of her son-in-law's request until many years later. But from that day forward, she trusted him less.

Talk of abortion was dropped, and Derek grudgingly came to accept that he was to be a father in the fall of the year. They moved into a larger apartment too. Derek's parents had bought a multiple-unit building as an investment the year before. It appeared now that the tenant in the two-bedroom basement apartment was moving out. Derek's parents offered it to them at a reduced rent in exchange for the money he had lent them to buy the building. Lexie was so pleased to now have a nursery for the baby that she happily agreed. Besides her mother-in-law would live in the same building, and Lexie felt sure she would want to help out by babysitting occasionally. She'd had very little contact up to this point and felt confident all those terrible jokes about interfering mother-in-laws were just that—jokes.

They scrubbed. They cleaned and scoured, and they moved in several months before the baby was due. She would soon be finished teaching for the year and was looking forward to spending her summer preparing for her baby's arrival. Part of that, in her mind, involved the buying of nursery furniture and decorating the room the baby was to occupy. Here, she and Derek clashed head-on. He had no intention of spending money on anything more than the bare necessities for his new member of the family. The colour of the walls was fine the way it was, he argued. He had a buddy who would sell him a used crib for $10 and the old multi-coloured drapes his mother no longer wanted would be good enough for the windows. No matter that nothing was new or matched. He simply could not understand why Lexie was making such a big deal of all of this.

She got stubborn again. What was it when it came to this baby? Derek noted his wife could dig in her heels about this like nothing she had ever done before. Lexie cried and pleaded. She would not let the matter drop. Usually when Derek got angry and roared out his ultimatums, she would accept his decrees as the final word and fall into sullen silence. Not this time.

This time her stubbornness blinded her to the warning signs. She had always suspected Derek had a temper. She had glimpsed that glazed-over, out-of-control look only once before in his eyes, but it had been enough to make her fear the potential of this man's rage. In that instant she had known Derek was capable of hurting her. His anger could reach such a flash point that it blasted through all the barriers of self-control and demanded expression no matter what the cost to himself or others.

She didn't see it coming. They had been arguing bitterly about furniture for the baby's room. Lexie was determined not to give up the quest. It was not for herself that she was asking but for another, who with each squirm and kick, was becoming dearer to her. It frustrated her so because she knew they had more than enough money saved to decorate several nurseries. She naturally wanted the best for her unborn child.

He hit her full in the face and sent her swollen seven–months-pregnant body sprawling. She had been yelling at him, desperately trying to make him understand how important this was to her when she saw his jaw clench, and his hand raise as if in slow motion. The realization of what was coming paralysed her. The back of his strong hand went smashing into the side of her face sending her reeling. She crashed into the floor. Stunned, she looked up to see him standing over her, breathing rapidly, his hand poised to strike again if she protested.

Picking herself up silently, her hand to her swelling face, she turned away from him and walked into the bedroom closing the door quietly behind her. As she lay herself across the bed in the semidarkness, muffling her tears in the pillow, an overwhelming sense of strangely comforting self-pity wrapped itself around her. What had she done to deserve such shocking treatment? How could he not come to comfort her? He knew how much the baby's room meant to her. If he loved her, wouldn't what's important to her also be important to him?

Drawing her arms closer around herself, she rocked back and forth sobbing in the darkness. The tears came harder and faster, but still there was no soft knock on the door. She knew he would never apologize, never admit that he had done anything wrong. He would twist the situation so she would bear the blame for his actions, telling her she was wrong to keep insisting—she had driven him to strike her.

As she cried on into the evening, thoughts kept going around in her mind like a squirrel in a cage. They started with, *I'm a good wife. I treat him with respect and compassion.* The thoughts ended with the question, *How could he do this to me?*

How could he do this to me? Never once, as the darkness descended, did her conditioned mind think to ask a new question.

How can I allow him to do this to me?

Such enlightenment would have set her free.

Instead, she accepted the treatment she had received, she took on the responsibility for another's act of violence and fearing more of the same resolved to be an even better wife. She never again wanted to see that flash of rage in Derek's eyes, and if she was always good, she believed she never would. He became someone to please and placate for her own protection. Someone to be pushed so far and no further for he had proven he was capable of hurting her. Could he ever be trusted again?

She should have left him, right then and there, packed her bags and out the door, but that prospect frightened her even more than Derek's fists! What would she do with a baby on her own? How would she manage? Desperate thoughts swirled around in her brain. She had never felt so vulnerable. There had to be a way to feel safe again. Her thinking began to shift. Perhaps Derek was not so bad after all. He had his good points, and he had only hit her once. She probably had driven him to it with her incessant demands. Surely, he was sorry but just couldn't tell her. Poor Derek, he was so locked within himself. If she could just give him more love, more under-standing, she was sure she could make him better. She wouldn't tell anyone what had happened. You know, not make a big deal about it. Maybe she had gotten what she deserved after all. Just let it go. It just wasn't that important. Besides she needed Derek's support with the baby coming. Once the baby arrived things would surely get better.

She repeated these thoughts to herself so many times that her litany of denial began to make perfect sense. Abandoning her own right to outrage, she abandoned herself. Fearing the power of her own anger, she sacrificed all in order to feel safe. To minimize and deny appeared the easiest way to survive.

She cooked his breakfast the next morning as if nothing had happened.

She contented herself with the used crib, the mismatched drapes and the sterile walls; she told no one what had occurred. She made it appear she and Derek were in agreement on the decorating for to do otherwise would reveal the imbalance of power in their relationship. Lexie did not even want to admit the imbalance to herself, let alone her friends.

She had underestimated those around her. Lynn, without saying a word, had seen through the situation and had come forth with such a gesture of generosity, it became a moment of pure joy for Lexie.

She saw the curved strips of wood first as they were thrust through the front door. Lynn was beaming at her, looking through the slats of a huge, comfortable rocking chair. *How had she known?* thought Lexie. In her mind, no nursery could have been complete without one! But there was more. Next came a beautifully painted and decorated toy chest. Lynn herself had painstakingly painted scenes of favourite nursery rhyme characters. She was overwhelmed with the expense and time her friend had invested in order to give her such a gift.

"I tried to match it to those drapes. I hope everything works together okay." Lexie noticed Lynn just couldn't hide the way her nose crinkled up in disgust each time she looked at them.

Lexie was filled with a warm glow as she smiled at her friend.

Everything was ready. Everything, it seemed, but the baby. The due date came and went. Lexie endured countless people calling only to say, "Are you still here? We thought you'd have had that baby of yours by now!"

Finally, when her doctor said labour had to be induced for the sake of the child, she agreed. She had put herself passively in the hands of this elderly, round-faced doctor who spoke in a clipped foreign accent. She was so young and inexperienced and this doctor was such a strong, no-nonsense type of man, she readily accepted his assertion that he knew what was best for her and her child. Attending prenatal classes really wasn't necessary he had informed her. Women had been having babies successfully for centuries without them, he said, so why change now? Besides, he would be there to help her through, and if things got too much for her, he would simply give her something for pain. He explained the procedure whereby, in the final stages of labour, she would be immobilized from the waist down by an injection at the base of her spine and consequently not feel a thing. He made having a baby sound like a painless interlude where he would have the solution for everything if she would just trust him and put herself in his capable, fatherly hands. His idea of answering questions was a condescending pat on the backside as he ushered her out of his office assuring her with the soothing phrase that the doctor always knows best.

She prepared for the birth by knitting and waiting rather than exercising and practising her breathing. She read books on how to care for the baby after it arrived, but was only vaguely aware of the process by which it would come into the world. That, she had been told, was her doctor's responsibility. She handed her body and its contents over in complete trust.

Her doctor had booked her into the hospital for nine o'clock on a Wednesday morning. Derek sat fidgeting beside her hospital bed. It was now noon and he was getting very nervous about the time away from his job. He worked on a flat rate system and if he was not actually working, he made no money. The doctor on call had appeared around ten o'clock and informed them that Lexie's doctor would be unable to be there to start the process, but would check in later as labour was progressing. Thus, a man she had never even seen before instructed her to open her legs wide and without explanation, placed her bare heels up into the cold steel of the stirrup supports. He left her wide-eyed with apprehension, as he came at her with a long, sharp instrument and slid it up into her exposed vagina. As it advanced inside her, she could feel its smooth coldness and then a dull aching pain spread like fingers radiating out and drawing into her the whole heaviness of her lower body. She knew this pain well. It had been part of her each and every month. The doctor withdrew the instrument releasing a gush of amniotic fluid. It now would begin he informed her. She should expect the first labour pains anytime for he had ruptured her amniotic sack—broken her water—he explained. They would keep an eye on her, but now, he explained, they were to let nature take its course. Being a first-time mother would probably mean a lengthy labour—twelve hours or more.

Just like a man, Lexie thought wryly to herself. *Stay long enough to get things started and then leave the real work to a woman."*

Derek obviously subscribed to the same philosophy. He could see no practical purpose in staying to watch his wife wince in pain every twenty minutes, and so informed Lexie she really didn't need him and returned to what he did consider important—making money. He would see her at dinnertime, he said, and with a kiss on the cheek he was gone. Lexie was left alone with her fear and her pain.

She had known Derek would not be present during the actual birthing process. Strict hospital rules dictated no one other than sterile medical personnel was to be present. In their infinite wisdom, the administrators of this mammoth building of sickness had decreed it was not a healthy thing for a new life to first be greeted by the loving touches of the individuals who had shared in its creation. Rather it was to come into an atmosphere of scrubbed, white sterility devoid of warm, welcoming colour, soothing sounds, fragrant sweet smells, soft textures, and sensuous touches. None of the promised pleasures of the waiting world were represented. Instead there lay a frightened birthing mother strapped down on sterile, rough-textured sheets, harsh, glaring lights in her eyes, surrounded by masked, expression-less faces, their bodies robed and covered exposing no sign of warm, human flesh, holding sharp, piercing instruments in their hands and communicating in a code of abbreviated grunts. They, who partici-pated daily in the amazing human event which ensured the very survival of the species, proceeded with detached efficiency. The goal of a successful birth consumed them. The quality of the process escaped them. The setting and scene was more appropriate to a sacri-fice of new life than a celebration of it.

So it was that Jessica Alexandra entered the world. She came without a whimper. Whole and perfect, round of face and plump of body, she exuded a healthy robustness. As she had been pulled from her mother's body, Lexie, observing, had experienced a strange sense of detachment. There was no sensation at all. The long, silver needle had done its work. It had silenced her pain but it had also silenced Jessica. Lexie, not allowed to touch her child, also did not hear her child's cry for many more hours.

In order to be cleaned, Jessica was taken immediately. *How could one so perfect need to be cleaned?* Lexie wondered. Enthralled with this new life which had come from inside her body, she wanted to see her baby, caress her smooth skin, hold her and look upon her face. Instead she lay mute as her baby was wheeled away.

Jessica, tightly wrapped in hospital linens and lying inside a Plexiglass box under an amber warming light, was finally wheeled into her room. Lexie, still on her stretcher, was told not to touch her child, allowed to see her only for a few minutes before Jessica was taken to the nursery because Lexie needed to rest.

What she needed was to hold her baby and get to know her through touch and scent not just through her eyes. Again, she silenced her objections, subjugating her own needs in order to conform to the hospital's dictates of how birthing should be.

Across the room those silent, new eyes, drew her. This was not the blank, expressionless face of a newborn infant. There was something—a timelessness—here. With each knowing blink Lexie felt drawn, pulled into a feeling that wonderful wisdom, wrapped in unconditional love, had come to her through this new soul. Like windows into a place where they had known each other before, their eyes held fast, and a string of words whispered by a tiny, new voice, passed like precious pearls through Lexie's mind.

"Mother, Mother mine. We have known one another before this time.

For love of me, a lesson learned through pain, will be yours and mine."

And then it was gone. The light of knowingness faded, and the child became once more, innocent and new—a blank slate upon which some of what the world was would be written.

CHAPTER FIFTEEN:

READ IT AGAIN, MOMMY!

ॐ

She shoots! She scores!
She leaps! She soars!
Afraid to be just who she is,
A frightened girl inside her lives.
Her feverish drive for perfection
Leaves no time for reflection.
Again and again the same script is read,
Round and round the refrain goes in her head.
Do it again! Do it right! Do it more!
In perfection there lies acceptance.
Society states its litany of deliverance.
To be equal, of the female requires more.
Weary on then, daughters of All is One,
Know in the grand scheme of things
Each, both male and female, come to be healed.
Not frivolously by what each has feverishly done
But instead, to each, in time, may be revealed
The true garment of Superdom.
When all else seemed useless travail,
To have loved the self was the test
That laid all emptiness to rest.

"You're like a bloody witch, Lexie!" Derek's friend sputtered. "How the hell do you know who's going to win every damn hockey game? It's uncanny the way you do it all the time, you know."

Lexie smiled to herself. She was getting used to this way she had of just knowing things. It could not deliberately be called upon. It just happened. A feeling of certainty about an outcome would inexplicably settle in her mind. At first she had kept track of her hits and misses only in her head, but as her accuracy began to grow, she ventured to jokingly share her predictions. She enjoyed the open-mouthed incredulity of others when they came true.

Having her baby had increased her capacity for feeling and thus for knowing. Her awareness heightened by the intensity of love she felt for this tiny, helpless bit of life, she became filled with a sense of purpose and power. This gave her courage to explore and accept unquestioningly the strange new ability bestowed upon her. In becoming a mother, she had discovered more of herself.

Yet, her new gift fed her sense of "otherness." It heightened the illusion that if she could just predict and thus control everything around her, she could feel safe, whole. To avoid feeling her own sense of emptiness, she also became an obsessively devoted mother. Her child now became the centre of her existence, the vortex around which all her energy swirled.

No one could meet Jessica's needs as well as she, the consummate mother, could. Derek's fumbling initial attempts to care for his infant daughter were scorned. Discouraged by her condescending criticisms, he gave up the attempt. As Lexie became bonded to her infant daughter, there was less room for Derek. Turning to her daughter for love and validation, her baby's trusting, adoring eyes provided a new mirror for Lexie. One that reflected back all the love she could focus upon it. Her child's constant neediness was sucked in greedily to fill her void. An emptiness still haunted her, walked with her, could not be avoided even though she believed she had paid the price of happiness. Did she not always do what was expected, what everyone else thought was right? Was she not always the good girl? Now, in living out society's role of the perfect mother, Lexie had found a powerful new way of filling the emptiness inside. Thus, mothering both nourished and consumed her.

As she held her beautiful baby in her arms, looking down at her as she contentedly suckled, Lexie came to feel, for the first time, true unconditional love. She would do whatever it took to ensure her baby would thrive—even if that dictated putting the child's needs above her own and doing it all alone.

She just accepted she would be the one to crawl groggily out of bed in the dark of night in answer to those tiny cries of hunger. Derek, always a light sleeper, would be awakened first. A kick would let her know she was expected to get up and care for their child. As she sat alone with her baby in the dimly lit room, rocking gently back and forth, the minutes sleepily ticking by, she would often feel the urge to snuggle them all cosily together in their big bed, with both pairs of adoring parental eyes drinking in the wonder of this child. How comforting it would have been to share these lonely, late-night feedings with another, but it was never to be. Derek insisted he needed his undisturbed rest.

She never discussed it with anyone, but Lexie had another reason for wanting company on those late, dark sojourns in her daughter's nursery. It would always begin the same way. She would be startled awake by the baby's cry or Derek's kick and as her eyes would open, she would see the same vision flash before them. In that fleeting second before she could shake off the sense of foreboding, she was aware of a long, dark figure standing over her daughter's bed. She knew it was a tall, slender man who stood staring down at the tiny, helpless child.

Shivering, she would attempt to shake off this vision. Steeling herself to go into her child's room, she would content herself that what she saw was no more than an overactive imagination at work. Entering her baby's room, she would see only the elongated shadows the furnishings cast upon the walls. The soft glow of the night-light gave the room an eerie cast, and she would often shiver with more than the cold as she scooped up her hungry baby and cuddled her to her full breast. Then settling into the chair, her eyes would come to rest lovingly upon the tiny rosebud mouth and perfectly formed nose and cheeks and her apprehension would melt away amid the sounds of contented sucking.

The nights flowed into days, the days into weeks, and the weeks into months. Jessica grew sturdy and strong. She was generally a contented baby, crying only when hungry or wet. Because of this,

Lexie allowed herself to be convinced she should occasionally get out without her child. Derek's mother, Maria, who lived two floors above them, appeared willing to babysit. All seemed to go well until the third time she was left to look after her granddaughter.

Lexie had returned earlier than expected, and as she unlocked the door, an eerie quiet greeted her. It was the silence of an apartment devoid of a caring, protective adult presence. Lexie went searching for her mother-in-law only to find Jessica totally alone in the apartment. When she angrily pounded on Maria's door and demanded an explanation, the older woman, contentedly chewing on her lunch, shrugged her shoulders, saying that she saw no problem. The baby was asleep. The fact that the child could not be heard from two floors below seemed not to be a consideration for this particular grandmother whose main concern seemed to be the state of cleanliness of the laundry room adjoining Lexie and Derek's apartment.

That had been another source of friction in a relationship which was steadily deteriorating. Lexie, only finding time to do the baby's laundry late at night, had found an angry note on their door the next day, informing them that the room was not to be used after six in the evening! It further admonished Derek because his new wife was negligent about cleaning up after herself! Lexie had left some of the baby's sweaters blocked out to dry on the top of the washer.

The more Lexie came to be around Derek's overbearing mother and silent, ill father, the more she came to wish for a place of their own. It was true what they said about mother-in-laws in those jokes after all. Nothing her son's bride did was ever good enough. The woman could not be pleased and often took it upon herself to take over and show how, in her opinion, something was to be done. One day, Lexie found her rehanging all the pictures in their apartment because, she said, they were hung too high. The fact that she used her key to let herself into their apartment whenever she pleased finally forced the issue of a move.

It was a Sunday morning. The sun was streaming in through their bedroom window, and Jessica was contentedly sleeping. It was one of those mornings when things felt right with the world, and Derek was in good spirits. He reached over and made it known he desired her. It was warm in the apartment, and they had thrown back the bedcovers. As their two naked bodies entwined, they heard behind them a slight gasp and then a stifled, nervous giggle. Derek jumped up like he had been shot and stood face to face with his mother!

She had assumed they were out and for whatever reason, had decided to let herself into their apartment. Slipping noiselessly down the hallway, she had inadvertently become a witness to their lovemaking.

Derek was shaking with rage.

"Get out!" he screamed at his mother. As she retreated, he threw the bedcovers over Lexie's nude body then paced the room declaring emphatically that he had absolutely had enough of his mother's meddling. Immediately, they would start looking for a house of their own.

True to his word, their search began the next weekend. The particular small town north of the city where they concentrated their search was divided into two sections by the railway tracks running through it. The side to the east of them was unofficially labelled the wrong "side of the tracks" with the west side being known for its beautiful pond and luxury homes.

Their real estate agent, when made aware of their budget, toured them through house after house on the east side. Finally in desperation, Derek asked if there was anything better to be had.

When they pulled up in front of its wide front lawn with its three stately pine trees standing like sentries at the corner of the long, low west-side bungalow, they immediately fell in love. This was more like it, they chorused in unison. The perky structure boasted blue-and-white, striped awnings over large plate-glass windows that went all the way to the floor. There was a large, two-car garage that, although separate from the house, was joined to it by long, white beams that ran from the roof line of the house to the roof line of the garage. Between the two structures was a sunken patio surrounded by garden boxes filled with shrubbery, and on one side the lawn sloped down to meet a rock garden alive with colour.

It was something out of *Better Homes and Gardens* as far as Lexie was concerned. She knew she wanted this house. Whatever else she saw, she was now convinced this house was definitely the most their money would buy.

They stretched their resources to their very limits and succeeded in making the house their own. They were to move in the day before Jessica's first birthday. It seemed like a good omen.

Moving day dawned dreary and cold. The whole experience of buying a house had felt like a hosing of ice-cold water. In their naivete they had neglected to allow for land transfer tax and legal fees. Consequently they had had to approach the bank for a further personal loan on top of their already substantial mortgage in order to complete the purchase. The loan officer had shaken his head as he advanced them the required funds. "I wish you luck," he said as he shook their hands good-bye. It was becoming obvious Derek was not as knowledgeable about finances as he had led Lexie to believe. Consequently, he did not object when she suggested, that because she was home and had the time to do the banking, she would take over the management of their accounts. She would need his permission for all purchases and was expected not only to manage on his wages, but save money as well. Derek's rule was, "Always pay yourself first." By that he meant that ten per cent of whatever was earned immediately went into a savings account and was not touched. You then lived on what was left as if those savings did not exist.

He need not have worried about restraining her spending. By this time she had no desire to face his stinging tongue. After all this time of being with someone so critical and controlling, Lexie had internalized his values. Now when the temptation came upon her to spend freely, she would see his disapproving face and hear his harsh voice. As she looked at her new home in the dreary light of their moving day, devoid of the camouflaging furniture of the previous owners, she knew it was pointless to pine for what it could again be.

Derek would kill me if I spent that much! Better wait. I guess we can do without, she thought.

She would again make do with what they had. Even years later when money was no longer a problem, that internalized critical voice would continue to rob her of the joy of buying something simply because it was desired. The struggle to becomd financially secure had left her unable to enjoy being there.

But Lexie could be stubborn at times. She insisted that even though they had moved into the house with only a few dollars in

236

the bank, they would nevertheless invite all their friends and family to a combined celebration. It was to be a celebration to mark the passing of their daughter's first year and to initiate their new home. Somehow, she argued, she would pull it off without spending a great deal. Lord knows, she had seen her mother do it often enough.

The date was set, all were invited, and Lexie set about preparing the food. She worked hard planning, cooking, cleaning, and being determined everything was going to be absolutely perfect - everything, that was, including her.

The one fatality during her pregnancy had been her hair. Once long and lustrous, it now hung limply on her shoulders, a nondescript shade of brown. She had been a "bottle" blonde in her late teens, but had gone back to her natural shade of brunette, convinced that the harsh colour treatments were about to make her the first bald female teacher she had ever known.

Did a part of her still believe that blondes had more fun? Whatever the reason, she was a sitting duck at the Wanda the Wonderful wig party. She had been surrounded by a group of giggling, mop-headed women when the smiling sales girl had plopped the halo of beautiful, blonde curls on her head. Out popped her wallet. It had been a reflex action that had left her stomach in knots later. How was she going to explain this one to Derek?

She was developing a strategy for just such occasions. It went something like this. When she broke down and bought something she really wanted, Lexie brought it home and hid it in the closet. She then felt appropriately guilty about what she had done every day for two weeks or so. She didn't use or wear what she had bought, thereby depriving herself of any pleasure and then, when she had done enough guilt work, she would nonchalantly trot out the purchase. When Derek's eyebrows went up, and he asked her if it was new, she could say quite convincingly, without a trace of guilt, having worked it all through in her own mind, "Oh, this old thing? I've had this for ages!"

Thus the guests were greeted the day of the party by an excited, blonde hostess. She had worked so hard to make this party a success, she just knew everything was going to be perfect.

She had read one of those fancy bridal gift cookbooks and had decided this was the perfect time to try out some new recipes. All the guests were seated in the living room talking when it was time to pass around the hors d'oeuvres she was heating in the oven. Excusing herself, she went into the kitchen and yanked open the oven door, sticking her head inside to inspect its contents. She checked and rechecked the food because her nose told her something was burning. They were done, but certainly not burnt. As she kept her head inside the oven, inspecting each piece for burn marks, she could hear a crackling sound and even when she pulled the trays out of the oven that burned odour cooks dread still surrounded her. Brushing it off as her imagination, she placed the hot tid-bits on a serving tray and headed into the living room. She was having such fun with all of this, entertaining the way it was done in the movies, passing the tray around the room, elegantly handing out hot canapés to her guests, the perfect hostess in her new domain.

"Lexie, what's wrong with your hair?" One of her guests was staring up at her in open-mouthed amazement. As she reached up to touch what was left of her beautiful blonde wig, her hand landed on a brittle bunch of charred nylon strands, which with her touch, disintegrated and fell upon the food like blackened bits of shredded wheat. It was years before she lived down her reputation as the hot headed hostess! When the subject came up, she later could laughingly say that obviously hot blondes didn't belong in kitchens and since she couldn't give up kitchens, she'd given up being a blonde instead.

Lexie recovered her composure, the wig went in the trash, and she went on to enjoy everyone else enjoying the main attraction of the day—a small child dressed in pink frills, laughing and gurgling at everyone until she signalled she'd simply had enough by rubbing tiny fists into tired eyes, popping in a contented thumb, and proceeding to go to sleep in front of everyone.

The day, however, was not over for Lexie. She had made an exotic cake for dessert, and she was determined to serve it even if the guest of honour was asleep. She had to confess she was a little concerned about it because she had somewhat altered the ingredients. Instead of layering the rows of chocolate wafers with whipping cream as directed, she had decided it would taste better with chocolate frosting. The directions specified the cake also needed to be refrigerated for several hours to allow the biscuits inside to soften.

There was a hush as she brought the cake out to be served. The outside of her creation was a frothy mass of whipped cream covered with curled shavings of rich, dark chocolate. All gathered around to watch her cut into her work of art. She had to admit that even she was impressed by how it had turned out. With all eyes on her, she pulled the knife down through the layers of whipped cream, into the cake, and then further into the centre of chocolate wafer biscuits. Here, she met with firm resistance. Trying not to show she was having difficulty cutting into this form of perfection, she simply tried harder. She exerted more pressure. The cake resisted - more pressure, more resistance. By now her forced smile barely covered her clenched teeth as all waited expectantly for the interior of the confection to be revealed.

As is often the case in life, things are not on the inside as they appear on the outside. The frothy, soft layers of this creation hid a core as hard as granite! Bearing down with all her weight on the knife, Lexie finally sliced through to the bottom. As the knife abruptly hit the smooth, slippery surface of the glass plate, it acted like a hockey stick hitting the slick surface of the ice in a slap shot. The piece of cake, finally freed, shot across the room like a puck fired at an open net. The crowd roared as the piece of cake went bouncing across the floor only to land, stuck fast to a wall. Lexie, horrified, knew she had once again scored a place in the Hostess Hall of Fame.

As the winter snows piled up outside, Lexie thrived inside, cocooned in the safe, secure world of her home and child. With Derek gone all day, she could order her life as she pleased. She enjoyed the solitude with no one looking over her shoulder or telling her what to do. Like a hothouse plant, tended and nurtured in a protected setting, Lexie blossomed. These were days of contentment.

With the night came Derek's arrival — a shudder on the surface of her serenity. It seemed they were always at odds with one another now. The fear there would not be enough money to meet their needs gripped at him constantly. He coped in the only way he knew how. He closed his world in around him, contracting all that they did, hanging on so tightly, allowing no more money to pass through their hands than was absolutely necessary. Their new home became a darkened symbol of his mistrust and fear as Derek compulsively shut down its heat and light. After a day flooded with sunshine, warmth, and freedom, Lexie's home nightly became cold, dark, and oppressive to her. If she turned on lights, he turned them off. When she turned up the heat, he turned it down. He spent his evenings in the dark hole of a basement with only the flickering, blue light of the television for company while Lexie worked above him.

They fought often. Lexie was coming to bitterly resent the way Derek controlled all aspects of their life together. She withdrew more into herself, becoming sullen and uncommunicative much of the time. She expected him to instinctively know what she needed for her happiness and to provide it. When instead he met his own needs and followed his own agenda, she would seethe with resentment. This would build like a volcano within her until at last, unable to contain her wants any longer, but still fearing to communicate them directly, she would vent her energy in small, constant, and manipulative bursts of nagging words.

Nothing was ever resolved. The same issues would surface again and again, each time carrying more emotional charge. Their marriage was becoming a power struggle. Lexie coming more into her own sense of who she was, was demanding more often that her needs be met; Derek, feeling threatened and uncertain of where this would lead, only hung onto his power more tenaciously.

One night they had been fighting over money, as always. They each wanted to control it. Derek wanted to shut down and save. Lexie wanted to experience and spend. He believed there would never be enough of it to go around, thus he had to amass as much of it as he could. She trusted there would always be more. Lexie had faith in her ability to create money. Her philosophy was, if you needed more money, rather than cut down your expenses, you went out looking for ways to create more revenue. Her belief in an ever-expanding, abundant universe clashed head-on with Derek's conviction that he was alone against a scarce, stingy world.

In sheer frustration, unable to compel her to accept his beliefs, he backed her into the small room. Nothing he said or did could make her stop arguing and agree with him. The rage of not being able to control her boiled over in him. He knew he was going to hit her with more than angry words. She knew it too.

240

The deliberate moment of decision was reflected in the set of his face and the tensing of his arm even before his hand came up to swing at her. When she saw it coming, she crossed her hands over her head and chest to protect herself and crouched down into the corner. There was nowhere to go. As the blows smashed into her arms, something inside Lexie broke. He had gone too far this time. What did it matter if he hurt her more? He had hurt her too much already. She could take this no longer. From somewhere deep inside her came an energy that rolled upward through her uncoiling body and burst forth with flailing arms and a roar of anguished protest.

"No-o-o!"

Her hands flew out at him, blocking each one of his continued attempts to strike her. She was fighting back.

Her eyes were bright with fear as she matched him blow for blow. Not his equal in strength, that no longer seemed to matter for she felt she was fighting for her very life. He would not inflict enough damage to rob her of her physical existence. She had no fear of that. No, she was fighting for her right to live with dignity. To Lexie dignity was the same as life itself. For to live always in fear-filled oppression was not to be truly alive.

His anger finally spent, still heaving from exertion, he looked at her with disgust and turned to leave the room.

But to Lexie it was far from over. That night as they lay silently together in bed, the energy unleashed by defending herself carried her forward into a plan.

The next evening Derek returned to a dark, cold, empty house. Lexie had taken Jessica and gone. There was no note, no explanation, no sign she intended to return. For three days he had no knowledge of where she was. Every attempt he made to track her down failed, for she had deliberately chosen to stay with a friend whom Derek did not know. She knew she would return, but Derek did not and that was just as she wanted it to be.

At the end of three days a stronger Lexie walked through the door of their home. Nothing was initially said, but Derek knew by the way she carried herself that there was a new set of rules. As she put Jessica into her crib, she looked back over her shoulder at Derek and simply said, "If you ever touch me again, I will leave you for good."

Derek only nodded his agreement. He would do what he had to do to keep her. This battle may have been lost, but it was not the war. It was simply a time to change strategies. He would find another method of control.

Deceiving themselves they now had a resolution, never speaking of the incident, they continued instead to imitate intimacy. He never again dared to strike her as long as they lived together as husband and wife.

The spring before their daughter turned two, they decided Lexie should return to work. Even Derek had to concede the restricted lifestyle they were leading was not satisfying for either of them. Lexie was weary of the powerless position of a woman without income. She had almost forgotten what the inside of a restaurant or movie theatre looked like and now lived in her 'uniform' of jeans and turtleneck sweater with her long hair pulled back in a pony tail. Makeup and hairdressers had become luxuries to be trimmed from their budget. Their sole form of entertainment had been getting together with friends to play cards and drink homemade wine.

When she stared into her closet wondering what to wear for her upcoming job interview, she realized she had a problem. There were just too many bare hangers staring back. It also seemed styles had changed radically since she had last been in a classroom and what she did own was no longer acceptable.

As she slipped a borrowed dress over her body and looked into the mirror, Lexie felt transformed. A tall, competent teacher stared back at her. Helped by a friend's packaging and a recommendation by her former principal, Lexie landed a job teaching in a school forty-five minutes from home. She felt fortunate to have been rehired by her old school board during these times of severe cutbacks and nonexistent maternity leaves. The employers and the teachers' union itself had not caught up with the concept that women would now often be in and out of their profession in order to have their families. Lexie had been told to resign when she became pregnant. Her male employers had made the assumption she would stay home until her last child was raised. Society still clung tenaciously to the myth that it was best for everyone if a woman's place was in the home.

The playground was deserted when she pulled her car into the parking lot. The gravel crunched under her feet as she stepped onto the path leading to the door of the grey-stone church. As she descended the steps into its dark, cool basement her stomach seemed to be sinking deeper into her body. Was she really going to leave her tiny, young daughter here day after day?

She had done her research carefully and this centre seemed the best choice. After much soul searching, she had decided upon it instead of a private individual. Even though they were a revolutionary new concept and not very common, Lexie felt strongly that the socialization Jessica would receive here would be what she needed rather than the isolated environment of an individual's home.

Not yet two, Jessica Alexandra was a softly passive, loving child. She had made best friends with the thumb of her right hand, and it bore two tiny, raised callouses as testimony to the thumb's soothing effect. She was also a familiar passenger on her mother's hip as the two had been inseparable, Lexie taking her child almost everywhere with her. Jessica was well received wherever they went for she most often settled contentedly into her new surroundings as long as her mother was within sight or sound.

As she toured the centre, asking question after question of the staff, she tried to ignore her racing, painful heart. How could she even be considering this? She felt her sadness expanding, filling her whole chest with an aching throb, choking off her very breath. She climbed slowly, sadly back up the stairs and out into the brilliant, summer sunlight. As she stood squinting into its brightness, Lexie felt confused and disoriented, sensing she had just consented to sacrifice something very precious.

She took Jessica there every day for the next week. Packing her child up each morning with her diapers and her favourite blanket, off they would go to spend a few hours at the centre. It was called a desensitizing process, designed to allow Jessica to become comfortable with the surroundings while still in her mother's presence. For Jessica, however, the most exciting thing in the brightly painted rooms was still her mother's leg. For there she clung as she watched all the activity go by. Occasionally she would venture forth to explore, but always making sure her oasis of safety, her mother, was not far away.

Finally, the staff, recognizing this little one would have a difficult time making the transition, reassured Lexie that even though tears and trauma were inevitable, they were not a permanent condition.

She had been so caught up in concern for her daughter that she was unprepared for the impact of her own feelings. That first day as Jessica was pulled crying from her arms, Lexie felt as though part of herself was being ripped away. For the next several weeks, she drove to work each day with the streets and roads passing by in a blur of tears. She returned each evening with a knot of guilt twisting in her stomach. She hated leaving her child, but she also hated herself for getting lost in her work, thinking of Jessica only occasionally throughout the day. She hated coming home each evening tired, exhausted, and wanting only to have no more demands placed upon her. In Lexie's mind this was certainly not the profile of a perfect mother, and she hated herself for that. She did not allow herself to feel the grief of separation, the joy of work, her legitimate sense of weariness at the end of a productive day, and most of all she did not allow herself to ask for help. Instead she dug deeply into that inner costume chest of fierce independence and cloaked herself in the steely garments of her own relentless expectations. She would be all things to all people. She was that new breed of woman. Genetically engineered for both home and workplace, designed to work long hours, prepare meals with the speed and dexterity of a chef, wash and fold sheets and shirts like a Chinese laundry, perform the duties of chauffeur, maid, gardener, teacher, counsellor, entertainer, financier, nurturer, and lover and to do it all cheerfully with a minimum of maintenance or complaint. Last but not least, she even came covered by a lifetime replacement warranty. There were many more models just like her to choose from she was told. Like the mythical Clark Kent, Alexis Alexander, stepping into her inner phone booth, stripping away her own healthy boundaries just as Superman stripped away clothing, at last emerged, transformed. She was now 'Superwoman!' If not able yet to leap tall buildings in a single bound, at least able to do almost everything else

"Read it again, Mommy, and this time don't leave out the middle part!" The thumb had come out of Jessica's mouth just long enough to give this dictate and had then been plugged firmly back in. Three-year-old Jessica contentedly squirmed further into her mother's lap. The story reading, seated cosily in the ample rocking chair, was a nightly ritual. Each evening, Lexie arrived alone at the centre, bundled her charge into the car, chatted with her about her day, then let them both into the empty, silent house to make dinner. Lexie cooked while her daughter would watch, convinced that "watch helping," as her job was called, was just as important as what her mother did. They ate at the small, round kitchen table together, then filled the tub with frothy soap bubbles for Jessica's nightly bath and splash. Finally, scrubbed then wrapped in cosy pyjamas and favourite blanket, Jessica would snuggle into her mother's lap as the teacher in Lexie shared the wonderful world of children's books with her enthralled young student. The cadence of the words, the rhythmic movements of the rocking chair were only occasionally punctuated by the little one's queries or Lexie's own sips from her tea cup.

Often Jessica was tucked into bed for the night when Derek arrived home to his supper kept warm on a plate in the oven. He worked hard. He most often worked late, but even when he didn't, the routine never changed. On those nights, he would eat with them, but then disappear into his basement den to forget his day, becoming entranced by the flickering shadows of life portrayed and projected on a television screen. Thus with no eyes to see nor ears to hear, the drama of his own family life unfolded unheeded around him as he chose to absent himself from most of its truly important scenes.

Another winter passed in the trance they called living, the long months having taken their toll. Lexie came and went each day in the darkness. Growing weary with the routine of living, she longed for the sense of aliveness that awakened in her with the arrival of the sun. For Lexie had discovered a new love. This love had been a gift to her from Inga, Derek's sister. On her one and only visit (after Derek and Lexie were married), Inga had spent time with Lexie introducing her to the joys and mysteries of the garden Lexie had inherited with her new home. As they had walked the grounds, Inga had pointed out the many weeds Lexie had allowed to grow undisturbed convinced they were the wanted residents known as flowers. Uncharted territory, this was something new to master. Inga patiently instructed and then left Lexie with lists of books to read on the subject. Lexie remembered the beautiful rose garden Inga had tended behind her own home. It had taken skill to produce beautiful, full blooms in that insect- and fungus-friendly climate. As she taught Lexie how to care for her own rose garden, Inga's great affection for this velvet-petalled flower had become obvious.

Her hands were wrist deep in the soft, brown soil when Derek called her into the house. She had been uncovering her rose bushes from their long winter sleep, scooping the mounded soil away from their woody stems and feeling the warmth of the spring sunshine on her back and the cool dampness of the just-thawed earth under her knees. Brushing the earth from her hands and jeans, Lexie came up the walkway, and when she looked into Derek's face, she knew something was terribly wrong.

"My sister's dead." The words came out in a hoarse whisper. He turned silently from her, and she followed him into the house in stunned silence. Slowly and haltingly he told her what details he had. He never once cried. Lexie expressed the grief for them both. She held him, and she cried for him. The energy of his pain trapped within, he kept his body rigid, unyielding, refusing to feel its flow. He was stoic stone.

They flew to California to be with Inga's children. The stories of how she had died were all so confusing. She had been separated from Eric and her children now for more than a year. Lexie again recalled Inga's last visit. It had been shortly after she had left Eric. She had not spoken of it, but Lexie knew she had had angry words about it with her parents. They had expected her to go back to her husband and her children. She remembered Maria had packed up boxes of china and silverware to send back with her daughter for her home. She just refused to accept the idea that her daughter's marriage was over. Everyone also seemed to refuse to accept the strange scars Inga had on both wrists. Lexie never asked and Inga never volunteered an explanation.

Derek's mother had been the one to hear the news from Eric. She had become hysterical, and it had been impossible to get an explanation of how her daughter's death had occurred. She kept blubbering on and on about her daughter having had leukaemia. When they arrived for the funeral, Derek and Lexie found only more secrecy.

Eric was barely civil, saying he could not put all of them up and asked them to stay in a hotel. The two children were staying with Eric's brother, and Lexie and Derek were denied the right to see or talk to them.

Ugly suspicions about how Inga had died began to grow. Lexie and Derek had visited them once more in California when Lexie was expecting Jessica. The trip had ended in violent disagreement between Derek and his brother-in-law, and Eric had thrown them out of his house. Pregnant, Lexie had spent an uncomfortable night sleeping on an airport couch while Derek had arranged an emergency flight home. The two men had not spoken to each other since. It seemed to be a common way of dealing with family disputes in the Gaust household.

They had not expected to be particularly welcomed, but the veil of secrecy was very unsettling. Derek went off on tirades where he fantasized that his brother-in-law had deliberately had something to do with Inga's death. This line of thinking eventually led them to the coroner's office to request a copy of the death certificate. They were told it could only be released to the parents or husband. Totally frustrated, they arrived at Eric's home on that final day after the funeral to pick up Derek's parents and take them to the airport. As they turned down the street, Lexie could not believe what her eyes were seeing. There, standing on the driveway, with suitcases strewn around them, stood two lonely, old figures.

As they drove up and loaded everything into the car, Lexie noted Eric was nowhere to be seen. From the air of tension in the car, she could also tell no one wanted to discuss what had happened. The trip to the airport was shrouded in silence, just as the whole matter of Inga's death had been. Perhaps, they believed if they did not talk about it, they would not feel the pain.

For many years to come, as Lexie spent more time with Maria, the agony of her daughter's death poured out in an endless stream of tears. She could not seem to let go of the guilt she felt. Lexie would hold her hand and reassure her that she had done all that a mother could have done. From Lexie's perspective, a mother, of course, would be there for her child. How could it be otherwise?

It was only years later, as Lexie was going through Maria's papers preparing for her move to the nursing home, that she came across a small, folded piece of paper bearing the Marin County coroner's stamp. As she unfolded it with shaking hands, the words jumped off the paper.

"Cause of Death: Drug Overdose."

Had Inga really meant to do that to herself? Lexie wondered?

Her mind drifted back to that confusing time and to a strange, compelling event that had taken place the night Inga had died.

They had been visiting Lexie's parents for her father's birthday celebration and had arrived home very late. Jessica had been sleeping in the car, and Lexie had carried her directly into bed and then turned in herself. She had no idea how long they had all been sleeping, when she was ripped awake by a blood-curdling shriek coming from Jessica's room. The sound of the voice made her hair stand on end and sent a shudder through her whole body.

As she bounded breathless into her young daughter's room, Jessica's words took shape in her mind.

"I want to live! I want to live! I want to live!"

Lexie stood frozen in the door only to see her child sitting up in her bed, staring straight ahead as she emitted those agonized cries.

Then it was over. Jessica had quietly lain back down in her bed, totally unaware of what she had said. As Lexie stood over her, her hand gently brushing her child's smooth forehead, watching the rhythmic rise and fall of her sleeping child's chest, she noted how peaceful she looked.

"What was that?" Derek asked as she climbed back into bed beside him.

"I don't know. I really...don't know." Lexie answered absent-mindedly.

She was busy trying to figure it out herself.

They received news of Inga's death three days later when the police discovered her body in her apartment. She had been dead those three days.

Secrets, secrets, secrets, thought Lexie sadly, as she folded up the piece of paper and tucked it away. She had heard it said once that a family was as sick as its secrets. Denying the truth had helped to

destroy Inga and—even after her death—had caused ruptured relationships. Lexie wondered if Derek knew his parents had refused
to pay half of their own daughter's funeral expenses and had thus
ended up unceremoniously dumped out in Eric's driveway that day.
Years later when Lexie had discovered that piece of information, she
had felt ashamed to be a Gaust.

"Mommy, I'm a girl, you know." The tiny voice whispered through
her mind. Lexie abruptly stopped stirring the dinner on the stove and
reached down to touch her swollen stomach. She was seven months
pregnant with their second child, and she had been hoping it was a
boy she was carrying. The little voice had an impish lilt to it, and she
had no doubt as to its correctness. Lexie had been having many such
psychic insights over the last few years, and she had learned to recognize the inner way of knowing she possessed. Steadily drawn to books
on the subject of psychic phenomena, she found herself hungry for the
information on their pages. The subject of psychic phenomena held an
inexplicable fascination for her.

Perhaps Lexie felt compelled to explore other worlds because
she was so often unhappy in this one. She felt different from other
women because of her psychic gifts. Derek did not share her fascination. In fact, she and Derek shared very little at all.

In many ways Lexie wondered why she had decided to have this
second child. Perhaps she had just come to expect so little from her
marriage, and it was less threatening to stay than to go. For whatever
reason, she decided Jessica was not to be an only child. Derek had
agreed but had insisted she time her pregnancy in order to complete
her teaching year before having the baby. Lexie had been using the
birth control pill and, after discussing it with her doctor, had decided
to come off it three months early in order to allow its hormones
to clear her system before getting pregnant. They would simply be
careful in the meantime.

Lexie sympathized with women who had trouble conceiving. For
her, though, it was as easy as falling off a log. She had been careful,
but she knew she was pregnant ahead of schedule even before she
had gone to the doctor for confirmation. Because breaking the news
of her first pregnancy had been such a disaster, Lexie was determined to do it right this time.

She shopped for all his favourite foods. She chilled the wine. She set the table elegantly with candles and flowers and she awaited his arrival home for dinner. They would celebrate this wonderful news together.

He might as well have slapped her. His words wounded her just as much. He stood there facing her in the kitchen as he flung his rejection at her.

"You can eat your damned supper alone! What's to celebrate? You just got pregnant early so you could quit work sooner! You've always got to have it your way, don't you Lexie? Just like last time. Well, I've had it with you!"

He left Lexie standing openmouthed in the middle of the kitchen as he stormed out. Tears of humiliation rolled down her cheeks as she sat down to eat. With each bite, she stuffed down the hurt. With eat bite, she stuffed down her outrage. She managed to swallow the pain whole. When she at last excused herself from the table, she had digested it enough to excuse Derek's behaviour. She told herself he would come around. He'd get used to the fact that she was pregnant early.

Again she bore the responsibility for his bad behaviour. She excused it, minimized its effect on her, and felt noble for silently bearing the hurt. She knew she had not become pregnant by herself. Why then did she accept the blame?

Her only defence against the hurt was, as always, to try harder to be more perfect. She would do everything perfectly this time. She signed up for prenatal classes. This time she would take control of her own body and the birthing process, determined to have this baby naturally.

Derek refused to go with her to the classes. He wasn't the one having the baby he said. After a great deal of coaxing and pleading, Lexie managed to get him to agree to think about being present during the actual birth. He seemed to enjoy keeping her off balance with his non-committed response. It was rather like a cat toying with a mouse. He would make her wait until the last possible moment to inform her of his decision. It afforded him a position of power, and he had used this same technique often with her.

Hospital rules had changed a great deal in four and a half years; fathers, properly gowned and masked, were now allowed into the delivery rooms. Lexie could only hope Derek would decide to be there for her and their child. In the meantime, accepting his minimal involvement, she went off each week to prenatal classes by herself. Perhaps a part of her wanted to keep the experience of motherhood for her very own. Perhaps a part of her had realized the more she begged and pleaded with Derek, the more she played into his hands.

The sound of raucous male laughter coming from the basement below greeted her as she came into the house that night after her class. Her foot was on the step ready to descend when what she heard stunned her.

"Did ya see the hair on that one! It was all the way down her legs. How'd ya like to screw that?"

It was Rick, a friend of Derek's whom Lexie had never liked nor trusted, who was speaking.

Lexie shivered again as the other men chorused a bawdy reply, hooting and hollering, obviously enjoying the bump and grind movements of the women as the stag movie rolled on before their eyes.

Lexie was not a prude, and she did indeed understand the need for sexual stimulation and release, but the contrast of where she had just been and where she now found herself was just too great to bear. The child she carried inside her was a symbol to her of the commitment between a man and a woman. It was the result of cherishing life, all life, female as well as male. Woman as mother represented to her all that was most unique and beautiful about her sex. To witness women now reduced to repositories of male lust, objects to be used and ridiculed, unleashed in her the floodgates of rage. Without thinking, for she was far beyond that, she deliberately descended the stairs, each step propelled by white-hot anger. She did not address them. She did not rant nor rave at them. She simply dismissed them with a disgusted, "Get out! Get out of my house!"

They scattered like a group of scared schoolboys whose mother had caught them reading dirty magazines. Lexie too, fled the house, finding refuge with a neighbour and friend. She sobbed out her hurt and disappointment. She felt shamed by her husband's actions, as if he represented all that was wrong between men and women. Most of all, though, she felt fear - fear of Derek's wrath. She knew she had humiliated him.

When she had the courage to return to the house, she found Derek strangely subdued. He never spoke of the incident, acting as if it had not taken place.

It seemed they dealt with many issues that way. A conversation was like a walk through a minefield. There were so many unresolved issues that constant vigilance was needed lest they touch off a conflict. Thus, as the years passed, there was less and less they could talk about. Fewer and fewer topics were safe territory. They touched less and less in other ways too. Sex had deteriorated into a brief encounter twice a month or so, always leaving Lexie unsatisfied. She did not know what it was to experience sexual fulfilment at the hands of her husband.

She rarely woke during the night unless it was in response to her child's cry, so it was with surprise she found herself startled awake this night. It was the differentness of the room that had summoned her back to consciousness. Something was not as it should be. Derek was not there beside her.

She crawled noiselessly out of bed, and went seeking him, concerned something might be wrong. As she relentlessly yet silently searched each corner of the house, she came upon him huddled and naked, hidden in the basement. They stood there silently staring at one another in the darkness. He offered no explanation, and she asked for none. She turned on her heel and headed back to bed, a heavy sadness within her. So, their marriage had come to this. There was now so little connection between them, that he preferred to meet his needs on his own. Lexie, too, driven by sheer frustration, had some time ago taken her sexual gratification into her own hands. It was easier than asking for what she needed. They had become like two ships slipping noiselessly past one another in the night. There was no recognition, no acknowledgment of one another's rights or needs. They both were steaming stubbornly ahead on their own timetables, going in opposite directions, their lights becoming more and more distant on one another's horizon, no longer any lifeline connecting them.

"You're doing wonderfully!" The nurse patted her hand as Lexie was wheeled into the delivery room. She had just come through five hours of hard labour and knew her child's birth was imminent.

Derek had sat beside her through it all, holding her hand limply, totally absorbed in what he was reading.

Lexie, believing there was merit in stoicism, had not cried out as the pains had ripped through her. She had not asked for the loving touch of the back rub that would have eased her pain. She did not scream at Derek that she didn't give a goddamn about the statistics he was quoting her from the article he was reading. No, she stayed stubbornly within herself. She didn't need anyone. She could do this all by herself. Besides, was Derek such a dolt he couldn't see what she needed? If he hadn't figured it out by now, she would punish his insensitivity by shutting him out even more.

If he's not there for me, I'll be damned if I'll let him in. This pain-fevered logic ran through her brain as she bore down silently and pushed new life into the world.

She had been surprised when he entered the delivery room, wearing the required cap and gown. Just like him. He had left her in uncertainty until the very last moment. He sat down by her shoulder as her legs were raised into the stirrups and the mirror adjusted to allow them both to witness the birthing process.

"Push! Push again! Good girl!" Her doctor coached her on.

She felt exhilarated by the pain. With each push, her excitement mounted. This was the easy part. This was the home stretch.

She looked over at Derek between pains. He was leaning forward, his mouth hanging open in amazement, his eyes wide. He, at last, was being drawn into the drama of life. Impacted, perhaps for the first time ever by a realization he was connected, through his act of creation, to this tiny new life struggling to be born.

"There it is! There's the head!" The doctor, too, was caught up in the excitement.

They heard her almost as soon as they saw her. She was determined to announce her arrival in the world.

"She cries like a girl, Lexie! I don't think you're going to get your boy this time!"

Two more pushes proved the doctor to be right. As he held her up for all to view, Lexie's breath caught in her throat. She was perfect, absolutely perfect!

They placed her lovingly across Lexie's stomach. She reached out and stroked her child's velvet skin, wanting nothing more than to see, touch, hear, taste, and smell this tiny being—to gather her child into her and to drink in the wonder of this new life with every sense she possessed.

Mesmerized by her new baby daughter, Lexie only became aware of Derek by sensing his absence. When she asked, the nurses joked that they had asked him to leave before he himself had become a patient. He had been so pale they were afraid they might be soon picking him up off the floor.

Lexie was content. As she lay gazing at her tiny daughter, she was satisfied. This time, she had done it all perfectly.

Jade Emily was a breathtakingly beautiful child. Every feature of her tiny face was perfectly formed as if shaped by a loving sculptor. With dark, almond eyes, alabaster skin, a soft blush of pink on her cheeks, and lips in a perfect cupid's bow, her loveliness was startling. She was a contented child as well, peacefully eating and sleeping away the first few weeks of her arrival.

Lexie was then surprised when a new pattern began to emerge. After nursing contentedly for several minutes, Jade would inexplicably pull angrily at her nipple, break free, and wail in frustration, then come back and suck tenaciously again. Lexie focused on what might be wrong with Jade to cause such behaviour. After weeks of taking her baby to the doctor and filling her with medicines to counteract what she believed to be an intestinal disorder, she finally accepted the truth. There was nothing wrong with Jade. The problem was her.

After the initial first weeks when Jade had been her whole world, she had gradually begun to allow other concerns to intrude. In her belief that she could be all things to all people, Lexie did not allow herself to lessen her responsibilities or to lower her standards of performance. She simply added Jade to her list.

Derek helped no more than he had with Jessica's care, and this time Lexie had a house to run, a preschooler to care for, and her garden to tend. She did it all, and she did it to the same standard she always had. It was not surprising, then, that the stress expressed itself through her body. She was holding on so tightly, her perfectionism driving her beyond her limits, that she held on to the very thing her child needed in order to thrive.

Sadly, Lexie scooped Jade up and settling into the rocker, put the bottle to her baby's lips. She took it immediately, sucking greedily, and Lexie knew she had denied her child enough nourishment because of her stubborn, perfectionistic pride.

Jade smiled up at her mother contentedly as Lexie laid her back into her crib. *Poor child*, Lexie mused. *You tried to tell me didn't you?* She was overwhelmed with love for this little one who had been so patient, so accepting that life did not always give her all she needed. Her perfectionism had blinded her to her child's needs. It should have been a valuable lesson.

The arrival of this beautiful jewel of a child wrought many changes in their lives. Her birth gifted Lexie with a new acceptance of her body and its functions. Because she had been there, really there, working with her body to bring new life into the world, she had come to have a deep and profound respect for its grace and power. At the age of twenty-six, she began finally to embrace and accept the mantle of womanhood.

False modesty had been stripped from her during two child-bearing experiences. She could now see her nude self reflected in the mirror and accept its image. Walking naked among the fitness-conscious females at her club, she no longer struggled to cover herself. She stepped into her femaleness as one might slip into a garment that was, at last, no longer too big. She took ownership of her body and all that it was capable of experiencing for her, and she could no longer ignore its whispered sexual promise.

She knew she had found the right book when her hand fell upon it. Pulling it from the shelf, she glanced around to see if anyone was watching her as she leafed through its pages. This would do, she thought to herself. She would read it first and then find the courage to discuss it with Derek. She knew she had to. She could not go on any longer suffering in silent denial. She walked out of the bookstore with a copy of *The Joy of Sex* tucked determinedly under her arm.

They had been married now for six years, had had two children together, and Lexie still did not know what it was to experience an orgasm during their lovemaking. Because of both ignorance and shyness, she had allowed herself to suffer frustration again and again, always stuffing down the feeling and telling herself it didn't really matter to her anyway. Sex was just not that important.

Derek had simply accepted that his wife was incapable of more. Lack of knowledge and his own sense of sexual unease allowed him to content himself with their dysfunction. Denial relieved him of taking responsibility.

If Jade's birth had been a revelation for Lexie, it had been a veritable explosion of awareness for Derek. It had given him a new profound respect for the power of the female to create life. He had been awed by what he had witnessed — awed and humbled. He began to see Lexie in a new light. To see her as mother, nurturer, source of life, had drawn Derek closer to her and to himself. In witnessing birth, there had also been a rebirth. He had come face to face with the wounded child within himself.

As this need had opened within him, he feared it was greater than his ability to meet it. Deceived and terrified, he sought out Lexie's physical touch, wanting to be near her all the time. He developed the habit of calling her several times a day just to hear her voice. Having witnessed her bring life from her body, she now became his touchstone — his connection with aliveness. Now he would not only be nourished by the powerful elixir of control but would also suck from Lexie all the nurturing she would give, letting her do for him what he could not do for himself — what he had not even known he needed to do for himself. She would love him, and her love would be the very proof he was lovable. He could define himself in terms of it. He would find a mother for his wounded child.

She was not far away. He had married her.

These awakenings breathed an appearance of new life into their unhealthy union. They began slowly, tentatively to explore the realms of sexual pleasure together. Derek now sought out the warmth of her body at night, and they slept like two spoons nested together. They read their "how to" book, and Lexie slowly came to trust Derek's touch enough to let herself respond. Physical release came at his hands, but, inexplicably, she was left feeling there was still so much more. Their sexual encounters, though now satisfying enough, never moved her with the passionate abandon for which she yearned.

And so life once again settled into a predictable routine. Their finances were decidedly healthier this time around, and Lexie stood firm in her determination to stay home with her children. Her days revolved around their needs and her evenings around her own. Because she and Derek had little in common, Lexie filled her after-dinner hours with creating. She began with handiwork and crafts and then moved on to the work of the mind. Learning was a way of life for her. To cease to grow would signal her purpose in living was finished, and so she began a project that would span many years. She set to work on her university degree.

She did not know where it would take her. All she knew was that for now, it satisfied her driving need to achieve, quelling her discontent at being "just" a housewife and mother. Perhaps if it had been left only to her to judge the worthiness of what she was doing, she would have labelled herself content. Yet, the values of a newly emerging societal norm left her feeling restless and incomplete. She must do more. The dictates of others said there must be more, always more.

Jade Emily, although healthy enough, remained thin. This filled Lexie with guilt. Furthermore, her slenderness was sharply accentuated whenever her friend Lynn arrived with her children to visit. Lynn had had her third child, a robust, chunky girl, at the same time Jade was born. Although Lexie loved Lynn dearly, she did not always look forward to her frequent visits as she would arrive in a whirlwind of disorder with three children, two dogs, and a station wagon loaded down with diapers, empty milk jugs, dirt, and other debris of disorganization. She was certainly different from Lexie for Lynn was as disorganized as Lexie was organized.

In the past this difference had caused only minor ripples in the tranquillity of their friendship, but that was now about to change.

Returning from a doctor's appointment, Lynn had decided to drop in. Borrowing Jade's utensils to feed her baby, she had neglected to tell Lexie that her daughter had been very ill with an intestinal virus which caused severe dehydration. Leaving in a flurry of activity, she never even mentioned her baby's condition.

A few days later, Lexie was shocked to get a panicked phone call from Lynn's new nanny. The woman was positively hysterical.

Between sobs, Lexie managed to coax out of her what was so terribly wrong. Lynn and Taylor had left this woman in charge of their three children and gone on vacation in Bermuda, only indicating to her that the little girl had been ill, but was now better. With the return of symptoms, the nanny had called the doctor only to learn she had been left to care for a baby with the same condition which had caused her own tiny child's death years before.

Beside herself, as with each day, the nightmare of her own child's demise appeared to be playing itself out again, she had reached out to all the names on the emergency contact list. Taylor and Lynn could not be reached.

Lexie was stunned to learn of Lynn's callousness for she had known of her nanny's loss! Counting on the fact her baby was getting better, she had decided to risk the situation, escaping from the stress to their destination in the sun.

Dread flooded Lexie as she unpinned Jade's diaper. There it was, the sign she had so feared. It explained her baby's listless behaviour and raised temperature. The virulent virus had found a new home.

Unable to keep anything in her system, all that she was fed caused pain and cramping and passed right through Jade's tiny body. The doctor prescribed a diet of distilled water with some dissolved sugar. Nothing more could be done, he said. The virus would have to run its course. The sugar water should prevent dehydration, the main reason for death in these situations.

The days were leaden for Lexie, seeming to stretch on forever as she watched her listless child become thinner. Lexie's frequent calls and visits to the doctor's office always elicited the same advice. After two weeks Lexie was crazed with fear—her baby was becoming too weak to even cry! Silently, she lay limply in her crib, her dark eyes staring helplessly from her pale, little face. It was as if she had resigned herself to this slow starvation. She was, one might suppose, no stranger to the pangs of hunger.

Lexie sobbed out her panic to her doctor. He agreed to hospitalize Jade the next day. He had resisted up until now, assuring Lexie her baby was receiving better care in her hands than a hospital would provide. They would now put her on an intravenous drip connected through her skull, he informed her. This mental picture drove Lexie wild with concern. There had to be something she could do. She had been reading lately of the healing properties of the friendly bacteria to be found in yogurt. It was worth a try. Anything was worth a try. Surely the grip of the intestinal virus was weakened by now.

Jade responded listlessly as Lexie fed her the creamy substance. Eating seemed like too much of an effort for her child. With each spoonful Lexie prayed. She fed her again, and she prayed some more. Mercifully the cramps did not come this time. Mercifully the diaper stayed unsoiled for hours. Encouraged, she dared to hope and continued to feed Jade small amounts each hour.

Tears of relief poured down Lexie's face when her baby began to greedily suck in all that was on the spoon, smacking her lips together and looking for more. It was finally over! If she could take nourishment again, she could thrive again.

Unable to forgive her friend's irresponsible behaviour, Lynn's unannounced whirlwind visits to Lexie's home were stopped. They did not see one another again for many years.

The other irresponsible person she could not rid herself of quite so easily. He lived with them. Derek had chosen to distance himself quite literally from the whole situation. He made plans to be away with "the boys" each weekend leaving Lexie to cope on her own. On the final weekend before Jade was to be admitted to the hospital, Lexie had begged him to stay home with them. She had found the courage to tell him how very frightened she was, to admit her weakness, clinging to him and crying as he said his good-byes.

He simply shook her off, telling her she was overreacting. There was nothing to worry about. The baby would be fine in her capable hands. She could handle it. Unable to get away fast enough, he had literally bolted out the door, leaving behind a wife who once again hardened her heart to him. Derek was running out of chances at redemption.

Jade did eventually thrive, becoming her mother's shadow, following her everywhere, asking question after question, eager to grow and to learn. Lexie's world became filled with her children, her home, and her studies.

Discovering the realms of Eastern philosophy and and intrigued by the promise of an inner serenity, Lexie decided it was time to learn the practice of meditation.

It was a warm, balmy day with the spring sunshine streaming into her living room as she sat cross-legged, bathed in a pool of sunlight, her eyes closed, concentrating on slowing her breathing. Following what she had read about meditation, she began to repeat over and over a single-syllable word she had learned was called a mantra.

Out of the calmness came a rushing, roaring sound in her ears, a flash of brilliant white light engulfed her as her living room swirled around her. The brilliance had come from somewhere behind her eyes, sending her head reeling backwards with the sheer force of its expression! With eyes rolled back, her head begin to sway gently as if she was swimming in a sea of whispers. In that blinding flash was a promise of more.

In recognition, she let herself flow at first tentatively and then joyfully forward, seeking to become one with this brilliant light. The boundaries between her and it blurred as if she was flowing out of herself and into something vast and incredibly inviting. To become part of it was never to desire a return. She strained forward into this joining, this celebration of expansion. Yet at the same moment a mutiny was building within her. Another part of her clawed back into itself in sheer panic. To let go was to surely die to what she was. Every part of what she projected herself to be here in this physical reality went into open rebellion. To see with these new expanded eyes was to know the truth of being. The reality of the five senses that she was so emotionally bound up in was not all there was. There was more to this experience of life. But to accept this truth meant to deny all she believed herself now to be. That part of her, the part that defined her reality, that part known as ego, could not let this trans-formation take place. It did not understand this joining of self to a greater spiritual reality to be assimilation but annihilation. To know more was to die to what was known now.

This terror engulfed her as with each rapid breath she clawed her way back to the surface of consciousness. Her eyes flew open to again take in the comfortable reality she knew. In the flick of an eye it was decided. She would no more venture into an inner world, the portal of a vast unknown. The books on meditation were put back on the shelf. Lexie was not ready to be more, only driven to do more.

Erroneously Lexie had assumed closing the books had also closed this larger reality to her, but it continued to seep in through cracks and holes and continued to live in her mind. It even assailed her through the five senses she knew and trusted so well.

Her night visions continued. As Lexie moved through the dark hall to answer the summons of a crying child, her housecoat clutched tightly around her, she would happen to glance down the hall's long, dark length into the large open living room at its end. There, before looking fearfully away, she would often make out a white formless shape seated on the end of the chesterfield. Shivering ,she would convince herself it was no more than a shaft of light streaming in through the window from a street lamp outside. She ignored the whisper in the back of her mind that said, *But the drapes are always tightly closed!*

Lexie lived with her nameless, shapeless shadow just as she had lived with Jessica's tall, dark man. She shrugged them off as tricks of her imagination.

Not so easily fooled are the senses of a child.

Seated in the kitchen eating their dinner, just the three of them for Derek was working late, they were talking animatedly about their day and four-year-old Jade was busy telling her mother what story she wanted read to her that night. Their kitchen looked into the living room to the very spot where Lexie's mysterious night shape lingered. Suddenly, Jade stopped in mid-phrase, and her body went completely rigid. All the colour drained from her tiny face; Jessica and Lexie watched in open wonder as Jade appeared to ready her body to receive a blow. The child was in absolute terror of some-thing, of this there was no doubt, but there was nothing to be seen. She held her rigid, fearful posture for a few seconds and then just as quickly as she had tensed, she relaxed. A broad smile spread over her face as she looked up at Lexie and uttered an incredible string of words.

"It's all right, Mommy. Man kissed me. Now he's gone." She went on eating her dinner as if nothing had happened leaving Lexie reeling, searching for an explanation.

She knew Jade had seen and reacted to something, but what? As she puzzled on this the same realization kept coming to mind.

Jade had been born in the spring after Inga's death; the same spring in which Derek's long ailing father had died. The passing of his daughter had been too much for a body racked with emphysema. He had died a broken, frightened man a few days before Jade was born, not living long enough to see his new baby granddaughter.

It gave Lexie a sense of peace to believe he had spent her baby's first years watching over them and had now come to say his good-byes. Perhaps it was just a coincidence that the late-night shape was no more seen at the end of the long, dark hall.

"Read it again, Mommy! And this time don't leave out the middle part!" Jade's voice echoed through the house as she climbed up into her mother's lap that night. Lexie opened the well-worn book Jade knew by heart. The house felt so lonely; she felt so weary. Like the book she read to her child, life seemed to repeat itself over and over, with the same words upon each page. A restlessness was stirring inside her. Was it time once more for a change? She thought about going back to work again.

She tucked her children in and wandered aimlessly into the living room. There on the table was the local paper. She plunked herself down and began to leaf through its pages. Her eyes fell on a tiny want ad and it beckoned seductively to her. It taunted her with a challenge as its bold heading asked impertinently, "Can YOU qualify?" Her competitive nature was alerted, and she wanted to know more.

Was she ready to attempt another job? Lexie had thrived on the excitement of being out in the work world, but it had not come without a price. It had, however, given her a taste of her own power.

She read the ad again.

CHAPTER SIXTEEN:

CAN YOU QUALIFY?

๛

Your smiling face upon the stage,
Your liquid, flowing words deftly arranged,
Your taunting eyes, your velvet throat,
The promise of love given with every note.
Long, soft-hued hours spent talking,
Thirst quenching forays to the well of the soul,
You came; you went. I remained.

You, an oasis amid long years of drought,
A brief encounter in time
When your secret desires were as known as mine.
Seeing ourselves in the eyes of another,
A shiver of recognition pulls us together.
For I am you; you are me
Travellers on our trip through eternity.
Briefly touching in the night
Risking all for love's brief insight.
To discover in human weakness and fear
What can transform and bring near
The image of our own perfection.
Reflected, as if in a mirror,
In the eyes of the trusted one

We chose, with whom, for a moment,
To know love, not fear.

"Why don't you just fuck off!"

The words hung, suspended between Lexie and Derek, the mouth they had just left open in disbelief. Lexie had said "that word." She had never said that word in her entire life. Surprised, she realized the explosion of feeling it had released had made her feel very powerful. Turning on her heel, she marched out the door of the expensive hotel and hailed a cab while reaching into her purse to make sure her "mad" money was still there. Carried along by her anger, she ordered the cabby to take her home. She'd just had it with Derek! He could act like such an insensitive jerk. He had known how much this evening had meant to her, how she had looked forward to it for weeks. It had been bad enough he had decreed she could not spend money on a new dress, but now this!

It was his company's annual Christmas dance and for Lexie it was the social highlight of her year. She had tried so hard to look elegant, but with no money to spend, it had been a challenge. When she waltzed out for Derek's approval she knew she had not pulled it off. He was not pleased with the way she looked. She had put on extra inches since Jade's birth, and he cruelly pointed out that her outfit did absolutely nothing to hide that fact. Derek regarded one of his jobs as her husband to be her official trainer—monitoring her weight gain and muscle tone as strictly as a coach with a star athlete.

Determined she would not let Derek ruin this night for her, she had held back her tears. She would put up with his insults for she had waited far too long to dine and dance in the glamorous setting of the hotel ballroom. This evening was as close as she ever came to her fantasy life.

The tension between them had escalated moment by moment as they had walked through the corridors of the hotel searching for the ballroom. Derek was strangely uneasy about attending his company party. He had counted on his beautiful wife to create a stir of admiration allowing him to feel like more with her on his arm. She was a prize, his badge of merit, but tonight her appearance made him uncomfortable. He was angry at her, for she had failed to fulfil her part of the bargain. He worked hard to provide for her, and in exchange she was to make him look good. He did not like to admit it, but his once-beautiful bride appeared dowdy and drab.

"Christ, Lexie! How could you be so god damned stupid and leave the invitation at home? This whole thing just pisses me off! Who wants to be here anyway? I hate these god damned stiff-necked parties!"

Derek raved on. He was on a roll now, and Lexie knew what was coming. He didn't care that this evening meant the world to her. No, he would trample all over it, ruining every bit of pleasure they might have gleaned from the time together. He had to vent his frustration with no awareness of what it did to her.

"Let's get the hell out of here!" Derek exploded. "Who needs this shit anyway?!"

"No-o-o Derek. I really want to stay. I've looked forward to this for…"

"Who gives a shit? If I say we're leaving, we're leaving!" Derek reached out and grabbed her arm. Lexie wrenched herself free and walked quickly down the hall and out onto the street.

Alone in the backseat of the cab, she sat thinking about what this freedom ride would cost her. Surprisingly, she felt empowered as if she knew she had just made an investment in her own future.

It was indeed time for a change.

Derek lost his job. He was fired, although to hear him tell it you'd never guess. In the last few years Derek's ambition had seen him promoted first to foreman and then to manager. He was good to the men who worked under him, getting a power charge out of helping the underdog, but when it came to dealing with anyone in authority, his magnanimous facade broke down. He both feared and hated anyone with power over him. Consequently, he could not help himself when his ambivalent feelings caused him to outwardly support yet subconsciously subvert all that his superiors tried to do. Derek pumped up his feelings of potency by referring to all those in authority as complete idiots whose main flaw was that they didn't appreciate him.

Lexie was devastated when Derek was abruptly fired. She felt the pain as keenly as if it had happened to her. Derek's shame was her shame. She felt somehow that she had failed as his helpmate.

With a shock, she also realized her financial well-being was tied to whatever befell her husband. She had not performed poorly at work; Derek had, but she suffered the consequences nonetheless.

They had their savings, and their home was nearly paid for, but those facts did not ease the stress in their minds. They had worked so hard to build those savings that it seemed inconceivable they should spend them. The amounts in their accounts were like shrines to Derek. If that money was always there, he could feel safe. To see it eaten away day by day just for living expenses was a nightmare for him. He struggled to find another job as fast as he could. They would live on what unemployment insurance there was and any other sources of revenue they could find. He cast an eye in Lexie's direction.

Because she had been home now for four years, he decided it was time she looked for work.

Finding a job was not going to be easy. It was midyear and all the teaching positions had been filled; none of the school boards were hiring. In fact many teachers were being classified as "redundant" due to the lack of student enrolment. Lexie had resigned after Jade was born. She had been so worn out and weary after her double duty of mother and teacher that she had hoped never to have to teach full-time again.

It seemed logical to say yes when her neighbour suggested she apply for the job at the hotel where she worked as a dining room waitress. Lexie had served plenty of meals to her family during the course of her life, so she figured, *What could be so hard about being a waitress?* She would give it a try.

She applied for a job and she got one. The only trouble was it was not the job she applied for. They didn't need waitresses in the dining room. The management took one look at her and suggested she work in the cocktail lounge. Being naive, Lexie figured it would be more fun and less work. It certainly was that and more.

Working the Pink Cloud Lounge now for about a month, she was pretty comfortable with the job. More than that, she was actually enjoying it. Working mostly evenings, Lexie got to spend all the time she wanted with her kids and none of the time she didn't want with Derek. On weeknights she worked the floor serving drinks, but Saturdays she spent behind the bar making them. The evenings were fast paced and exciting, the room a smoked-filled, hazy world where music, sex, and booze brought some life to meaningless existences. Here any man could be a king; everything was for sale. With their plastic and their cash, they bought their friends, their lovers, even a sympathetic ear. Often as Lexie poured, she would hear an old, bar-worn veteran whine and say, "Ya know, Lexie, I'm here because my wife really doesn't understand me the way you and the guys do."

They'd often slobber out their sad stories while they stayed and made love to the liquid they held most dear. As Lexie looked across the bar at the same faces, she'd find herself thinking, *It's no wonder your wife doesn't know who you are. You're always here!*

They got what they needed from her, and she got what she needed from them. She nourished them with a smile and a full glass; they gave her lusting eyes and a bulge in their pants. There was no doubt that many of them wanted to bed her, and she loved the attention. After years of being told her body was too fat, that if she'd just lose that five pounds she'd be perfect, she rejoiced in men who found her body a full-fleshed fantasy.

Her pulse would quicken as she donned her sleek, black, bottom-hugging pants, put a slash of red across her lips, and tousled her long hair. At work, she felt beautiful, desirable, powerful. As she moved through the room of mostly men, she was aware of their raw sexual energy. She loved the sight and scent of them. She saw the desire in their eyes, and her body responded. It swayed seductively as she worked, bending suggestively over tables outlining her tight rear end. She knew she was being watched, her body devoured by lusting eyes. She knew it, and she loved it. She often handled the bottles lovingly as she placed them on the bar. Her hand would linger over them like one might tease and stroke the hard part of a man. She drove them wild, and they cheered her on. She couldn't help it; she was awash in a sea of sexual fantasy, turned on all the time by the abundance of adoring men around her.

And then there HE was, his face staring back at her from the poster propped up on the bar. He was coming to town next week. She had heard so much about this new entertainer. He played the piano almost as well as he played the ladies. He was in the business of selling romance, and he could croon out a seductive tune with the best of them.

Her eyes connected with the deep, dark pools of his as they stared back unflinchingly from his picture.

I'm going to fall in love with him! the thought gasped through her mind. She knew it to be true.

He stood close behind her, his hot breath falling on her neck.

"Do you fool around?" he asked bluntly in his raspy voice.

Lexie could feel the heat from his body as he pressed closer. They were alone for a brief moment in the tiny storage room behind the bar. She had come in to retrieve something, and he had followed her. All that night he had watched her as he'd played one romantic song after another, cheered on by an eager, adoring crowd. He was striking in appearance, seated behind the large, ebony grand piano on the stage. A dark man with sleek, black hair and smouldering eyes, he groomed himself immaculately and dressed elegantly, from his well-manicured hands to his expensively cut tuxedo.

Losing himself in his music, the man exuded an air of elusive mystery. He was everyone and no one. Emotions would ripple over his expressive face as he released the stories held captive in his songs. Drawing his audience in as he touched both their pain and joy, he made love to them. When he stepped down from his stage at the end of the evening, all felt intimately connected to this strangely compelling man.

So much so, that many of the women had experienced more of him than his music. It was rumoured, however, that even though many women had loved him, none had succeeded in keeping him in her bed for long. He remained polite, attentive, and charming, but always distantly aloof.

He was waiting for her answer. Experience had given him the confidence to be direct, and the patience to await its rewards. He had watched the way Lexie had moved seductively through the crowded room that night, her eyes often meeting his, her body a beacon for him. She was new, exciting, and beautiful. The only question still left unanswered was whether or not she was willing.

Flustered by his physical presence, her heart was racing, her chest heaving as her breath came in shallow, rapid gasps. Her face was aflame, and she was thankful for the soft, dim lighting which helped to hide her aroused feelings.

"I'm m-m-married." She managed to stammer out a reply at last.

"So?" He snorted out a contemptuous response. "Why should that stop us?"

"I don't do that." Lexie continued to stammer. "You know. I mean, I don't cheat on my husband."

By this time she had turned around to face him and was staring up into his eyes. He received her reply with a big grin. He liked the fact very much that he flustered her. Her innocence was an aphrodisiac.

"Well, if you ever change your mind, you know where to find me." He left her with a wide, warm smile, but he wasn't going to give up quite that easily.

Waiting for her at the end of her shift, he knew just how to head off any objections she might have. He only wanted to have a drink with her and talk, he said. He needed to unwind after a night of performing as he couldn't sleep for several hours after a show, and besides, he really wanted to get to know her. He spun out his line so smoothly, Lexie convinced herself he posed no threat. She could handle just one drink.

As they talked into the small hours of the morning, something happened that this salesman of romance hadn't counted on. As he looked into her soft, gold-flecked eyes, he felt himself being drawn in. She listened, really listened to all that he said. What was more important, she heard what was behind the words—the resonance of loneliness threaded through the tones of his strong, confident voice. She sensed the ripple of fear ruining all the attachments with his legions of clinging women. A fear that sprang from a belief that he would be swallowed up by their all-consuming need. He heard himself confess how he never felt real to his lady loves. They were in love with an idea, an image, not with him. Representing all that was romantic, he was the perfect package. All they had to do was to plug him into their lives, and he would be there to play out their fantasies. He lived his life on a stage, always performing, always attempting to fill that enormous, dark void yawning out in front of him, pouring his talent out to desperately lonely women who naively, hopefully attributed to him the power to fill their ache. They didn't care about him. They only cared about what he could do for them. He was so tired of being used.

He poured out his heart to Lexie night after night. He had started out simply desiring her warm flesh, but now he felt warmed by her presence. Slowly, he began to tell her of his own fantasies. He longed for a strong woman to take him away to a lush, tropical love paradise and minister to his every need. He dreamed of a woman who could take responsibility for her own happiness, leaving him to enjoy his own. He wanted to be off his stage, no longer held hostage by the image he himself had worked so hard to create.

He began, over the next few days, to spin a fantasy of the two of them as husband and wife. He wanted to feel, to try on for size, what it would be like to be connected intimately to a woman like Lexie. He introduced her to others in the bar as his "Mrs." Every night he sang a special song for her, finding her eyes in the crowd as he did. They sat together sharing drinks at the end of every evening, talking until the early hours of the morning. They did not embrace or kiss. Her handsome singer respected her belief in marital fidelity. He was receiving from her just what he needed even though their bodies never touched. Sensing her unspoken desire for him, he would look deeply into her eyes and say softly, tenderly, "Never mind, Lexie. We've made love a thousand times in our minds."

For you see, Lexie could not give herself permission to have him with her body. She dared love him only in her heart, even though every part of her yearned to join with this erotic man. She wanted to be enfolded by him; to drink in his affection; to feel love because she was adored. His secret vulnerable needs, shared with her in their early-morning conversations, were in truth her own. She could be there for him, understand what cried out in him because she was like him. Both judged by their packaging and their ability to perform, they had lost touch with who they truly were. They believed themselves to be the image they projected. When their feelings did not match this image, they were silenced, strangled, leaving the true self lost and abandoned. The recognition of self in one another had set the stage for seduction.

It was his last night at the bar. Friends and fans were gathering at a nearby home for a farewell party. Lexie knew she shouldn't attend because she would get home very late, but she had to take that risk. She had to be there to say good-bye.

Staying late to close up the bar, she arrived after the party was well under way. The music was blasting, the liquor was flowing, and the house was alive with the energy of people talking, laughing, and dancing. As soon as she arrived, she was told that the guest of honour had been asking for her.

When he pulled her into his arms and onto the dance floor, she knew she was in trouble. As their bodies moved to the music, she seemed to melt into him. Her head rested on his strong, broad shoulder as both his arms encircled her waist. She couldn't help it. A profound sigh of longing escaped from her lips as her body went limp and yielded to its desire. She was exactly where she had wanted to be. She was doing exactly what she had dreamed of doing for weeks.

He responded to her sighs by holding her closer with one arm while caressing her hair and shoulders with the other. They moved as one as the soft, seductive music swirled around them, oblivious to anyone else in the room, two lonely people, clinging to one another, seeking to find what each of them so desperately needed—a love without conditions, a love simply here and now. To be lost in the sheer pleasure of touching and being touched, of finding in one another a safe accepting haven, if just for this one night, was all that mattered to them now.

They danced away the hours, talking only with their bodies. There was no hope of more, no fear of less. They knew tonight was all they would have. Both were starved for affection—he awash in a sea of self-serving female adoration, she stranded in a desert of male control. Without words they understood completely what was needed. For these few hours they opened to one another, finding the courage to believe in being loved for just who they were.

Lexie's need to be held, stroked, and adored was so great that she would risk anything now, even Derek's wrath. Her skin hungered for touch. Her eyes desperately needed to see the look of love on another's face. Her ears greedily drank in the sounds of her lover's sighs and moans. The warmth of his body warmed her heart.

The crowd around them gradually dwindled. As there were fewer eyes upon them, their desire for one another felt free to escalate. Their dance together had been exquisite foreplay, and the sweet promise of more beckoned.

"I want to kiss you, but I want to kiss you where no one can watch," he whispered huskily into her ear. "Come with me."

He led her off the dance floor and into the lower level of the house. She followed him silently, obediently, down the stairs and along the hall to a bedroom. He stood in the doorway as she stared at the beckoning bed. His eyes held his question.

Her body answered as she moved into the room and lay down on the bed awaiting him, her arms and legs enfolding him as his body slid over hers. He began kissing her, slowly, gently at first and then with more urgency. A sudden explosion went off in her brain.

Oh, my god! What am I doing!? She froze in silence. Her panic went unvoiced. Instead it spoke to him through her body. She stopped responding. She became limply passive. As she lay closed in his arms, he sensed the change in her immediately. He pulled back to look into her face, and his eyes said that he understood her reaction perfectly. He knew exactly what to say to her.

"It's all right, Lexie," he said softly. "I know how you feel about all this. I'm not asking for that. I only want to be with you, to lie with you, to touch you and to feel your warmth just for tonight. I know there can't be more, but it's enough for me. Be with me here in the dark a little longer, will you?"

Feelings of incredible love and tenderness washed over her. He understood! He was willing to accept just what she could give. She reached up and stroked his face. Her lips found his, and she pressed her body against him. He lay his head on her breast and relaxed with a deep sigh. She held him lovingly, her hands stoking his soft hair as he drifted off to sleep. As she lay awake watching the first rays of sunlight filter through the blinds and listening to the peaceful rhythm of his breathing, she wondered how she could ever explain all this? Who would ever believe that it had been nothing more that two needy people reaching out to one another in the dark?

With the arrival of the morning light came reality. Lexie soothed herself, believing that because she had not consummated the love affair, she had not been unfaithful. But in her heart she knew she had been adulterous. She had wanted this man desperately. Yet, perhaps, had she been kinder in her judgement of herself, she would have seen that her crime was not one of passion, but one only of basic human need. It was his loving of her she wanted. It had not been so much erotic desire that had driven her forward, but need. She mattered if someone loved her. The physical act itself was secondary. What she had needed had come from his soft words and loving looks. The ripple of joy in his voice when he sang for her, the light of love in his eyes when he had looked at her had been enough. She had received already what was important to her. Reflected in his eyes she felt lovable.

Her feelings went in a file labelled "beautiful memory," and believing it was all she could hope for, all she deserved, she prepared to return to being the self-sacrificing wife and mother. Her brief respite produced such guilt that she resolved to work harder at saving her loveless marriage. Blinded by her lack of faith in herself, she could see no other way of providing for herself and her children. The dull ache of love lost would simply be added to the burden of sadness she already carried with her every day. It was not so much the loss of her singer she mourned, but the euphoric belief in herself as lovable which he had inspired.

"You're nothing but a bloody slut, Lexie! Where the hell were you all last night?!" Derek raged.

She stood her ground, trembling, but not daring to defend herself lest she inflame him further. She prayed only that his anger would soon spend itself. He paced around her, his words tumbling out in a fury of hurt and frustration. How could she do this to him? He had looked like a bloody idiot not knowing where his wife was all night! Did she really expect him to believe that she hadn't had sex with this guy?

On and on went his litany of blame. He accepted no part of the responsibility for his wife's desperate foray into unfaithfulness. It never occurred to him to wonder why she had sought comfort in the arms of another man. This whole scenario was, of course, her fault. She was somehow lacking. How dare she not follow the dictated role of his loving, faithful wife! She was to be his until death parted them, no matter how unhappy she became. She was his possession. How dare she behave in a way that shamed him!

He hadn't bothered to hide his rage from the children. They, too, were an extension of him, there to meet his needs. He had to dump his anger on someone. If Lexie wasn't been there to receive it, then her children would do. Spewing out a string of curses, he informed nine-year-old Jessica and four-year-old Jade what a slut their mother was. If he was in pain, they would share it with him.

Lexie knew what she had done was wrong, but she also felt she wasn't totally unjustified in her action. She wanted to defend herself, but how could she explain that it was not for love of Derek that she had stopped short of the ultimate act of betrayal, but because she did not have the courage to end her marriage? She wanted out desperately, but she thought she couldn't provide for those two beautiful children she loved so much. Alone, she could not give them all the things she and Derek could give them together. In the weeks of her infatuation with her piano player, she had run the scenario over again and again in her head. No matter how hard she tried, she could not envision how it possibly could work. She knew, in her heart of hearts, that her infatuation was just that. In the cold light of day, her practical, maternal side rejected him as a partner because he could not, would not, provide the stability required to raise a family. Her exploration into the world of affairs had been about her needs, not about her children's. When the two were stacked up one against the other, there was not even a question about whose came first.

She would stand and endure Derek's tongue-lashing, preparing herself to grovel for many weeks, to do whatever it took to put their family back together again. Raising children well, she knew, was an indomitable task. She did not believe she could do it alone. To have a verbally abusive, shaming husband was better than to have none at all, wasn't it? Perhaps, if she was just more loving, he would be better. She would try. She would really try to make this up to him. More attentive, more considerate, she would work harder at being the perfect wife and mother and maybe, just maybe, they could put this behind them. Maybe she could fix their family's brokenness with the glue of her self-sacrifice.

She knew she had to stay when Derek slammed out the door with the words, "I'd rather see you dead than see you with another man!"

The sound of that door shattered any hope of escape. He would never let her go. His violent need to control and her fear of abandonment had meshed together to create a state of bondage for them both. All she could now do was put all her effort into making her home the best prison on the street.

In the ensuing months her renewed efforts to be the perfect wife and mother brought her no peace. Her brief brush with romance had unleashed an energy in her, an aliveness that could not be denied. Like a caged animal, her energy drove her thoughts and feelings in circles going nowhere, seeking, always seeking an outlet, a way out, but always denying her need to leave her marriage. There had to be another way to express this energy that kept pushing her towards the freedom she both longed for yet lived in terror of. There had to be a way of distracting herself. A way to deceive herself into believing she had control of her life while staying safe.

While working in that den of men, she had thrived on the adoration she had received. That was now gone. Her life as a barmaid had been quickly put behind her after her night of passion. Quitting her job at the bar to appease her husband, she had thrown herself into mothering, cooking, and cleaning, but those tasks were not enough. There was a restlessness in her, a yearning to express more. Long ago she had given up on Derek ever being able to receive and return her loving energies, but now even her children and home were not enough. Ready for a challenge, yet not strong enough to make her escape, her swelling energies devised a way to at least rattle the bars of her cage.

She had to know. Picking up the newspaper again, its challenge seemed to speak right to her.

"Can YOU qualify?" The words taunted her.

Qualify for what? Lexie wondered as she picked up the telephone and placed her call.

CHAPTER SEVENTEEN:

A MATERIAL WORLD

ॐ

Picture, picture on the wall,
Who is the fairest of them all?
Queen of sales, wizard of winning,
Your life in the spotlight just beginning.
Because of your growing business empire
To be like you, your fellow women aspire.
Your smiling face, in the picture frame hangs,
Enfolded in fawning furs,
Sparkling with successful gems,
As Icon, words of wisdom you impart.
Your message of happiness urges,
In material success,
The true potential of women emerges!
In your realm of possibilities
A single dimension you were deceived to see.
Money and wealth, though a comfort be,
Are not the prime fruit upon the tree.
For to strive in sole focus
With wealth the only goal
Leaves so much of the self unsaid.
With the exclusive worship of the material world
Comes the condemnation
To remain spiritually dead!

The woman had incredible skin. It seemed to glow with aliveness, a moist softness about it. Taking in her features, Lexie noted her makeup was applied as if an artist had skilfully arranged the colours and hues upon her face. Her piercing blue eyes were framed in soft clouds of pale powdered colour, and her lips formed a perfect bow of pearlized pink. She was a woman in her late fifties, but she took care of herself, that was obvious. From her shaped and styled hair, to the tips of her well-manicured hands, to the cut of her business suit and the fine leather pumps on her feet, this woman was a walking statement of exquisite grooming and fashion detail. She made the best of what she had, of this there was no doubt. That, it turned out, was her business.

The response Lexie received to her call had left her curious. She had spoken with a woman who was very reluctant to give details over the telephone and had been persistent about meeting Lexie personally. All she would tell her was that it was a sales position and that she would be required to undergo an interview. Feeling that she had nothing to lose and perhaps much to gain, Lexie's curiosity pushed her forward.

The tinkling of a bell over the door announced her arrival at the small office. The advertised position was a sales representative for a company called "Fashion Now Cosmetics." The gold lettering on the door told her this was the place. Letting herself in, she had a few moments to gaze uninterruptedly around the elegantly comfortable room. Directly in front of her was a dark oak desk behind which she assumed a receptionist would normally sit. As she moved further into the room, she became aware of a small sitting room with plush couches, a coffee table, lush green plants, and walls covered with elegantly framed photographs. They were of women, and they were everywhere.

As Lexie peered at each one in turn, she discovered her heart was beginning to race. In every shot were women, ordinary women like herself, who, perfectly groomed and coiffed, were being draped in mink coats and dusted in diamonds. Beaming down on her were faces of females crowned like regal reigning monarchs, their names embossed in gold letters under their smiling faces. The titles read like a directory of royalty—Queen of Sales, Star Recruiter, Senior Sales Director, Car Winning Manager, Woman of the Year—Lexie had never experienced women's accomplishments honoured in such a powerful way.

When the strong feminine voice spoke behind her, Lexie turned and looked directly into those piercing blue eyes, and she knew instantly she had found a home. She would do whatever was necessary to qualify for the way of life framed on the walls of this room.

With a new look and a new mission, her purple display cases grasped firmly in her hands, her newly made over face set in determination, and a manual for success tucked under her arm, Lexie felt more alive than she ever had before. She had been told that if she would work hard, every dream was within her reach. If she would plan her work and work her plan, she would have all the recognition and material wealth she had ever wanted. It was all there, within her grasp, carefully described in the Fashion Now Manual and Marketing Plan. It was a step-by-step guide to star status.

The restless energy of doing had already been pulsing through Lexie, pushing her to explore new worlds—the rocket fuel had been there. When she had stepped through that gold-lettered door, she had, like an eager pilot, slipped into the waiting vehicle that would take her to her stars. Here, she could have the safety of her marriage and the exciting, powerful elixir of self-expression too. She could have it all!

The woman with the piercing blue eyes was called Audra, and she became Lexie's mentor. Audra had been born Audrey Shelby in a poor, rural town of northern Ontario, oldest in a large, brawling family of town drunks and welfare waifs. She had married young, too young, only to escape her abusive, drunken father. With her drinking, truck-driving husband she had had five children—four daughters and one son. On her own much of the time, she had struggled to raise them in an old farmhouse without running water located miles from any town, its only advantage being cheap rent.

Sixteen when she had married to escape, Audrey watched bewildered as each of her beloved daughters did the same. Wounded by each departure, she nevertheless accepted their explanation that they were eager to make their own way and to cease being a burden to her. The reality was, they too, like their mother before them, fled an abusive parent. Only when the last daughter was out of the home did they feel safe enough to reveal an ugly secret. Their father had not only been a drunk, he had raped his own daughters, violating each one of them repeatedly, taking their sexual favours as his due.

In the world he may have been nothing, but in his home he was king. Made brave by alcohol, this failure of a man could feel powerful as he stood in the doorway of his daughters' room unbuckling his belt preparing to take what he rationalized was rightfully his from a child who did not know she had the right to refuse.

The day she learned, Audrey left him, never to return. With a few dollars in savings and her only skills those she had learned through years of mothering and housekeeping, she set about to rebuild her life. She, too, had searched the want ads, and she, too, had been led to those gold-lettered doors. Here, she was given back herself. Here, she learned week by week, year by year, how to sell, to hire, to motivate, and to train others. Here, she was given not only the desire but the tools to reshape her life into all that it could be. She became a walking advertisement for the products and the philosophy she sold, and all who heard her story could not help but be inspired. Now calling herself Audra Shelby, she became an icon in the industry of direct sales and marketing. Walking, talking, living proof that human beings have the power to rise above the worst of their beginnings. She demonstrated belief in the self as the beginning of transformation. It had been the awakening to her own self-worth that had propelled her forward out of dependency and into empowerment. The woman who once had carried wash buckets of water to scrub endless piles of diapers, who did not know what it was to see or speak to another adult for weeks on end, and who had endured years of abuse, now breathed life into the deadened hopes of the women who witnessed the example of her life. Now through her ability to teach and inspire, she reached out and mobilized the hidden potential in the women around her. "If I could do it, anyone can," her motivating motto.

Success bred more success. As cooperative teams, supporting one another, legions of women, with their purple cases and marketing manuals, grew in number and wealth. Audra's own life was made infinitely richer by her example of personal freedom for many fellow women who were still in self-imposed slavery.

One of those women was Lexie. Each time the novice would balk at the next step in building her business, Audra simply would not accept her fears as legitimate excuses not to try. She facilitated Lexie's growth in self-esteem and tutored her in all aspects of her being, stating that if others before her had been successful, she would be too. The Fashion Now marketing plan became Lexie's bible and blueprint for a new way of life. Consumed by her drive for success, she worked to bring her vision into reality twelve to eighteen hours a day. Such was her passion for what she did that she did not regard it as work for it energized and empowered her. From her very first sale all the way to accepting the keys to her new, white Lincoln Town Car, she had loved every second of it.

Her business thrived, for what you love is what you give your attention to, and Lexie was now in love with all that this new way of life provided. Because it was a business about fashion, it gave Lexie the opportunity to be glamorous. Even though she worked her business from an office in her home, she arose early each day, and after seeing her children off to school, began the process of transformation. As she slipped into the expensive, new clothing her money had bought, carefully and skilfully applying her makeup, a new woman would emerge. They had a saying in the business that if you make a woman pretty on the outside, you make her pretty on the inside too. Lexie experienced that each and every day. Because she looked the part of successful entrepreneur, Lexie began to act the part. With each accomplishment, her self-esteem grew. As she believed more in herself, she achieved more. As she achieved more, she believed more in herself. It became a self-perpetuating cycle. Every day the face that looked back from her mirror liked what it saw more and more.

Her days were spent in the home office her money had built, arranging appointments on the business telephone line her money paid for and then driving to those appointments in the luxury car her abilities had earned. Zealously, she took her vision to other women. Her contagious enthusiasm convincing them to change their lives sometimes with as little as a new lipstick or other times with as much as a new career.

She sold her product easily for she passionately believed in it. She sold the way of life easily for she passionately lived it. She built a strong organization, one woman at a time, and she never asked them to do anything she herself had not already proven could be done. Like her mentor before her, she too taught by example. When training the new recruits in her organization, she used the "Show Me" rule. If a novice in the business needed to learn a technique, she would become Lexie's shadow as Lexie would "walk her talk," giving the novice the proof that the task *could* be done while at the same time demonstrating *how* it was done.

The Fashion Now life nourished Lexie. For the first time, she found herself surrounded by women who had the courage to outwardly express all that she had secretly felt, but hidden. These were women who believed in themselves and in the power of positive thought, women who did not minimize their own talents and abilities, women who dared to look beyond the limits of society and who structured their lives to put their own needs first. They believed in taking responsibility for the quality of their own lives. The core strategy of the Fashion Now philosophy was simply to align the company's policies and goals with the movement of thousands of women engaged in the process of self-actualization. The company could not fail to grow as the abilities of these ambitious women also grew. This innovative cosmetic company, led by women of vision, provided this emerging consciousness with a vehicle—a way to take their place in society as productive, intelligent, and creatively equal beings carving out for themselves a place of respect and achievement in the arena of business and of life itself.

And, oh, how it celebrated those who achieved. With all the pomp and ceremony of an Academy Awards night, the most successful women were invited each year to walk the long runway called, "The Royal Road to Riches." Amid the fanfare of flashing lights, pulsing music, and roaring applause, they would take their places on stage to be honoured by their peers. It was a night of glitter and glamour. A night of fabulous fantasy! The very air itself was full of magic which transformed even those who had previously thought themselves undistinguished. Sprinkled with daring dust from the wand of possibilities, even the ordinary believed dreams could be the property of all. They came to celebrate and to share in the moment when even the simplest among them could feel like Cinderella, at last slipping her foot into that perfect glass slipper.

It was an intoxicating atmosphere, and it fed Lexie's addiction for excitement and recognition. It filled the emptiness left by her barren marriage, the void in her soul. In her all-or-nothing way of thinking, she was prepared to sacrifice everything for the sense of completeness her success provided. She zealously poured in her love, her devotion, her time, and her energy. Derek, now replaced as Lexie's primary validator, accepted his new wife as he realized she could now provide what was most important in life to him.

Late each night, home from her evening of selling, Lexie would crawl into bed beside Derek and hear his voice in the darkness. The question always came. "How much did you make tonight, Lexie?"

He was willing to give up a warm body in his bed if it put money in his bank account. Basking in the glow of his wife's success, he convinced himself he was largely responsible for it. He had chosen to let her express herself. Because he was such a magnanimous and understanding husband, his wife had the freedom to achieve. Had he not approved of what she was doing, he could have worn away at her fledgling sense of confidence, eroding it until she had abandoned her first attempts at business. He puffed himself up with the belief that because he had not crushed her first attempts, he had allowed her success. Because she now possessed the things in life he valued most—money, beauty and status—she was an asset. Not only did he now have a beautiful woman on his arm, but one who was also successful. By extension, that made him more of a man.

Sadly, the only ones not provided for in the Fashion Now manual for success were children.

Jessica was nine and Jade four and a half when Lexie put her brush with marital infidelity behind her and went looking for another route to fulfilment. Up to that point she had been the consummate mother, her entire world revolving around her children. Now, it seemed, they were well enough on their way, and she could begin to include other interests. What she had not counted on was that this new way of life would so intoxicate her that she would become obsessed with it. Not only was she now a very successful business owner, but she often had to make a conscious effort to remind herself that she was still a mother. Even though she was thoroughly enjoying her new life, her list of responsibilities had become considerably longer.

Derek did not move in to close the gap. The pattern of interacting with his daughters only to discipline them had been firmly established. It was openly acknowledged that Lexie was the nurturing force in the family. She was the one the children always confided in. To go to their father would only mean subjecting themselves to stern advice on how to handle the situation his way, never really understanding that children, often knowing their own solutions, need only a sympathetic ear and confirmation that they can handle their challenges. In Derek's mind he was always right, and he saw the role of father as solver of his children's problems whether they agreed with his methods or not. The result was often shouting matches with his oldest daughter while his youngest, observing their interaction, came to a resigned understanding that communication with Dad usually went only one way. Rather than fight, she simply withdrew.

Derek was terrified of his daughters' emotional neediness, feeling that their neediness reflected his own. Consequently, when his children showed their insecurities, he saw them as his weakness. As this was intolerable to him, Derek would do anything to give himself the comforting illusion of control. Using anger, threats, or the withdrawal of approval, he became a critical and distant father who was more than willing to allow his wife to be the emotional glue of the family.

Over time, although it was never plotted nor consciously thought about, Lexie and her daughters became aligned against Derek. The three of them formed a united front, ignoring Derek's frequent nagging and sharing a bond of understanding among them. They were female, and he was male so how could they possibly hope to understand one another? Lexie saw nothing wrong with this aligning of loyalties in her family. In fact she was very proud of the close relationship she had with her girls. As they grew older, she confided a great deal in them, leaning on them for emotional support and running interference for them with their father, acting as a mediator in their disputes. Becoming the peacemaker in a household fraught with unspoken tensions, she sought from her daughters the love and acceptance she no longer wanted or received from her mate. On the one hand, she was not involved enough with her daughters, her mind often distracted by her drive for success; while on the other hand, she was too often overinvolved, seeking from them the love and support she should have received from a husband. An emotional child raising children, like so many others of her time, she had not yet learned to nurture herself and thus she was unable to fully nurture others. Her own needs kept getting in the way.

Lexie's children also had another competitor for their mother's love and attention.

Even before Lexie's business had become successful, she had had dreams of a larger home with a swimming pool where she could sun herself and watch as her children splashed and played. Derek had completely dashed this dream as economically unrealistic and became angry every time she brought the subject up. Lexie suspected his anger had more to do with his own feelings of inadequacy than with her desires. He felt, and rightly so, that his wife was driven to always have more, powered by an engine of insatiability. Even though he wanted the large, expensive home as much as she did and for many of the same reasons, he dared not voice this desire. To admit he wanted something he was not sure he could provide was like admitting an inadequacy. Thus, when Lexie dreamt out loud, he felt compelled to ridicule her, pointing out all the reasons why a larger home was frivolous.

Lexie reacted to him the way she often did these days. She ignored him and went on hoping. She set the attainment of a new home as one of her goals, spending time visualizing it, feeling the feelings its achievement would bring. Lexie, through the many women now around her, had seen positive belief influence an individual's reality. If she could truly convince herself she was deserving of her grand new home, she knew she would be guided to work toward its attainment.

She persisted in viewing the many homes that eager real estate agents showed her, becoming an expert on all the available properties for sale. Because she did not want to move out of the area and there were very few new homes being built, the selection was limited. When the sales trailers went up signalling a brand new development just south of them, Lexie was immediately there, collecting glossy brochures and working on a plan to get Derek out to have a look.

Perhaps her frequent dreaming out loud had conditioned him or more likely, he saw an opportunity to tie his restless wife even more firmly to his side. He knew she would not be content until she had the home of her dreams and now with her ever-increasing income, she was becoming more and more capable of providing it for herself. She had already shown Derek where discontent could take her, and he did not care to experience a repeat. The thought of losing his wife frightened him. If a large house would keep her busy and happy, perhaps she would not have the time or the inclination to look elsewhere for fulfilment. Providing her with material things would ensure her loyalty and in buying a new house for her, he would ensure his position as head of the family and provider. Not above offering a bribe to keep what he had, Derek knew he had to reach deep into those locked pockets or risk losing his wife to the pursuit of her dreams.

He signed the papers, and the new home was bought. They had chosen the largest lot in the development in order to comfortably install the inground swimming pool of Lexie's dreams. Their westside bungalow was put on the market and snapped up within two weeks. Derek and Lexie had worked very hard at keeping it immaculate and in good repair, and it had shown well. They had six weeks to wait until their new home would be ready.

They visited the building site every week or so and watched their dream progress from a hole in the ground to a framed structure. Then, over the next few visits, they noticed that little was being done on their particular house. They were scheduled as one of the first families to move in, so this caused some concern. Other houses seemed to be taking shape faster than theirs.

Derek came back from the construction shack cursing and swearing. He slammed himself into the driver's seat of the car where Lexie and the girls were waiting for him. The sick feeling in the pit of her stomach told her something was wrong.

"I'll be damned!" Derek cursed. "Those bastards have stopped working on our house, and they didn't even have the balls to let us know!"

"What do you mean, they've stopped working on our house?!" Lexie was incredulous.

"I mean because our lot is the only one that fronts on the old street, the house is too damned big for it. It's something about coverage. They had the old bylaw amended for the rest of the subdivision, but because of where our lot is, it was overlooked. Now we have to wait six weeks or so until everyone in the area is notified of the proposed change and until town council can approve it. Then they can start work on the house again. Can you believe our bloody luck?!"

"We haven't got six weeks. We've got to be out of our house in four! Dear god, what are we going to do, Derek?"

There was a pause and then he answered calmly, "Call the real estate agent we used the last time we bought. Tell him we're in the market for a house!"

And that's how it came about that Lexie got more of a dream house than even she had dared hoped for. She knew even before she picked up the phone to call Mr. Hughes, their agent, that there was nothing to be had in the area in their price range. Nevertheless, the distinguished, greying gentleman came to their home, listing book in hand, and took down all the details of their situation. He had a calm, orderly way about him that inspired confidence, and Lexie could easily understand why he was so successful in his chosen business. When they had bought through him years ago, he had been a struggling broker. Now he was the highly successful owner of his own office. Yet, he was never too busy to service his own personal clients and to make them feel as if their business truly mattered to him.

In his supportive, fatherly way he assured them that perhaps they had been too cautious in what they thought they could afford. He also pointed out all the additional costs of the pool and other upgrades they had wanted to add to the house and suggested that he had a property in mind that provided everything they wanted already in place.

Lexie became nervous as he began to flip to its description in his listing book. She knew that the further he went into the book, the higher the prices would be. Finally, he thrust the picture of the house he had been looking for under their noses. Incredibly, there it was. It was the exact house she had always seen when she had visualized her dream! It had everything they could possibly want and the address was perfect. Would anyone believe it? It was on a street actually named "Easy Street." How could life get any better than that?

She swallowed hard when she looked at the price. It was many thousands more than the other house. She looked over at Derek in complete shock when he said flippantly, "Let's go have a look at it!"

After a whirlwind tour of only fifteen minutes she knew. This was it! It was like a fairy tale come true. How many times had she driven by large, spacious homes like these and wondered how it was that people could afford to live so grandly? Now this was to be hers. She felt as if she had finally arrived!

There was one small hitch. Derek, of course, had to try to buy the house at a ridiculously low price. He nearly succeeded in getting distinguished Mr. Hughes thrown out on his ear by an insulted owner. He then made a reasonable counteroffer, committing them to thousands more than they had originally budgeted.

Lexie was amazed that this man who would refuse to spend a few dollars taking his wife out to dinner on a Saturday night could now calmly commit them to such a huge debt. Derek could still surprise her. She also knew that she was not about to be the voice of reason when her dream was so close at hand. She would do whatever it took to have this house! Besides Derek knew what he was doing, didn't he? At least according to him, he always did. It was a comfort to hand the worrying over to someone else. To take responsibility for their financial success or failure had been Derek's role up to now, and Lexie was content to let him continue. She might be struggling for financial independence and personal freedom, but all that could be put aside when she was going after something she had always wanted. If they succeeded she would share in the glory. If they failed, Derek would take responsibility and find a way to bail them out. She had always counted on him for that in the past. It was why she closed her eyes to so many of his character defects. In this uncertain world, the one thing she could count on was Derek's unbending strength. He was her rock, protecting her from the disasters of life. She clung to him like sea moss buffeted by swirling currents, not yet courageous enough to take the responsibility for charting her own course in the streams of life.

As it turned out, she needn't have worried so much about the extra cost of their large house. It proved to be a gold mine in a way she had not foreseen.

Because of her ability to inspire others to join her, Lexie had become successful in her cosmetic business. Paid a generous over-ride on everything sold, Lexie prospered as her organization grew in numbers and profits. Now, when she brought prospective new recruits to her office in her lavish new home, she told them this was the house that Fashion Now bought. In a sense it was true, for she had earned much of the savings for the down payment, and she had agreed with Derek that she and she alone would make the mortgage payments from her business earnings. The young, ambitious women she was bringing into the business saw all that she had accomplished through the Fashion Now way of life. Thus, her white Lincoln parked in the driveway, her imposing home with its plush office, and her enthusiastic rhetoric all conspired to assure them that they too could have it all, and they readily signed on the dotted line.

Success bred more success, and Lexie soon became the largest distributor in the entire company. Now HER face beamed down from the gilded frames in the mead office. Now, women looked up to HER in awe and admiration. Pointed out in hushed tones as she entered sales meetings, she felt like Cinderella arriving at the ball. Indeed, she was living on Easy Street!

At last, she was about to see the lives of the rich from the inside - lives, which in her ignorance, appeared to be free of trouble and pain. In her fantasy, those who had money had nothing else to worry about. Had not money worries dominated most of her life? What else could there be to worry about?

Mentored by Derek, she had been trained in the making and saving of money for most of her adult years. Her black or white way of looking at the world did not allow for all the shades in between. Rich meant happy. Poor meant worry and stress. That's just the way it was. Now that the trappings of wealth had arrived, she was convinced happiness would follow.

Life has a peculiar way of presenting us with a gift that, when unwrapped, is only a further gift to be undone. Like a traveller on a spiralling journey, Lexie kept arriving at destinations, with each arrival simply a new quest for greater understanding.

The move brought with it an almost imperceptible shift in family patterns. Looking back on it, she recognized something had begun to change the day they entered their spacious new home. Perhaps its large, empty rooms were a metaphor for the large, empty spaces between them. Each member seemed to drift away from the other, isolating in his or her own private, spatially defined territories. Consumed by her business, Lexie renovated their entire basement and turned it into a studio where she held regular meetings and training sessions with thirty or more women in attendance. Her office on the main floor was equipped with two business telephone lines, and she was at her desk from early in the morning until late in the evening. In the home, but not really there, her mind was constantly occupied with business and the pursuit of success.

It dawned a typical enough day, yet one which would mark another subtle surrender. Lexie reached over to turn off the alarm and crawled out of bed. She would have a half-hour at her desk before she would awaken her daughters. Six-year-old Jade—shy and dark eyed—who so often moved silently and unobtrusively through the house, had become a bed wetter.

Because she asked for so little, Jade was often lost in the shuffle of life. She worked at being invisible and succeeded in escaping conflict except when Derek would rant and rave about her "problem." Lexie had come to accept Jade's nightly accidents as something to be endured until the child outgrew it. Derek, on the other hand, treated it like a dread disease to be cured as quickly as possible. Bed wetting was a mark of imperfection and as such was not to be tolerated.

Their doctor, however, shared Lexie's view. He explained it away saying simply that because Jade was so tiny and petite, her bladder was underdeveloped and simply could not last the night. This seemed reasonable to Lexie, and she arranged the morning schedule to allow extra time for Jade to bathe and for her bed to be changed before going off to school. It seemed pointless to scold a child for something beyond her control.

Control. That was the key to it all as far as Derek was concerned. He would severely reprimand Jade, convinced that if he shamed her enough, she would learn to control her body functions out of fear. His mother never would have tolerated his wetting the bed. She had beaten him for less, he would often say. Derek had been no stranger to physical punishment while growing up. What he had not received at the hands of his mother, he had received at the hands of the good Catholic Sisters who had taught him to read and write and obey rules. It was what he knew, and he was convinced the method had worked. In his opinion, their treatment of him had only made him stronger. He was determined that no child of his was ever going to be weak. He would raise his children the way he had been raised. It had been good enough for him, thus he believed it was good enough for them.

The day came when he could no longer tolerate what he saw as Lexie's ineffectual way of dealing with the situation. Lexie was going to make a sissy out of this child if she kept on with her pampering and tolerant ways. The time had come to take matters into his own hands. He would fix the situation. Jade could be whipped into shape.

This particular morning, Jade had not responded to her mother's call. Derek, a poor sleeper who often rose before the alarm, was already prowling the house. Jade had delayed getting up because she knew two things. First, her bed was wet, and second, her father was up. He had told her in no uncertain terms what the consequences of another wet bed would be, and she had no doubt he would act. He would take his belt to her as promised.

Like a frightened, caged animal awaiting its punishment, Jade waited. There was nowhere she could go, nothing she could do but accept the inevitable. She knew her father well enough to know his had not been an idle threat.

"Jade, time to get up! Right now! You've slept far too long! Don't want any kid of mine being late for school now do we?!" She heard his voice bellow up from downstairs, and she shakily began to peel off the layers of wet night clothes. Maybe he wouldn't ask her. Her cereal was pouring into her bowl when he entered the kitchen. He asked.

"Well, did you wet the bed last night, young lady?" He stood belligerently waiting for her answer.

There was nothing she could say. Her mouth had gone completely dry. She couldn't have formed the words, even if she had wanted to. Her eyes grew wide with fear and the frantic phrase ran through her mind. *Where's Mom? I need Mom!*

"Well, I can tell by the way you look that you did. Didn't you? Answer me, child. You did, didn't you!" He was advancing now on Jade, becoming angrier with each step.

Instinctively backing away from him, her eyes wide, her breath coming in short gasps, her head silently nodded in answer.

"Go up to your room and wait for me. I'll be there in a minute to deal with you!"

She darted quickly past him and raced up the stairs taking refuge in her room. It did not occur to her to go looking for her mother. Her father had told her to go to her room. To do otherwise was to risk further wrath. Yet, all the while, the panicked question ran through her mind. *Where's my mom?!*

Too frightened to call out, paralysed by fear, Jade waited silently, helplessly, for what was to come.

Lexie met Derek on his way up the stairs. She had come out of her office alerted by his raised voice. *What was he ranting about this time?*, she wondered. She froze as her gaze came to rest on the leather belt tightly wrapped around his hand.

"Derek, no!" The words came out in one incredulous gasp as he pushed past her.

"You had your chance to fix this kid, Lexie. Now we'll do it my way! I've made up my mind about this. Something has to be done. This has gone on far too long, and I've had it with her! She's got to learn!"

In that moment Lexie felt so weak, so powerless, so weary of the struggle. It seemed they couldn't agree on anything any more. If she saw it as white, he would call it black. Constantly, she defended herself and her children against his incessant criticism, rationalizing and making excuses to others for the way Derek's behaviour disappointed and embarrassed her. His verbal abuse had escalated over the years and was now a habitual response, a daily occurrence both in public as well as private settings. He passed it off as teasing, but Lexie knew what it truly was. It was a carefully designed and executed method of keeping her off balance—to make sure she never became confident enough about who she really was and what she truly could do. Constant and effective, it wore her down. Each day it became harder to fight Derek's energy, harder to believe there could be ways of doing things other than Derek's way.

In Derek's domain, there were certain unchanging principles. Like a declaration of codependence, they laid the groundwork for unhealthy relating. One: never admit to being wrong and never apologize. Two: never, never tell your wife she was good at what she did because she might come to believe she could manage on her own and leave you. Three: never give approval to anyone in your family for they might cease striving for it, and you would lose control over them.

This, then was the secret of his power. Skilfully, he kept them entranced in a self-defeating dance of codependency. A dance which he brilliantly choreographed and directed. The script he followed was simple enough. Its design dictated he never reveal his true feelings. Others could need him, but to let anyone know his need would bestow the power he feared most—the power to abandon. Always, at all costs, he was to be the master of himself and others—in control. Control your feelings, thus, control life. Promote the big lie. The one that said, "They need you, but you don't need them!"

These steps, carefully planned and executed, would guarantee Derek the thing he most needed to feel safe—power! If the power of the family was in his hands, then there could be no emotional surprises. It was like handling a dangerous explosive. He had convinced himself that if he knew where all the trip wires were, he could keep his emotions bottled up forever. He had to control others lest they disturb the delicate balance that kept him intact. In this designed dance of codependency, Derek knew he must always lead. Only he knew the patterns and steps that kept him safe.

As he pushed by Lexie into Jade's room, she didn't stop him. She well knew Derek's potential for violence and god help her, in fear and hopelessness, she sold out. Her shoulders sagged and a long sigh escaped from her tired body.

"Let him try it his way," she thought wearily to herself. "Peace at any price."

In her heart of hearts she knew what he was about to do to this beloved child of theirs was wrong, very wrong. Her heart cried out to her daughter. Why was it then that she felt rooted to the spot? Could it be that part of her wanted to believe his twisted logic? He was so sure he was right. Or was the horrible truth of it simply that it was easier to accept the unacceptable rather than resist? For years Lexie tortured herself with the question of why. Why had she not stopped her husband from brutalizing their daughter?

Sadly, the conclusion formed over time that she had taken the course of least resistance. The only way she could live with this revelation was to over and over again minimize the effect of Derek's actions. It was the only way she could accept her abandonment of her helpless child. And so the thoughts that allowed her to go on pretending and accepting ran daily through her mind. *It wasn't really so damaging. It wouldn't really harm Jade. Derek was just doing what he thought was right. Why make such a big deal about it anyway?*

Many years of throwing herself against the iron will of this man had left her with a deep sense of hopelessness. It just didn't matter what she did, nothing ever changed. He had to win at all costs, and he usually did. He respected no boundaries in his relationships with others. He took what he needed no matter how his need to dominate damaged others. Derek did not build relationships, he took hostages. Those close to him were kept bound by threats and demands. He saw others as there to met his needs. If they refused, he resorted to manipulation, deception, and threats. His daughter had shamed him by her behaviour, and he simply could not tolerate that. There was never any thought given to the reasons Jade acted out as she did. Her point of view never came into consideration. Not seeing her as a person with thoughts and feelings, he saw only an extension of himself.

Having repressed memories of his own childhood terror, Derek's forgetfulness allowed him to become the very thing he had hated. The abused became the abuser. Standing with belt in hand, Derek acted out with his own daughter the very scene he had experienced with his mother. Standing helpless, quivering and naked, himself a tiny, defenceless creature, he had been taught to accept whatever this tall, yelling, hitting person was doing. The world was not a friendly place he had learned, for if a tiny, innocent being received pain and humiliation at the hands of the very one entrusted with his protection, what then did that foretell?

Jade, like her father had done before her, began to build walls around her inner child. If the world indeed was such a hostile place, at all costs she would protect herself from needing it or anyone in it. As in nature where oak trees only produce more oak trees, and maple trees only more maple trees, why, then should it be any different with the human species? We produce after our kind. A blighted tree does not produce healthy fruit.

Their sickness was systemic. The disease had been passed on to the parents from their families of origin and now was infecting their children just as they had been infected. This sickness of their souls sprang from a sense of being imperfect, of being somehow marred or defective. Supported by layers of damaging rules, beliefs, and inhumane practices—many sanctioned by society—the disease took hold and grew in each child as he or she took responsibility for the pain acted out upon them by caregivers. The dysfunction was passed on as the wounded child inside obsessively set out to recreate what he or she had known. For some, emotional pain had become so familiar that it was confused with love. Jade was destined to become like the very thing she feared most. In order to protect herself from him, she would become like him. It was what he had done exactly one generation before. "The sins of the fathers" passed on for generations.

"Mo-m-m-y!" Jade's blood-curdling scream made Lexie's hair stand on end. She left her customer standing open mouthed as she bolted up the stairs from her basement studio. Something was horribly wrong.

Coming breathless to the top of the stairs, she took in a horrifying scene. Before her stood Jade, rivetted in fear, the matches still in her trembling hands while the bulletin board behind her was a mass of bright, orange blazing flames! In the split second it took Lexie to react the streaks of fire had greedily licked their way up the wall devouring all the papers in their path.

She shot forward, grabbed Jade down off the chair she had pulled up in order to reach the bulletin board and deposited her safely in the centre of the kitchen. In one continuous movement she reached under the sink, pulled out a bucket and filled it with water. The flames had grown in heat and intensity and now were curling themselves around the wooden cupboards above the bulletin board as they looked for new fuel to consume. With a fervent prayer for success on her lips, Lexie threw the water at the wall of fire. Her prayer was answered by the sizzling sounds of dying flames. Another bucket of water ensured her success, and she then turned her attention to the trembling little girl standing in the centre of the kitchen.

Scooping Jade into her arms, burying her head in her hair, holding her tight, she repeated over and over again to reassure them both, "Thank God, you're all right! Thank God you're all right!"

When Lexie could finally release Jade from her protective hold, she shuddered when she noted what her daughter had been wearing. Her thin little body was covered only in a filmy, nylon nightgown. A nightgown that could have gone up like a torch if it had come in contact with those all-consuming flames! She said a prayer of thankfulness again as she tucked Jade back into her bed. She had been home sick from school that day, and Lexie had been preoccupied with business as usual. Lexie prided herself that, because she worked in her home, she could be there for her children when they were ill. She was very glad she had been there on this particular day.

When she asked Jade what had possessed her to do such a thing, the only response she received was a quivering lip and shrugged shoulders. When Lexie finally turned to leave her daughter's room, however, she did find her voice long enough to form one question.

"You won't tell Daddy, will you Mom?" came her small voice.

Lexie was not surprised by the question. It was one she heard often. She took a moment to think through her response. She often did hide things from Derek simply for the sake of peace - but this?

"Your Daddy will want to know what happened to the wall, Jade. I'll have to tell him. Don't worry, I'll explain that it was an accident, that you didn't do it on purpose, honey. All kids play with matches sometimes. I did when I was little. I know you'll never do it again now, will you?"

She returned to stroke her daughter's furrowed brow. The damage was not severe, and she knew she would minimize the event when she told Derek about it, confident she could manage Derek's reaction. Perhaps sensing this, Jade wiggled deeper into her bed, relaxing under her covers, contenting herself with her mother's reassurances.

Yet as she turned to leave the room again, the question haunted her. Whatever had possessed this sensible, well-behaved little girl to do such a thing? She herself had been somewhat of a rebel as a child, often doing the forbidden, but Jade never caused problems. She was a shy, quiet child, always obedient. Lexie found the whole event strangely unsettling, but she could not dwell any longer on it. She had a customer waiting. She shifted her attention and put her focus once again on business.

Years later, after Derek was out of their home, the truth about that day finally came out. Jade had not been playing with fire without a reason. She had had a definite purpose in mind when she had pulled the chair across the kitchen floor and up to the bulletin board above the telephone. There were many papers and cards tacked up on display, but one in particular was Jade's mission. A sense of power and fascination had washed over the little girl as she lit the match and held it to one special card in front of her, watching with a sense of cathartic satisfaction as the flames curled and consumed the words, "Happy Father's Day!"

Lexie did manage to smooth things over so that Jade was not punished for her misadventure with matches, but she was not there to protect her daughter when twice more Derek's belt bit across Jade's small, bare backside. Out making sales calls, she had come home to a quiet and withdrawn little girl and a smug, self-righteous man. He was convinced his course of action was working. Jade was having fewer and fewer accidents at night, wasn't she? It was little wonder for she lay awake in fear.

Eventually, as the bed stayed dry, Lexie convinced herself the situation had corrected itself with no permanent harm done to her daughter. She wanted desperately to believe that the bubbly, energetic baby girl who had been joyously inquisitive about everything was now shy and withdrawn because it was her nature. To see the truth would have been too inconvenient. It would have led Lexie to ask too many painful questions about herself and her family. It then might have led to making changes, major changes in the way they lived. Lexie could not cope with changes right now; threatening clouds loomed on the family's economic horizon. Financial survival once again became her focus.

They had just celebrated their first year in their new home when Lexie heard familiar words that sent fear ripping through her. They were words she had heard several times while she was with Derek.

"Come and pick me up, Lexie. The fucking assholes have fired me!"

The clunk as he slammed the telephone down resounded like the thud of a court gavel.

Panicked, she thought, *Was this some sort of judgement against them? Why us? Why always us? What have we done to deserve this? What have I done to deserve this? Doesn't Derek know how it terrifies me when he's out of work? How are we going to manage?*

As she drove in on that grey, blustery day, Lexie saw her defiantly angry husband standing alone and windblown in the empty parking lot. She watched as he handed the keys to his company car over to a clerk and then walked silently, head down, toward her. At that moment, she felt a sense of shame wash over her. She, too, felt as if she had done something wrong and had been fired for it. It was impossible for her to distinguish where Derek left off and she began. She felt so totally responsible for all he did and all that happened to him. Right along with Derek, she would suffer the agonies and insecurities of being unemployed. She had been there before.

As they drove home together, she experienced the full range of Derek's emotions. Bristling with a sense of injustice, he complained angrily that his abilities had never fully been appreciated, then going on to recite a scathing condemnation of those who had fired him. Empathizing, she nodded, propping up his wounded ego by accepting all he said as truth. Even when it occurred to her to challenge the accuracy of his perception, she chose to keep her thoughts to herself. She was to be the supportive wife, understanding and unquestioning. Her role was to stand by her man, even if the truth was sacrificed in the process.

Derek, too, made it easy to believe him. He was so convincing. Not for a heartbeat did he allow himself to think he had brought this dismissal upon himself. There was nothing wrong with him! This was an obvious act of injustice!

Lexie tried very hard to ignore the small inner voice that kept whispering to her, making her squirm in her seat.

Could everyone else be wrong so often, Derek? Was the world really that full of assholes?

They managed. In fact they managed quite well. Lexie's increased business efforts brought substantial profit increases. Increases that carried on, even after Derek found another position. Derek's dismissal, however, had only been the first in a series of ripples disturbing their financial tranquillity.

For some time there had been troubling rumours rumbling through the Fashion Now ranks. It seemed the aging founder of this family-owned company wished to retire. He also wished to retire as wealthy as possible. In order to do that, he was in the process of negotiating with a foreign buyer. It was this investor and his way of doing business that was fanning the flames of fear. Wild stories spread of how this particular male, because of his culture, refused to have female executives present during negotiations. He had been quoted as saying that even though the broad base of this cosmetic company was built on the efforts of countless studios owned and managed by women, it was not the women's role to set company policy.

The flames were further fanned by the disclosure of secret talks discussing the fact that the product formulas were mainly what interested the investor, and he really intended to concentrate on exporting to the European market. It became clear that this potential new owner had neither the desire nor the expertise to manage a large network of demanding and troublesome female franchise owners. His vision was to market through retail outlets.

The rumours rolled around like dice in a drum, with speculation rampant. News changed week by week, leaving franchisees disgruntled and fearful of losing their investments.

Through this smoke screen of confused, often conflicting memos and directives, Lexie continued to build her team. Even though it was becoming harder to convince others to build offspring organizations under her recruiting umbrella, she managed to do so. If it meant she had to wear blinders to what was going on in her company's head office and operate only on faith that everything would work out, that was what she did. Refusing to believe the company's founder, whom she idealized, would sell out the legions of hard-working, dedicated women who had devoted themselves to building their businesses and consequently his, Lexie believed in what she had been taught by her Fashion Now mentors. This was a business based on cooperation. Team work, along with an almost karmic belief that prosperity resulted from a system of reciprocity, had built a company of women who believed that as they sowed, so they would also reap. The belief in enough business for all was the thread that bound everyone together in cooperative growth. Lexie herself had two bold banners mounted on the wall of her studio. These served as a constant reminder of the Fashion Now way of doing business. In bright company colours the words on one banner proclaimed, "Team—Together Everyone Achieves More!" while on the other, the words formed a symbolic karmic circle, reminding all that, "What Goes Around, Comes Around."

For Lexie that pretty much summed things up. As she supported the unfolding potential of the many women in her organization, she also benefited from their increasing achievements. She was both teacher and student; giving and receiving. Having benefited from her mentors, she now did the same for those who came after her. The secrets of success were willingly shared with the newcomer, not jealously guarded or hidden in professional jargon or bureaucratic code. No one here felt threatened by another's success. Instead, they rejoiced in one another's achievements. With their perspective, if success was possible for one of them, it was possible for all of them. Consequently, Lexie never saw her business in the form of competition. For her, it was never to be conducted like a game which produced winners and losers, but rather as a process to empower all. She believed there were already winners inside all of them.

Still the inveterate teacher, Lexie played her role like that of a coach, handing out the tools and rules for success during her frequent training sessions. She bandaged up damaged egos and charted and devised positive, corrective strategies through the countless reenactments of sales scenarios. Lexie always sent her charges forth with words of encouragement ringing in their ears. She provided opportunities for each recruit to feel the rush of personal success as she met her goals. And Lexie made sure of one very crucial thing. It was positively essential, she believed, that every player on her team not achieve in a vacuum. They were to hear their crowd of peers give forth a resounding roar of recognition as they achieved things they never before believed possible! All personal and professional growth was cause for celebration. If women do indeed, as the Chinese say, hold up half of the sky, Lexie rejoiced in the fact that she and her fellow sisters celebrated it.

This connectedness was what she loved most about her business. It nourished her to know she mattered to others. Many even credited her with their success. She thrived on the affection and adoration emanating from those around her, and she was at home with the high ideals of her company. Like a sturdy seedling, rooted in and nourished by the deep soil of common belief, showered often with the waters of recognition, and warmed by an all-encompassing aura of affection, Lexie had grown stronger and happier in her Fashion Now family than she had ever been before.

CHAPTER EIGHTEEN:

A STRANGER IN
A STRANGE LAND

Hold me under the stars,
Tell me I am not alone.
Why do I feel at times so unreal
A traveller just passing through
Stranded here on the way to somewhere new?
Why am I here? What am I to do?
Strangely compelled, feeling there must be more
Somehow, I've forgotten how to do.
In this strange land I call home,
I see in your face too,
You often feel lost and alone.
Could it be that we were all
Meant to be one under our sun?
Now, fragmented, split and on our own
We struggle with vague memories
Flashes of insight that say
Parts of us have gone astray.
If once one family we were among
Why then does each feel like an unadopted one?
In this journey we call life,

Full of its toil and strife
Will we ever, at the end of our day,
Feel at home, welcomed to stay?
Complete, peaceful, our fears at bay,
Friend in a friendly universe,
Knowing intimately all that is.
Living no more, each in a strange, isolated way.

Lexie met the postman on the driveway. Returning home after an afternoon sales call, she was climbing out of her car, when he walked over and placed the envelope in her hand. Impressed by the grainy feel of the fine quality paper, she turned the envelope over, seeing something that stirred a vague memory. The back flap was sealed shut with an embossed sticker bearing a crest of crossed shields and swords. Under it, in bold, intricate letters, were the Latin words *Per Aspera, Ad Alta.*

"Through Difficulties to the Heights," Lexie whispered softly to herself. She remembered those words well for they had represented the ideals of her home school, Gibson High.

As she slid her fingers under the seal, breaking open the envelope, her excitement began to mount. It was a reunion!

Lexie planned every detail of her return to Gibson High. She would go without Derek, of course. Lately, he seemed happy when Lexie spent time on her own because it helped justify his weekends away without her. These were her memories, her friends, a world Derek had not shared, and she had no desire to include him now because when she was with him, she felt like an exotic butterfly trapped and pinned under glass for observation. Always dissecting her behaviour, Derek was relentless in giving constructive criticism as to how she could improve herself. Having no desire to be constantly evaluated and redirected like some experiment gone wrong, she preferred not to have him around.

Planning what to wear and where to stay, she was excited to learn that her sister Tess had also received an invitation and was planning to attend. Celine and Millicent had chosen to attend the other high school in Whitfield—the one where the children of blue-collar workers were more prevalent. So, it was Tess who would be with her on this, her triumphant return.

"Local Girl Makes Good." Lexie envisioned it all. Pulling up in front of her high school in her new white Lincoln, she would step out wearing designer clothes, her makeup and hair absolute perfection with her list of accomplishments ready to be recited.

Not that any of this was consciously planned out with such ruthless detail. That wasn't Lexie's way, and she never would have admitted such an agenda. It would not be nice to want revenge on those who had slighted her at Gibson High, revenge for the parties she had never been invited to, revenge for the feelings of inadequacy every time she watched the other girls swish down the halls in their new, expensive wool skirts with their Peter Pan collars and their sweater guard pins. She could still see the way they had thrown back their heads in haughty disdain as they passed her, their gleaming-white, soft suede shoes seeming to squeak out a refrain as their feet touched the smooth surface of the corridor floors. A refrain that sang out in Lexie's brain, "We're better than you. We're better than you. We're better than you!"

No, she would never have admitted, even to herself, that she was seeking vindication. She saw herself as too noble for that. So out of touch was she with who she was that she could not even allow herself success. Straightforward honesty about her accomplishments and acceptance of the subsequent admiration of others would have served her well. The best revenge is living well. Instead she played the game of pretending not to care while caring too much. Lexie had not learned the incredible freedom that can come when you regard what other people think of you as none of your business.

Her agenda hidden even from herself, Lexie went to her reunion, armed with her new success, to erase old pain caused by others who had measured her by the yardstick of dollars and cents and found her lacking.

"What crowd did you hang around with? I don't remember you." The small, attractive brunette circled her, her eyes narrowing, her voice dripping the acid of envy as she snarled, "Who invited you here anyway?"

"Back off, Melody. You're drunk!" The voice came from a tall, thin man slouched against the bar Lexie had been heading for when the hostess had intercepted her.

Geoff Courtland. The recognition rippled over Lexie as she took in his tall, handsome form. There he was, still so in control, yet at the same time appearing incredibly vulnerable, still capable of seducing every woman with the hope she was the one to fill his aching emptiness.

Taking her hand softly, yet awkwardly, he said, "I'm sorry. It's Lexie - Lexie Alexander isn't it? You have to excuse my wife. She gets drunk and well, you know, she says things she doesn't mean. You're here with Mark Shepherd aren't you?"

My god! He'd married Melody! Lexie was stunned. What's more, she couldn't believe so may of the others in her graduating class had also married their high school sweethearts. Had so few escaped the Whitfield society indoctrination process?

"Yes, I came with Mark, but Mark and I aren't married if that's what you mean. We've just seen each other tonight for the first time in years." Lexie answered. "I think he's over there talking to one of his old buddies."

As Geoff didn't respond, Lexie moved in to fill the conversational gap, her sales training having made her good at doing so.

"It's really amazing to see so many of the old familiar faces again, isn't it? The boys from the band, the teachers...It's really good of you to invite everyone back to your home, Geoff." Her voice trailed off as she found herself strangely struggling to know what to say. His silent appraisal of her was unnerving. Remembering the awkwardness of their only date so many years ago, she wondered if they were still worlds apart.

"You look terrific, Lexie," he said softly, his eyes lingering curiously on her face. His puzzled expression seemed to say, *How did I miss out on this one?*

"Here's your drink, Lexie. Sorry I took so long," Mark interrupted.

As she turned away from Geoff, taking her drink from Mark's outstretched hand, she touched the glass to her sensuously curved, smiling lips, and slowly sipped the sweet nectar of smug satisfaction.

The weekend became everything she had hoped for and more. Everywhere she went, Lexie was amazed at what she, a girl from the wrong part of town, had managed to achieve. So many of the brightest stars of Gibson High had fizzled in their home skies. Most, too content where they were, had never ventured away from Whitfield. They worked there. They married and raised their children there, with lives as secure as their bank investments, yet many, nearing middle age, felt betrayed. They had done everything the right way, the safe way, the way their parents had taught them, only to wake up one day with a sense that there had to be more. Was this all there was? A restlessness drove them to ask the question, to look everywhere for clues to what had gone wrong. The system had worked for their parents, hadn't it? What, then, was wrong with them?

Now here was Lexie, someone who had gone away and had returned seemingly so full of life, so vibrant—someone who had come from nothing and succeeded on her own. Curious, they now wanted to know someone they had not cared to know before.

Lexie thrived on the attention. She had always loved a party and this night she felt like queen of the prom. Making another mental check on her internal scoreboard, she wondered where all this adoration had been, when hurt and bewildered, she had watched a less attractive girl cradle an armful of roses and waltz by her to wear the crown? Naive, she had not yet learned beauty alone was not enough. An outsider, she had never even been considered by those who decided such things. Now as these same individuals compared their lives to hers, they seemed to have a vague sense that they had missed something along the way.

And then there was Mark. She had hoped he would be at the reunion. There had been a few brief encounters after the spring of their breakup, but none now for many years. Just before she had gone off to college, he'd called to tell her he was leaving for Australia. Having failed his senior year, he was at loose ends. Lonely, without a girl in his life, perhaps his parting words had been an attempt to ease the pain of change, to go back to safer, softer times.

"Why did he have to come into your life anyway, Lexie? You know Derek's not right for you. You know that, don't you?" Mark's voice was filled with unhappy resignation.

Lexie's throat tightened with tears. She knew what was coming, and she knew what she would say in response. Unable to give Mark what he needed, she listened in silence.

"Damn it all to hell, Lexie!" He spit out words of frustration. "If it weren't for him, you might still be mine."

There was an intake of breath and a pause. Then the tentative question came. "What do you say, Lexie? If you tell me to stay, you know I will. I want you back, Lexie."

His last sentence had come out in a barely audible whisper, then silence.

"It's best if you go, Mark." She heard herself say the words she knew were the right ones.

Three months later, while attending school in the big city, she had received his only letter. He wrote that he was working as a lifeguard on an Australian beach; as Lexie had pondered this, the finality of their separation at last penetrated. He had been her first love and now that was gone. Feeling utterly alone, Lexie had sat perched on a stool in the middle of a drab kitchen with the grey November day closing in around her and let the tears slide down her face and splatter the letter still in her hand. In that moment, she had missed him so. She had missed his warmth, his smile, his funny, tender words. She missed how he had adored her. Why had she not been satisfied? Mark had been so devotedly hers and she had not appreciated him. She had cried that day for the pain she had caused him.

But Mark was not done with her yet. More than two years later when she had the independence of a monthly pay cheque in her purse and the restriction of a wedding band on her hand, she was grocery shopping when her eyes fell upon a familiar broad back and blonde head. He was in his "uniform" again. Her eyes travelled up over the work boots, black pants, white shirt to the familiar butcher's apron, its strings wrapped and tied securely around his waist. There he was, stocking shelves just as he had done when they had dated. She sucked in her breath. The sight of him could still do that to her. She remembered well the enfolding touch of his naked body, his strong protective arms, his warm masculine scent, and his softly curling blonde hair.

Feeling awkward and excited at the same time, she had stood behind him, close enough that she was sure he could feel the heat seeping up into her face. He turned to face her, his broad smile shining down on her.

"Hi, Lexie. It's good to see you," he had said simply.

As she walked home, her groceries firmly held to her chest, she couldn't really remember how the rest of the conversation had gone. Shutting down, she had become cold and impersonal. A married woman, she couldn't allow herself to feel anything for Mark. That would be dangerous.

She didn't say, "It's good to see you too, Mark. I've missed you in my life."

Instead, she acted as if he had only been a casual friend from long ago. They exchanged pleasantries. She told him about her marriage. She lied and said she was happy with Derek. She chirped away that wasn't it great that they had bumped into one another after all this time, hiding her feelings behind falsely cheerful, meaningless chatter.

What she really wanted to do was hold him in her arms, tell him how sorry she was that she had hurt him, and that she was grateful it had been him, with his tender ways, who had been her first lover.

None of these things were said. How could they be? She didn't dare to even feel them!

That had been the last time she had seen him until now. As she walked into the classroom where her graduating class was gathering, she could sense his presence. His energy was there. She could feel his tension.

And then he was in front of her, standing first on one foot and then on the other, just as he had on the night of their first date. His face was flushed and smiling, and his eyes sparkled hello. He was happy to see her, of that there was no doubt, but there was also an air of expectancy about him.

Inseparable for the rest of the evening, they went to the classrooms together, talked to all their former teachers together, and walked through the gymnasium doors into the same dark room filled with undulating bodies moving to the same songs they had danced to almost twenty years before.

He held her. They danced and talked, but they touched less than they had that night years before. Lexie teased that he no longer stepped on her feet. He replied that she still sang off-key in his ear.

Still there for her, Mark again played the part of male protector and provider. This time it wasn't a coat placed around her shoulders in the rain, but a banner tugged down from a wall.

During a break while they were enjoying a cold drink in the school cafeteria, the banner had caught her eye. From the moment she saw it, she knew she had to have it. On the end wall of this huge room hung a banner, three feet wide and five feet long, crafted by former students especially for the reunion. It bore both the crest and school motto painstakingly hand painted in purple and gold.

Lexie could not have explained why she wanted it. She just did. As she sipped her drink, she cocked her head to one side, and then said boldly, "I want that."

No sooner had she said it than Mark nudged his buddy, who gave a knowing nod that said, "Your wish is our command." Off they went on their quest.

Like clowns in a vaudeville act, they worked the unsuspecting crowd. Folding up the cloths from vacant tables they threw them over their arms like waiters and began moving their way down to the end of the room where the banner hung, all the while pretending to be solicitous members of the catering team. It was late, and the crowd had thinned considerably so no one paid much attention. Those who did were too busy enjoying their Laurel and Hardy antics to question just what they were up to.

As they moved they juggled empty glasses into waiting garbage bins, balanced full trays of dishes on upturned palms and whipped cloths off empty tables like matadors flourishing capes at imaginary bulls, moving down the room as if participating in a well-choreographed musical play. It then seemed a logical next step when Mark beckoned his buddy to pull over a table up onto which he leapt. In full view of everyone, he then reached up to his full height and unhooked the banner freeing it with a flourish from the wall. With his prize in hand, he turned to descend.

Rivetted, he stood there in a split second moment of hesitancy, then his eyes met Lexie's. She couldn't believe what he had done.

Alone and exposed on top of a table, he stood with her prize amid a room full of people. He too, realized in that moment just how blatant an act of thievery he was committing. Fear flicked over his face only to be quickly replaced by a whoop of triumph as he snatched the banner to him, bounded down off the table, and came flying across the room. He caught Lexie by the waist, and spinning her around, they then made their getaway doubling up the banner and themselves in hilarious, giddy laughter as they went.

The banner stashed securely in the trunk of Mark's car, they made their way to Geoff's party. Once there, they reminisced until the wee hours of the morning, the banner-snatching incident becoming a lively topic. It was very late when Mark offered to drive her back to her parked car.

He made a detour on the way. She recognized the place as soon as they pulled in for it had not changed much over the years. Still secluded, the cliff overlooked the lake, and provided a great parking spot for amorous teenagers.

He turned off the car and slid his arm around her shoulders, pulling her to him. As she nestled in, she heard him sigh. Squeezing her tight, the side of his face coming to rest gently on the top of her head, he said softly, "I've missed you, Lexie."

Her only response was the rippling shudder of her shoulders as a small sob escaped her throat. She felt like she could cry for a million years. Mark had touched a deep sense of sadness that seemed to go beyond the pain they had shared.

As his fingers passed over her face gently wiping away her tears, Lexie could feel a huge lump building in her throat. He was going to ask what was wrong; what could she say? Did she even know?

When the question came, Lexie straightened herself in the seat and looked up at the vast canopy of stars above them. She knew what she wanted to do.

"Mark have you still got that old blanket you always carry around in your car?" she asked cautiously, knowing what such a request would start him thinking. "I just feel like being under those stars tonight with you to hold me."

Looking into the vastness of the warm summer sky, Lexie struggled to put into words the longing living inside her.

"Do you ever feel like you don't belong here, Mark? You know, like this planet isn't your home?"

"I don't know. What do you mean exactly? I know it wasn't big enough to hide from the pain of losing you. Is that what you mean?"

"Yeah, sort of. You know, feeling disconnected, lost, alone even though you're with people. No, more than that. Feeling like you're lost even to yourself. You know, sort of like everyone else knows what's going on here on earth, but you somehow missed the orientation class, like they built this great body for you to experience life with, but shipped you down and forgot to send the operating manual with you."

"Where's all this coming from, Lexie? You were having a great time tonight. My god, you were the envy of just about everyone there! What's going on with you?"

"I wish I knew Mark. I really wish I knew. All I do know is that no matter what I do, I walk around feeling like I'm not really here, you know, like a stranger on this planet. It never feels like home to me. Ever since I was a little kid, I always felt like home was somewhere else. Did you ever feel that way?"

"No. I don't think so. I've always kind of liked it here."

"Well, I guess I'm just nuts, or maybe I'm just unhappy about something in my life. I don't know. All I know is that most of the time I feel uncomfortable inside my own skin. My life feels foreign and uneasy, like it's not my natural way of being, like I'm meant to be someone else or somewhere else, like I'm acting my way through life. Doing what I'm supposed to do because I don't know what else to do. Sometimes, I just don't feel anything at all, know what I mean? And when I do feel things, I wonder if it's what other people would feel. Sometimes I feel like a real alien, like what's going on inside of me isn't the same as what's going on inside of anybody else."

She rolled over against his warm body and wrapped her arms about his waist, letting out a sigh of exhaustion. All too complicated to unravel, she was tired now of thinking about it. Was it time to go back to that place in her mind where she didn't think, to put the lid again on her Pandora's box of emotions and go back to being Lexie, the one-dimensional success?

"I bet I know what could make you feel better." Mark nuzzled against her, kissing her neck.

"No, Mark. I couldn't. Derek may not be perfect, but he doesn't deserve a cheating wife. I couldn't do that to him."

He laughed out loud at her response. "Hey, that would be great, and I admit it crossed my mind, but, no, I was talking about breakfast!"

Weeks later, Mark, who was now a travelling salesman for a grocery supply chain, was in her town and called to ask her out for a drink.

Sliding in beside him, her eyes took in the muted tones of the dimly lit bar. He had positioned himself in one of the plush, private booths and the surrounding room was awash in the colour red, with rose and crimson hues cascading off its surfaces. With music pulsing in the background and her body cradled in the deep softness of the booth wrapping itself around them, Lexie felt she had stepped into a secret, sensuous chamber.

That room, like a beating heart, nourished the bringing to life of a secret.

Mark having married a town girl from Whitfield with parents who were well to do, could pursue a less-than-ambitious lifestyle. They'd had a daughter together, but that did not stop Mark from doing what he had always done best. As he travelled from town to town, he sold more than his supplies. In each isolated small town, there was always a lonely woman needing to hear she was beautiful, special. One who spent her lonely evenings in front of her television set, her evening snacks arranged around her like lovers. Seeing the need in her eyes, it did not matter to Mark if she was plain, short, fat, or thin. All that mattered was that she could need him. In countless rooms above countless small stores, he filled their empty beds and hearts.

Making no secret about what he could and could not offer, they still accepted the limited love he could give. Most knew about his wife and child, some even knew about the others. To have him in their bed whenever he passed through town was enough. They were grateful for what they could get.

Lexie listened in disbelief as Mark told his tale of seduction. This man who could be so honest with so many about his activities had not told the one who most had a right to know. His wife never knew of his insatiable need.

Sexual connection fed Mark, letting him know he was alive. He had convinced himself he made love to his many women because they needed him and perhaps that was true, but the truth was he needed them more. Addicted, he thrust himself inside another, hiding in the lie, if just for the moment, that he was not alone, but connected to life. The heady high of an orgasm filling him with power and purpose, it seduced him into believing he could live forever. Then came the narcotic of relaxed release, far more seductive for him than any drug. When he made love he felt needed, powerful, complete, and in control. Afterwards, relaxed and renewed, an addict having satisfied the need within, he could face his world again - a world where truly needing another terrified him. Instead, sex—his drug of choice—provided the illusion of intimacy.

"How could you do this, Mark? It's so unfair to your wife and all those other women..." Lexie's voice trailed off into stunned silence.

"Some know. Some don't. The ones that do accept me for what I am."

"And the ones that don't? Your wife, does she accept this?" Lexie was becoming more upset.

"No, she doesn't know." His head down, he answered in a soft, shamed whisper.

"Mark, I don't think we should talk about this any more. I can't deal with it. I don't want to deal with it."

Lexie could feel dangerous feelings coming to the surface. A rage was building. How could he do this to so many women, deceiving them to meet his own needs? Didn't he care how they felt or how his wife would feel if she knew?

Lexie prided herself in not judging others, in being open and receptive to the many different ways people chose to live their lives. Besides, it would not be nice to tell this man what she really thought of his behaviour. If she started, she might lose control and say something threatening to both of them. It was better to deny her sense of outrage. It was his business, not hers. She supposed the signs had always been there in Mark. It was not her problem any longer. Instead she would choose to cherish what he had been to her. This newly revealed man was a stranger to her, and she wanted no part of what he had become.

Emotional walls came down, as her protective facade went up. The rest of the conversation focased on meaningless, safe details. She told him again how good it was to see him and prepared to make her escape. She'd judged and reached a verdict, but she did not have the courage to tell him to his face. Instead, kissing him softly on the cheek, as her gaze fell upon the room key he held in his hand, she said simply, "I don't think that's a good idea, Mark."

But she didn't say no as he called after her. "I'll see you next Thursday. I'm back in town then. Same time, same place!"

Instead, she picked up the phone that next week and to the wife on the other end, she said calmly, cooly, "Would you please tell Mark, I'll be unable to keep our date today?" and hung up.

This way, she never had to admit to herself what she had done, convincing herself it had been an innocent phone call designed only to keep Mark from being inconvenienced. The power to minimize and deny had become a useful tool, allowing her to do her dirty work without even getting her hands soiled. Her rage had found its outlet after all.

The reunion had brought a sense of closure, strengthening Lexie's belief in herself. They say you can never truly go back, but perhaps in the attempt she had learned to see with new eyes, to let go of an old, worn-out sense of being inadequate, of feeling less than those who possessed large bank accounts. Their lives could be just as meaningless as those not blessed by financial fortune, she'd discovered. She'd also stumbled upon the answer to a puzzling question.

Her friend Jayne had also been at the reunion. Since Jayne had married and moved to another town, Lexie had lost touch with her. They had managed to spend some time together during the course of the reunion weekend. Now, older and more self-possessed, Jayne revealed how she had so often been able to steal many of Lexie's boyfriends.

Perhaps reunions do that to people—make them more confident about revealing things in their past. Maybe it's because they don't believe they will ever see these people again so they find the courage to set the record straight, so to speak. Or was it something as simple as the four or five rum and cokes Jayne had had? Whatever her motive, while reliving the intense relationship of two young girls struggling with the raging hormones of early womanhood, Jayne decided to unburden herself that particular night.

"Lexie, didn't you ever figure it out? I mean, after a few times I thought it would be obvious to you. You know all those nights I'd get you and your date to pick me up from wherever I was and then get him to drop you off first? What do you think happened after you were gone? God, I thought you'd know what was up when he'd ditch you to start dating me. How did you think I got him interested in me in the first place?"

There was stunned silence between them as Lexie let Jayne's words sink in.

"Holy shit, Jayne! You mean you slept with most of my boyfriends? Well, I'll be damned!"

As she focused her attention on her friend, gradual smiles of mutual knowing began to slowly spread across their faces.

"Well, son of a bitch! While I was busy guarding it like the crown jewels, you were giving it away for free! You slut, you!"

By now Lexie was laughing. Laughing at herself for being so uptight and self-righteous back then. Laughing at the thought of Jayne snatching pimple-faced, sex-starved young men out from under her very nose. Laughing at herself for caring so much, always questioning what she had done wrong. She hadn't done anything wrong. She simply hadn't done anything. How could she compete with a friend whose underwear so often went missing in the back seat of a car?

Lexie stood back to admire the banner. The fact that it hung in her meeting room and not some stuffy high school office seemed a triumph of courage, daring, and the ability to break free from convention. By an act of total indifference for authority, she had felt liberated, as if she had taken back her power, disdainfully demonstrating to Whitfield society that she no longer cared about their rules.

Mark had championed her that night, taking risk in his stride so she could have her symbol. What she had wanted had been more important than stuffy protocol.

The banner's words stood as a testimony for all the nobodies from the wrong side of town who conquer the greatest difficulty of all—the enemy within. In accepting the evaluation of others, as so many do, Lexie had deserted herself and lived her life feeling the pain of those limiting labels. Now, as her banner hung securely, it became a constant reminder that she need not live under the oppressive weight of the judgements of others. Only she would determine the heights to which she could aspire.

Having laid to rest much of her past on this reunion weekend, her future waited to challenge her.

CHAPTER NINETEEN:

THE ZOMBIE YEARS

Smiling, serene face
Carry me home.
Drug induced haze
Lost and alone.
Out of the dark
I came into the light.
From the black void of the deepest night.
The words of a song I had once sung
Reminded me of where I had begun.
Sick and broken I have become.
A weighted, weary, worldly one.
The key to my martyred prison be
All this time hidden within me.
Asleep, I now awake.
Called by remembrance from my past.
My Friend, I had forgotten Your name.
Yet, the touch of your garment be enough,
The sight of You through my haze,
My heart and spirit to raise,
And my grateful soul inspire to sing.
Now I see the potential of being
In each small, wondrous thing!

Lexie, excusing herself from behind her desk, left her four branch mangers sitting in her office as she went to answer the door. The mailman handed her the telegram and left. Walking back to her meeting, Lexie's curiosity rose with each step as she tore open the envelope. A quick glance revealed it was from the Fashion Now Head Office. Her hand began to tremble, her eyes moving unbelievingly over the text again and again. She could not accept what they were telling her. Stunned and dazed, she stepped back into her office, back to the group of women drawn together by her drive and determination.

What could she tell them? How could she possibly say what had to be said? In that one moment she had known it was all over. The printed words had proven to be the death knell for her business, for all their businesses. It was finished—years of hard work gone just like that.

What a devastating stroke of pure genius. Lexie had to admit it had been a brilliant manoeuvre on the new owner's part. When the company had been sold to a foreign interest, there had been reassurances that things would remain substantially as they were. After initial resistance most distributors had settled back into business as usual. They had good reason to feel secure because the new owner had signed binding contracts with each of them guaranteeing the same discount structure and commission overrides. Lexie had continued to build her organization confident that, although the family atmosphere provided by the founder would be missed, this new owner would run the company much as before.

But, this! This was dazzlingly devious, accomplishing all the new owner's destructive objectives without allowing for any legal recourse. For months it had been rumoured that the new owner's only aim was to procure the formulas for Fashion Now's exclusive creams, caring little for the direct sales network that allowed thousands of successful women to earn their living. With one directive, he had put all the distributors out of business.

Between the home office and the distributor, there was one privilege the home office held exclusively—only one. Product price had never needed to be negiotiated—the market had taken care of that. Either their new owner was not a sensible business man, or he had definite reasons for destroying his new acquisition. The dictate of destruction stated simply: "Effective immediately, all prices are subject to a 100% increase."

That was it—seemingly innocent words with a devastating effect. The suggested retail price of the product dictated what the distributors would have to pay for it. Without any warning, all monthly quotas would have to be filled with product at double the price. If sales representatives failed to do so, they would immediately be in breach of contract, and their right to distribute would be revoked. With a single stroke of his pen, the young, rich foreigner had effectively nullified all contracts.

Lexie knew she could not sell her already exclusively priced product for double. It was ludicrous to even try. It was simply over. Their young, rich Persian investor had pulled the rug out from under them all. Lexie's next step would be, as gracefully and painlessly as possible, to wrap up her obligations to her organization and her clients.

As soon as the word had gone out about the collapse of Fashion Now, the competitors had come knocking at the door. To acquire Lexie and her organization would be quite an industry coup. She could have stepped from being a high-profile distributor with one company right into the same position with another. They knew, as did she, that most of her organization would follow. They were looking to her even now for leadership.

But, she just couldn't do it. So emotionally tied to the Fashion Now way of life was she that it would seem like personal betrayal to work for its competitors. Thoroughly indoctrinated with belief about the product superiority, she had become a zealous, closed-minded convert. In adamantly believing their way was the only right way of doing business, Lexie had ceased to be open to other possibilities. Blindly passionate, she could not envision another company taking its place in her heart. The very devotion that had helped to make her successful now hindered her, standing as it did in the way of rational decisions. Thinking with her heart, she could not let go of her misplaced loyalty. The company had been like a lover, providing her with all she needed. It had been there to guide her as she grew in ability, applauding her each step along the way, sustaining, nurturing, and making her feel special, filling the void left by an unhappy marriage. How could she let go of that? To consider other proposals now would make Lexie feel like a widow flirting at her husband's funeral. She was not about to jump into bed with another "lover" only to be deceived again for she felt as if most of what she cherished had been ripped from her. All the high ideals were now nothing more than empty rhetoric. She felt used, abandoned, betrayed. Instead of accepting what she felt as righteous anger and using it to move herself and her organization forward into a new future, she chose to withdraw into pain, to shut down. She would do no business anywhere.

Calling her organization together for one final meeting, she outlined their alternatives and made it clear they were free to go wherever they chose, but that she would no longer be active. For her, the love affair was over.

Many tried to coax her, to convince her of her mistake, but her mind was closed. She had given this business everything she had, and life had not turned out as she hoped. In her all or nothing way of thinking, her black-and-white world, Lexie could not conceive that her business could go on in any other way than it had in the past. To sell and promote a product she had previously competed against was not in her range of adaptability—not even if it meant the survival of a very lucrative way of life. In this her heart ruled her head much to the dismay of many of the women in her organization. Leaving them without guidance or direction, the doors of her studio were shut, no more to provide a place for women to grow and explore their own sense of being more.

Yet, if Lexie were completely honest, there were more reasons for withdrawing other than her fierce company loyalty and subsequent sense of betrayal. As events wound down and excitement ebbed, she found herself with time on her hands. Every minute of every day was no longer scheduled and planned, and she no longer lived each day in hyper time, rushing to fill it with accomplishment. As the tasks she had to do began to dry up, Lexie found there was nothing left she wanted to do. Just sitting and staring out at nothing at all, she was no longer able to motivate herself to do, do, do. All she found herself wanting to do was sit, sit, sit. An incredible lethargy washed over her, and a realization began to seep in. She was exhausted. Her wellspring of seemingly unlimited energy had dried up, and she was running on empty.

Now that her frantic, constant activity was no longer pumping adrenalin into her system, her body's weariness could finally make itself known. For all those long, late nights spent out selling; for all those times she had ignored her sense of weariness and pushed on to one more sale, one more training speech, one more hiring interview; for all of her reckless use and abuse of her body's precious resources; for all of that and more her body was now presenting its bill. Success bought and paid for by workaholic obsession has its price. Her constant fixation on achievement had sent her soaring to the heights. Now that same obsessive thinking was plunging her to her depths.

Unable to admit that her extreme reaction was caused by a repressed sense of rage at having been abandoned by a company she had loved with all her heart, Lexie suppressed her feelings. Cultured, educated women did not rage. Instead, she turned the anger inward and manifested self-pity and lethargy. Instead of railing at injustice, speaking out, and using her anger as a tool for positive change, Lexie did what society has come to expect of the fairer sex. She became depressed. Women who work out their pain in quiet desperation are far less threatening to the established order than women propelled into action by their anger. She lied to herself, explaining away her lack of energy saying simply that she needed a rest anyway. That's what she told everyone around her. The lies in her mind grew and with each telling she came to believe them more. She had been growing weary of the business with its constant challenge to achieve, she said. She minimized the impact its demise had on her, saying it was probably all for the best. Addicted to denial, each repetition of her litany of self-deception acted like an injection of a powerful drug dulling her pain. Soon her true feelings were lost in the haze of medication. Even she came to believe she'd accepted it all.

The truth was that she was so devastated, she couldn't allow herself to feel anything at all, becoming a body going through the motions of living. Doing what she thought she should do, acting in the ways she thought she should act.

Yet, still denying herself what she truly needed, not yet ready to give herself permission just to be, to feel the pain of loss and betrayal, she forced herself to rally one more time. A direct sale jewellery company had approached her to recruit and train a sales force for them. They were willing to give her a salary as well as overrides, and she knew this would make Derek happy. He had made it clear he still looked to her to maintain the mortgage payments as they had originally agreed. Fashion Now may have deserted her, but the monthly bills hadn't. Lexie knew herself they could not manage on Derek's income alone. She would start again - this time with a totally different product and with a company whose owner wasn't a male. Perhaps an organization led by a female would be different. She allowed herself to believe perhaps this company truly practised what it preached.

The company struck her as odd from the very beginning. Warning bells began ringing, but she minimized her feelings. Thinking back, she knew from the very first moment she had walked into their head office that something was wrong.

There, directly in front of her, taking up almost the entire wall, was a huge portrait of a beautiful young woman. The subject was the heart and soul of the company which was named after her. There was only one thing very unnerving about all of this. The beautiful young woman in the portrait was dead. Jenny Lynn Jewellery had been dedicated to the memory of its owner's dead daughter—a company founded on a mother's guilt - a mother whose ambition had caused her to leave her children unattended once too often in pursuit of success. Jenny Lynn had been the oldest of four siblings left alone in the house the evening her mother had been out on yet another sales call. Beautiful and capable, even at the age of fourteen, she was well practised in the role of caregiver. Abandoned by their father years before, their mother worked hard selling jewellery she fashioned late at night in her basement workroom. By day she worked as a department store clerk, so Jenny and the others were very used to being on their own.

Their home was poor, a somewhat isolated old farmhouse in a rural area now carved up for a housing development. The wooden frame house stood like a lonely reminder of harsher, more primitive times amidst houses of more modern design.

Jenny's mother had been told many times to get rid of the old cast-iron cookstove still set up in the back shed, a remnant left over from earlier days when it had served as a summer kitchen. Surrounded by other discarded pieces of equipment, it was forgotten and ignored.

Ignored, that is, except by mischievous boys. The shed and all its treasures acted like a magnet for Jenny's brothers. That fateful day they had decided they absolutely did not need their sister's help. If she was too busy to cook for them, they would simply do it themselves! Who needed a girl to cook anyway? How hard could it be, they wondered, to put some paper and wood into the old stove and then light it up? They had great plans to fill the frying pan they had secretly brought to the shed with the potatoes they would peel and slice. Having seen their mother do it a hundred times, they would create that greatest of delicacies for themselves—french fried potatoes.

Jenny would be sorry she had been too busy to make them. They'd show her they could do it themselves. Chatting excitedly, the youngest brother, straining to reach the stovetop, slopped grease into the pan. It sloshed out over the black enamel surface soaking the corner of his sleeve and trickled down the front of the stove. He wiped his shirt off carelessly, impatiently, across the front of his jeans, then turned to see his brother coming towards him ready to light the wood within the stove. Fascinated, he watched as the flaming torch approached. Then, a sudden implosion of sound, a whoosh, and the flames greedily sucked in the air, travelling along a trail of oil on the way to flesh.

Piercing screams reached Jenny. Instinctively, she dropped the bundle of washing she had been carrying and bolted for the shed. Smoke was curling out through every gap and crack of the ramshackle structure. Before her very eyes, the ancient, dry wood exploded into flames, the tongues of fire licking their way up the walls like caged beasts starved for food. Without a thought for herself, Jenny charged into the smoke-filled shed and scooped both frightened boys up under her arms, carrying them to safety.

They tried to stop her when she went stumbling back in, but the roar of the flames blotted out their protests. She was looking for one more. There had to be one more brother in there! They were always in threes! The thick blanket of smoke had just hidden him from her view. She had to save him too. She was the oldest. She was responsible for them.

Jenny never came out of that fire. The brother she sought had not been there, sent earlier to get more wood for the stove.

Flames ripped mercilessly through the rest of the house. Their mother came home to the flashing lights of ambulances and a charred pile of rubble where her house had been. Her sons were badly burned, and her beautiful daughter's body was unrecognisable.

Never able to forget, the mother became obsessed with the belief that she could make Jenny live again if she could create the dream they had shared. Working day and night at her creations, she sold her jewellery at every market and boutique she could find. Her compulsion drove her to build a company to bear her daughter's name. Each step closer lessened the pain of her guilt.

And then it happened. A man walked into her life. He liked her work, and he liked her. Along with a marriage proposal he also made her a business proposal. He would help her realize her dream, and thus Jenny Lynn Jewellery was born.

Joan Charest was as different as her company. Her signature blonde hair, white miniskirt, and cowboy boots made a startling first impression as she climbed out of her low-slung, white corvette. As she extended her hand in greeting, eyes would become rivetted on the huge, milky-white diamond on her hand. It could have been a small doorknob it was so large! But like many other things about her, it unfortunately was not quality.

So great had been her drive to build a wildly successful company that her obsession had taken over, corrupting her values and allowing her to do whatever it took to succeed. If that meant cheating her suppliers, delaying their payments until they were forced into bankruptcy, then so be it. She operated her business with total disregard for the welfare of anyone or anything else other than the shrine she was building to her daughter. Jenny Lynn would live again through this company, even if others had to suffer in order for it to happen.

This was what Lexie walked into. Within six months she knew she had made a mistake. Customers and recruits alike were calling her complaining about the shoddy quality of the product, missed deliveries, and discrepancies on their bills.

Joan Charest had been no different. In fact she had been worse. She used her feigned female incompetence to escape responsibility, playing the role of dumb blonde when it served her purposes. The rest of the time, she was excessively charming, dismissing queries of concern with a wave of her manicured, jewelled hand. "It's nothing," she would say. "Don't worry. Everything is being looked after!"

Lexie learned the hard way that breasts instead of balls don't ensure business integrity. She handed in her resignation feeling even more numbed and lost than before.

Wandering listlessly about the house one day, she happened into Jade's room where her daughter was seated at her desk, busily intent upon her homework. Attempting to chat with her, Lexie's eyes fell upon some of Jade's drawings tacked up on her bulletin board. One in particular looked as if it had been there some time for the paper was yellowed, the picture faded. When she looked closer she could discern a crayoned drawing of a woman with the childish words scrawled underneath, "My Mom."

"Jade, is this a picture of me?" Lexie asked, unfastening it from the wall in order to get a better look at it.

"What's this bulge at the side of my head?" she asked.

"Oh, Mom. I drew that when I was just a little kid in kindergarten. That bump's supposed to be the telephone! You were always on the phone!"

Jade's response rivetted Lexie to the spot. So that's how her small child had seen her—a mother with a telephone as a permanent part of her anatomy. The message was crystal clear. Her tiny daughter had seen her as always connected to somewhere else. There, but not really there. That one picture had spoken a thousand words.

Perhaps that was why, with a heavy heart, she put in her application for supply teaching. At least working again as a teacher, she would have time to be with her children. The frequent school breaks and the lack of paperwork associated with occasional teaching would allow her to be home at the same time as her daughters. Once again she would be there to prepare their meals and to talk with them about their days. More importantly, she could spend her evenings at home.

To return to teaching, leaving behind the glamour and excitement of the sales world, was not what made her happy. Yet, she did not have the heart to again build a business from nothing nor did she wish to be apart from her children the long hours required to do so. The choice seemed obvious. Teaching would meet all the requirements but one. It was no longer what she wanted to do, but something she had to do. She saw no other alternative.

With the perception of lack of choice comes a sense of numbing hopelessness. It was not that returning to her profession was in itself such a disagreeable thing. It was Lexie's perception of all it stood for—a symbol of her defeat in the business world, the result of not being able to champion herself, of being unable to stand against Derek and refuse to return to work until she was healed enough to make better decisions. Giving up her own happiness for the sake of her family, she would play the role of martyr. But, more than even that, she felt like a failure. Teaching adult women to be the best they could be had felt like her mission in life. To return to the world of children seemed not to make full use of her talents. No longer would she be surrounded by women who loved what they did. Now she went to work each day with tired and worn-out individuals who often felt used and abused by the system in which they tried, often unsuccessfully, to live out their ideals. Lexie had known it was time to move on from teaching children, and she was angry to find herself once again facing a class of ten year olds who did not particularly want to be there.

Was there no safe place to express her anger and frustration? Who would understand? She would only be labelled selfish and idealistic. What was wrong with her anyway? Most women would be happy to have her career in teaching. Why couldn't it be enough for her? Did she think she was somehow too good for it? Why did she often say she was *just* a teacher, the way she heard women say they were *just* a housewife. What was wrong with her anyway? Why was she so discontent with her lot in life? Her thoughts chased themselves round like mice in a cage, never going anywhere, always leading back to the same place.

She did not admit her anger, her sadness. She didn't grieve her losses, rage, or cry. Instead she went to work like a good girl, brought home the expected pay cheque, and lived with a deepening depression day after day, month after month, year after year.

To see her no one would ever know. She always wore her smile— such a "nice" person. If anyone asked her, she was fine. Just fine. Later in life, a new awareness would allow her to chuckle at the insightful meaning assigned this group of letters, making it into a cryptic acronym. In the world of polite, meaningless, and nonthreatening communication, "fine" should be seen for what it is—a code word growled through clenched jaws while pretending nothing is wrong. A new understanding of the word would give refreshing honesty to all such replies. The word fine is code for: Fucked Up, Insecure, Neurotic, and Emotionally Unstable. Without a doubt that was Lexie's state of mind, but to ask her, she was just fine.

She had waded deep into that symbolic river in Egypt—the one called Denial. It had served her well in the past, and she needed it now. Go with the flow, don't feel, don't talk about what you feel, don't admit to pain. Lexie had a job to do. She had two beautiful kids to raise who in all respects seemed to be normal, healthy, and happy. Determined to keep it that way, Lexie ignored the constant churning in the pit of her stomach. It seemed a small enough price to pay.

The witch arrived on Halloween Day and didn't leave. At least that's what the kids at St. Martyrs Christian School often said. The phone by her bed had jarred her awake at six thirty that morning. It was the dispatcher from the local Catholic school board asking her if she could replace the teacher of a grade five class. Lexie groaned to herself. It was Halloween! That meant classroom parties, with costumes to pin and zip up, faces to paint, and excited children running in and out of classrooms fuelled by the power of sugar. It would definitely be one of those days where she reached for the headache pills as soon as she came home.

With her most pleasant voice, she said that of course she would take the assignment. She had been doing a great deal of work for the Catholic school board these days because they called earlier in the morning than the public board, and consequently she had ended up working almost exclusively for them.

This had caused her some trepidation at the beginning as she found it unnerving to walk into a school and come face to face with the naked figure of a man hanging on a cross. Educated in the secular system, Lexie had taught initially there and had sent her own children to its schools. A relatively inexperienced Catholic, having been raised in the Protestant tradition, her only exposure had come when Derek informed her he absolutely insisted on being married in the Catholic church. This surprised her enormously for as far as she knew, Derek had not darkened the door of any church for a very long time.

He, however, had remained stubborn about this, and she had agreed. Somehow in her way of thinking it had seemed almost destined to be—a form of closure. Lexie's mother, the youngest of twelve children raised in a Catholic family, had been excommunicated when she had married Lexie's father, a Protestant. Her mother's parents had even refused to attend the wedding. It had been a point of pain for many years with only time bringing eventual healing and acceptance by her family. Lexie's mother, bitter about her church's rejection, had made a commitment to raise her children in the Protestant faith. When Lexie had returned to the Catholic tradition to be married, there was a sense she was doing something that would vindicate her mother.

Lexie had attended the compulsory marriage instruction classes with Derek. Before she could be confirmed as a Catholic, she was told she must confess her deepest, darkest sins to a total stranger—a man at that! One who had never been married and probably had very little idea about the sin that was uppermost in her mind. She was going to have to tell a perfect unmarried, male stranger that she, a supposedly pure and virginal bride to be, had been sleeping with her boyfriend. Not bloody likely! Wondering if hell's fires were as hot for lying as for fornication, she had decided to risk lying. There was absolutely no way she could accept the concept that she needed help to talk to her creator. She had a direct line, and as far as she was concerned this whole confessional stuff had been dreamt up to keep the priests off the unemployment line. Lexie had realized that when it came to Catholicism, she would have to take the best and leave the rest. She just couldn't buy it all.

Derek, it seemed had a similar philosophy, wanting all of the benefits of a faith without any of the work. He had expected his church to be there to marry him, bury him, and save his children from hell's fire through baptism, regarding his only duty as a Catholic to be one of showing up when he needed something. Derek had insisted on a Catholic wedding, but he had no intention of ever attending mass. The church did not see Derek again until the baptism of his first child.

It is strange how things turn out, though. Lexie, the convert, grew to have an affinity for the cool, reassuring interiors of her adopted church and came to enjoy the ritual and ceremony of the Catholic services. She and her children often attended without Derek, and Lexie became a far better Catholic than Derek had ever been.

This then, paved the way for the offering of a permanent teaching position at St. Martyrs. The Catholic board had a hiring policy which stated only confirmed Catholics could teach in their schools. Lexie obtained the obligatory letter from her priest and was hired on an occasional contract. That meant she would replace the former teacher, Mrs. Payne, for the rest of that year. She felt like asking if the contract she was signing included a provision for combat pay. By now she knew she had committed herself to teaching in a war zone. Hadn't Mrs. Payne already been one of its casualties?

The classroom was in a total uproar. The teacher had left no plans for the day, and as far as Lexie could tell, that had been the case for some time now. Textbooks were in short supply, bulletin boards were bare, and there was no timetable or seating plan anywhere in sight. What work was in the students' books had not been checked in weeks. It did not take Lexie long to figure out that these children had spent the first two months of this school year accomplishing absolutely nothing.

Nothing, that is, except trouble. This did not surprise her, for idle children find their own things to do, and they are not usually the things adults want them to do. Crying out for structure and direction, children will resort to just about anything to be noticed. Negative attention is better than no attention at all.

This Halloween Day, filled with emotional outbursts, was hardly a party. One large, angry boy overturned his desk in frustration, ranting and raving that he could not do his arithmetic. Flying into a rage, he yanked his belongings from the desk and threw them across the room. Another boy kicked a classmate in the face during a playground scuffle, and a group of girls had approached her, one in tears, complaining bitterly about the cruel teasing by another student. With no plans made to have their Halloween party, they were the only class in the school not in costume and enjoying treats. Room C was filled with angry kids acting out their frustration.

"I wouldn't blame you if you didn't want to come back," the principal said to her. "I'd understand really. I know they're totally out of control, but, you see, we're in a real bind. The classroom teacher, Mrs. Payne, well, ah, you see, she's had, ah, well, a relapse." He cleared his throat nervously and went on in hushed tones. "You know—emotional problems. I'm not at liberty to say too much, but we're not sure when she'll be coming back or even if she will be back." His eyes flicked appraisingly over Lexie. "You seemed really good with them today. I'd really appreciate it if you'd hang in there with us for a week or so until we know what's going to happen. If it works out, you never know, it could turn into a permanent job for you, and they're hard to come by these days. What do you say?"

Growing weary of supply teaching, of always being called out to different schools and with this school just around the corner from where she lived, she was considering accepting. True the class was a handful, but she knew they were basically good kids. They just needed a lot of attention and good, fair discipline. She was confident she could do it. In fact it might be just the challenge she needed. Lexie hated to see anyone in pain, and these kids were so obviously unhappy. Besides, no other career alternatives had presented themselves in the last months. It was beginning to look like she wasn't destined to leave teaching children just yet.

"Sure. I'd be happy to help out." She smiled as the principal reached over and shook her hand.

"It's settled then. Welcome aboard!"

She stood at the door the next day to greet them as they filed in. She didn't smile. She didn't dare. It was cruel, Lexie knew, to present such an austere face to these children, but she also knew from experience it was critical to let them know she was in control. Later she could mellow and allow them to see her human side, but now her first task was to establish order in the midst of chaos.

That first morning she outlined her expectations, defining what acceptable behaviour was, and setting out the consequences of bad choices. She did not yell. She didn't even raise her voice. It was a simple matter of cause and effect. If they treated her with respect, she would treat them the same way. She gave the impression that she expected the best from them and that they would fulfil that expectation. The rest of the day was spent talking about what they would learn in the next few weeks and discussing some of the exciting things they could explore as a class. And last but not least, Lexie did what she always did with her classes each day. She gathered them around her, allowing them to sprawl comfortably wherever they chose, and read to them from one of her favourite books. She knew that no matter how angry, how tough, how uncaring these young individuals appeared to be, they were still frightened children inside. All children love to explore the world of possibilities held within the pages of books. Passionately, Lexie put her all into sharing stories that told of children just like them.

As the days went by, Lexie filled their time with productive activity, words of praise, smiles, and gentle touches on their shoulder as she passed by them, their heads lowered in concentration on their work. And each day, the noise became less of a raging roar and more of a well-tuned hum. She was firm, of that there was no doubt. She often referred to herself as the witch in room C. It pained her that these children still needed so much external control. But if she called herself a witch, the children had another name for her, affectionately referring to her simply as Mrs. G.

Christmas gave her the best present of all. A cocky young troublemaker, who had been one of her greatest challenges, passed by her desk on his way out the door. Stopping in mid-track as if something had suddenly struck him, he walked back and stood beside her desk lost in thought.

"You know, Mrs. G., I just noticed something. Since you came, the days have shrunk! It just seems like morning recess, and already we're going home!"

She wanted to reach out and hug him. Instead she let the warm, tender feeling wash over her as she watched his head bob happily out of her classroom. *Thank you, God*, she said silently to herself. Perhaps she was in her right place after all, for now anyway.

"Time flies when you're having fun!" she called cheerily after him.

"Mommy, when's the priest going to say my favourite words?" Jade had reached over and was twisting Lexie's wrist so she could read the dial on her watch.

"Shhhh, Jade. We're in church, remember. You're supposed to listen to the priest and think about what he's saying." She knew it was an empty instruction. A ten-year-old child could not possibly understand the intricacies of Scripture being discussed. All she could hope was the teachings would somehow sink in by osmosis.

Holding his arms up over the crowd, the priest gave them his farewell blessing as he said Jade's favourite phrase, "The mass is ended. Go in peace."

"Hooray, it's over!" Jade bounded out of her seat. "Let's go, Mom. Come on, mom, hurry!"

Lexie looked around her to see if anyone had heard her disrespectful daughter. The four of them were heading out of the church on their way to a restaurant. It had become a Sunday ritual that Lexie and her two daughters would pick up Derek's mother and take her to mass and then to lunch afterwards.

"What restaurant would you like to try today, Jade? Any favourites?"

Lexie was asking Jade because she especially wanted her daughter to be in a happy mood today. She had something to tell her that she knew would be upsetting.

She waited for the right moment as she was tucking her into bed that night.

"Jade, honey. How would you feel about going to a new school in September?" she asked quietly. She knew this was not going to be easy.

"No way! Leave all my friends, Mom? Why would I do that?"

Lexie plunged in. There was no soft way to say what had to be said.

"The Catholic board has offered me a full-time teaching position at St. Martyrs next year. That means I'll be teaching every day in the same school. It means more money for us, and it would be easier in a lot of ways on me. I've decided I want to accept." Here, she took a deep breath before she continued.

"The only thing is, they won't hire me permanently unless I become a Catholic school supporter and that means that you, Jade, have to transfer to a Catholic school. You have to go where my tax dollars go. I'm really sorry about this, Jade, but I can't see any other solution." Her voice lowered in sympathy as she finished her sentence.

"What about Jessica then? Doesn't she have to change too?" Jade shot back her angry reply. It was so unfair. She wanted company in her misery. Why was she the one to suffer?

"Jessica isn't affected because she's going into grade ten. They have different regulations about high schools."

"Oh," came the flat reply, then a long pause and finally a sad, "Do I have to, Mom?"

"I'm afraid so, Jade. But there is one bright spot in all of this. You'll probably be in my grade five class! St. Martyrs is the closest Catholic school, and it has only one grade five teacher—me!"

Jade looked skeptical. "Isn't that against the law or something, having your mother as your teacher? I've never heard of that. Are you sure?"

"Pretty sure. Look, Jade I know this will be hard for you, but look on the bright side. It's a chance to make lots of new friends."

"I like the ones I've already got!" Jade turned her face into her pillow, and Lexie knew they had discussed the subject long enough.

"You'll get used to the idea in time," she said as she left the room. "You'll see. It'll all work out fine." Her words made her feel better. She wasn't sure if they helped Jade.

September came, and that first day of school Lexie arrived with a small, frightened ten-year-old daughter in tow. The word spread in a flash that Jade was a teacher's kid and that helped break the ice somewhat. Anyone who wanted to impress Mrs. G. in the hopes of getting better grades went out of his or her way to be nice to her daughter. Unfortunately, the same dynamic worked in reverse. Jade was to find out that anyone upset with her mother would take it out on her.

"You only won because you're the teacher's kid! Your speech wasn't that good!" Lexie rounded the corner in time to see the gang of kids surrounding Jade. The moment they saw her, they scattered, and she knew instinctively they had been up to no good. Her daughter was in tears and after some coaxing Jade sobbed out the whole story of how jealous classmates had dismissed her hard-won victory in the public speaking contest as favouritism.

"I hate having my mother as my teacher! I always have to be perfect, and everybody treats me like I'm different! I hate it! I hate it!" She stomped off yelling, "I don't want to talk about it! What good would it do anyway? We can't change anything, can we?" Jade threw the words over her shoulder as she walked away from her mother.

Lexie was left standing alone in the yard wondering if she had made a terrible mistake, sacrificing her daughter's happiness for her own convenience. If she allowed guilt to fill her, if she paid the price of feeling it, would she have to do anything about changing the situation? Would her misery be payment enough? Unable to see how she could change anything anyway, she convinced herself she would make it up to Jade in other ways.

Lexie's life settled into a numbing routine. She would go to work each day only to come home and start her second job. As she walked through the door each evening, she would head to the kitchen, tie on an apron, and begin to prepare the family's dinner. Even now, with Derek working in sales and often home ahead of her, she would still find him sitting, waiting for her to come home and cook his evening meal. When she complained, he would make excuses that he did not know what to cook or how to cook it. When she asked to occasionally eat meals out, he would ask her where she planned to find the money for such extravagance. In Derek's mind they were still poor even though they had successfully paid off the mortgage and now had many thousands of dollars in cash savings. Money always came first. That was the message she was beginning to receive loud and clear. No matter how much money they accumulated, Lexie realized that there would never be enough. The amassing of money had become an end in itself; the state of Derek's bank account was more important to him than his wife's happiness.

Worn out from years of arguing about money, Lexie did not have the energy to fight with someone who, in her mind, could be so blatantly uncaring. It seemed hopeless and pointless. How could she reason with a man who saw nothing wrong with an exhausted wife working alone in the kitchen while he sat and watched television? It was how he had been raised, all he knew. His mother had toiled like a draft animal both at work and at home, and he expected it of his wife as well. Instead of fighting with him, Lexie would burn with silent resentment. That was all she knew. Never having witnessed open conflict in her home, where feelings of frustration and resentment had been dealt with by martyrdom, she had watched her father play it that way for years. Thus, instead of challenging Derek, she used her anger like a fuel, driving herself further into perfectionism. There must be something wrong with her to bring this unfair treatment upon herself. It did not occur to her that the dynamics that she had witnessed in her family of origin were intrinsically unhealthy. Placing her parents on pedestals, the fault, therefore, must lie with her. They had made it work hadn't they? She kept trying to recreate what she had known with her parents. Because she had won their love through achievement, she would do the same with her husband. She would just try harder, continuing to be the perfect, uncomplaining, all-nurturing wife. Then, she continued to believe, if she just got it right, Derek would treat her the way she wanted to be treated.

The payoff for Lexie in this stance of self-pity was that if Derek continued to be a selfish oaf, then she at least was without fault. Puffing herself up with noble self-sacrifice, allowing herself to feel a smug sense of superiority, she would revel in the thought that she was never as cruel and uncaring as he was. She was above that. She was better than Derek.

Rooted in falsehoods, nurtured by dysfunction, blighted by misperception, life in the Gaust household resembled life in the families of its founders. How could it be otherwise? On the surface all appeared unrippled, yet beneath, turbulent, unresolved emotions bubbled. The message was clear. The appearance of happiness was to be projected at all costs. No one had ever openly declared it to be so, but the leaders of this family, Lexie and Derek, clearly modelled what was expected. Actively living a lie, promoting a false image, not allowing themselves to live according to their true feelings, how then could their children possibly grow into the truth of who they were when the wise, all-powerful adults in their life had failed to do so?

Receiving the silent but potent message that disturbing feelings were not to be talked about lest they upset the facade of tranquillity projected by her family, Jade never again risked an outburst about being placed in her mother's classroom. She appeared to accept and adjust. Only once or twice to her mortification did she slip and reveal her vulnerability by calling Lexie "Mom" in class. Lexie soon found she could treat her daughter like any other student. It was strange, but her persona as "Mrs. G." seemed somewhat detached from who she was at home. Perhaps it was because it was just a role she played. More and more as time went by, Lexie found it easier to slip in and out of the required personas. Skilfully adept at fulfilling the expectations of others, like a chameleon, she could become whatever was required, being all things to all people, the essence of who she was disguised by her many layers of camouflage.

One of those roles was that of happy, dedicated teacher. She did her job well, but so much of the time she was on autopilot—doing what she was supposed to do, saying what she was supposed to say, and all the while, becoming less and less in touch with her own needs and wants, her own happiness.

It is strange how things unfold at times. Sometimes life seems to hold up a mirror for us when we most need to see ourselves but have refused to look. When Lexie walked into the staff room and saw Mrs. Payne, the teacher she had replaced two years before, sitting like a zombie, recognition hit. Was that to be her one day?

The conversation hummed all around the seated teacher, but she remained oblivious. She sat in a world of her own, walled in by her drugs. Her eyes closed, she had no desire to speak to anyone or to have them speak to her. Content to let the energy of life pass her by, there appeared nothing she desired to do.

Lexie, somewhat shaken, nudged the teacher beside her and asked, "What's with her?"

Her friend took her by the arm and steered her out into the hall. There, in hushed tones, she told Lexie the story of this woman who so obviously did not want to be there.

It had started the year before Lexie arrived at the school. Mrs. Payne had her first mental breakdown. Pumped full of drugs, she had been sent back into the classroom the following September only to be replaced by Lexie two months later. Now she was back once again as an occasional teacher. A tight feeling began to grow in Lexie's chest as her friend described a life pattern chillingly like her own.

Beginning as a young bride freshly graduated from teacher's college, Mrs. Payne had gone on to teach for twenty-three years, even though she and her husband, being good Catholics, had had four children in quick succession. Because his mother was available to come and care for their children during the day, the husband, who was now advancing to the position of principal, felt his wife should not abandon her career but continue to teach. With short breaks of three months or so off after the birth of each child, the new mother went dutifully, resentfully back to work. This was made possible, even in the days before maternity leaves, through the influence and contacts of a husband who was rapidly rising in the administrative ranks of the school board. When their youngest child started school, he lost no time in presenting his wife with a new agenda. Being a stellar achiever himself, he felt that it behoved her to get a university degree now that she was less needed by the children. He encouraged her by telling her over and over again that if he had done it, she could also. He, however, had not been slowed down by the duties of caring for a legion of children, leaving that to his wife and mother. His job, as he saw it, was to be the family provider, and he had thus set out almost immediately to obtain his degree, seeing himself as the primary breadwinner and as such responsible for all major decisions in this family he led. Even though his wife had always worked, he saw her contribution as secondary to his, and he felt justified appropriating her salary in the name of effective financial planning. Managing and supervising her career as diligently as his own, he pushed her to enrol in university night courses. Seven years and countless assignments and essays later, his wife attained the prize her husband had been after all along. Not only did this driven man want the social status of being an administrator of a school, he had also wanted the perks that went with two high-paying salaries. His wife's new qualifications added significantly to her net worth. Money, it seemed, was becoming her husband's primary motivation.

In no time at all, he lived up to and surpassed their new level of earning power. Their steady pay increases were gobbled up by a new, large and spacious home, a sleek sailboat docked at an exclusive club, and a late-model car for the husband. His appetite for status surpassing all other things in his life, he was creating a prison of debt from which his exhausted wife saw no escape.

She left the only way she knew how. Because he had never truly listened to her, she ceased to communicate. Because she no longer wanted to be in a classroom, she found nothing she wished to teach. It was true she placed her body there each day, but she was as much a piece of furniture as the desk she sat behind. She was there, hour after hour, day after day, staring blankly out into space.

They found her that way the day she failed to come home. Her husband walked down the silent deserted corridors of the school with a growing sense of uneasiness. It was unlike his wife not to return home directly after work. She always left on time, eager to be free at the end of her teaching day. Darkness had fallen by the time he had freed himself from yet another evening meeting and come home to his family. Immediately, on learning that his wife was not yet home, he had checked the calendar where he insisted the entire family write their schedules. His wife did not appear to have any commitments that evening. He didn't know why he had bothered to look. She rarely went out anywhere these days.

He had driven to the school, somewhat relieved to see her car in the parking lot. What was she doing here so late?

As he turned the corner in the corridor, he could see her room at the end of the hall in blackness. He headed instead for the staff room. Perhaps she was there. After a thorough search of the school failed to reveal her whereabouts, he returned to peer into the dark emptiness of her room.

"Ida? Ida, is that you?" he called softly as he narrowed his eyes trying to make out the shapeless shadow behind the desk. He flicked on the lights. "My god. It is you." His voice showed irritation. "What's wrong with you—sitting in the dark by yourself all this time?"

She didn't answer. Too weak to challenge him directly, she would do it the only way she believed she could. He had always been too powerful a persona for her, twisting and manipulating what she said, leaving her to feel her needs were unimportant. Worn down and defeated, she had simply withdrawn from the conflict that had become her daily life.

When she failed to respond to anyone or anything, hospitalization was decided upon. Her fear of abandonment had caused her to bottle up her rage year after year, believing it was not safe to express anger to those she loved. Instead she had turned the anger inward until now it completely immobilized her. In so doing, her goal had finally been achieved, giving her what she needed for survival. Her mental breakdown had freed her from living the agenda of another human being and, at the same time, guaranteed she would never face what she feared most—being left alone. She would always, as long as she remained ill, be surrounded by those who would do for her what she could no longer do for herself. Mission accomplished.

A shudder of recognition ran through Lexie. Mrs. Payne's story felt distrurbingly familiar.

Lexie clutched the warm coffee cup tightly in her cold hands, and as she paced over the hard, blackened surface of the playground area, her anxious thoughts swirled around in her head. Oblivious to the school children playing around her, she was caught up in her own pain. Over and over she relived the scene in her principal's office, wincing at the memory of her harsh words. How could they? How dare they think such things about her? The principal's blunt statements still smarted.

"The parents think you're not doing your job, Lexie. There's talk of launching a formal complaint with the board."

Reeling with shock, she hardly heard the list of specifics upon which the parents had based their complaints. Had she had the strength of belief in what she was doing, she would have systematically defended her methods. Instead, part of her shrivelled as her mind accepted there must be some basis for their unhappiness. For some time now, Lexie had desperately not wanted to be in a classroom, and it was obviously beginning to show.

This was the year Jade would graduate from St. Martyrs. The symbolism did not escape Lexie. Perhaps, it was time for them both to move on. As this last year had unfolded, Lexie had become progressively unhappy. Smiling less and less, she found her passion for learning fading as she taught the same subjects over again. Becoming more aware of the systemic shortcomings of the institution of education, Lexie faced daily the reality of her own ineffectiveness. She could never fix all the students in her care, take away their pain, or solve their problems. She spent her time applying simple anaemic, academic bandages to wounds she felt the system itself often inflicted.

Less convinced each day that the best interests of children was being served by classroom containment six hours a day, Lexie had an aching feeling there had to be a better way. She knew the rigidity of the school system had evolved to prepare children to function in a mechanized, industrialized society of time clocks and linear hierarchies of power, but as she watched young creativity often wither and die at the hands of teachers who told students what should be, Lexie often felt more like a jailer than an educator. The system originally created to facilitate the development of humankind now lived to propagate itself, becoming an insensitive, unresponsive bureaucracy defying dismantlement. It was not so much that there were no solutions that might inject life into the anaemic performance of many of the school system's students and teachers. The answers were there. It was just that no one asked the right questions. Many teachers, it seemed, had forgotten why they were there. Lured by the generous salary, ironclad job security, and the numerous holidays, many said teaching would be the perfect job except for one thing—the kids! It disheartened her, when policy decisions were being made, that the question most often neglected was, "What's best for the kids?"

Perhaps the lethargy and hopelessness Lexie saw in the system was a reflection of what lived in her mind. As she circled the playground, her eyes looking out over the children, but not really seeing them, a huge lump of frustration filled her. The stifling suffocation came welling up from the pit of her stomach tightening her throat, constricting her body, forming tearful pinpricks of self-pity behind her eyes. She had done the best she could, coming to work day after day to a dingy, dust-laden classroom, sacrificing her own happiness to stay in a place where she did not want to be and now this. What a slap in the face. How could they be so ungrateful after she had been so unselfish? If they didn't want her, if she wasn't good enough for them, she'd show them all. She'd leave.

As self-pitying tears spilled briefly out over her eyelids, she lifted her head, jutted out her chin in determination, and calling on all the invisible powers that be, spoke fervently into the grey, spring sky, "Lord, get me out of here! Just let me be free!"

Two weeks later she awoke one morning to find she could not move. So contorted in spasm were the muscles in her back that the effort to roll out of bed brought excruciating pain. Her desperate prayer had been answered, if not in a way she would have wanted. Imprisoned by her flesh, she had been set free.

There's an old saying that warns our feeble human race against the power of our own thoughts to create reality. Its wisdom entreats us to be careful what we pray for—we just might get it! Seeing no other way, Lexie's mind had engineered her desperately desired escape. What she would not do for herself, her body had done for her. The rumour was now circulating that Room C at St. Martyrs must be jinxed. The sudden, unfortunate departure of its last two occupants had not gone unnoticed.

The diagnosis was immediate. Lexie had suffered a ruptured disc in her spine. It was impossible to determine exactly when the injury had happened. Because Lexie had been so hard on herself physically over the years, working right alongside her husband lifting and carrying heavy objects, she was asked by her doctor, after he viewed her x-rays, if she had been working as a bricklayer in her spare time. Lexie was paying the price for her stubborn pride in being able to do almost anything a man could do.

To sit or stand for extended periods caused her unbearable pain. She was bedridden for several months as she awaited the procedure that would restore feeling in her right leg and alleviate her discomfort by removing the bulging spinal disc pressing on her sciatic nerve. Even with her world blurred by painkillers, Lexie nevertheless still tenaciously struggled to direct it. Sending countless instructions to her replacement as the school year drew to a close, Lexie also insisted that she was the only one able to prepare the final report cards on all her students. In her mind, no one could do them as well as she, and her students deserved an accurate appraisal of their year's work.

Propped up on pillows in her bed, a large plywood board resting on her knees to provide a flat working surface, she wrote all thirty reports by hand.

Even though she was scheduled for surgery immediately thereafter, she managed to be present to see Jade graduate and to wish all her students a safe summer holiday.

Lexie was not the only one who did not accept the limitations of her condition. Derek was furious. Unable to cope with the fact that his strong, capable wife could no longer be constantly by his side, he flew into a rage, unwilling to accept that she couldn't travel for three hours in a car and stay in a strange hotel room overnight to assist him in all his duties as best man at a friend's out-of-town wedding. Lexie had suffered through a sales conference at a resort two weeks before because he had insisted. Defying her doctor's orders for strict bed rest, she had forced herself to sit through long business lunch-eons and meetings, excusing herself often from the table, her face white with pain. Hopeful Derek would be sympathetic this time, she had expressed she had no desire to repeat the experience. Instead of understanding, he spewed out words of self-centred immaturity.

"You selfish bitch! I won't forget that you weren't there for me when I needed you! You can go to hell for all I care!"

With that he peeled out of the driveway and left Lexie standing, mortified, too numb to even cry.

Her body healed, but Derek's words left a wound. He had made it very clear he had no patience with a wife who was less than perfect, a liability rather than an asset. Sickness, as far as Derek was concerned, was something that only befell the weak. He, himself, was never ill. He would not allow it.

To be incapacitated and at the mercy of your body's inability to respond was a revelation for she, too, had always taken her good health for granted. Her body was speaking to her now, and she was getting the message that without her health all else would fade into insignifi-cance. Would life be worth living? It was a question she hoped never to have to face, and she vowed that if she was restored to her former vigour, she would revere and care for her physical well-being.

With Lexie's illness came compassion for anyone encased in a physical body that did not allow the full range of human experience and an appreciation for the daily heroism required of anyone who is disabled. Also for those dedicated to the art of healing, she learned a profound sense of gratitude

Encountering many healers, some effective and some in need of healing themselves, perhaps it was more good luck than good management that she made her way through the treatment process and came out on the other side whole and well. The whole experience was bewildering, painful, and frightening, but what other options did she have? Because she did not intend to spend the rest of her days lying flat in bed pumped full of mind-numbing drugs, Lexie handed her broken body over once again to doctors.

A specialist diagnosed her condition and recommended a very new, but highly effective procedure rather than traditional surgery. It involved injecting the ruptured disc with a chemical much like a meat tenderizer. It would simply dissolve the disc allowing the two vertebrae to fuse and thus removing the pressure on the nerve. Patients usually felt relief within a few hours. It sounded like an appealing alternative, and Lexie agreed. The doctor then informed her she would first be subjected to a test known as a myelogram. What he failed to tell her was that she could suffer painful side effects and that she would have to be completely awake during the entire procedure for a very important reason.

The myelogram went well enough considering that a long needle pierced her vulnerable spinal column sending a dye into it. The aftermath of the test became the problem; Lexie could not sit or stand or in any way deviate from a horizontal position without feeling as if the top of her head was about to lift off. The headache was excruciating, and each time she rolled over to retch, she seriously considered death might be a viable alternative. Finally in desperation after days of this, she agreed to go into the emergency ward to have another procedure done. This one was designed to equalize the pressure of fluids in the spinal column and end her headache. Lexie knew she was in trouble when the nurse who was standing beside her stretcher glanced at her nervously. Lexie had been prepared for the procedure and now waited for the doctor on call to perform it. Assured he was capable, nevertheless, one look into his eyes sent a shiver of apprehension through her. His pupils were so dilated it was like looking into two deep, black holes.

"My god," thought Lexie. "This guy is wired on drugs!"

Having heard the stories of how many doctors used chemical stimulants to keep up with the demands of their job, there was absolutely no doubt in her mind she was about to let a doctor who was high inject her spinal column with a potentially paralysing, three inch needle. She knew enough about these things to know that if he missed his mark, she could suffer paralysis.

As he nervously paced the room asking the nurse several times where things were, the doctor revealed that he was definitely in a highly hyper state. Lexie looked up questioningly into the nurse's face, but she only shrugged her shoulders as if to say there was nothing she could do. She then clasped Lexie's hands in her own and instructed her to curl up into a tight little ball. As Lexie brought her knees up under her chin, she squeezed her eyes shut and prayed.

With a sharp jab the needle entered, then she felt the release as it pulled clear. The nurse rolled her over and smiled as she helped her into a sitting position. Wonder of wonders! She could still move and the headache was gone. Lexie said a silent thank you under her breath, not stopping to dwell on the fact that, once again, she had passively handed herself over, willing to risk her physical well-being rather than create a scene. She could have become a cripple that day, but at least she had been polite.

Now she would prepare herself for another date with another doctor bearing yet another long silver needle.

He informed her as he slid the sheet partially off her naked body that he had only done three of these procedures before and thus had another doctor, an expert, with him to assist. This did not exactly inspire more confidence as she lay on her side on a stretcher in the brightly lit room, her bare back to the two gowned and gloved doctors. Above her head was a complicated setup of television screens and computer hardware. Told she would be awake during the entire operation, she was encouraged to watch its progress on the screen above her head. What she was not told was the critical reason she needed to remain awake. Only later, did she learn of the small percentage of patients who had an immediate allergic reaction to this chemical injection and went into cardiac arrest. The patient had to be kept awake as any use of any anaesthetic would only endanger recovery.

The doctors standing behind her discussing her condition had fallen into a strange silence as they slid the sheet further off her body. Their eyes roaming her back, an air of uneasiness settled over the room, until finally the nurse pulled the sheet over Lexie's legs and on up to again cover most of her body. At that point, her doctor cleared his throat, picked up an instrument and preparing to begin said sheepishly, "Bit of erotica right here in the operating room, eh?"

The nurse shot her an understanding look, and Lexie was grateful for her considerate act. *How could they be thinking of sex at a time like this?* she wondered. *Men were indeed strange creatures. Did they really think a sexual thought three times a minute as the research said?*

As the needle entered her body, she watched its path on the screen, not needing to be told when it found the ruptured disc. Her body jerked wildly up off the table as a searing pain ripped through her. They held her down, the doctor saying, "That's what we needed to see! We've got the right one now!"

It was all over in a matter of minutes, and Lexie was wheeled into recovery where a series of regular painkilling injections was started. Without them, all the muscles in her back would go into spasm causing extreme pain. The good news, however, was that she had feeling in her right leg again.

Ladies in white padded softly into her room every four hours, rolled her over and injected her flesh with vials of pain-reducing chemicals. Soon her buttocks were sore to the touch, and the nurses had to search for new target areas. Lexie lay like a leaden slug in her bed, with little desire to eat or drink, wishing only to remain in her drug-induced haze, free of all pain.

Struggling to the surface of consciousness as day blurred into night, encased in darkness, fear enveloped her as it seemed no different if her eyes were open or closed—she was floating in a black void. Wide-eyed panic set in as her body failed to respond to the thought, *Raise your arm, Lexie. Ring for the nurse, Lexie.* Instead, she lay motionless below. An undulating, dark tunnel like a silent, whirring tornado pulled her deeper into its blackness drawing her ever closer to a small patch of white shimmering at its end. Then like a newborn thrust into the world, light and sound exploded around her, as if it had always been there, awaiting only her awareness to bring to life a blindingly brilliant scene long forgotten. Drawn down, down, down until, with a start, she realized she was looking out through the hazel eyes of a young, blonde, fair-skinned girl sitting in a choir docket, adorned in white ribbons and a frilly dress singing out with all the passion of a pure, young heart. At once she knew where she was.

Gazing down on the congregation through twelve-year-old eyes, she was in church, singing in the choir. She had loved to be there, her body resonating with the rich, deeply melodic tones of the organ. Unself-consciously she had sung, expressing a burgeoning love of life. Each time she looked out over the other singing souls bathed as they were in the rippling, iridescent, coloured patterns of stained-glass-windowed sunlight, she would be uplifted, nourished, and sustained by a sense of something greater than she.

She came here because her parents did, but she sang because she loved how it made her feel. Thriving on the stories in the softly bound leather book that told of justice, bravery, and noble acts of self-sacrificing courage, this was a world she could love - a world where goodness and patience were rewarded, where there was always someone who would protect you.

When she was alone in the church, she would sit for many long minutes gazing at the man in the portrait. She was drawn into the kind, liquid eyes which seemed to know about the pain of this world and yet accepted it, knowing it for what it was. A calm steadiness radiated from that strong, gentle face, framed as it was with a glowing halo of soft hair. It took her breath away to look into those knowing eyes and filled her with a longing to place her hand in his. This man had walked the earth long before, yet his presence lived and breathed in the quiet solitude of this tiny, country church. She came to clean it each Saturday, and she sat in quiet communion with someone who became a special friend. One who had championed the small, insignificant, wounded, and worried of the world. In her child's understanding of things, this kind, gentle man was the rescuer who brought swift, noble justice when the bullies of the world descended. That was how Lexie chose to see him, anyhow. He was her Saviour, there to protect and guide her. Inspired to be like Him, Lexie had felt she was connected to what He was. Had the seeds of His potential been sown in every human being? Had He walked among humankind to demonstrate how to unlock the spiritual potential in each of us? Had He been one of the greatest teachers who had ever walked our earth? Lexie had believed so.

It is said that when the student is ready, the teacher appears. Lexie as a child had been an eager pupil, intuitively understanding the power of unseen energies within - energies that allowed the boundaries of self to blur, as consciousness stood still in a timeless emptiness full of the pulsing beat of life. As a teachable child, she had known that she was not alone, that she was connected by the very rhythm of her own breathing, moving in and out of all that was. Now, as a spiritually arrogant and forgetful adult, she had been humbled enough to allow herself to once again remember. The teacher had become teachable.

As the hymn built to its crescendo, Lexie knew she was about to step back into that tunnel of time and leave her childish body behind. She had been sent on a journey of remembering to renew an old acquaintance and breathe life back into a body and soul wearied by the weight of worldly existence.

She awoke to the cheery good morning of the nurse and the sound of breakfast trays clattering in the hall. This day looked, sounded, and felt brighter than many, many before it.

Her journey had left her changed. A new strand had been woven into her tapestry, its presence a wash of sunlight on a dreary day. Changing her perception, the experience gave new meaning and brought into sharp, clear focus the magnitude of the simple gifts she had to offer. She could make a difference in the young lives around her. She was not *just* a teacher. She realized the greatest contributions are not always made with fanfare, but can often be given quietly, consistently over time. This new thread, strong as steel, soft as silk, came from her simple gratitude at being alive and able to return to her livelihood, to earn her own way in life. Healed physically and spiritually, she took up the job in her bright new school with enthusiasm, determined to be the best teacher she knew how. Like a prodigal, she was welcomed with open arms. The more love and dedication she poured out, the more she received. Soon she was one of the most loved and respected teachers in the school.

Learning to let go and trust that events were unfolding as they should, Lexie gave more power to her students to shape their own learning experiences, and their creativity blossomed, spilling over from her classroom into all areas. The incredible ability of children to create, solve problem, and have compassion for one another never ceased to amaze her. Her room became an oasis of music, art, literature, and geography visited through books and maps; Lexie also discussed and debated morals and values with the children. The greenery of plants, the comfort of carpets, and the beckoning security of an old, worn chesterfield filled her room, which was flooded with the soft glow of lamplight as the harsh overhead lights were snapped off. Insecurities and false facades of rude, obnoxious twelve years olds seemed to melt away as they stepped into her welcoming classroom.

The first order of learning was to make this room, their room, a safe place to be. A place where all were accepted just as they were, no matter how they performed. Here, in their secret and confidential diaries, they could share with their teacher all the dark torments of their budding teenage world—a world fraught with self-doubt. Lexie, when invited to read their deepest feelings, never condemned nor evaluated, but often asked the very questions they needed to ask themselves. They usually carried their answers within them, she simply facilitated their discovery.

It seemed ironic that everything had climaxed in a rupture of her physical support system, her back. She had felt as if the weight of the world had been upon her. Often the words had run through her mind, *If only I could get out from under. If only I could get other people's expectations off my back!*

Yet now, by allowing herself to acknowledge her own weakness and to be vulnerable, she had opened herself up to receiving support. As Lexie removed herself as the controller of all that had to happen, a new dynamic began to emerge. As a teacher, she got out of her own way, and in so doing she pulled forth all that was loving and capable from her students. By allowing them to help her, she empowered them. The dynamic became one of mutual respect and caring. If there were days when she felt less capable, tired or worn out, she admitted it to them openly asking for their help instead of hiding her weakness beneath a mask of stern authority. Grateful to be able to give to her, they always came through. Those were the days she would hear them say to one another, "Can't you be quieter? Don't you know Mrs. G.'s not feeling well?"

Their days together began and ended peacefully in quiet reflection and simple prayer. Each day a different student opened their time together by reading a short piece of Scripture and then proceeded to tell what it meant in his or her life. Often the beginning of the day's first class was delayed as eager twelve year olds grappled with the concepts of justice and morality. Then all would settle for a few quiet moments to explore how others saw their world. They would explore the world through books, magazines, newspapers, filmstrips, the writings of another student, whatever form of communication they chose. The only requirement was that it be done unobtrusively, allowing everyone the opportunity to settle comfortably, undis- turbed, into the vast world of the word.

It was a ritual all looked forward to and revered. For twenty minutes each day, everyone in that room settled into the peaceful pursuit of sharing another's mind through the magic of print. They were free to travel in space and time, the only passport being the active imaging of their minds. They sat or sprawled, all connected in a bond of consciousness, yet each separate, as the clock peacefully measured off the ticks of time.

Day was ended with quiet reflection upon the prayerful request penned by a humble Bible scholar, "Grant that we may not so much seek to be understood, as to understand."

For Lexie this seemed to sum up a great paradox. When we cease our struggle to control everything in our life, our life suddenly becomes more manageable. Turning within, trusting that still, small voice, handing over the illusion of control, brought peace. Perhaps to understand our world, we must first understand ourselves, and to master our world, we must first master ourselves. Had truth seekers long ago stumbled upon this simple truth? Was it no accident that the ancient Greeks, the harbingers of great wisdom, had carved such simple words above their temple at Delphi? "KNOW THYSELF." Did they believe the gateway to all knowledge lay through self- knowledge? Are we simply a microcosm of all that is, the mirrored patterning of the universe within the very atoms of our being?

As Lexie had embraced gratitude, she had then experienced so much more to be grateful for. Rejoicing now as she led her students in discovery, she watched as their world grew ever fuller, their lenses of perception ever expanding. To know yourself more fully is to know more of everything. As we close our senses to something, it ceases to exist for us. Life strives to collect and store experience like a vessel collects and stores its contents, but perception is the valve of admittance.

Her new attitude of gratitude allowed her to move more easily in her world. As she shook her fist less and less at the inequities of life, she found her world less clouded by black hopelessness. To resist is to suffer. Repeatedly, she had thrown herself against the walls of her perceived prison only to be broken down by them. In her stubborn refusal to take the keys of freedom into her own hands, she instead had looked out through her self-imposed bars of limitation to shake an accusing finger at everyone and everything else upon which she heaped the anger and the frustration called blame. Becoming a prisoner of her own rigid, entrenched, self-defeating thinking, she had built such a burden of self-abandonment that its weight had literally broken her back.

Moving into acceptance, but sadly, not the true liberation of taking full responsibility for herself, she now looked at her prison with new eyes, seeing what there was to be grateful for, but still focussing on the bars and not the spaces. As a result, it became a softer, easier jail, but still a jail, for she was not yet ready to see that change could set her free. It was true, she suffered less, because she resisted less. She had moved into acceptance, but it was the ultimately self-defeating acceptance of her imprisonment.

Her job became a living oasis as life in the Gaust household became even more barren. Derek had not changed. He remained cold, distant, and judgmental. Jessica had moved away to attend her first year of university and Jade, bereft at the loss of her sister's company, had gone away too—if only to her bedroom. There she stayed, isolated, rarely coming out to interact with Lexie or Derek.

They all had become somewhat accustomed to Jessica's absences as she had been going away every summer for the past three years to work, eager to experience life away from her controlled home life. Jade had simply chosen another route of escape. Although present, she spent most of her time locked in her own world sharing little with her parents.

With Jessica's departure, it was as if an invisible hand had reached out and removed one of the family figures from a delicately balanced mobile. The remaining figures were left to bob wildly around seeking a new equilibrium, and a whole new set of family dynamics began to emerge. With her sweet-tempered, pleasing daughter gone, there was no one Lexie could turn to for unconditional love and understanding. Jessica had been her confidant, the one she had often complained to about Derek's nastiness, the one she had conspired with to keep secrets from the self-declared head of the household. Jessica had been her supportive ally. Jade could not, would not, fill that role for her. Being more like her father, self-contained and less expressive, she had no desire to nurture her mother. They became like a wind chime suspended, its rough porcelain figures bumping and scraping against one another, trapped and meshed by the ties that bind, yet suspended at different levels of understanding, unable to touch or connect for more than the briefest of moments, buffeted by the unvoiced resentments between them, they bumped, hard surface against hard surface, only to spin away from one another in confused bewilderment. Lexie knew something was terribly wrong. What she did not know was how to fix it. Rarely did they take meals together any more. When the three of them did have a meal together, both parents spent the whole time trying to pry information out of Jade about her school and social life. Lexie desperately wanted the charade of the happy family, but Jade refused to live the lie. Her terse, limited responses ran the gamut of, "No," "Nothing," "I don't care," and when asked how she was feeling, an emphatic, clenched-toothed, "Fine!"

As both parents no longer had Jessica, their firstborn, to focus their attention upon, Jade became the new recipient of their compulsive need to control. Unable to cope, Jade withdrew further into herself and what Lexie had not seen before now became glaringly obvious to her. Her youngest child was deeply depressed.

Wading once again into the river of denial, she convinced herself Jade was simply pining for her sister. There was an element of truth in this, and thus Lexie didn't delve any deeper. She could have asked why the bond between the two siblings was so incredibly strong, but she didn't. Lexie had taken great pride in the fact that her two daughters had rarely fought; that they spent a great deal of time in one another's company even though there was nearly a five-year age difference. Jessica was also very protective of her younger sister. Had she asked herself, she might have arrived at an answer. These two, as frightened young girls, had banded together against an external force—someone they perceived as a threat.

CHAPTER TWENTY:

YOU MAKE ME SICK!

Put it in. Take it out.
Purge. Purge.
That's the urge.
What's unclean within me
I know not.
God, help me! I can not stop!
For my body I must control.
Slender of waist, flat of breast,
My body's growth I must arrest.
I dare not express the woman within, without.

Daily my secret claws and shouts,
Silenced and gagged,
It struggles to get out.
The watchful warden of denial
My pain, its cause, has jailed
Within a secret, internal vault.
Yet, can all this be, comes the whisper,
The result of another's fault?
My body destined to win
In its self-destructive drive to disappear.
My only hope of salvation to be,

Facing the memories that live
Hidden within my fear!

Lexie was watching the movement of her daughter's mouth, but she was hearing only the roaring rush of her pulse past her ears. Sitting across the table from Jessica, Lexie let her daughter's words bounce off the hard protective shell of denial forming around her. This can't be true! I can't be hearing this! This can't be happening!

As the sounds came at her, relentless in their need to be accepted, Lexie could feel her insides turning in on themselves. Her body twisted like a corkscrew, every drop of life was being wrung out of it. Bile built and burned in her throat. The urge to vomit became overwhelming. She wanted to run, to purge, to rid herself of this horrible knowledge, to be anywhere but seated at the other side of the table, listening to her daughter's words.

"Mom, I don't know how to tell you this. I'm so scared, Mom. I have to tell someone. I'm frightened by what I'm doing to myself. I can't stop it, Mom. It's like it takes me over, takes control, you know. Every time I do it, I promise myself I'll never do it again, and then I find myself right back there, doing it. Mom. I'm frightened, really scared. What I'm doing isn't normal. I know that. I just don't know what else to do."

Jessica sucked in her breath and charged on in her confession before her mother's comforting responses could silence it. If she allowed her mother to speak before the horrible secret was completely revealed, Jessica knew she would clutch at her warm sympathy, receiving reassurances that she was indeed all right; that nothing she could ever do could be that bad, and she would miss the window of opportunity her fierce sense of self-preservation had now wedged open. She must not slip again beneath the calm, unruffled surface of denial.

Instead, she plunged on into the icy water of truth. If anyone was going to throw her a life raft it had to be one made of more than empty platitudes minimizing this secret obsession which had tortured her now for over three years.

The summer she was seventeen, it had begun. Ecstatic at obtaining a job at one of the beautiful, northern Ontario provincial parks, she was looking forward to the sun-filled days outdoors, the laid-back, quiet pace of life in a northern town, and most of all, the freedom from critical parental eyes.

At seventeen, Jessica was herself a sun-bronzed wood nymph, tall, slender, somewhat boyish of figure, small of breasts and hips, with a mop of sandy blonde hair crowning a face with unusual almond-shaped blue eyes, an upturned nose and a brilliant splash of white teeth under full, pouting lips. Combining her mother's prettiness with her father's inscrutable air of mystery, Jessica's looks had been unique enough to warrant the interest of the modelling agency Lexie had taken her to.

Mother Nature had other plans, however, for at the age seventeen, Jessica's face had erupted in angry red bumps. The acne had arrived along with health problems which all stemmed from the lower half of her body. Her previously painless menstrual periods now became occasions for excruciating discomfort and embarrassing fainting spells. Calls from the high school informing Lexie that her daughter had once again passed out in the washroom became almost as commonplace as the calls she had received about her young daughter vomiting in the day care centre. In both instances Jessica seemed to recover rapidly with very few aftereffects. In fact the processes of vomiting and fainting both seemed to alleviate her distress.

Nevertheless, from that age onward, Jessica experienced one health challenge after another. She went from infection to infection, depending more and more on the use of antibiotics to balance her system. Lexie put it all down to the growing pains of adolescence. No one, especially Jessica, recognized it for what it was. Her body was in open revolt, a silent war raging inside of her.

Seemingly unaffected, denying that there was anything unusual about her frequent illnesses, Jessica continued to live out the life of the perfect teenager. Accepting that the prospect of a modelling career was remote even if she had wanted it, she concentrated instead on her social life, boys, school work, boys, piano lessons, boys, dance lessons, boys, and all the other things a normal seventeen-year-old girl is supposed to be interested in. Lexie admired the way, that even with her face in full bloom, Jessica never slowed down. She was always the extrovert, forming around her a tightly knit group of other beautiful girls who rapidly became the barometer of what was "in" and accepted at their high school. Where her mother had been on the outside looking in, unable to afford the price of admission, Jessica was given all the material things needed to create the illusion of worth. Beautiful clothes draped over a beautiful body, a beautiful home in the right part of town, friends who had been with her from preschool — all these things combined with a flashing smile and a bubbly, sincere interest in the feelings of others made for a winning combination.

Up to this point, Lexie had been able to observe her one daughter's bubbling popularity, and her other daughter's budding beauty as she had dutifully chauffeured them from one extra-curricular event to another and had convinced herself they truly were the model family. All of them were certainly pleasing to look at with all the trappings of wealth doing all the things required of successful families ranging from community involvement to expensive vacations in exotic places. They hosted parties boosting their daughters' popularity further as their guests splashed and sunned around their swimming pool. On the surface it appeared the Gaust family could have substituted for the characters in any of the many popular television shows depicting perfect family life. Lexie, always perfectly groomed and coiffed, the smiling dispenser of emotional support; Derek, stern and silent, the undisputed head of the household; and Jessica, secure and accepted older sibling, acting protectively towards Jade who was struggling awkwardly into adolescence. They played out their roles as carefully as if they had been scripted for them. Without the script's direction, they would not know how to act. Locked in their roles for so long now, they struggled to know the person behind the character they had created, their perfect images as false and without substance as the two-dimensional characters in a television drama.

Jessica rarely came home the summer she was seventeen, enjoying instead the raucous, freewheeling social life of barracks living. Employees' quarters were shared by both males and females and supposedly chaperoned by older supervisors who also lived on the grounds. Jessica shared a room the size of a closet with one of her closest friends from the city and appeared to be having the time of her life.

In many ways ignorance can be bliss; because she was not confronted directly with Jessica's behaviour, Lexie was freed from the pressure to direct and control it. She was quite sure her daughter was sampling more of life's pleasures than she might have preferred, however, she also knew attempts to stifle the process of an adolescent reaching for adulthood would have about as much success as trying to prevent a seedling from reaching for the sun. The process could be postponed, but not prevented.

When Jessica had returned home that fall to complete her final year of high school, Lexie had noticed her usually slender daughter had gained weight. She put it down to a diet of calorie-laden junk food and thought nothing of it. Derek, however, made quite a bit more if it. He had been Lexie's self-appointed diet agent for years, and now he took it upon himself to perform the same function for Jessica. Being one of those individuals who could eat all he wanted and never gain weight, he enjoyed a smug air of superiority, unable to understand anyone who fought the battle of the bulge. He made no secret of the fact that he found heavy women extremely unappealing.

"You know how Dad feels about anyone who's fat, Mom. I just couldn't stand his constant remarks!"

Jessica's statement jolted Lexie back to the present. Now, once again, she remembered the horror of what she had heard her daughter say.

Playing the words back in her head, she hesitated. What was the phrase with which her beautiful, young daughter had turned her mother's world upside down?

"I make myself sick everyday now, Mom."

Yes, that had been it. Short, simple, and devastating. She envisioned her daughter at the toilet, sticking her fingers down her throat, her body contorting in retching spasms, spewing up the food consumed only a few moments before.

"The first time I did it, I didn't think it was any big deal. We had been stuffing ourselves on pizza, and I felt so bloated, so fat, so ugly that I remembered I'd heard one of the other girls mention what she did to get rid of that feeling, so I thought, *Why not try it this once?* Some of the other girls did it once in a while; I knew that. It seemed like such an easy solution. Pig out, throw up, stay thin. Easy!

"I got to like it, Mom. I got to like the way it made me feel. I felt so empty, so light, so free after I did it, and I liked the way my body looked."

It was true. Jessica had lost weight rapidly after that first summer away and now for the first time in a long time, Lexie allowed herself to really look. Jessica sat dressed in what had become her uniform—large, oversized baggy clothing with her sweatshirt nearly to her knees, hanging over equally lose-fitting pants. Lexie had just believed her daughter was shy about her body and that was why she had never worn revealing clothes. It had started young, these camou-flaging dressing habits. From the first days they had the swimming pool, Lexie remembered, Jessica had always covered her bathing suit with a baggy T-shirt. Her extreme modesty had become so accepted, everyone around her ceased to comment on the healthy young girl who refused to draw attention to her slender, attractive body.

Lexie did admit that, on the occasions when she had hugged her daughter, she had been appalled to feel bone so close to the surface of her flesh. It was with shame that she remembered herself then thinking, "It's better she's a little too thin than the other way. I'm so glad she doesn't struggle with being fat."

You can never be too rich or too thin. Those were the values so many lived by. Had Jessica become a victim, sacrificing her health on the altar of society's definition of beauty?

In stunned disbelief, Lexie had listened as her daughter's confession came spilling out. Like a sleepwalker now suddenly shaken awake, she cleared her throat, focused her attention on her daughter, and began to search for her words. Slowly, she swallowed, her lips began to move, and the first sounds of speech rattled in her throat. Drawing from a deep pool of unquestioning love for her daughter, Lexie fought for the strength to respond.

Shakily, she began, "Jessica, you need help with this. We need help with this. This is too big for either of us to handle alone. I'm so grateful you trusted me enough to come to me. Sweetheart, it's going to be all right. Don't worry. We'll get you help." Staring blankly, Jessica did not cry, nor did she move. It was as if she was no longer present. Even as Lexie enfolded her thin body, wrapping her protective motherly arms about her, Jessica remained mute and motionless, tears beyond her reach. Drained emotionally, she longed to slip back into denial, to pretend she had told someone else's story. She could handle just so much truth on one day.

"I'll go through the counselling service at work, Jessica. I know they will recommend someone competent, and it will be kept strictly confidential. I'll call first thing tomorrow." Lexie was rocking gently back and forth cradling her child in her arms like a baby. "It'll be all right, honey. You'll see. You'll see. You're strong. You can get over this. You can do it, I know you can."

Lexie pulled away to look at her unresponsive child. Looking her daughter directly in the face, she said, her voice filled with concern, "Are you all right, Jess?"

Silently, she nodded her head. What else could she do? What words could express the insanity of what she had been doing? Her behaviour could lead to her obliteration. Yet she could not prevent herself from being compelled to do it again and again. Was it that possessing the potential power of self-destruction was the only thing that kept her alive? Did having control over life and death, deciding to feed or starve her body, give her ultimate power over it? Dictating what stayed in it, did that make her master over her own body? Was to vomit to have control?

Having shared her horrible secret, fear now paralysed her. Without this power, would she indeed choose not to live? Was the umbilical-like thread of her mother's love enough to keep her from purging herself into oblivion or would it snap under the strain of her secret guilt? Could their connection survive the all-consuming self-loathing threatening to crush the very life out of her? She did not understand why or how it had come about. She only knew an ugliness inside her was satisfied only when it clawed its way up her throat and out. In that brief moment of release, she felt purified. If that now stopped, where would she put the shame?

This all-pervading, numbing shame had propelled her to live away from home as much as she could. Living in a small university town now, she was in her second year, studying for her degree in psychology. For a child who had struggled academically, it had seemed impossible that she would realize her dream of attending university. Through sheer will, diligently working late into the night on assignments, she had pulled off the required grades. Lexie, too, had been involved in her success story, challenging the academic bureaucracy more than once on behalf of her child.

Bubbly, friendly Jessica to her friends, she rapidly became a withdrawn, silent, submissive individual when confronted by authority figures. Teachers often mistook this for lack of ability, and Jessica had consequently been overlooked by many of them. This had caused problems more than once for her. Jessica had been in danger of failing her grade three year, and Lexie had gone charging in determined to rescue her child from this fate. After listening to all the reasons, she emphatically refused to allow it. As a teacher herself, she knew she did not actually have the power to dictate the promotion policy, but she also knew if she made it difficult enough for them, the school would reconsider. With a promise made to tutor her own daughter, Lexie had left with the assurance that Jessica would move on with the rest of her classmates. A twinge of guilt came over her at the memory of her daughter's brush with failure. It was the year she had worked at the Red Cloud Lounge, a difficult year for all of them.

It seemed easy to fight for her children. Lexie, could at times, be fierce in the face of an injustice done to one she loved, understanding as she did, that children were often treated like nameless, faceless commodities in our society. Some adults even considered children invisible, stepping in front of them in lineups, refusing to serve them in their turn, waiting instead on the adults present, and ordering children in their charge around as if they had no right to refuse whatever was asked of them. Children—seen but not heard—that was the motto many adults still used.

Her daughters told her of the rudeness often experienced at the hands of adults when they shopped or ran errands on their own. No more than children in big bodies, some adults took the frustration of their own powerlessness out on those who could not fight back, enjoying the opportunity to feel superior to someone, anyone.

How could she not have seen her child's anguish before this? How could this have happened? She thought she had been a good mother. Perfect mothering would produce perfect children, wouldn't it? Hadn't she done everything right, reading all the parenting books, treating her children with loving respect and giving them every advantage, as well as providing for all their physical needs? Where had she gone wrong? She knew that at times her focus had been elsewhere, that at times she had been distracted, but she also knew she had done the very best with what she knew. How then had this horror happened?

Finally, she found the right question and like a loose thread on a hem, as Lexie tugged at it for clues, loop after loop came undone, leaving her with a string of clues and a final, inescapable conclusion.

Having hidden her feelings so well, she had convinced herself her unhappiness rarely showed. Were not she and Derek a happily married couple as far as her children were concerned? Taking great care never to ague with Derek, she had taken his cruel, sniping comments in stride, either appearing to ignore them or laughing them off. No one, she believed, saw her anguish. Only later, her sobs hidden by the splashing of the shower, would she cry. Never actively showing displeasure with Derek, instead she appeared kind, loving, and patient with his immature outbursts, always calming and soothing his ruffled emotions. The peacemaker of the family, Lexie prided herself that on the surface, her family ran smoothly. The children rarely challenged Derek's authority, and if they did, Lexie was always there to soften his punishments. Deceived by her denial, she chose to believe her children seemed happy. Derek was happy. What did it matter if she wasn't? There must be something wrong with her. A weakness, a flaw which caused her to walk around each day with a gaping gash of unhappiness, a source of actual physical pain, a feeling she was open, raw, and vulnerable. Hadn't her depression been a small price to pay to keep her family intact?

But this! A child does not throw up every day into a toilet unless something is horribly wrong. That fact had hit her square in the face. There was no running from, no minimizing this one. Her child was in danger. Now, nothing would stop her from looking, from knowing why. Frozen emotions were finally about to thaw, drop by painful drop, a river of healing tears.

Lexie pushed her foot down hard on the accelerator, merging her car with the expressway traffic heading north, going where you can always find answers when you need them.

Her mother had picked up the phone when Lexie called, listening quietly as the secret had been told. In that strange way of knowing that Lexie had, she sensed her mother held a key.

They sat at the kitchen table talking late into that first night. Her parents had moved back to the northern town of their roots, her father retiring to build the country homestead of his dreams. Creating something out of nothing, they had bulldozed a road deep into the bush and built their cedar-plank and fieldstone home on a piece of land bequeathed by Lexie's grandfather, a hundred-acre parcel from an original homesteader's grant. Lexie's father felt great pride when the newly created road leading into it was named in honour of his family. Alexander Road wound lazily over its short distance to end abruptly in the front yard of the new homestead.

There, in their country kitchen, Lexie's parents breakfasted with people from all over the world. Her mother had always had a talent for working with food and her savoury home cooking along with homemade jams and jellies, honey from her apiary, freshly baked muffins, and farm-fresh eggs made her newly opened bed and break-fast business flourish. It seemed fitting that her mother should now earn a living doing what she always did so well. Her kitchen table, well-worn teapot, and sympathetic ear had for years acted like a magnet drawing people.

No different now, the teapot was there as was the sympathetic ear. When Lexie had finished pouring out her heart, her mother said simply, "Lexie, there's something you should know."

"After you were born, I was anorexic. I didn't bother to eat, I just lived on cigarettes and cola. You probably don't remember, but it was when we were working so hard at the taxi business. I just put it down at the time to the stress of overwork. Looking back now, I know my problem with food went even further back than that. As a teenager, I used to throw up in the outhouse on the farm. No one ever talked about such things back then. I had no way of knowing anything about the horrible sense of shame I felt, and the way I was choosing to deal with it. Things eased up a lot when I met and married your father. He was six years older than me and it was a good thing. I was only eighteen, and he needed the patience of a saint to put up with my wild mood swings. I'd get so depressed sometimes, and I didn't know why. All I knew was if I didn't eat, I felt in control."

She took a deep breath and laughed. Lexie was looking at her strangely. "I know, I know. I don't look like someone who never ate do I?" You only remember your mother with her bulges don't you?" With that she patted the generous roundness of her middle.

"After your sister Celine was born and your father was spending so much time away, I discovered food could be my friend. I know I used to excuse my weight saying I just never lost what I put on with my pregnancies, but the truth was I ate for comfort. I ate when I missed your father, I ate when I was angry, I ate when I was depressed, and I was depressed when I ate. Soon I was eating all the time, often not knowing what I was feeling. What scared me most of all was that most of the time, I didn't feel anything at all."

She sighed and went on. "Don't you remember the diet roller coaster I was on? I must have tried every food plan, organization, and club out there! Even with my kitchen jammed with weight-loss products, I was still fat most of the time. Not only was my relentless pursuit of diets not helping, it was giving me exactly what I needed—an excuse to focus on the thing I had come to depend on above all else—food. It became my drug of choice."

She threw back her head in a chuckle, "There was one benefit of my compulsive fascination." She paused. "I became a great cook, and you kids always ate well!"

It was true, Lexie reflected. When living at home, everyone in the family had wrestled with weight problems. The trouble had been the temptation of bulging cupboards, home-baked deserts, and a freezer always stocked with a stash of forbidden goodies supposedly for company. When they had all in their turn raided this secret supply, they had found the comforting presence of a rich chocolate brownie or syrupy-sweet butter tart good company indeed.

Lexie had just accepted the fact that her mother was overweight—most were in those days. If a woman was in her forties, no one realistically expected her to have a good figure. It just wouldn't have been motherly.

"Do you remember about five years ago when your father and I went to Florida with your Aunt Susan?" her mother asked, and Lexie nodded. "Well, that was when I was at my heaviest. I had managed to reach over two hundred pounds."

Lexie was shocked. She never would have believed her mother could have weighed that much. She had hidden it well.

"Well, that's when I realized I had a problem. A problem no diet was ever going to fix. What was wrong with me went much deeper than calorie counters and weigh-ins could ever correct. It was your aunt I have to thank for shocking me out my destructive behaviour. I was living only to eat, literally digging my grave with my teeth!"

"What did she say that made such a difference?" Lexie was curious.

"It wasn't so much what she said as the fact that she had to say it. I was busy dragging her into yet another restaurant, planning our trip according to where we would eat next, not even finishing one meal before planning the next, when she finally stopped dead in her tracks and said in exasperation, "All I've seen in Florida on this bloody trip is the inside of restaurants! You, Emily Alexander, have a problem with food. Get yourself some help and do it quick before you're too fat to even waddle around in your own kitchen!"

"Wow! That must have hurt!" Lexie was aghast at her aunt's honesty.

"Yes, it wasn't much fun, but after the shock of it, I was forced to admit she was right. I needed help. Nothing I had ever tried before had worked. I had to go in a new direction. Rather than treating the symptom of overeating, I had to look for the cause. What drove me to eat, even when I knew the self-loathing my shapeless body would cause? I couldn't stop what I was doing. Food was in the driver's seat, and I was out of control!"

"Is that when you started that support group?" Lexie knew her mother had been the first in her area to start a group for overeaters based on the twelve-step programme of Alcoholics Anonymous.

"It worked where everything else failed, Lexie. I had to admit I was powerless over food just as an alcoholic has to admit he or she is powerless over alcohol. The alcoholics have one advantage over us, though—they don't have to ingest their addictive substance daily in order to stay alive. They are free to put the bottle down and never pick it up again, but we face our monster three times a day, everyday."

"So, how does this work?" Lexie was intrigued by this concept of powerlessness. It was one she knew well.

"Better to show than to tell. There's a meeting tomorrow. Why don't you stay?"

She came away from her visit with as much of an answer as she was ready for, seeing how admitting you needed help was the first step in healing. Impressed by the simple, commonsense wisdom she heard in the meeting room, the door of her mind had been wedged open a crack. Not yet ready to see how her own life was coloured by an unhealthy addiction, she came away convinced it was only her daughter who needed the love and support offered in such rooms. She would talk to Jessica. Joining a support group surely couldn't hurt, could it? In her naivete Lexie didn't recognize that the process was designed for exactly that—coming out of denial into acceptance hurt. The only way out of the pain was through it.

CHAPTER TWENTY-ONE:

TROUBLE IN PARADISE

City of timeless, ancient stone,
I stand within your pulsing centre,
Directionless, amid all wisdom ever known.
Confused, afraid, seeking to find,
The one, unknowingly left behind,
Lost in the search to find self in another,
Rings, rocks, crumbling columns of towering temples
Fill my eye with the ruin of you and I.
With each word of love unsaid,
With each tender deed undone,
The cruel hand of indifference
Its eroding work has done.
Temple of union now in ruin,
Vain sobs whisper through its voids,
The god of the material heart
Enthroned upon its altar,
And there beside it,
No room for you or I.

Lexie stood on the street corner, under the grey, smog-filled sky with small foreign cars whizzing by her, the tears of frustration and anger streaming down her cheeks. She didn't know where the hell she was; she was lost, completely, totally lost.

"How could he do this to me? What a jerk he is—so self-righteous, so immature, so stupid!" She was grasping for any invective she could think of to hurl at Derek who had deserted her, leaving her alone in a strange city where she didn't know one street from another! Finally she settled on the perfect phrase.

"Cheap, ungrateful bastard" seemed to fit the magnitude of the crime, and she let the refrain run through her mind.

It was the summer of their twenty-second wedding anniversary, and here she stood, abandoned, in the middle of a busy street in Athens, a blue-sapphire ring, newly missing one of its diamonds, still on her hand.

The trip had been Derek's idea. He had been excited about it ever since they had sent her parents on a Greek Island cruise for their fortieth wedding anniversary. In the last decade they had done so well financially, Derek and Lexie had been able to travel the world during their vacations. It was the one time Derek could usually be counted on to open his wallet, as if he rationed out permission to enjoy life, allowing himself a few weeks of fun each year.

Lexie was thrilled to travel to far-off places, escaping the humdrum routine of everyday living, and having a glimpse of how she imagined the rich and famous lived. Yet, as she and Derek travelled from one paradise to another, Lexie always felt the same. Feelings of heaviness pervaded her being. Wherever she went, there she was. She could not escape. Everything seemed like an effort, an imposition. Her movements seemed slow and cumbersome like those of a deep-sea diver, weighted and hampered by the resistance of the all-encompassing water. Living in a sea of melancholy, nothing held any joy for her. She seemed to be wading slowly through her life, waiting for it to miraculously change. Someday, perhaps she could feel light again. For now, she could only see herself doing more of the same. Like a disoriented diver, lost and confused in an underwater maze, she too, had distorted perception. She too, had lost sight of the surface above her. There was a way up and out. All she had to do was enlarge her understanding of who she was, who she was responsible for, and what she had control over. Instead she chose to believe and think more of the same.

In yet another hotel room with the sound of yet another ocean crashing against the shore, she would drift off to sleep, the same haunting thought always echoing in her mind. Surrounded by perfection in her tropical paradises, there was always the presence of this same yearning which ruffled her surface tranquillity. A sigh shuddered through her body, and once again she heard herself think her now familiar refrain, *If only Derek were different, I would be happy.*

"It was only a ring. A stupid ring, but couldn't he see how much it meant? He's such a jerk!" Lexie was muttering angrily to herself, all the while, struggling to find her way back to the jewellery store.

"Well, if that's what he wants. That's what he'll get and just see if he ever gets near me again! He'll be sorry he's such a cheap jerk!"

On went her self–righteous, muttered dialogue until she found herself in front of the store where less than a half hour before, she and Derek had purchased the ring with the row of diamonds surrounding the central sapphire.

"That's what started all this! If one of those dumb diamonds hadn't fallen out right after we left the store, Derek might have been all right."

Angrily, she plopped the ring down on the jeweller's counter and demanded her money back. The young man who had waited on her before, opened his mouth in protest, but seeing the flash in her eyes, changed his mind. This was a determined woman, and she was very angry about something.

"I'm sorry, madam. Ah, this very rarely happens. The stones must have been loosened when we sized the ring for you. We're truly sorry. Are you sure you will not change your mind? It is truly a beautiful ring and such a good price too!" He was all over her with his politeness trying desperately not to lose a good sale.

"I'm sorry." Lexie said flatly. "My husband has decided not to buy it for me after all. He won't change his mind, I'm afraid." She ended the statement with an air of wounded self-pity. True, Derek did not want to buy it for her, had never wanted to buy it right from the beginning, but what about her money? They had recently separated bank accounts in an attempt to alleviate the constant bickering about who spent what, and she had more than enough in her account to pay for the ring. The truth was, she would not allow herself to buy it. If Derek didn't want her to have it, she could not give herself permission to have it. In her mind if he did not feel she was deserving of this luxury, then that was the way it was. She would abide by his judgement of her value.

That was what this was all about. Lexie would never have admitted to it at the time, but this was very definitely a test of Derek's love. During the entire trip, she had watched her friends' husbands purchase jewellery for their wives. Many of them took great pleasure in surprising the women they loved with extravagant evenings out, dining and dancing, and then ending the evening with a gift expressing the love and respect they felt for their mates. Lexie's heart had withered when she heard these stories for it had not escaped her attention that their anniversary was rapidly approaching, and Derek had made it very clear not to expect anything lavish. In fact he had suggested that they not buy anything at all, for he was worried once again about his job. *The same old story*, she thought. *There's always a reason why he can't spend his money.* They had thousands of dollars stashed away earning interest; they were debt free, and he still couldn't see his way clear to spend a thousand dollars or so on a piece of jewellery that was worth three times that much back home.

Her memory flicked back to the time when Derek had been out of work and they had been living off her tips from the Pink Cloud Lounge. She had cleaned out the last two hundred dollars in her account to buy Derek a watch for their anniversary. He had bought her nothing. She could build a list of such occasions. There was also the time when they had been vacationing in Spain several years before this trip, when an 18-karat gold bracelet had caught Derek's eye. Unable to give himself permission to buy it, Lexie had written the cheque. That was the way Derek was. He had such a hard time parting with his money that she had to buy everything for him, including his clothes. Providing a shop-at-home service for him, she dragged everything from the stores and would then sit as he selected what he wanted. It was the only way she could get him to dress decently. Derek would rather have money in the bank than good clothes on his back.

Derek had a problem with money, of that there was no doubt. Every Christmas was ruined as he ranted and raved at Lexie's spending. She could not deny her children so she would spend anyway. There would be cold, angry silence between them until the time came to unwrap the gifts. Then Derek, who had done absolutely nothing at all, would take full credit, puffing himself up like the great benefactor of his family. Many Christmases were ruined for her in this way, but she allowed it. It was a game they played about money. It was expected that Derek would always say no and she would decide which expenditures were worth his anger.

The Christmas before this trip, Derek had insisted she buy him nothing and she had complied. Absolutely not one gift was under the tree for him. As he covered his stunned sense of hurt with a forced smile, she could not help but enjoy her revenge. It was short lived, though, when she saw the look of stunned sadness etched on their children's faces. Their nearly grown daughters had been hurt by their parents' immaturity.

As she left the jewellery store, her hand barren of its beautiful sparkling ring, she sighed. "Nothing ever changes, does it? With Derek, money always comes first."

Calmer now, Lexie wound her way slowly back to the hotel picking out the landmarks as she went, knowing she could find her way. Still able to see his angry, stiff back as he had walked out of the jewellery store, Lexie started thinking about what she would say to him. True, she had coerced him into buying it, insisting they go into the jewellery store just to look.

Of course she had found a ring she absolutely had to have and as Derek sat sullenly, she had shamed him into buying it. The two young men waiting on them were so anxious to make a sale they were tripping over themselves to do whatever was needed. Under that kind of pressure, how could Derek refuse his beautiful, beseeching wife? He would have looked so blatantly insensitive that even he knew he would have felt ashamed saying no. She got her way. The ring was on her hand as they walked out the door with Derek marching angrily, silently ahead of her. *He'll get over it,* she thought. *He'll come around like he usually does.* With that thought she had glanced down one more time to admire her ring.

It was then that she saw the yawning emptiness of the missing stone. It seemed to mock her, laughing at her saying, "Not this time, Lexie. You're not going to get your way this time! See, you don't deserve us after all!"

"Derek, stop, wait. Look at this!" She was breathless as she called out after him.

The veins in Derek's neck stuck out, and his face went red with rage. "Well, you stupid bitch!" He spat the words out at her. "You had to have your way didn't you? It looks good on you. They've taken you to the cleaners on that ring! It's probably a piece of junk!" He turned to walk away, hesitated, then came back in for the final blow.

"I've had it with you, Lexie. Find your own god damned way back to the hotel, you stupid bitch!" With that he had turned and walked off.

As she turned into the street leading to their hotel, she looked up and saw Derek standing in her path. She walked by him, and saying nothing he fell into step with her. She could tell by his expression that he had cooled down. Once inside the dim, quiet semidarkness of their hotel room, Derek made amends the only way he knew how. His version of an apology was given with head down, shoulders slumped, a shuffling of his feet as she sat on the bed looking up at him. He sheepishly said, "I don't know what you were so bloody upset about, Lexie. It was only a stupid ring."

That was all the apology she was going to get. In Derek's mind the situation was dealt with by minimizing its importance. If he could convince himself the whole thing was no big deal, then he could let himself off the hook and he wouldn't have to feel guilty about the way he had behaved. All that was left to make his absolution complete was for her to agree. If she refused to express her anger, then he could ignore the small voice within him whispering, *Take your wife in your arms. Tell her you need her and that need frightens you. Tell her you have to act strong with her even when you don't really want to. Tell her you're scared to show her how much you love her. Tell her how you fear you can never give her enough, be enough for her, so you pretend that you never need to give to her at all. She's in pain. Can't you see? Reach out to her before it's too late.*

But the voice inside him was silenced by Lexie's own words. Words that told him he was right. It was no big deal. He was forgiven. Words that said he could hide his need a little longer, play the role of strong, controlling man a little longer. A part of him had withered with her words. Her forgiveness signalled the inevitable death of their relationship. No longer caring enough to fight for them, no longer able to hope, she had become indifferent. The opposite of love was not hatred, he knew. It was indifference. With enough passion to fight, there was a glimmer of a chance. In his wife's defeated sense of acceptance, there was no promise they could ever be different. Gone now was his last reason to redeem himself.

He watched her as she sobbed, her tears further absolving him.

"It's all right Derek. I understand. I pushed you into buying it. I knew you didn't want to, but it was just that all the other husbands were buying things for their wives to show them they loved them, and I…I hoped you would too. I know you're worried about money. I'm sorry. I shouldn't have expected it. Let's just forget it."

But, she couldn't forget just yet and unable to forgive her own submission, she continued to weep for her own weakness. Derek moved away from her, turning his back and staring blankly out the window. It was the beginning of the end. He sensed he had gone too far. Today had been some kind of test, and he knew he had failed. He slid his hand down inside his pocket to touch the tightly wadded roll of bills. At least his money was still there.

CHAPTER TWENTY-TWO:

RETREAT TO FREEDOM

Jewel of my eye,
Home of my heart,
Feast for senses, soul, and mind.
The green of your hills,
Beneath sunset-washed skies,
Prayerful, silent and tranquil,
Your blessings, your gifts,
Live with me still.

For the beacon of your light,
Called another to this place.
A healer, dark-eyed disciple,
Who walked with me through
Morning mist and soft moonlight.
Seeing through his eyes and spirit,
I knew,
That which I had come to do.

That day in Athens, her hope having died, Lexie stopped fighting her demons. Accepting her life with Derek would always be the same, she ceased hoping for deliverance.

When she returned, friends remarked upon the change in her. Gone was her quick smile and laughing eyes. Always one to find the wry humour in her situation, to poke fun at herself and the capricious nature of life, she was now quiet a great deal of the time, rarely bothering to make light of her unhappiness. Numbed to her emotional pain, she mechanically went through the motions of living. Her forty-third birthday was looming, and here she sat, treading water in her life, asking herself the time-worn question, *Is this all there is?*

Where had she failed? Where had she gone wrong? How could she fix her life? Her eyes saddened when she thought of her children. What could she do to fix them? Every time she thought of Jessica retching up her life-giving sustenance into some waiting toilet, she shuddered. Each time she talked to her daughter, she could not bring herself to voice the question she so wanted to ask. How do you casually say, "Oh, by the way, did you throw up today?"

She didn't ask, and Jessica didn't offer. All she could do was pray. She was doing a lot more of that these days.

Jessica didn't come home from school much, choosing instead to stay and work summers in her university town. In some ways it was a relief not to face the thin, boyish body of her daughter and to hear how she was now dating less because relationships had become too painful. This revelation puzzled Lexie when she allowed herself to think about it. Her daughter had not had a successful relationship for a very long time now. The only bright spot in her daughter's life was that she loved what she was doing in school. Jessica had blossomed academically in university, finding the subjects of sociology and psychology to be her true loves. Well on her way to completing her graduate degree, she was now talking about doing a Masters in Social Work, having decided she would make her life's work in counselling. Perhaps we do teach what we most need to learn.

While Jessica's condition worried Lexie, she felt, deep down, her daughter would be all right. She possessed a courageous sense of what was right and wrong in life, and she cared deeply about people. Lexie and this daughter had often talked late into the night about anything and everything. They could communicate through touch as well. Lexie had been a demonstrative mother and Jessica still accepted her hugs.

Jade on the other hand, was a totally different matter, having walled herself in early, cutting herself off from any physical touch. As Lexie reflected back now, she was reminded of an incident when Jade was very young which should have signalled her child was shutting down emotionally.

One warm summer day at the homestead, when the grandchildren had all been playing outside, Emily Alexander had stuck her head out her backdoor and had given their famous dinner bell a hearty ring, and everyone had trooped dutifully in for dinner. All of them, that is, but Jade. When she didn't appear after a second call, Lexie went looking for her. Out behind the garage in a lean-to shed, she found her daughter huddled in a corner, tears streaming down her face. Still a tiny child, even at six years of age, she seemed lost amongst the various pieces of garden equipment scattered around. Lexie still remembered the eerie cast of the soft sunlight as it was filtered down through the coloured, corrugated roof. As she came closer, she could see Jade sitting with her knees pulled tightly up under her chin, rocking herself gently back and forth, one hand tightly clasping the other.

"Jade, honey, are you all right?" Lexie's voice was full of concern. "What's wrong honey? You didn't come in for dinner. What's wrong with your hand?"

The sound of her mother's love seemed to give permission to feel. Jade's little face crumpled, her tiny chest heaved, and sucking in gasps of air the words came out in shuddering sobs, "A h-h-hornet, Mom. It was a h-h-hornet! It st-stung m-m-me!"

"Oh, baby! Why didn't you come and get me? I know how that can hurt!"

Lexie knelt down beside her child, placing her arms around her in comfort.

"Why didn't you say something to someone instead of staying out here all by yourself?"

The only response was a shrug of her tiny shoulders.

Why did her child chose to hide her pain? Why did she not trust enough to ask for help?

Year after year Lexie bumped against Jade's rejection, as if her child was angry with her, irritation always bubbling just under the surface. If pushed to interact, Jade would stomp out of the room refusing to discuss the problem, considering her statement, "I don't want to talk about it!" the final word. There was so much they couldn't talk about that it left nothing to say. Their days began with a distantly polite good morning. Upon arriving home, they asked each other about their days, and ended with an endured kiss as Lexie tucked her daughter in each night. Many days very little else was said. Lexie knew there should be more, and she ached to reach out to the angry little girl living inside her armour of prickly attitude, but Jade remained in her "shed," the sting of the world blotting out all else.

Lexie had given up hope their family life would ever be any different. Everywhere she turned she felt she was bumping into walls, like living in a box with no way out. She had made a wrong turn in her career, too, it seemed. After spending seven long, hard, years to obtain a business degree, her graduation seemed somewhat anticlimactic as she realized no large corporation was beating down the door to hire her. Coupled with the fact that the last years in teaching had locked her into an increasingly lucrative and secure position, she found herself trapped. Her job was too good to leave now, everyone reminded her. Might as well stick it out and retire with a nice, fat pension. It was beginning to look like she had outsmarted herself. While working toward leaving, she had inadvertently made it harder to go.

Her goal had been to graduate by the time she turned forty, and everything else in her life had been secondary to the unending assignments. Many summer days she had locked herself in her study, working, while her family splashed in the pool. Graduation day she had felt absolutely deflated, with nothing left to work toward. Feeling disconnected, lost, she looked at the smiling faces of her graduation party guests, and she couldn't stop asking herself, *What now? What next?* Her shiny new degree had failed to open any doors. She gave up hope her career would ever be anything different.

Every day became more of the same. The disappointments piled one upon another, yet she remained. Even conceding defeat, accepting there would never be change, she still could find no peace. Every night just as she was about to drift off to sleep, she heard the same whispered words, *You need to l-e-a-v-e!*

She didn't leave, but she began her retreat. Not courageous enough to do what inevitably must be done, she nevertheless began to prepare. Not consciously, for most actions with Lexie never were, and it was only by looking back upon a decision that she was ever able to see how she had begun moving toward it. In retrospect she knew she had begun by talking to her friends about her unhappy marriage. She was selective, opening up to a few of the most trusted ones, admitting to them she'd been unhappy for a long time, her marriage a mistake from the beginning. The next stage was to admit to herself something she had known for many years. She would never grow old with Derek. Every time he had hurt her, she had soothed herself with the phrase "forty and out," as if by age forty, she would have done her time, and—with her children raised—she would be let out early for good behaviour

That last Christmas she had taken the camera and documented every room of their house, as if this was the end of an era. The photographs came back filled with the smiling images of a perfect family. There they had all been, seated around the family table, Derek at its head.

When she booked the flight, she never would have consciously admitted it was the beginning of the final steps away from Derek. All she knew was that the opportunity to be alone doing what she now loved most had presented itself, and she was going to take it. Only one thing held any joy for her these days. Finding the world outside to be too painful, she had retreated within, returning to the practice of meditation. Now more mature and ready for such things, through meditation, she had begun to feel connected to a power greater than her fears. A still, small voice whispered to her that she had an intrinsic right to pursue her own happiness, that it was not a selfish desire to wish to be treated with respect. She began to listen to the guidance given, and although she was terrified, Lexie began to prepare to do what the still, small voice asked.

She would always remember the day vividly. It began like any other day with her lying in bed in the early morning, struggling with an inner sense of despair as she seemed to so often these days. Suddenly, a revelation! The awareness stunned her with its simplistic brilliance. In a flash of insight she understood her constant struggle for control was by its very nature futile. She was simply not capable of healing herself by herself. The purpose of the veil of ignorance shrouding all of humankind, there by divine design, was to lead all life to seek answers. In that process we learned who and what we were. The process itself was the prize. But there was more. In struggling to know, we would come face to face with the realization that there was more. The test of existence was to see if human life would recognize that there was a force of which they were a part, but which was greater than they were alone. Human despair was not something we could fix by ourselves. It was not within our capability to do so. If we believed there was nothing greater than ourselves, we as a species were doomed never to transcend what we were. There would be nothing greater to become.

In a flash of insight Lexie realized her years of trying to understand and heal herself through her intellect had been a form of ego worship. Like all practices of narcissistic self-love, it had made her feel better, but had accomplished little beyond momentary relief. She had been going in circles, always ending up back at the same place. If anything in her life was going to change, Lexie needed to get outside of her own restrictions. She needed help. She had to hand over control of her life in order to have control of it. She had to get out of her own way. Like so many living mysteries, this seemed to be a paradox, but she knew now what it meant. There was a power in this universe of which she was a part, but it was a power greater than she. This creative force and only this creative force could unravel the mess and mindless maze she had made of her life.

With this understanding came gripping fear. She would have to give up control, trusting in something other than herself. She was to put her life in the hands of this higher power, believing the power knew what was best, that there was indeed a divine plan. What was best for her would probably not be what she would choose for herself in the short run of things. She knew it would mean change, and change meant pain and upset. It was because she had actually known the truth that she had resisted for so long, and her resistance had brought her suffering. Lexie feared the pain. She feared the change. Yet, on that day, lost on the streets of Athens, the pain had reached a critical point. It had become more painful to remain the same than to change. The critical mass had been reached; the process that had led her to this gloomy day, thrashing around on her bed had begun. The unknown could not be more debilitating, more fearful, than what she had now. Ready to step into that void of the unknown, she would finally admit that she was powerless over her own life and that it had become unmanageable. She needed the help of a power greater than herself.

Her body resisted her decision. She thrashed about some more, burying her head under a pillow to stifle her gut-wrenching wails. What if the changes brought more pain than she could bear? The fear of the unknown felt like it would swallow her whole. She rolled about some more, her body going into involuntary ripples and spasms. She felt open, raw, wounded, unprotected, vulnerable. For so long she had had no boundaries, no sense of where she started and others ended. Whatever happened to those close to her, Lexie always felt their pain as her own. Without a complete sense of self, everyone, every interaction and relationship, could and did hurt her.

Gathering the sheets in her hands, and clutching them to her chest, she cried out to the empty room, "Take me! Do with me as you will! Lead me where you must! I put myself in your hands! Dear God in heaven, help me!"

In that moment, the agony subsided to be replaced only by an eerie inner calm. She felt strange, different. There was no miraculous sense she had been rescued or saved, only apprehension. She had given permission for the pain of change to begin, and she was indeed afraid!

Only brief weeks later her mother called, excitement in her voice, and as one thing had led to another, Lexie had found herself booking her flight to freedom.

She would never have guessed that was what it was to be. Not evident to her was the hand of providence that now facilitated change, her cry for help having given permission for the process to begin.

It seemed only to be a wonderful opportunity to spend time with her mother in a peaceful setting away from the worries of her family and away from Derek. At this point, Lexie welcomed any chance to be away from his controlling, dominating ways.

Lexie and her mother were to spend two glorious weeks tucked away at a peaceful midwestern retreat surrounded by lush green rolling hills, enjoying the sunshine, the Olympic-size swimming pool, the world-famous meals, and the stimulation of hours spent in classrooms devoted solely to the pursuit of spiritual awareness. It was a retreat into the inner self, and Lexie became a sponge ready to drink in all that was offered, eager to learn how many before her had overcome the despair inherent in the human condition. If there was peace to be had in this earthly existence, she was now in dogged pursuit of it. Struggling daily with her sense of hopelessness, she had become convinced there was only one philosophical question in life. Once that was answered, there was no other choice but to engage in the pursuit of understanding. The alternative she had rejected. The philosophical question she had answered was simply this, "Suicide?" When she had made the choice to live, the only other choice she had was to decide how.

The flight was booked, the arrangements made, and Lexie soon found herself running to make connections in an airport in a midwestern city. Lexie and her mother had been unable to get a direct flight. Delayed in the first phase of their journey, they now found themselves with barely enough time to make their connection. The outcome of all this was that they were placed in the only available seating left, and their luggage wasn't placed at all. They arrived at their destination, but the luggage didn't.

Driving through the gates, down the treed boulevards, and past the fountains of the vast acreage of the Unity School of Christianity, Lexie and her mother arrived at the main office to check in. Here, after explaining their predicament and asking that when their luggage arrived it be directed to their room, a dark-haired, bearded man, whom Lexie had not noticed before, offered his services. He had a car here he said and would be happy to get anything from town they might need. Somehow his last words rang like an omen. "If you need help, I am here," he said softly as they walked by him into the dusk of that first evening.

In the following days a strange unsettled feeling came over Lexie. In this beautiful setting of perfect peace and tranquillity her own raw, troubled energies seemed even more discordant. It was nothing she could articulate or explain, but she came to fully understand what the expression, "to be beside oneself" meant. It was as if she were present, but she not really inside herself. As if part of her had already moved on and yet part of her was desperately, stubbornly staying behind. Feeling disconnected, unreal, she could not understand why her uneasiness persisted when all around her was peaceful. A restless discontent surged through her, and her energies, beneath the surface appearance of calm, were billowing like storm clouds gathering.

On the second day of classes, as Lexie listened to another student brilliantly articulate a difficult concept, it struck her. She was angry and disappointed in herself. This, the pursuit of spiritual awareness, was to be the pinnacle of human experience. Through this pursuit she was guaranteed the attainment of personal peace, was she not? This was her last resort, the last "fix." Why then was it not happening? She was searching within herself. She was doing everything she could to bring about her spiritual growth, wasn't she? Then, why was she still so miserable?

Lexie couldn't believe how she quaked inside when called upon to talk in the group sessions. She seemed to be getting worse not better. Terrified to contribute an answer even when she knew what she had to say was insightful, Lexie wondered where her self-confidence had gone? What had happened to that woman who had spoken effortlessly to large groups of women only a few short years ago? What was happening to her?

Her mother, too, was concerned about her, surprised by her uncharacteristic silence. Lexie, her oldest, had always played the role of the superstar, the achiever. Nothing, it seemed, had been out of her grasp. Now, here was this same daughter afraid to open her mouth. This was not the confident, in-love-with-life girl she had always seen for Lexie had skillfuly hidden her marital unhappiness.

Lexie had sunk into a pit of self-deprecating worthlessness. It seemed there was nothing left to try, no "fix" to save her from the pain of her own despair. Even in a spiritual paradise, happiness eluded her. Would her life ever be any different?

Then she heard it, a voice from the row of seats ahead of her. She had been sitting in the lecture, her mind unable to keep from wandering, when she had been brought up short by the sheer brilliance of a statement.

Who said that? she wondered, as her gaze sought out the speaker. *Oh, it's him again. I should have known.* She paused to consider the young, dark-haired man who had been consistently contributing important intellectual insights throughout the lecture.

She found herself observing him more closely after that, learning his name and noticing he sat in the same seat during every lecture. Two days later, as she was ushering herself into a seat directly behind him, she bent down as she passed behind him and said, lightly, casually, "Hello, Philip."

For a split second, time seemed suspended. In that shimmering, crystal-clear moment, Lexie heard him think. She was inside his mind. The connection had been made.

She started at the sound of his voice as she heard and felt the promise of a beginning. *My God,* he had thought, *she knows my name!*

As she walked on past him, Lexie smiled. So, he has noticed me, and he does care that I've noticed him. She had come to know all of this in the split second of the encounter. She did not question it nor did she plan to act upon her new insight, believing that whatever was meant to be would unfold of its own accord. There was, however, no doubt in her mind that there was to be a special link between the two of them.

This, she thought to herself, *could prove interesting.*

Lexie settled herself into her chair, less distracted, less disconnected from herself. She had found her new focus. She had found her "fix."

Lexie and her mother, never the unsociable types, had begun to draw quite a nucleus of new friends. A mother and daughter team who appeared so close and accepting of one another was fascinating and even somewhat inspirational to many others at the centre. Consequently, they did not lack for company during many of the meals taken in the large common dining hall.

At just one such meal, as Lexie and her mother searched for an available table, they were called over to join a newly made friend. Sitting down Lexie found herself staring into two dark, deep pools framed by luxuriant black lashes. His steady, unflinching gaze drew her deeper and deeper down into their dark depths and she knew. In that moment, she knew she was destined to find there what so long had eluded her. In the very deepest reaches of her soul, she experienced recognition. This man was here in this place, a divinely purposeful traveller whose path was meant to cross hers. He was to help her do what she had been unable to do for herself.

Startled back to awareness by the voice of her friend, Lexie heard him say, "Lexie, do you know Philip?"

Where her answer came from she had absolutely no idea. True, they had just come from a Bible study class and perhaps that was on her mind, but she suspected there was more to it than that. She had a way of doing and saying outrageous things and calmly acting as if someone else had said or done them. Perhaps in this case it was someone else—a part of her that saw beyond the present moment.

"Not in the biblical sense," she quipped. There was a stunned silence and then the men at the table exploded into raucous laughter. It was clear they appreciated her racy sense of humour.

Philip smiled at her, his eyes twinkling in amusement as if to say, *I like your wit. When I look at you, I think of making love too.*

His dark, liquid eyes appreciatively scanned her face, eager to drink in all that she was.

Not yet willing to acknowledge their physical attraction, they set about getting to know one another as friends. They listened attentively when either of them spoke in the group, gleaning whatever information they could without seeming to be too obvious. It was with surprise that they realized Philip had been the dark-haired man who had spoken to them the night of the lost luggage. Lexie had barely taken notice of him then, certainly not looking for someone to become interested in. She was still a married woman, even if an unhappy one; it had not been her intention to become intimately involved with any man.

Nevertheless, intrigued, she now allowed her eyes to take him in fully, appraising his physical appearance. He had a heavyset build, with broad, full shoulders and a narrow waist and hips. Dark, natural curls softly fell around an attractive face. His smile revealed flashing white teeth. Bearded and with dark good looks, Philip reminded Lexie of the disciples of long ago; he would not have appeared out of place in daVinci's painting of *The Last Supper*. Seated among them now, he enthusiastically articulated his ideas, his eyes sparking with passion. How he loved to discuss the universe and its workings.

Then, turning his focus on Lexie, his eyes flicking over her face, they would soften and a smoldering question would linger in them. Would there be more?

Lexie watched as the strong muscles of his legs defined themselves as he stood to leave. Solidly built, he exuded physical strength. The generous proportions of his body said that here was a man who embraced life fully, one who was open to the abundance of all it had to offer. Lexie had never realized it before, but Derek's thin, sinewy body seemed to symbolize his way of moving in the world. Derek believed in scarcity, holding on tightly to himself and everything else. Philip's full body represented generosity and openness—two things Lexie had great need of.

Lexie watched from her room as he left on an errand. She quickly picked up a book and stationed herself by their door convincing herself she had a sudden desire to sit outside and read.

At the first sight of his return, Lexie heard her own voice erupt from her lips. "Hi!" she called out, and her body followed with an enthusiastic wave indicating he should come and join her.

When he did, settling casually down on the ground beside her, he lay on his side, his weight supported on one arm, his face turned toward hers. Under the brilliant noonday sun, she warmed to him, no uneasiness between them; like an old friend, he felt familiar, reassuring, safe.

Lexie literally came to life in his presence. She told him her history, hearing as she did, the many things she had to be proud of in the way she had conducted her life. It seemed she had somehow lost sight of that. His comments and appreciative looks reminded her she was indeed a beautiful, accomplished woman. Memories flooded back as she saw herself anew in the eyes of this vibrantly alive young man. Her pulse quickened with possibilities. It felt good to be with someone who was filled with a passion for life.

He was young. Younger than Lexie by twelve years, but his story was so much like hers. Only thirty-one, he regretted that he had lost much of his youth, dominated by an aggressive, progressively abusive woman. He now felt ecstatic to be free. It was as if, by ending his marriage, he had ended his bondage, and a whole world of possibilities had opened up for him. Lexie, it seemed, was being considered as one of those possibilities.

He chuckled rather sheepishly, giving her a sidelong glance when he confided he had always been attracted to older women. The woman he had lived with and eventually married had been fifteen years his senior. At the tender age of twenty, Philip became involved with a mature woman of thirty-five who was just coming out of a marriage breakup. She had a daughter almost as old as he was.

They had lived together off and on since then with Philip pursuing his undergraduate degree as she rapidly climbed the corporate ladder. A highly capable and efficient business woman, she had risen to a position of prominence such that shortly before they separated, their city's chamber of commerce had declared her "Woman of the Year."

Philip made no bones about the fact that he was attracted to beautiful, strong, dominant women. It had been his undoing he said. For years he had followed C. J. (she preferred using only her initials, believing it made her appear more decisive), around like a lovesick puppy and putting his academic career on hold in order to join her in business. The venture was successful, and they made a great deal of money together. At that point Philip stopped asking her every six months to marry him. Having given up hope of her saying yes, he had moved into an acceptance of their relationship the way it was. He had begun to focus on himself and where he was going in life.

It was this change that caught C. J. completely off guard, having come to depend on his devotion. She had felt a tremor of uncertainty shake its way through the very foundations of her emotional security. Without his constant pursuit, she had lost her sense of equilibrium. Her self-esteem depended a great deal on daily worship.

Swift to rectify the situation, C. J. married Philip six months later. He knew almost immediately it had been a mistake and consequently the dynamics of their relationship deteriorated. Always flagrantly taking his generosity and goodheartedness for granted and now made even bolder by the bonds of marriage, C. J. became blatantly abusive, humiliating him often in front of others, ordering him about and never, never letting him forget who was the high-profile sales leader of the electronics company they had founded, even though without his brilliant research there would have been no product for her to sell.

With ever greater success came ever greater stress and C. J. became increasingly unreasonable. One final selfish act became the straw which broke the proverbial camel's back.

Not yet forty, she had gone into this marriage knowing full well Philip wanted to have children, and she had agreed she would not use any birth control. Philip looked forward eagerly to becoming a father.

He had been in her office one day rifling through documents looking for a report he needed, when his hand had fallen on a paper with their doctor's letterhead. It was a bill for services rendered and it was dated for only a few weeks before. Philip had enough medical knowledge to understand the terminology in the report, and his hand began to shake as the reality of what it meant began to dawn. His heart sank as he realized there was no hope for them. An ultimate act of betrayal, she had lied to him. She had had no intention of ever having his child. He held the proof; she had murdered their child without even telling him. It was there in black and white, the bill for the abortive process of having the lining of the uterus scraped and cleaned. The consent form was signed in her own hand. She had known full well she was carrying a viable fetus—Philip's unborn child.

Sick with shock, unable to believe C. J. could be so cold, callous, and uncaring knowing what becoming a father had meant to him, Philip's sense of outrage erupted. How dare she make that decision without him!

Storming out of the office, not daring to face her now, afraid of what his anger might cause him to do, he knew he needed time to think, to plan how he would react. As he walked, he calmed down enough to resolve to confront her on the weekend. They had been planning to take a trip together to a city known for its festival of lights celebration. Actually, Philip had been planning it for weeks. He had read and heard so much about this waterfront city's incredible incandescent beauty that he had been as filled with excitement about it as a child with Christmas. It would be a good time, while they were away alone together, to talk about their marriage. Perhaps he should give her the benefit of the doubt. Maybe she had to have it done for health reasons. He wanted so badly to be able to excuse her behaviour.

The weekend of the trip C. J. had seemed listless and uncooperative, complaining of being tired. Philip was ever hopeful she would perk up in time to stroll the city that night to take in all the glory of a city dressed like a woman going to a ball, decked out in its finery, strung with strands of jewelled lights.

He had gone out to do some shopping on his own with the understanding that C. J. would rest and then dress. Stopping at the florist to pick up a single white rose, her favourite, he had then come bounding excitedly into the room eager to enjoy the excitement of the night with the woman he loved. He entered the bedroom to find her lying listlessly there, not yet dressed and with obviously no intention of joining him.

As he stood stunned in the doorway, he heard her groggily mumble something about being too tired and that he should go without her. In that moment, something snapped and a realization hit him full in the face. This woman was never going to change. She thought only of herself. She had always done so. Why hadn't he seen it before? He had been making excuses all these years for someone, he now realized, he didn't really even like? Someone who thought so little of his feelings she had murdered his child and felt it was such an inconsequential act that she hadn't bothered to tell him about it? What a fool he had been.

Throwing the rose across the room, he marched to the closet and yanked down his suitcase. With a sense of determined rage, he filled it. In response to her sputtered surprise, he said simply that he was spending the night elsewhere and needed time to think. He left her with her mouth hanging open.

Most of that night, he paced the floor of another hotel room, his gut in turmoil. At the first light of morning, exhausted and confused, he ventured out to a coffee shop. On his way he passed a newspaper box and decided to distract himself with what was going on in the world. As his hand reached in, his eyes came to rest on the full colour front page. There before him was the city in all its shining glory. Lit with thousands and thousands of bulbs, the city shone like a beacon. The headline jumped out at him, "SEE THE LIGHTS!" But to Philip it read, "See the Light."

The decision solidified. It was over. He was never going back. Wrenching the paper out of the box, he stuffed it under his arm and marched determinedly in the direction of his hotel. He had a great deal to do.

He left it all—her and a thriving business, and he did what he had really wanted to do all along. He went back to school to study for his doctorate, knowing now he had never belonged in the world of business. His first love had been research, especially the world of robotics where he had designed and built artificial prostheses for the disabled. Yet, with little or no regard for their overall impact or benefit, C. J. had taken his genius and used it to fuel only projects with the highest moneymaking capability. This fundamental difference in the way they valued life, now brought fully into focus by her last brutally selfish act, had made it intolerable for him to stay.

A sense of admiration filled Lexie as she listened to Philip's story. He had had the courage to remove himself from pain. A thought was beginning to take hold, and Philip's presence was steadily strengthening her.

The shadows grew longer under their tree as they talked away the afternoon. Lexie, too, had shared her story.

Today had been a beginning, and Lexie knew what she wanted— more! Obsessed, Lexie thought of Philip day and night. Yet, she was torn; happily married women did not act on their infatuations if they cared to keep their marriages intact. *What about unhappily married women?* Lexie mused. Where then was this taking her?

"Philip's quite good looking isn't he?" her mother asked casually that night at dinner. Lexie had been scanning the crowd looking for his face.

She blushed, "Oh, Mom. Yes, I guess he is good looking. We're just friends; that's all. There's nothing between us."

"Well, that's a shame."

Lexie's jaw dropped. Abruptly, she looked at her mother. "What do you mean?" she asked breathlessly.

"I mean that I've known you've been unhappy in your marriage for years now. It's about time you put an end to your pain. Don't you think I've noticed the way you glow when Philip is around? You light up like the Christmas tree in Times Square!"

Her mother's words were a shaft of sunlight in a darkened room. Suddenly, everything seemed sharply defined. Her mother could see her pain! She was not alone in her craziness. Someone, a very important someone, was validating the wisdom that had for so long whispered through her brain. It was now a shout! Her mother was giving her permission to leave her husband.

She wasn't crazy. The marriage was abusive. She had a reason to hurt. She needed to leave Derek in order to save the very essence of who she was - an essence that had been slipping away from her for so many years. Her mother's words had confirmed what she had felt for so long. Not having trusted her own judgement enough, Lexie had always teetered on the edge of the precipice. Today, she had been given a shove. A shove into freedom and a free fall of gut-wrenching fear. The thought of leaving her husband of almost twenty-three years absolutely terrified her. It would mean redefining her life; redefining who she was. Long into that night, Lexie talked with her mother. By recognizing her daughter's pain, Emily Alexander had given her daughter permission to speak about it. No longer did Lexie feel she had to hide what she felt, to play the role of the perfectly happy wife. With the barriers removed, a flood of feelings burst forth. Talking and crying together, they mourned the death of the young, vibrant girl who had so meekly handed her power over nearly twenty-three years before.

"Lexie, I should have told you to leave him when he hit you the first time. Do you remember when he came here looking for you the time you disappeared for three days? Your father and I knew something was terribly wrong between you, but we felt it wasn't our business to interfere. Then when you were working at the Pink Cloud Lounge, and you came up to the Homestead that one weekend to visit, I knew then that you were thinking about leaving him. I could sense you'd met someone else. You seemed more alive than you had been in years, but I also knew that you had two young children to raise. I was worried about how you would manage alone, so I kept my mouth shut again."

She stopped and looked lovingly at her daughter.

"This time, honey, I'm not going to keep quiet. I'm not going to let you down. I'm going to be there for you. If you can find happiness with someone like Philip, then you deserve it. Your father feels the same way I do, Lexie. Do you know what he said when I called him last night?"

Lexie looked at her mother in surprise. "You called Dad about this last night? How did you know what was coming?"

Emily Alexander sighed as she looked at her daughter, "Let's just say I had made up my mind to speak to you about this even before we left on our trip. Then when I saw you and Philip together and I saw the way he could make you smile and laugh like the old Lexie, I knew I had to act. Your dad couldn't agree with me more. When I told him I had decided to encourage you to leave Derek, his only words were, 'I don't want my little girl to suffer any more. She's suffered enough.'

"So there it is Lexie. Both your dad and I are with you all the way. We'll do whatever we can to help if you decide to go. You know you and the girls will always have a place with us."

Lexie embraced her mother in the soft, dim light of their room.

This can't be happening! I can't really be planning to do this! Part of her was in deep shock, detached, observing in disbelief the earnest conversation that was calmly takin place as Lexie planned how she would leave Derek. Another set of frantically whispered words inside her brain said it could not possibly be true.

Mother and daughter, coconspirators, were seated side by side on the large jet plane carrying them home. Home. Back to Derek. Lexie still couldn't believe what she was about to do. So much of it still seemed unreal to her. She felt anaesthetised, numb, unreal, with a nagging sense that she would not have the courage to do what her words said she was going to do. The whispers in her mind were saying, *Don't make any waves, Lexie. This will be too hard. Just go back to what you know. It's safe there.*

But somewhere inside her now there came a stronger, steadier voice. It did not speak to her as often, allowing instead the mind-less, fear-filled chatter of denial to clatter on. But it was there and it was rooted in a deep, primal sense of herself—an instinct that knew this had gone on long enough, that leaving had become a matter of survival. Strong, purposeful words settled firmly in her conscious-ness. Like sediment that had swirled endlessly in a dirty water glass, those words so long unheeded amid the flotsam of her faulty thinking now formed a foundation of determination, the clear water of new perception sparkling above them.

You can do this. You will do this. You must do this! became a refrain washing over her like a flood of determination, and with each new wave, her courage and conviction grew.

With each mile, Lexie's acceptance of what she had to do grew. Relaxing somewhat, she shifted her weight in her seat and turned her thoughts to the last days of the retreat—the last days with Philip.

After their sojourn under the tree that day, Lexie next saw Philip in the tiny bookstore on the grounds. She and her mother had entered, their laughing voices announcing their arrival as much as the tinkling of the bell over the door. It was a room bright with sunshine, filled with the sweet aroma of burning incense and filled most significantly for Lexie with the Philip's presence. He was there, in front of a huge stack of books, one open in his hands as he stood reading it.

His presence drew her in. She went directly up to him and joked about bumping into him here. He, always the intellectual one, described the merits of various books, and Lexie, always the needy one, did not even hear a word he said. So great was the pulsing energy of her arousal, she stood beside this man oblivious to all around her. The blood roared past her ears silencing all thought, all perception. All of his being was speaking to her so loudly that she could not hear what he was saying. She was overwhelmed by his physical presence, the sight of him, the smell of him, the exquisite promise of his touch. He broke off what he was saying midsentence, looked at her for a moment and asked, tentatively, hesitantly, "Do you mind if I tell you something, something personal?"

Lexie could do nothing else but say yes. She had to know what he was thinking.

He leaned closer, lowering his voice as he whispered hoarsely, "You are the most gorgeous woman I've seen in a long time. You're a very attractive, classy lady." He then straightened, recovering quickly. He knew he had let his guard down momentarily as he had unabashedly expressed his awe at her appearance.

It did not matter that he moved quickly to minimize the emotion expressed. She had heard the admiration in his voice. His words had been like balm to her wounded self-esteem. Derek had never complimented her. Never!

For his kind words alone, she loved him. So needy, so vulnerable, so long without love and admiration from the primary man in her life, all she was reached out to this new, kind man and opened up to him like flowers to the rain, asking only, *Give me more. I thirst. Give me more.*

She had only formally met Philip on the Thursday of their first week here and now the end of that week was rapidly approaching. Saturday was soon upon them along with the social gathering planned in the main lounge. Anyone who wished could take part in an impromptu talent show. Philip did. She didn't. She could not find the courage to contribute something to the show. She found herself feeling inadequate and envious as she watched the others perform. It was typical for Lexie to beat herself up for not being the best. She had this internalized, demanding parent inside of her who always pushed her to excel at everything, robbing her of peace. Why did she always need to be admired to feel whole?

She tried not to feel "less than" as Philip basked in the afterglow of his performance. It had been a simple thing, singing with a group, but he had been energized by it. Perhaps that's why he was one of the first to agree when an excursion to go dancing was suggested. He had a car and would be willing to drive. He looked at Lexie, as a large group of them stood around in the parking lot trying to organize car pools.

"I'll take Lexie and her mom with me," he volunteered.

Looking at her again, he asked, "You're both coming of course?"

They drove the twenty minutes or so that took them into the heart of the nearby city, chatting amiably with the fourth person they had added to their party who knew her way around well, having done this many times on her various visits. Lexie loved the people she met at this retreat because they were a lot like her, not looking at her like she had two heads when she talked about psychic phenomena. She and Philip also shared this common interest; he from the perspective of the scientist, she from that of spiritualist.

A whole crowd of them arrived at once, tumbling out of their cars and descending upon the dance club. It was dark, loud, and cool inside; as they wound their way through the crowd, Lexie could feel the excitement of the place. This was Saturday night, and it was packed. The immense room was crammed full of small round tables, chairs, a long bar spanning the length of one wall, and in the centre of all this, a dance floor.

Philip was moving through the crowd ahead of her as she heard music which caused her heart to race and a sense of excitement to build in her. In that same instant she felt the warmth of Philip's hand as it grasped hers and pulled her forward onto the dance floor. It was about to begin.

"C'mon. Let's dance. I love this song," he said simply.

She slid into his arms. Their bodies fit together effortlessly as if designed for one another. The dance floor swirled around her, everything blurring by. She shut her eyes, leaning against Philip, lost in feeling.

It was like her fantasy come true. Months before, away for a weekend with a group of girlfriends, the seeds of this particular vision had taken hold. They had all gathered pyjama clad, in one of the hotel rooms, wine bottles in hand to enjoy a movie night together. Lexie had never heard of the particular movie they were about to watch, but her unfamiliarity with it was to end abruptly that night. For months afterward it would live on in her mind, taunting and teasing her with a strange unsettling sense of premonition

Rivetted right from the beginning, Lexie watched as a young girl, going on vacation with her family, talked about the fact that everyone in her family called her "Baby' rather than her name. A bolt of recognition hit when the character commented that, up to that point, "it had never occurred to her to mind."

I know what's that's like, thought Lexie. *It's as if you're not really a person, like you have no true identity. By renaming you they put their label on you, taking away your power to be what you truly are.* For years Derek had dehumanized her, insisting on calling her "Babe" rather than her given name. Lexie had begged him to call her by her name, but he just laughed and made the excuse that his pet name was too much of a habit. Perhaps, but it was one she didn't like and wanted changed. He had even tried to move into calling her "Mom"—anything to avoid calling her by her name and giving her identity. She had put a stop to that by saying, "I'm not your mother. Don't call me that."

No wonder she didn't know who she was, for she was rarely called by her own name. She was someone's wife, or someone's mother, and at home she was "Babe." It made her feel like a powerless child.

The movie had hooked her, appearing to have been scripted just for her. Describing the sensations of falling in love for the first time, the picture was a celebration of the passion of youth. Having been a sleepwalker through her young life, not taking control of what had happened to her, never fully enjoying with complete abandon the pleasures of her own passion, Lexie experienced a deep, painful sense of loss as she watched. Having been far too concerned with servicing the passions of others, she wondered if it was too late for her to enjoy her own passionate self.

She watched the scenes play out as the characters met, and embarked on a voyage of discovery. Their task, to perfect a dance together, became a metaphor for the young woman's coming of age. Disciplining all that she was to reach the ultimate goal of performance, she took what life had to offer, passionately pursuing her partner. Brave, beautiful, and committed to having all that life had to offer, she went against the dictates of society, breaking cultural and economic barriers to go after what she wanted—an older, sensuous, less-educated man—a man she knew her physician father would not approve of. When the relationship ended, as all knew it must, she did not apologize. She had been true to herself, had loved unconditionally, and in the process earned her father's respect when the object of her affection proved himself to be a noble, caring man.

That brave, young character had touched Lexie's heart. Lexie wanted to incorporate so much of the young girl's character into herself. Spellbound, she had watched as the characters on the screen had moved as one, celebrating with total abandon their joy at being alive, living, breathing in the music surrounding them as if it was food for their very souls. Oh, how she had yearned for a moment of such total aliveness! The greyness of her life had overwhelmed her with sadness and an aching desire for the joyful splashes of colour being fully alive could bring!

Now it was here—the strains of the very song that had pulsed its way through her fantasy and into her heart. Music that had celebrated the fullness of life, its title telling the world there were times that were indeed the pinnacle, the height of all that we can feel. There truly were moments that were "the times of our lives."

This was one of those moments. As Philip reached for her and pulled her into him, Lexie knew she would never forget this night. So full of her own power, she had reclaimed her heart and was now free to give it to whomever she pleased. No more would she live her life defined by Derek's needs and wants. Tonight, and from now on, she would choreograph her own dance.

She had never felt passion such as she felt that night, never having allowed herself go there before. Always too self-conscious, she had been unable to lose herself in feeling. Consumed with expressing all that she was feeling for Philip, Lexie was, for the first time, unself-conscious about what a man thought of her. It was so simple. All that time she had spent focused on others, waiting for them to make her happy—what a tragic and pathetic waste of her energy! The potential to feel had always been within her. She had always had the choice; she had simply needed to pay attention to what her instincts told her. Had she given herself permission to act on her feelings, to make choices based on them, she would not have found herself, at the age of forty-three, experiencing for the first time the thrill of unbridled, joyful passion.

Others might dismiss it as lust, and if that was all it was, then so be it. Whatever it was, it was life-giving fuel, catapulting her out of her tomb, giving her courage to act. Philip was what she needed, when she needed it. Her feelings for him had reminded her she was far too young to be dead from the neck down. That night on the dance floor, just like the young heroine in the movie, Lexie claimed her power, rejoicing in the fullness of being. Philip had been a gift, a catalyst bringing about a long-overdue stage of her growth. Lexie, at last, felt free to do whatever she decided she wanted to do.

That night, Philip and Lexie danced together, his lips brushing against the soft skin of her face, his arm firmly around her waist. From a distance, Emily Alexander looked on with approval. She had never seen her daughter this happy.

Later that night, they all piled into their cars and left the bar. It had been a night to remember with its nostalgic music, barroom walls hung with the memorabilia of eras past, and, most notabe of all, the eye-stopping sight of a vintage pink Cadillac, fully restored, parked in the centre of the dance floor in all its glory, from which the disc jockey played songs filled with the hopes and dreams of their youth.

When they arrived back, everyone seemed to just melt away leaving Lexie and Philip alone. Their attraction for one another had become evident when Philip had dared to kiss her full on the mouth during a dance. Even before he said the words, Lexie knew what he wanted.

Moving closer to her, he put his arms around her and whispered huskily into her hair, "Where can we go?"

Without hesitation, she replied, "I'm not ready, Philip."

The fact that she had not hesitated in her answer, that she had known her own mind so readily, surprised both her and Philip.

He pulled back from her somewhat startled. "I thought that was what you wanted," he said puzzled.

"It was. It is. Just not yet. It's too soon, too fast. I'm still technically married, you know. Even if in my heart I left him years ago, it wouldn't be fair...I just couldn't do that to him. Do you understand?"

Philip smiled softly, "Yes, I do, and I know one thing."

"What's that?" she asked.

"I know that I'll like both you and myself more in the morning!"

He chuckled good-naturedly. "It's not what I want right now, but I know in my heart you're right. It's better for both of us if we take this slow."

He added, "I'll walk you to your door. That will accomplish two things. First of all you won't have to make any explanations to your mother about where you were all night. And second, I'll get a kiss goodnight."

With that they turned and walked arm in arm toward her darkened room.

The rumours spread like wildfire. By the next day, Sunday, everyone they had come to know in that first week was aware of their romance. They were being labelled an item and good-natured questions were being asked about their relationship. How could they explain to anyone what was going on when even they themselves didn't know?

That day was spent lying on a grassy knoll by the pool finding out all they could about one another. Were there any other bonds between them besides a powerful physical attraction? The day was spent in discovery.

They discovered a recurring theme in their personal stories. Both had given up having a self in order to have a relationship, fixated on pleasing the significant other in their lives. Also central was the importance of children. Lexie could not have imagined going through her life childless, and Philip's greatest goal now was to be a father. They looked at one another as Philip asked, "Lexie, how old are you?"

It had come out innocently enough, but Lexie knew the question was loaded with implications. First of all, Philip had been attracted to older women in the past and was now beginning to question why. Secondly, it would soon become obvious that her child-bearing days were over.

"I'm forty-three, Philip, and I can't have any more children."

"I see," he said quietly. "There are other ways, you know. I've spent enough time studying human biology to know that." Then he seemed to hear what he had said along with its implications, and he laughed nervously. "Why are we talking about all this? We're really getting ahead of ourselves aren't we? I was the one who suggested slowing down. Guess I'd better remind myself of that more often!" He laughed and changed the subject.

The next day in class, a very strange thing happened, leaving Lexie bewildered and hurt. They were sitting next to one another listening to the lecture when she leaned over and whispered something to Philip. It was simply a comment on what the teacher was saying as far as she could recall, but obviously it had touched off old memories. At the end of the lecture, Philip got up abruptly from his seat and without a word marched quickly out of the lecture hall. Lexie was stunned. The first question that came to her mind was, *What did I do wrong?* To her, Philip's upset was somehow her doing.

The rest of that day he avoided her. Wandering the grounds, Lexie had hoped desperately to find him. Searching in vain for his face in the dinner crowd, she had felt absolutely miserable and abandoned.

Then, there he was directly in front of her. He was walking toward her with a serious expression on his face. He took her arm as he passed by her and steered her in the direction of a small, secluded gazebo nestled amongst a thicket of lilac bushes.

He slid in beside her as Lexie felt the cool, stone slab of the seat beneath her. He looked so serious when he took both her hands in his and began to speak.

"Lexie, I want to start by saying I'm sorry. I know I hurt you by my actions today, and you deserve an explanation. I've been wandering around in town all day today, trying to figure out why I acted the way I did." He sucked in a big breath and plunged on.

"What you said was innocent enough, but it was the way it was said. It just had that ring of condescension that C. J.'s voice always had. That superior smother-love type of attitude that seems to say, "Only I know what's best for you. Listen to me because I'm always right.""

He paused and looked away. He did not want to see the bewildered and hurt look on her face. If only he could make her understand what he was feeling. He struggled on.

"I guess it was just combined with everything else that was happening. There you were, always by my side, sitting with your arm wrapped in mine in class, and it was all so fast, so public, with everyone talking about us and everything and, Lexie, you are older than me just like C. J. was and that scared me. Am I making the same mistake again? That question keeps going around and around in my head. You're like C. J. in a lot of ways and it scares the hell out of me!"

He finally looked up at her, his eyes pleading with her to understand. He did not want to experience her anger. He did not want to hurt her. He only wanted her to understand that he too was not ready for this. His wounds were still too new, too raw. With his journey of self-discovery only just begun, he feared getting lost in someone else.

There was a seed of understanding in Lexie, but it had not yet come to fruition. The necessity of the struggle to become whole within oneself was not yet evident for her. To grow leaning against another inevitably brings about collapse as their support shifts and changes. Philip was struggling to stand on his own, to be his own best friend, and he had begun to feel the disequilibrium brought about by her presence. It would have been so easy to hand over his wounded self to her for nurturing. She was more than willing, it seemed, to pour her healing love over him. Further along in his awareness than she, the warning rumble through his emotional foundations had alerted him to his slide, once again, into enmeshment with another. All he had worked so hard to establish—his belief in who he was and what he was to do with his life—had been threatened by his overwhelming need for a passionate uniting with another. If he concentrated on meeting Lexie's needs, on "fixing" her, he could forget about meeting his own needs. Needs that, even admitting their existence, brought pain.

Because Lexie was just embarking on this same voyage of self-discovery, she could not yet fully understand what Philip was trying to tell her, the sea of self-awareness still stretched out before her. She could only appear to understand, to forgive, to minimize the effect of his actions. She was very practised at appearances. To survive she'd had to learn to forgive a great deal.

No, she did not understand what was going on inside of Philip, only hearing what she could understand, only that which would allow her to pursue her goal—the goal of replacing one man with another. If the man in her life was different, then her life would be different.

What she heard was—it was not her fault Philip was unhappy—it was because of some strange sense of self-commitment he had. A sense of self-commitment that she was as yet incapable of understanding. She heard only that there was still hope for their relationship as long as they slowed things down. That seemed simple enough. She would still have him in her life. Things would just not happen as quickly as she wanted them to.

She had not thought beyond making this man her lover. All she wanted now was to be free of Derek and to be able to experience being passionately in love. Philip would most likely only be the beginning of her adventures. Perhaps this unspoken expectation, more than anything, was what caused Philip to shy away from the ultimate intimate encounter. Could it be that he sensed Lexie was about to use him, that her passion was all about her and not him? So great was her neediness, it would innocently yet tenaciously suck all that he had to offer into its void. What he was would be of little significance. He would be used up to fill her.

Lexie heard only what she wanted to hear, but Philip sensed so much more than what was said. We often hear what we want to hear and see what we want to see. This day Philip's perceptions, purified by the white-hot, blanching effect of painful emotional honesty, were far less clouded than Lexie's dark delusions of denial.

Even though there could be no true understanding, being light-years apart in their truths, they both contented themselves that they had made themselves understood. Lexie was convinced they would soon be lovers. Philip was equally convinced that he had escaped the enmeshment of a sexual commitment.

With the agreement to put raw, physical passion on hold could have come friendship, as Philip truly tried to reach out to her in understanding and compassion. Everywhere lush greenness welcomed them as they went each evening for long walks amidst the beauty of the grounds. Their ears were filled with the songs of birds, their eyes filled with the treasures of brimming flowerbeds and blooming shrubs. An air of sublime peacefulness settled over the land each evening, and they walked hand in hand through its calm sweetness. He gave to her in so many ways, sharing his experiences of breaking free from the bondage of his relationship. He tried, gently, to make her understand that she did not need anyone else to define who and what she was or could become. He prodded her, through the stories of his own awakening, to take responsibility for her state of pain. Above all, he gave her his unconditional affection, caring genuinely about her feelings yet refusing to take responsibility for what she felt.

Sadly, regrettably, Lexie missed much of what he could teach her, continuing only to focus on how he could complete her. For her, he was a way to bring life back to the desert of her existence.

Their last night together, as they walked the grounds hand in hand, they talked of the future. Lexie listened attentively as Philip sketched out all his plans to move to Boston and attend Harvard to complete his doctorate. She thought one thing and one thing only when she heard *Boston*—a weekend trip to visit him would be exciting. She would fly down for a lover's tryst several times a year. How perfect that would be! She would not have the demands of a man in her life on a daily basis, but would keep one tucked away, available when-ever she wanted him. How romantic and exciting. She could have her cake and eat it too—excitement without commitment. That was exactly what she was after now. She had been far too unhappy for too long to want to return to the smothering closeness of a committed relationship. Free at last! A man was going to become a disposable commodity in her new life. Having learned something about herself, she knew that with a man in her life on a daily basis, she would not be strong enough not to give her newly won power away.

Lexie did not consider that this arrangement might not be accept-able to Philip, that perhaps he was looking for something different. Although she appeared to be focused so completely on another, in reality Lexie was fixated on her own needs. Philip was going to be all that *she* needed. His presence in her life was going to make *her* happy. So consumed was she with him, of course he would want what she wanted! Weren't they one? He was becoming critical to her happiness. How then, could it be any other way? Blinded by her own desires, she could not see the situation from his vantage point. Her need dictated her view.

He handed her a small parcel wrapped simply in tissue paper.

"It's just a little something I picked up for you, Lexie. It's not much, really, but I thought of you when I saw it. I hope you'll remember me when you use it."

With that he sat waiting for her to unwrap his gift.

As her fingers closed around the fragrant bars of perfumed soap, drawing them out from their wrappings, she heard him say, "I want you to think of me when you take long leisurely baths. No more showers, Lexie. I don't want you to cry in the shower to hide your tears anymore. Promise me, Lexie. Promise me you won't cry in the shower any more."

With that he took her hands in both of his and sat looking into her eyes. "You've cried enough. You don't deserve to cry anymore."

He walked with her to her door, kissed her ever so gently on the mouth, and said good-bye. "I hope you find the happiness you deserve, Lexie."

As he turned to leave, she called after him, "I'll see you before I leave tomorrow, Philip. We'll talk more about my trip to Boston then. I love you!"

She had not heard the good-bye in his voice.

She sat on the plane thinking about him, the smell of his aftershave still fresh in her nostrils. Obsessed with him, she was convinced they would continue their relationship over time and distance. Distractedly, she looked out the window of the airplane, having a hard time reading the book on her lap, struggling as she was to finish a reading assignment one of the lecturers had given. The book blatantly betrayed her for there in front of her eyes was the very name her mind was trying so hard not to focus upon. Grabbing the text with renewed interest, she proceeded to read on. It was a metaphysical treatise written by the founder of the Unity School of Christianity, and it concerned itself with the twelve apostles of Christ. From his point of view, much accepted by followers of metaphysics, each of the twelve disciples was symbolic of a "great centre of action in the subconscious realm of man." This subconscious realm was further overseen by the Superconscious or, as he called it, the Christ Mind. Each disciple was an overseer, likened to department heads in the hierarchy, organizing specific functions of the body. For example the great apostle Peter represented the faculty of faith, residing in and presiding over the power centre of the body known as the brain. Love was represented by the apostle John and its energy centre resided, not surprisingly, in the area of the heart. It was when Lexie came upon the symbolism bound up in the apostle Philip that she was stunned.

Philip represented power, controlling energy vibrations throughout the body from the area of the mouth and throat. Through this centre and its power over the spoken word, spiritual faith could be inspired and quickened in an individual. The Gospel of John had begun with the phrase, "In the beginning there was the Word and the Word became flesh and moved among us."

Lexie knew the symbol of the living word referred to Jesus. What she did not know, and what struck her with awe, was what she read next. On the page, she found herself fully described, as the author talked about the body's back growing weak and disempowered under the burden of materiality. Those who suffered from chronic pain in that area were those who were burdened with material cares and worries. Constant feelings of fear and lack of faith in an abundant universe caused that centre to lose its strength. She saw herself again, as she realized that all through her life her areas of weakness and illness had always been the two areas about which she had just read — her throat and her back. Constantly she had struggled with weaknesses there.

But it was the mission of Philip that stuck her with true wonder. The text spread itself out in front of her like a road map showing her the way home. There, in the words dancing before her eyes, lay the explanation for all that had unfolded while away at her retreat. The long walks with Philip, his soothing presence as he gently told the story of his own liberation, the deep, dark pools of liquid reflection in his eyes that Lexie felt she could drown in. Yes, it was all explained. Had she been meant to dip herself into those pools to renew herself, to find her way out of her desert of denial?

Over and over again she read the paragraph, and each time the words were the same. There was no escaping its message. Was this all just a simple coincidence or was it more?

When a centre loses its power it should be baptised
by the word of Spirit. We are told in the Scriptures
that Philip went down to Gaza (the same word also means
desert) to baptise a eunuch.

('The Twelve Powers of Man' by Charles Fillmore)

There it was before her very eyes. Could she believe the conclusion stubbornly and persistently forming in her mind? She had known Philip had been a gift. He had been exactly what her wounded spirit had needed. Had he indeed been there to transport her from the dry, barren desert of her past into the passionately promising landscape of her present? She had, in his presence, truly rediscovered the power and joyfulness of living.

A spiritual and sexual eunuch, the life literally cut out of her, Lexie had been detached from her power, cut off from all that enables creation. In Scripture Philip had baptised and cleansed the eunuch of Gaza. For all who could see such things, this act stood as a symbol of the power of the baptism of new thought, new energy. For in the mind resides the power to create. Through thought's power to change and reshape, limitations that imprison creativity could be brought forth from the desert of passivity into the fertile crescent of action. Through the bodily centre presided over by Philip, the reality of the Word could live through the powerful expression of energy known as voice.

Her Philip had come to her while she wandered parched in her own desert. When he had left her it was with the living waters of her own internal oasis beginning to bubble forth. She knew she would now find all the words she needed to set herself free. The first to now echo through her were those of gratitude for her dark-eyed, gentle healer. Thank you, Philip.

With power born of new understanding, she was now ready to take on the formidable task of leaving Derek.

He stood there alone waiting for them. The first thing Lexie noticed was that his arms were empty. The very next day was their twenty-third wedding anniversary, his wife had been away from him for two long weeks, and he stood there with empty arms?

Not even a rose, a single rose to welcome me back. Why should I be surprised? thought Lexie.

How likely were flowers of greeting from a man who had to be told to buy his wife roses after the birth of their first child?

I guess I forgot for a moment, she thought to herself. *I've been around other men too long and I've forgotten my motto. Expect nothing, then you're not disappointed!*

She had to admit she had nothing for him either, having given up giving him gifts years ago when he had always berated her for doing so. Still, she had hoped. She had been away for two weeks, and it was their anniversary. If love was ever going to conquer all, this had to be the time.

It wasn't.

What he did have was an angry story. No sooner had she walked up to him and planted the obligatory kiss on his cheek when he started in on it. He had to tell her all the unsettling things that had transpired during her absence and how he had managed to fix them all.

Lexie's stomach had turned when she kissed him, but she had not wanted to risk the questions he would ask if she had behaved differently than usual. She almost always played the role of loving wife. The act would have to continue a little longer.

Her intestines continued to writhe and knot as she listened to the tale he had to tell. As they struggled with their bags and found their way out to the car, the story unfolded. Derek never missed an opportunity to show how well he thought he had handled something.

For years, he had had the habit of coming in from work and emptying his pockets of wallet and keys leaving them on the counter next to the phone. It had always bugged Lexie because of the clutter and also she felt it was being careless with money. A few years before, Jessica had had her wallet stolen from that very spot when a group of teens had been at the house for a party.

It was like listening to a replay of a bad plot as Derek laid out the details. It seemed Jade had also had a group of friends over a day or so before Lexie arrived home, and Derek had again left his wallet and keys by the phone. This group of friends also included some friends of friends that Jade did not normally associate with and, predictably, the next day Derek discovered two hundred dollars was missing from his wallet. He had flown into a rage. The one thing you did not take from Derek was his money. Looking for a place to lay the blame for this transgression, he had found his scapegoat. He drove Jade to the bank that very day and insisted she clean out the last of her savings to replace the amount stolen. Jade was now broke and bitter about it; Derek was convinced justice had been done. No move was made to track down the actual thief. Derek had his money back and that was all that mattered. The unfairness of the punishment escaped him entirely. Never once in his detailed accounting of the events did it occur to him to lay the blame where it belonged. It was not Jade's fault the wallet was in such an accessible and tempting place. Derek could not accept the fact that he had played a critical role in the unfolding of the theft. As usual he had maintained the integrity of his ego by finding someone else to blame.

Lexie and her mother sat in silence listening during the entire drive home. If Derek sensed something was wrong, he did not show it. He was content to have a captive audience.

Lexie's mother, fearing for her daughter's safety, had decided to stay overnight. She was to have Lexie's father come and pick her up the next day after Lexie had broken the news that she wanted a divorce.

All through the dinner hour, the atmosphere had been strained. Lexie had continued to play her role of dutiful wife, but the tension in the air was palpable. The sad thing was, her daughters were so used to tension that they failed to see what was coming.

Calling them up to her bedroom that night, Lexie left Derek downstairs in his usual spot seated in front of the flickering eye. As she closed the bedroom door and locked it behind them, her daughaters' bodies tensed. This was not like the mother they knew who believed in an open-door policy. She had almost always been accessible.

Lexie told them to sit down because she had something serious to tell them. Having given it a great deal of thought, she had decided to break the news to her daughters first before she even spoke to Derek about a divorce. Her reason was simple. She fully expected Derek to explode and rage through the house, and she wanted her girls forewarned of what was happening. She felt she owed them that much for the years she had lied to them about her feelings for their father.

They were looking at her with their mouths hanging open. She had used simple words to tell them what was about to happen. Sparing them the long gruelling details of why she was doing what she was, Lexie summed it up as gently as she could by saying that she had been unhappy in the marriage for a very long time, and she felt it was best to put an end to it.

Jade was the first one to recover. Her response too, was simple. She looked up at her mother, her face calm and expressionless. She simply blinked her eyes and said, "What took you so long, Mom?"

Jessica took longer to recover. She sat speechless and motionless. She had lived away from home now for over four years, and she had not seen it coming as Jade obviously had. All she could manage to stammer was, "If that's what you want Mom, we'll stand by you."

One thing that became abundantly clear as they talked on into the night; neither girl wanted to live with her father. Wherever Lexie went, that's where they would call home.

She fell into bed exhausted that night, not having found the courage or the energy to talk with Derek. She had made the excuse of exhaustion from her trip and had gone off to bed alone, pretending to be asleep when Derek had crawled in beside her.

During that fateful night of fitful sleep, she had been awakened by a shuddering beneath her. As she gradually came into an awareness of where she was, she realized Derek was sobbing in his sleep, his quivering body shaking the very bed. Lexie lay, her eyes wide, her body rigid in disbelief. As she stared into the black of the night, she heard only one more sound and then silence. A long, mournful moan from deep inside Derek finished in a long wail sending his body thrashing about, bedcovers wrapping and twisting about his body.

The sound filled her ears, the room seeming to reverberate with its primitive pain. Then there was only blackness, nothingness, leaving her to lie stiff with anxiety as the words played over and over in her brain.

"Lexie, n-o-o-o-o-o-o!" was the way it came to her again and again.

She closed her ears and heart against its sound. Tomorrow. She would think about what it meant tomorrow.

CHAPTER TWENTY-THREE:

THE COUNCIL OF ONE

Circle of being,
Flicker of light,
Council of One
Shining through my night.
Gesture of faith,
Unmistakable sign,
The More, my birthright.

For new works many
Will be commissioned,
Across our land moves
A spirit of omniscience,
Laying hands upon our souls,
Shaking us awake to old goals.
Can it be we only now remember
What we have eternally known?
From the One, all have come,
As gradually we awaken,
Preparing our journey home!

Two days later Lexie moved out of the bedroom. It took her two days because Derek pleaded with her to try one last time. Swearing he would change, he broke down and cried in front of her. Now, he was willing to go to a marriage counsellor. Now, he would do whatever was necessary to keep her. If he was willing to try, she owed him one last chance he said.

He worked on her until he sensed her weakening. The moment she wavered, he exacted the promise he wanted. Reluctantly, she agreed to give counselling a try.

Immediately, his mood brightened. With this small victory, he became confident he could put things back the way they had been before. Oh, he knew he would have to be on his best behaviour for quite a while if he wanted to keep her, but he felt sure this mood of hers would pass just as it had so many times before. He had her at home now, under his roof, his influence, no longer to be infected by the radical ideas promoted at that retreat.

This had been a close call. He had nearly lost his wife. But, already he could see her slipping back into her old pattern of doubt, vacillating, caving in to the pressure he was so good at applying. He was stronger than she was. She was the needy one. He knew her better than she knew herself, and he could use that knowledge to defeat her. It had always worked before. He was confident it would work again.

Sure he was going to get what he wanted, that she would stay, he made one more demand.

So desperate to have his needs met, he cared not if Lexie was happy, just as long as she was there.

He was right. She was unable to refuse him. Like a lost little boy, he had pleaded and she had responded exactly as he had known she would. She held him, she soothed him, she tried to mend his brokenness. The child in him brought out the mother in her.

She took care of his needs at the expense of her own. When he called her into the bathroom and silently handed her the soft cloth soaked with warm, sudsy water with which to wash his back, she did not say no. When he asked her to join him in the large, roomy tub, filled to its brim with swirling, fragrant liquid, still she did not say no. When he led her to the bed and laid her nude body down before him, she was silent. He laid himself against her, curling his slender frame around hers, entering her, thrusting away his pain, oblivious to all.

Through it all, her flesh lifeless, her eyes glazed, each thrust of his body pulled from her the last she could give. A vacant shell, her being was brittle, fragile, a skin stretched tightly over the vast emptiness inside her.

A conversation from earlier in the day played in her head, its words repeating the rhythm of their bed.

> A zombie I'll be if I stay, she'd said.
> Rather than be alone, he'd replied,
> I'll have you that way instead.
>
> His selfish assaults seeming to say, I don't care.
> It's better for me this way!

Later that night, she slipped silently out of his bed and into her daughter's room. Earlier, they had told them they would try counselling. Lexie knew, as she slipped between the sheets of this strange new bed, pulling its covers up around her, that the morning would bring a new story to tell.

She lay in the dark reflecting on what had just happened. *How much more would she allow herself to endure?* she wondered. How much more proof did she need than his reply today? It was better for *him* this way.

The meaning of his honesty seeped inward, cutting like acid through the thick layers of saccharine sweetness applied by Derek that day. Because dependency had for so long been Lexie's pattern, perception had once again been skewed by Derek's false charm. She had been drawn back into addiction. Dependency had for so long been her drug of choice.

But this time, the shroud of nonfeeling had felt cold, lifeless, like death. Revolted, she had lain like a conquered concubine, servicing his needs.

She had weakened, but she had not submitted. To continue this way, she knew, would be a type of soul-killing bondage.

The next morning dawned to find her moving back and forth past the marital bed, arms laden with clothes. Propping himself groggily on one arm, Derek struggled to open his eyes wide enough to take in what was happening. Silently, he watched as she removed her things. Not needing to be told, he flopped back down. He knew he had lost this round.

They lived that way for three months. She in one bedroom. He in another. It was especially tense, but they could see no other way. Derek had been out of work again now for almost a year, and Lexie had been carrying most of the financial burden, further increased by a string of investment losses the year before. Gone were the days of extravagant trips. They were barely able to pay their bills now.

When Derek's mother had been placed in a nursing home, she had signed over all her assets giving them joint power of attorney. Those assets consisted of a condominium which was now rented to cover her expenses and cash which they had invested speculatively in a new house under construction. Within months the real estate plummeted to below its mortgaged value and Derek had lost his job. Lexie and Derek were now staggering under the additional weight of that investment mortgage. Thus, there was no way they could see their way clear to finance separate living quarters. They decided they would sell the house they were now living in and each buy something smaller.

It sounded simple enough, but the fighting began almost immediately. It became impossible to agree on a listing price or even a listing agent. Finally, Lexie chose the agent, and Derek set the price. (A small victory she had assumed, but in hindsight she realized she had once again been duped.) He bullied the agent into setting the price unrealistically high, and Lexie resigned herself to living indefinitely behind a locked bedroom door.

Derek's moods became treacherously unpredictable. Each time Lexie tried to talk to him about the separation, he threatened suicide, then went on to wish them dead or thank them for setting him free. One moment Derek was charming and loving, the next, a raging madman slamming doors in his wake. Everyone was off balance. No one, least of all Lexie, knew what to expect from him.

Not only had she removed her clothing from the bedroom that day, she had also removed the shells from his shotguns hiding them in another part of the house. Truly afraid Derek might try to kill himself, she still lived with the false belief he would not hurt her.

Not knowing where else to turn, she sought help from family counselling. Even though the waiting list was long, Derek's threats of suicide were enough to have a counsellor assigned immediately to their case.

They all sat uncomfortably together for the first time in weeks in the small room of the mental health clinic. The tension in their home had been palpable and Jessica had immediately fled to her university town taking Jade with her.

Jessica had impressed Lexie with the way she had walked in, appearing calmer and more self-assured than she had seen her in some time. Therapy must be helping her, Lexie thought. Maybe, just maybe, this whole thing will turn out all right.

Very quickly the facade of functionality was shattered when Jade, the tough, unfeeling one shocked everyone. Strong and silent for so long, bravely carrying the burden of her parents' sick relationship, Jade now with the gentle prodding of this empathetic therapist broke like a damaged dam in a deluge, her hurt came crashing through. For just a few moments she again was the frightened, vulnerable little girl of her past. Catching everyone off guard, she broke the old patterns of relating. Jade was allowing herself to express what she truly felt, stepping out of her assigned role—a role which dictated she never cry. Always, she had been the stoic, scapegoat of the family—the silent, invisible child.

Jade's behaviour was new, and it flashed a message of courage. If Jade could change and express herself honestly, then perhaps there was hope for them all.

And so it went. The dance of relating began to change; Jessica followed Jade's lead by speaking out angrily at Derek's inability to see any point of view other than his own.

Lexie, too, changed her steps. No longer dependent on Derek's lead, she began exploring new patterns of her own. By changing her way of interacting, Jade had freed everyone else to do the same. In this dance of life, if one participant tries a new step, what choice do the others have? Moving through the resulting state of confused discord, they can either change to restore equilibrium or leave the dance.

Evident that the steps of the dance had definitely changed, all three of "his" women challenged Derek in new ways, daring to express anger, warning him his behaviour was no longer acceptable. He had two choices if he wanted to be a part of their lives, and he knew it. He must grow or go.

Purple with rage, he yelled over them in a desperate attempt to shout down what they had to say. Then choking on his anger, he became speechless, his words failing him. He wanted them to go back to the way they had been. What was wrong with everyone? Couldn't they see what they were doing to *him*? Couldn't they see how they were making *him* feel? It was their fault he became so enraged! They were always provoking him! Why wouldn't they just do what he told them to?

Speechless, frustrated, he stood glaring at them. Stuck in old patterns, his thoughts only served to inflame his sense of righteous indignation. They were all against him! Well, if that was the way they wanted to be, he'd show them! Who did they think they were, anyway? They were just a bunch of stupid women, and he didn't need them. He'd go where he was appreciated.

Shaking with rage, he managed to find his final words.

"You're just a bunch of stupid bitches, and I hope you burn in hell!"

Turning on his heel, his face and neck crimson, he stormed out the door, slamming it behind him.

His presence had been suffocating, sucking the life-sustaining oxygen from the room, his rage consuming all. When he took his energy out the door with him, the four women in the room collectively exhaled. Now, there was room for being. Now, there was room to breathe.

"That is a very angry man!" the counsellor exclaimed. "I'm going to recommend he see our psychiatrist right away."

Then almost as an afterthought she turned and added sadly, "If you want my opinion, I don't see much hope for your relationship."

Derek continued to make the same choices. No matter how the discussions were started, they always ended the same way. Unable to face the pain of change, he reverted to old patterns—manipulating with charm. When that failed, he resorted to threats. With his methods unsuccessful now, he would become enraged and storm out, unable to accept that his family was behaving differently.

Numbly, Lexie carried on. Having returned to work that September, she was teaching a class of grade seven students whom she grew to love dearly. Without giving them the details, she had told them enough to know she was going through a very difficult time. It was obvious she needed their support, and they gave it unquestioningly, with consideration and a gentle, nurturing respect. Not allowing any other students in the school to take advantage of her, they kept themselves as well as others in line.

Thankful for her work, she would lose herself in what she did during the day, but the nights were hell!

As Easter approached, Jessica had invited her mother and Jade to join her for the holidays. Lexie was looking forward to the change of scene and the freedom from the constant stress of living under the same roof with a volatile and unpredictable Derek. He was not invited to his daughter's for the holiday.

Sitting at the head of the feast, breaking bread with her two beautiful daughters, surrounded by the exuberant, laughing energy of their friends, Lexie was reminded of the potential of youth to possess pure, unconditional joy.

It's because their whole lives stretches before them, she thought to herself. *They have so much to look forward to - so much growing and experiencing yet to do. The world is full of endless possibilities for them.*

Smiling to herself, Lexie raised her glass in a toast. The light caught and danced its reflection through the mature, mellow tones of the well-aged wine. "Here's to the passion of youth and the wisdom of age! May we know them both!"

They stared at her, not understanding what she meant. It mattered not for she knew what she felt. That day, for the first day in a very long time, she shared their enthusiasm, their hope in a lifetime of better tomorrows.

Today I remember just how invincible youth can feel, she thought to herself.

The wine tasted sweet in her mouth.

The small, neat, white frame house perched sedately on the bank of the river flowing through the small northern town of her parents' ancestry. Having returned to the place of their birth to live out the last days of their lives, they had built their dream home on the legacy of land left to Lexie's father. That dream fulfilled, and with Lex Alexander's health failing, Lexie's parents had to move into town closer to doctors and a hospital. This, then, was to be Lexie's first visit north since saying her good-byes to the Homestead. It seemed she was saying a lot of good-byes lately.

Taking her suitcases from the car, she followed the path to the porch and stood looking out over the river. She could see why her parents liked living here. Watching it flow lazily beneath her, Lexie was reminded of all the rivers she had ever read about. How, as with so much in life, they appeared to represent a great paradox. Symbolizing the enduring and predictable nature of life yet, at the same time, their moving waters were the very essence of change. Rivers flowed ceaselessly to their destinations, only to dissipate themselves into a larger whole. Each droplet that had passed by her feet would give up its river identity and be caught up, transformed, changed, to a lake, ocean, or sea. Yet the river, the whole, always endured for in each part was the potential of the whole. Perhaps, thought Lexie, it is the same with us. Each of us a part of a larger whole, passing through this life just as the river flows. Each of us on a journey, droplet beside droplet, destined to meet with more until all that is flows together into one giant sea of being. I am in you and you are in me. The river, the blade of grass, the tree, all are no different. Here, as she stood and gazed out over the water, her view taking in also the hand of man with its bridges, buildings, towers, commerce, streets, and stores, all of this too, she thought, is part of what we are. *What is it,* she pondered, *that drives us to transform, change, arrange and manipulate all that is around us? Why can we not be content to be a droplet flowing trustingly to our sea?*

She stooped, picked up her suitcases, straightened, and turned to go into her parents' home.

Because she needed to be with people who loved her, Lexie had arranged for a few days' leave from work. Her children would be all right; they were together at Jessica's apartment. Derek was alone in their house this weekend. He was moving.

It was strange how things had worked out. Lexie of late had come to trust that some unseen force was looking out for her best interests, convinced that many times in her life she had been miraculously spared from the natural and painful consequences of her own foolish, ill-conceived actions. Now somewhat of a fatalist, she believed if something was meant to be, it would be, with circumstances transformed by faith.

As each day passed, she knew leaving Derek had been absolutely right. Not even for a heartbeat did she regret it. Terrified by the experience, yet strengthened by it, she knew never would she go back into that life of bondage. The only way out was through, and she had committed herself to experiencing and healing all the emotional pain that would come with growth. It seemed now even the forces of heaven moved to help her.

Completely unexpectedly, they had received a letter from their tenants stating they would not be renewing their lease. Up to that point they had given no indication they wished to move.

Like an answer to a prayer, Derek agreed to move into his mother's now-vacant condominium.

Perhaps it was not so much that he had agreed, but that he had come to realize he had no other choice. Lexie had remained firm in her resolve to end the marriage no matter what he had tried, and he had tried everything. His bag of tricks now empty, his only hope was to appear to be giving her what she wanted while hopeful the burden of such a large house, without his financial support, would force her to return to him within a few short months.

Derek rationalized that he needn't give money to a wife who didn't do as she was told. Besides, his kids were now both over eighteen. Why shouldn't they look out for themselves? He had! If they did not want him in their lives, they didn't deserve his support! He had cut others out of his life before. He could do it again. They would have to come crawling, begging for forgiveness, and only then would he rescue them. Let her try it on her own. Doomed to fail, Lexie would only be more humble when she came back. His plan made such perfect sense.

\Lexie had already been to see a lawyer, choosing a woman with a reputation for being tough. With each visit, though, it became clearer that the one who wanted out was the one who would pay most dearly. Wallowing in self-righteous rage, the spouse being left often operated from revenge not reason, and both parties suffered as a consequence. Difficult to accept was the advice that time would soften the situation, and Lexie's own impatience caused her much suffering as she pushed prematurely for a resolution. Having taken twenty-three years to get up the courage to leave, nothing was going to slow her down now, or so she thought.

Drunk with determination, she pushed Derek faster than he could cope, for she was as obsessed with ending the marriage as she had been with her unhappiness during it. Constantly, she came at him with proposals for dividing assets. Having never loved him, she could not understand the incredible pain of rejection he felt. High on freedom, she could not understand how he could mourn the demise of such a dysfunctional, bitterly unhappy union. She couldn't understand how, fearing emotional abandonment, Derek was fighting for all that had sustained him, for his very life.

He resisted. She pushed, failing to read signs of increasing frustration. The tension between them escalated becoming a living, breathing, palpable presence. Late one night, he'd come at her filled with fury, purging the pain of not being able to control her.

What had set him off, pushed him over the edge? They had been talking about money, about who would get what, and of course they were miles apart. That was the frustrating part. Her lawyer, experienced in divorce proceedings, had warned her to expect three points of view—the husband's, the wife's, and fair.

Derek's mantra, determinedly decreed through clenched teeth or yelled with purple-faced rage, was always the same.

"You'll get half of this house and nothing more! And you'll only get that because of the law! If it were up to me, you'd get nothing! Nothing at all!"

At those times, she'd whisper to herself, *God bless the Family Law Reform Act and the women who had fought to bring in legisla-*

tion so that wives leaving a relationship could go with more than the clothes upon their backs!

That night, the same argument, the same entrenched positions. Lexie naively believed if she just kept asking Derek to be fair he would be. Surely Derek wouldn't hurt himself financially in order to get back at her, would he? The concept shouldn't have been foreign. After all, hadn't she played the victim for so many agonizing years?

She'd had an insight into what drove such behaviour a few weeks before. It had been in the early evening, and she had just come in from swimming laps in their pool. She often swam to cope with her unhappiness. As she had stepped into the house, she realized she hadn't left the pain behind. Pain was becoming her constant companion, following her everywhere, no longer numbed by constant activity. Lexie walked around with a gaping wound in her middle. So intense was her emotional pain, it now manifested the sensation of a churning, burning, undulating wave as if something squirmed and lived inside of her. Focused on the hurt inside of her, she happened upon Jade and one of her friends helping themselves to a snack in the kitchen. Without thinking, Lexie lashed out at Jade with a viciously cruel remark that startled even her. Everyone stood, mouths hanging open, until Jade and her friend scurried away, hurt and bewilderment apparent on their young faces.

A bolt of poisoned energy had just flown across the room, erupting from the writhing turmoil inside of Lexie, like ripe ooze from a festering wound. The aftermath brought Lexie an incredible sense of relief, a blessed lessening of relentless emotional pressure, her words carrying her built-up, destructive energies away from her like the mushroom cloud forming after an atomic explosion.

That's what Derek does! The realization hit her full in the face as she stood alone in the contaminated wasteland of the deserted room. Her eruption had sent out shock waves, and evereyone had known instinctively to flee or feel the force of emotional energy out of control.

That's why Derek hurts others the way he does! He's so full of pain he can't help himself. In her moment of release she understood. Derek hurt others so he could continue to live. So much pain under such tight control had to be unleashed in small amounts, for he feared, if continually contained, it would literally annihilate him. To displace his pain falsely assured him he could control what he felt, thus giving some measure of relief. But, what if he dared to allow the monster out unfettered? Derek believed that to look the monster in the face, to name it and claim it as his own, was to give up that control. Instead he allowed it only brief excursions to intimidate and terrorize, only then to be hauled back inside, contained until the next time its clawing to be free became intolerable.

Now I may understand you, but I can't accept what you do, Lexie thought, the revelation only making her sadder. She went seeking Jade to make amends.

"I'll give it to the lawyers first before I'll see you have it!" Derek had roared. And so their arguments continued and escalated, as Derek and Lexie each recognized they could not make the other see their point of view. Lexie stood firm. Not this time could she be manipulated, cajoled, charmed, or convinced to change her mind. Desperate to have his own way, Derek reverted to a tested tactic of male dominance — brute force.

Lexie had heard a story once about her maternal grandmother, a diminutive French-Canadian spitfire, who had always faced her six-foot, strapping lumberjack husband with a broom firmly placed in her hands. "The great equalizer," she called it. Just such a broom was often given as a wedding present to the bride along with the advice that it was useful for more than sweeping floors.

It's too bad she didn't lived long enough to give me one on my wedding day, Lexie remembered thinking on this particular night, a growing sense of apprehension telling her she was going to need all the help she could get.

Backing her further into the room, yelling, bearing down on her, becoming more enraged with each answer Lexie shot back, Derek's fury built. She was not saying what he wanted to hear. Why couldn't she just forget all this nonsense about what *she* wanted and get back into line with what *he* wanted?

Nothing stood between them but the kitchen table; Lexie had moved as far into the room as she could, standing now with her back pressed against the wall. She'd been yelling back at him, something she had never done in all their years of marriage and each response only served to inflame him more.

She could feel it coming, could feel the energy building within him, reaching the point of no return. If she said one more thing, she knew he would strike out and send her head reeling, snapping it back on her neck.

Glaring, he stood daring her to speak, just waiting for her to give him the justification he needed. Nostrils flared, his hand twitching by his side, his breathing fast and shallow, he was getting ready to swing.

Every part of her tensed, getting ready to receive his blows, but she did not cower. Nor did she put her hands up in protection this time. She stood, bold and open, her head high, her hands calmly at her side, her eyes fixed upon his face and she said calmly, evenly, without a trace of fear, "Go ahead and hit me if you must. It won't make any difference. I'm not afraid of you any more."

Her heart stopped in her chest, her breath caught in her throat as the words left her lips. She braced herself for the blows she knew must come. Yet, she now knew, they could be no worse than what she had already allowed. Finally, she faced her truth. Derek had never had more power over her than she had allowed. She had met the enemy and it was her! Long, long ago, she had sold herself out and now she was at last facing that fact. What she was could not be destroyed by anyone else. Only she could be the author of her own destruction. In not championing herself, she had allowed the emotional beasts of others to feed unfettered, surfeiting themselves with all the power they could take.

In this still moment, Lexie unleashed the beast that lived within her, knowing now that its purpose was not to destroy, but to liberate. Its righteous roar of anger serves to defend the integrity of personal borders. It is the fierce dragon at the mouth of the primal cave, the warning that others should hesitate to tread on guarded ground. It is friend, guardian, the great equalizer, the force that pushes back when self-actualization is at stake. This beast lives within, allied with another force for, as she had come to discover, it is never tamed by the ego's illusion of control, but only by invisible healing energy that moves through all creation, the force she trusted would now keep her whole. Derek could no longer terrorize or intimidate. She had faced him, serene, at last recognizing the calm steady hand always resting upon the beast within. It was part of her, yes, this potentially destructive force, but it was not the whole of her, meant only as a tool for preserving the integrity of the self. In the wisdom of creation, was the whole more than the sum of its parts? Was this "something more" in Lexie now calmly, purposefully, fearlessly directing her? The anger she had carried inside her all those years was not a beast to be feared, but sprung from the love of self. In recognizing and releasing it, she had freed herself to move within that invisible force that governs all in the universe. In learning to love and thus champion herself, she had opened the way to love all that is. What a secret was this! Was there no force in the universe greater than love? She began to believe it could conquer all, for be it broom or beast that Derek saw beside her that night, he recognized she was a different Lexie who stood before him.

As he stared into those unflinching, hazel eyes, their flecks of gold burning into the deep, dark, depths of his pain, he reached flash point. His frustration engulfed him in a searing explosion of white-hot anger that travelled over the surface of his skin in prickly waves. The explosion came from his insides, radiating outward in concentric circles. No longer able to contain its energy, there came from his lips a scream of sheer frustration. What now protected her? Why was she now not afraid? He ripped her handbag from the table and funnelled all his frustration, rage and hatred into it as he mashed and mangled it between his strong hands. Swinging it high over his head in a gesture of blind, unbridled fury, he threw it down onto the tabletop, only to send it flying with a vicious backhand. Then, turning to give her a look of pure hatred, he fled the room, slamming every door as he went.

Lexie stood leaning against the wall, her hands now supporting her weight, holding her up as her body sagged with relief. She had done it. Staring him down, standing in the face of his irrational, explosive anger, she hadn't flinched. She knew it was over. He knew it was over. He couldn't control her any more.

Made brave by this discovery, she foolishly followed him up the stairs. So empowered was she by her newfound courage, she still felt safe sleeping in the same house. She believed the storm to be over.

Some minutes later, when she heard his voice calling from his bedroom, she assumed he had calmed down enough to talk. Stupidly, she crossed the hallway and stared into the darkened room.

"Lexie, come in here. I want to talk to you!" his voice barked in the darkness. Shameless in his attempt to control, Derek wasn't ready to admit defeat just yet.

Automatically, her foot moved forward in obedience. Then she stopped herself. Was she crazy, stepping into the dark with him? He wasn't rational. Who knew what he was capable of?

"No. You come out here if you want to talk," she answered cautiously.

"Why, you arrogant, little bitch!" the words flew at her just as he did. He lunged out of the darkness at her, and this time she knew no brave words would save her. Out of control, he meant to hurt her!

Diving into the bathroom, she threw her weight against the door to thwart his onslaught. As he crashed into it relentlessly, she held firm against each blow but couldn't get the door closed enough to lock it.

The wood began to splinter as he rammed his foot again and again into the door. He kept coming, and she began to weaken. With one violent shove he had the door open enough to reach in and grab her by the hair. Roughly, he jerked her out from behind the door and stuffed her head under his arm in a headlock. Dragging her out of the room and down the stairs that way, he moved toward the front door of the house.

Lexie knew enough not to resist. His fist was placed a hair's breadth from her jaw. One word would bring it smashing into her face.

"You stupid bitch. I'll show you who owns this house! I'll throw you out on your ass and lock the door! Then we'll see who's going to live here!"

All the way down the stairs, as she was being dragged and cursed at, Lexie had remained silent. As they neared the door, she realized she was about to be thrown barefoot out into the cold spring night. Perhaps the shame of it all was just too much to bear, their foolishness being exposed to the outside world, or perhaps it was just the fact that she hated the cold, but whatever it was, she knew she could tolerate no more whatever the price she had to pay. If he hit her, then so be it. She refused to live in fear of this bully any longer.

When Derek loosened his grip on her long enough to reach for the door handle, she had her chance. Struggling to work her way free, she began to move. An energy that had been building up inside of her burst forth in a desperate plea for sanity.

Her wail cut through Derek like a knife, bringing into focus just what he was about to do. Just as her last words echoed in the empty hallway, he loosened his grasp on her throat.

"You're acting like an a-ni-mal!!!!!" was all she had said, but it had been enough to jolt him back to reality.

He knew it was true. He had been out of control. As she slid out from under his arm and collapsed on a nearby chair, her hands running over the flesh of her bruised throat, Derek himself crumpled onto the stairs in front of her.

His head fell into his hands, sobs rocked his body, and his shoulders slumped. Appearing small and vulnerable, he became a sobbing mass of remorse.

Lexie sat in her chair and cried with him.

The scene of that night had played again through her mind as she sat telling her parents. Silent and sad, their faces reflected a deep sense of despair that their daughter's marriage had come to this.

Her father, a man of few words, but a man who had always lived life with a deep sense of personal integrity, quietly spoke when she finished.

"Lexie, you know we love and support you, and we had hoped to do the same for Derek. He has been a big part of this family for many years. I never condoned the way he acted with you, but I felt it was up to you to say how you would or would not be treated. You're both good people. No one is ever all bad you know. It's never just one person's fault. I think you realize that, and you're willing to look at the part you played in all of this. But, honey, somehow, I don't think Derek is there yet. He stands to lose more than he'll ever know with this violent, punishing attitude of his. You know, all I said to him when we first talked about your separation, was that as a man, he had an obligation to be fair to the woman who had worked by his side all those years to build something together. It looks like he didn't take my advice Lexie."

He stopped to reflect a moment and added, "But I guess if he was a reasonable man, you might still be with him, wouldn't you?"

With that he got up from his chair, softly touched her shoulder, and then left the room to Lexie and her mother. He knew they would talk about this situation for hours on end, analysing every detail. That was not his style. He had said what he thought about it all, and he was wise enough to know that if you truly wanted to change a situation, talking to others about it rarely solved anything. This was between Derek and Lexie. They were the ones who should be talking. If they couldn't, there really wasn't much anyone else could do except help them get on with the business of separating. He respected his daughter's courage to at last make changes. He had seen the unreasonableness of Derek's position on their last visit when Derek, convinced his in-laws were not cooperating with his efforts to convince Lexie to stay, had ordered them out of *his* home.

Lex Alexander, veteran of a world war, husband, father of four, sufferer of untreated bouts of depression followed by manic euphoria, now a heart patient facing the last few years of his life, had learned a thing or two during his earthly existence. Having paid a dear price for years of denying he had feelings, playing instead the role of stoic, able provider, he'd only sought help for his all-pervading sense of hopelessness a few years before. His involvement now in a spiritual programme of recovery designed for emotionally bankrupt individuals had brought him a great measure of relief. Reclaiming his feelings, he had at last experienced a calm acceptance of life. By changing himself, he had transformed all he experienced; by plumbing new depths in himself, he had brought a new richness of understanding to his life. He understood Derek. He understood his pain and knew how such pain could destroy a man if he refused to accept his own vulnerability. Pain had nearly destroyed him. Men have to feel. To believe otherwise is a prescription for insanity.

As he headed out for his evening walk, following the road, he said silently to himself, *My prayers are with you, Derek. May you become the man you were meant to be.*

Foreign words from the man who could never believe in the power of prayer because its effectiveness could not be demonstrated unequivocally, the man who had argued with his eldest daughter that there surely was no God, for how could a loving God allow so much pain? "There was nothing more," he had said. "Reality was defined by our five senses. This was all there was and when we died all that we were was extinguished, ceasing to be."

Filled with fear for so many years, he'd felt so alone. Were they fools, those who called on a deity, an unseen force, to help them in times of need? How could they be sure? Now, he laughed at himself. What a fool *he* had been. Had he not seen the hand of God working in his own life? How could he have been so blind? He had put God on the shelf, convincing himself that he—not God—was the ulti-mate authority in his life.

Shaking his head at these memories, Lex concluded that he was never meant to be a philosopher. A simple man he was, and the simple truth now stared him in the face. When he had been finally able to admit that there was a power in the universe greater than he, when he finally was able to hand over his terrors and trust that all he was would always endure in some form or another, he had, for the first time in his life, experienced a sense of peace. The fear that had clutched at him night and day had dissipated, leaving an under-standing that he could survive whatever life had to offer, yet not be destroyed by it. There were things he had the power to change, and there were things he did not. He set about changing what he could and accepting what he could not, at last accepting that there was divine order and that the universe was undoubtedly unfolding as it should. (Just because he didn't know the agenda didn't mean that one didn't exist.) With acceptance came relief from suffering. To resist the inevitability of life was the very essence of suffering.

As he finished his walk and neared the neat, white house he now called home, Lex knew his firstborn would be all right. Somehow, she had come into this world knowing all these things he had strug-gled most of his life to discover. She had always looked at him with such incredulity when he had asked her how she knew we were so much more than our senses allowed us to know.

"I just know it here, Dad," she would say as she rested her hand gently over her heart. "Don't you?"

He stopped to catch his breath as he climbed the final hill before his house. Yes, he knew. Because he had become teachable, like a child again, his student sojourn here on earth was soon to be through.

Dusk was descending. As he started again on his way, the light in the window of the house by the river beckoned him home.

"This is Tuesday night, Emily. Are you taking Lexie to *that*?" Lex Alexander appeared a little concerned about his wife's decision.

"Lex, don't forget who introduced us to all this years ago. It's just that we've had more time to pursue it of late than she has, that's all. She'll fit right in, don't worry. She'll be fine."

With that Emily Alexander handed a very curious Lexie her coat and said, "C'mon now. I don't want to be late."

Once in the car, Lexie couldn't resist the temptation to push her mother for an explanation.

As her mother headed the car up the long, steep incline to the top of the highest point in town, Tower Hill, she calmly said, "We're going to a séance."

"We're *what*?" Lexie asked astonished. "How long have you been involved in all this? I thought I was the only crazy one in the family."

"The group has been meeting regularly now for about a year. There are eight of us, and three of them are actively involved in what is called "channelling." I don't talk about it much, and I guess you can tell why. This is a very small town, and people often don't take kindly to new ideas. We keep a very low profile here."

By this time Mrs. Alexander had stopped the car in front of a large, rambling white house on the crest of the hill. From this vantage point, the sparkling bay below lay at their feet.

"This is where Cassandra and Michael live. They're convinced the physical setting lends itself to the awareness of spiritual presences. That's why they offer to host our group every week."

This is too weird, thought Lexie. *My own mother involved with séances and spirits. I never thought I'd live to see this day.*

She had to admit, though, as she climbed out of the car and walked up the walkway leading to the yellow front door, that she was intrigued. Nothing was going to keep her away from this experience!

The minute she stepped inside the house, she knew. It hit her in waves. At times, Lexie could read emotional energies. This was one of those times. The house itself seemed alive with personality, excitedly welcoming her, but also almost chiding her for taking so long to get there. Its energy of expectation was almost overwhelming, calling to her as she went from room to room, until she arrived at a large, open space where nine chairs were set in a ring around the dark, polished oak table. The soft light of candles sent flickering shadows up the wall. This was where she was expected. She knew exactly where to sit, and, placing herself at the head of the table, Lexie waited for the others to seat themselves. No one disputed her place, simply completing the ring of bodies around the table, joining hands in connection with one another, bowing their heads briefly in a short prayer and calling upon goodness and light to surround them.

They sat and talked casually for a while, introducing themselves to Lexie and chatting about their week. They seemed in no rush to begin anything that Lexie would have considered weird or spiritual, content instead to let the evening take its own course of events.

The only clue that they were expecting something to happen was that Michael set up a microphone and tape recorder in the centre of the table.

Lexie, wide-eyed, was taking in all of those around her. The six women and two men in the group all appeared normal enough to her. Then it struck her. Was she expecting them to look or act like freaks? She had been psychic most of her life, and she didn't consider herself a freak. True, she was very careful whom she spoke to about her abilities, but she accepted her strange insights as normal for her. Reassured, Lexie relaxed and decided to enjoy this foray into the unknown.

"They're here!"

Jolted her from her comforting thoughts, she stared agape as the speaker enthusiastically said spirits had entered the room and were all around them. Just at that same moment, the big, white cat lazily sleeping in the rocking chair abruptly rose, stretched, and left the room.

Fascinated, Lexie watched as one of the channels in the group, a large heavyset woman of Native American descent, placed her hands flat on the table before her, closed her eyes, and let her head bob gently to and fro. Soon she was speaking in a soft, almost unintelligible whisper, all her words running together producing a hypnotic humming cadence. Then suddenly her head snapped back and out of her exposed throat rumbled strangely primitive, hauntingly musical utterings. As they grew gradually in volume, then faded back again into near silence, Lexie recognized the rhythm of an Indian chant.

The woman, eyes still closed, next began speaking in a voice several timbres lower than her own. To Lexie's astonishment, it was the voice of a man.

She listened fascinated as what was said expressed concern for the environment, with warnings that mankind's flagrant abuse of Mother Earth could not continue without dire consequences. The voice dreided the human race for being in an insolent, adolescent stage of development, completely self-centred and self-involved. Mother Earth, the spirit said, had been a tolerant and forgiving parent, but now had reached the limit of her patience and endurance. If we, meaning humanity, did not change our ways and recognize our interdependence with all living things, including the earth itself as a living organism, we would risk dying right along with our planet, our physical forms forever banished from our home, destined instead to forage for expression amongst the distant stars, leaving behind us a dead, barren parent.

Then it was done. The message given, the spirit bid its good-bye, and the woman who had spoken slowly opened her eyes and asked what had been said, claiming to have no recollection of the information which had just passed through her.

Lexie had found the whole experience to be fascinating, but remembered thinking that what had been channelled was nothing more than common sense. One did not have to be a disembodied spirit to know what was going on with the earth's ecology. She was encouraged, though, by the message of stewardship, for she felt it long overdue that all recognize God had conferred upon them the responsibility to watch over the earth. We had not been given the power to use and abuse the planet's resources under the guise of a birthright of dominion. If the words of supposedly channelled spirits helped us stop our destructive, egocentric, polluting ways, then all might do well to listen, Lexie included. .

Next an individual beside her indicated a spirit wished to speak through her. She told Lexie that she always sensed their presence by a pressure on the back of the neck and an overwhelming sense of drowsiness. Lexie watched as the woman's head began to nod and her eyes gently closed. Her hands also stretched out before her on the table, but they were placed palm up. As the woman began to utter words of greeting to the group in a strange sounding foreign accent, Lexie could not help but wonder how many spirits were lined up waiting to come through. *Do they take a number or something?* She had visions of them, their little slips held patiently in their hands, waiting their turns. The whole experience was a bit unbelievabile, yet Lexie could not have left. Compelled to stay, she wanted to watch and learn.

Was it the soft light of the candles flickering in front of her eyes or the soothing voice of those who channelled that caused her head to nod drowsily? Never sleepy in public, this was totally out of character for her, and she was incredibly embarrassed. At one point her head had nodded so far that only as it involuntarily jerked itself upward did she realize she had been falling asleep. Red faced, she had looked up to see if anyone had noticed and eight pair of eyes greeted her with smiling recognition.

The woman channel who had been seated beside her got up, silently moved around behind her and said softly, "Don't fight it Lexie. They obviously want to speak through you. Trust that it will be all right. There must be something you need to know. I'll be right here beside you the whole time. Don't fight it, dear. Let go. It's all right. Let yourself relax...let go...that's good...you know how to do this..."

Lexie could feel herself drifting. Falling into the soothing voice that seemed to fill the room, her body sliding, turning into fluid, golden warmth as her muscles felt like creamed butter melting in the sun.

Liquid, borderless, floating, she was then in a big, open space, standing in the middle of a serene expanse of white. High above her the sun poured through what appeared to be openings between the slats of wood of a roof. Surrounding her was the fresh, sweet scent of pine, the lingering odour of fresh-mown hay mixed in. She was in a barn. So little was she that the space appeared cavernous! The space echoed with her aloneness. But then, she felt something soft and warm squirm in her arms. Looking down, she saw enfolded in her thin white limbs, the furry softness of a kitten. As if it was the last thing on earth that made her feel safe, she was clutching it tightly against her blue, cotton dress which was cinched so tightly at her waist that it almost cut off her breath before it flared out in the fullness of its skirt.

Her breath. What was wrong with her breath? She couldn't seem to get enough air to breathe.

And it was hot, so hot! The tickles of sweat ran in rivulets down her face and body. There was a stinging in her eyes and nostrils. In the centre of that barn, she stood, a child of eight, dressed in a blue, calico dress, clutching her tiny kitten to her breast, and she had burned! Burned to death! While outside the panicked voice of her negligent mother had come screaming, searching, too late to save her, only to hysterically collapse weeping while soldiers with their squat blue caps, their shiny boots, and their muskets and mounts had ridden in circles around the wooden building torching all that stood in their way.

As she watched the barn consumed in its fireball, the madness of destruction all around, Lexie cried out for the helpless girl. Her words came flooding from Lexie's mouth in a compelling cry seeking to free her young spirit from bonds of guilt. From beyond the boundaries of new lifetimes lived, the words of accusation came.

Sobs erupted from Lexie's mouth as the meaning of the vision became clear. Guilt was tied to this past lifetime event—a guilt that carried pain forward to this life and needed to be healed.

"Someone here was responsible for that death! Someone here still carries blame!"

Lexie wept at her own words. Then, the trance was broken. Her sobs subsided and she came to herself, fully aware now of where and who she was. As if retelling a movie, she knew she had described the scene to the group detail by horrific detail.

As they all moved around her to congratulate her on her first channelling experience, no one asked the question uppermost in every mind. Who? Who was the one responsible for that child's death? In a past existence, which one of them had been negligent and still carried the emotional scars into this lifetime?

Instead, the group went on to talk about karmic connections and how past life experiences can carry forward into the present one; how we can be held in bondage by energies that have been set in motion in a previous existence, and how we can only be set free by forgiving ourselves and paying back our karmic debts, restoring the balance of justice in the scheme of things.

Lexie sat dazed, bewildered, only half listening to their talk. Her mind still back in the barn, she was reliving the horrific scene. Slowly, like cold fingers sliding over her, came the realization.

In a barely audible whisper, came her words.

"I was the one responsible. It was me. I was the one."

No one knew what to say.

Late that same night, her mother asked her to join her in the dimly lit kitchen. She had been "directed" to help Lexie she said.

Lexie, still too dazed by her experience earlier that evening, did not ask who had directed her mother to help, but instead followed her to a table where paper and pen were laid out. She listened, mouth agape, as her mother explained she had had quite a bit of success in contacting spiritual entities through a process called automatic writing. There really wasn't that much to it she said. It just took the openness to believe and the courage to try. Everyone, she believed, had the ability to communicate with beings who, though they no longer took physical form, felt a great deal of concern for the spiritual development of humanity.

She became very serious when she relayed that some close friends had asked if she ever contacted evil presences. Everyone today has seen too many horror movies, she said.

"For some reason they seem more willing to believe unseen forces are out to hurt us—that they are sinister. I don't know why that is. I guess we humans only trust what we can perceive with our senses. But, I have to say that point of view hasn't served us all that well in the past. We've still been led down the garden path, so to speak. For my money, I find it more comforting to believe there is a force of good in the universe and that it can always overcome evil. You know what happens to the dark when you shine the light in don't you, Lexie? Darkness ceases to exist. I believe evil is just the same. It becomes powerless in the face of good."

With that she straightened herself, took a few deep breaths and gently recited her prayer of protection.

> I believe that I am more than my physical body and as such can perceive more than my physical world. May I be assisted in my search for Truth and Love by whatever means is appropriate to advancing my ultimate awareness. Divine Creator, please protect me from all negative forces. Thank you.

She looked lovingly at Lexie, then closed her eyes, again took a deep breath, and said, "I'm ready to begin if you are. Let's find out if they have more to tell us about tonight. I just know there's a reason you needed to relive that experience at this point in your life." With those words she gently readied the pen in her hand and waited.

Still trying to fathom all of this, Lexie remembered she had read thatspiritual entities were reported to move the hand of the person in a trance so that messages were traced out on the paper, but she had never seen it done before. Besides, she was confused. Just who were these entities anyway, and what could they know about her purpose here on earth?

Her mother quietly whispered her request that "they" reveal her daughter's purpose in life, that "they" would enlighten and guide her to understand the message received earlier that evening.

This is too much, thought Lexie to herself, but nevertheless, the process held her spellbound. She had to know more.

She, too, settled in to wait, breathing in rhythm, her chest rising and falling in time with her mother's. Waves of relaxation washed over her. She felt her body letting go, sliding again into that fluid state of being, her mind drifting, floating, wandering in and out of a beautiful vast space of white nothingness, where her thoughts seemed to stand still, where it didn't even seem to matter if you thought. In that space you were content just to be.

The jerking movement of her mother's hand on the table jarred her out of her relaxed state. Looking up, she saw that her mother's eyes were still closed. She seemed not to be aware of what she was writing. The words at first were scrawled in large uneven letters across the page. Then the movements slowed and the rhythm of the writing became more regular, more even. Lexie craned her neck to read what was being written, but she knew enough not to speak to her mother.

It amazed her how the words flowed, sentence upon sentence. Without looking, her mother automatically knew when to turn the page and to begin filling a new one. It positively amazed Lexie. With whose eyes did her mother see the paper?

And then, as abruptly as it had begun, it was over. The pen fell from her mother's hand and rolled across the table. Her mother's open palm lay limp and her breathing slowed. She sat like that for a few minutes, her eyes closed, her body relaxed, and then a broad smile spread slowly across her face. She nodded her head several times as if responding to an unseen speaker. Her face seemed aglow with an expression of complete acceptance.

Lexie sat holding her breath, waiting to see what would happen next, straining with anticipation to see what had been written for her.

"Wow!' she said as her mother slowly opened her eyes. "That was really something, Mom. How does it make you feel afterwards? Do you feel weak or tired?"

"I'm sure I feel just like you felt after your experience. Think about it. How did you feel?" Her mother smiled at her.

"At first, I felt really shaken that I had been responsible for that little girl's death, but then this incredible sense of peace came over me, and I can't explain it, but I just knew everything was all right, that I was forgiven. I knew that no matter what horrible things I had ever done, I was always loved and accepted as I was. Somehow I knew that all the bad things we do are meant only to teach us about good. It was strange, but I was never for one moment frightened by the experience. In fact I had never felt safer!"

"That's how it is for me too, Lexie. It energizes me to connect with that part of myself that knows there is more. When we channel like this, I believe we just open ourselves up to all the loving, healing energy that is always around us. We become receptive to learning about our true state of being—our spiritual natures.

"I can't begin to explain all of this, and your father is still a bit of a skeptic that's why he doesn't come with me on my Tuesday night outings," she rushed on excitedly, "and I'm still not comfortable talking to most people about what I can do, but I've quietly been keeping a journal of all the writings that have come through me in the last months, kind of documenting the information they've been giving me. And you know what? I've been surprised and amazed at the insights and guidance I've been given about my life."

She looked right at Lexie and said, "I was told to take you to that séance tonight, that your time had come. You've been hiding in the spiritual closet now for years haven't you Lexie? You know that you'll take to all this channelling stuff like a duck to water, don't you? It's what you were meant to do. It's why you're here. Take a look at what my guides have written about you."

With that she turned the paper so that Lexie could read what was written upon it. She watched her daughter's face carefully as the message impacted her consciousness.

In the dim light of the kitchen, Lexie softly read the message out loud.

"We send you both love and greetings. The one you call Alexis is a very powerful medium. Her power is just bursting to come forth. She must give us an outlet for there are many around her. She will come to know us as her 'Council of One.' She has many special talents, and she must use them to benefit mankind. The two of you are old soul mates and you are finally coming together in a meeting of the minds. Use it well, my darlings. Tell Alexis she must seek help with her gift. Like fine silver, she must be polished to shine in brilliance. It is no accident that she is a teacher, yet she grows weary of teaching the little ones. Her time there is finished. SHE HAS PAID HER DEBT TO THE LITTLE ONES. She must move on to higher things. She will always remain a teacher. God has chosen her. She is a special child of the Light. Help her and love her. Let her energy flow. Together or in a group of like-minded persons, she can do beautiful works. WE—there are many of us around her—will help her. Have no fear. Your child is much loved. We must go. Shalom. Your guide, Jasmin.

So there it was. The explanation they had sought. As Lexie and her mother worked through the words, they marvelled at the synchronistic symbolism of the message.

The little girl who had burned had been eight years old. Lexie had first started teaching eight-year-old children. When she had returned to teaching this second time, it had been exactly eight years ago. So, Lexie mused, my debt has been paid. She'd always known she would not spend all her days teaching children. The pull to move on to other things had become increasingly intense in the last year or so. *To resist is to suffer,* she thought to herself. They're telling me that it's all right to explore new paths.

She became more and more excited as she mined the paragraph her mother had written, extracting golden nuggets of self-awareness.

"That's why that happens every time I go away on a trip!" exclaimed Lexie.

"What happens?" her mother asked puzzled.

"Well, it's alway upset me," said Lexie, "that every time we're approaching the house after being away, I'm convinced I'm going to see it in a blaze of flames! It's always terrorized me that I would one day lose everything I cherished in a fire. Just a nameless, yet over-whelming feeling of loss would engulf me each time I'd been away. I guess I had been away on that day, hadn't I? That's why I'd blamed myself."

Lexie continued. "You know, another feeling I've always had? I've always known I would be a teacher. That's not a surprise to anyone, but I always also knew I was born to be mother. There was absolutely never any doubt in my mind that my life would include children. I just could not imagine it any other way. And you know why? I was determined that this time I would do it right, that this time I would always be there for my kids. I guess I still had something to prove, didn't I? You know the group was right. I can understand that if what I saw really was a past life experience, its effect has reached forward into this life. Maybe it helps explain why I always felt life was meant to be full of suffering. Maybe that's why I put up with so much unfair treatment in my marriage. I have a feeling I've carried with me a deep sense of guilt which made me feel unworthy of the love of my family. It does fit doesn't it? I was going to do it right this time, no matter how bad it got. I wasn't going to desert my kids. You know Mom, Jade is such a cat lover. I wonder if it could have been her in the barn . . ." Lexie's voice trailed off. She was beginning to see there was no end to the significance she could attach to her vision.

"There's no way we can ever know about all of this, Lexie. I think that it's purposely designed that way. It's easy to believe in what is tangible. That doesn't take anything extraordinary. But, to believe there is more than what our senses reveal to us, well, I think the Creator made it that way to test our spiritual strength. It's what is known as the leap of faith, Lexie. You just have to trust that there's something more there!"

With that she folded up her papers, walked around behind her daughter, and gave her a gentle kiss on the neck. "Don't stay up all night. The answers will still be there in the morning. I'm off to bed now. I hope you don't mind sleeping out on the livingroom couch? We just don't have the space here that we had at the Homestead. Ah, well, sometimes less is more. See you in the morning, dear." With that, she was gone, leaving Lexie to sit alone in the quiet light of the kitchen to ponder all that had occurred.

With thoughts buzzing around and around in her head, Lexie didn't feel the least bit tired. Excited by all that had happened, she still felt a little apprehension too. What if there was nothing more to all this than an overactive imagination? She was a practical person who believed the true test of the value of anything was whether or not it improved the quality of life. She really didn't need to know all the ins and outs of how something worked like some people did, all she needed to see was the result. If channelling and thus being connected to the spiritual realm could improve her life and the lives of those around her, then she felt compelled to learn more about it. She knew the power of tonight's insights and how they had made her feel, even if she was somewhat uneasy about being called a "chosen one." Lexie feared her own capacity for egotism at times. She often vacillated between feelings of grand superiority over others, believing that she was capable of anything and everything, to feelings of absolute worthlessness and powerlessness. She feared that egotistical feelings of superiority might surface now, effectively blocking any further self-discovery. She well knew that being convinced of your own self-righteousness always precluded the rigorous honesty needed for self-awareness and growth. Balance, like patience, had not been one of her stronger characteristics. Her moods, and thus her capabilities, tended to swing like wide arcs of a pendulum, high then low, rarely coming to rest at the midpoint of sustained consistency.

Yet putting all doubts aside, she could not deny that when she meditated, she felt an incredible sense of peace and well-being. As her parents now explored the spiritual way, she could also see a difference in how they lived their lives, an unruffled sense of calm emanating from them both.

With all these thoughts running through her mind, she absent-mindedly picked up the dishes left undone that night. Putting everything away, she left the counters clear, the sink empty, and as was her habit, the dishcloth neatly folded across the single-lever tap. There, she thought to herself, as she snapped off the light and turned to leave — everything tidy for the morning.

Placing the sheets her mother had laid out for her on the couch, then plumping her pillows and slipping off her clothes, Lexie slid quietly into bed. She skipped a trip to the bathroom to wash her face because that would take her right by her parents' bedroom where they were both fast asleep. The room where she was sleeping was directly between their bedroom and the kitchen, and she knew she would be awakened early when her father walked through to the kitchen to make his morning coffee.

Dimming the light above the couch, she settled in to do her evening meditation. Still energized by what had transpired that evening, she found it difficult to settle down. Disturbing thoughts began to crowd her mind. What was she supposed to do with all this new insight? Was she supposed to teach all this spiritual stuff to others? Stuff she barely understood herself? What's more, did anyone understand it? Sure, she had always believed in it in a general way before, but this was getting really specific. She could just see the looks on her friends' faces when she told them she had channelled. She knew they'd quickly change the subject. Being able to foretell the future with psychic predictions was one thing, but being in contact with spirits? That, she feared, was entirely something else.

Unable to resolve the conflict growing within her, she tossed and squirmed in her bed. She'd been given a mission tonight. She had been told what she was to do. It was time to go public. She just wished that "they" would give her some kind of guarantee that the limb she was about to inch out on would not be sawed off! She knew her Bible well enough to know better than to ask for a divine sign. Jesus Himself had admonished all not to test the Lord God. And Job, each time he had complained of his lot in life praying for a heavenly sign, had only received even more tribulation. But, Lexie just could not help herself. She had to ask!

"If you're all really around me as you say you are, give me a sign, something, that will tell me that I'm not going mad! There are times lately when I think I really am crazy! Leaving Derek, making all these changes in my life, who am I trying to kid anyway? Then you guys come along and tell me I'm to be prepared for even more change, that I'm going to go out and teach things people have been locked up for teaching in the past!"

Following this line of reasoning carried her deeper into the depths of her despair, and she found herself rapidly abandoning the serenity she had had earlier that night. It was easier to feel fear, to wallow in self-doubt. That felt familiar! That she could count on. What was it she had always said? Expect nothing, and you won't be disappointed. Tonight, perhaps she had revised that to believe: expect only what is tangible and real in life, no magic, no fantasy, no miracles. Then nothing can disappoint. To risk believing there could be more, that there just might be an eternal source of good flowing through the universe, was to open herself up to the bitterest disappointment of all. What if life was nothing more than a cruel joke? What if this was all there was? What if there was nothing more? The fear that this could be true made Lexie retreat into her small, negative self. Could she survive the crushing weight of disappointment if she ventured forth on the spiritual sea only to be swamped by bitter, disillusioned tears or run aground by gales of ridicule?

How can I even think of teaching something I'm not even sure of myself? How can you even ask this of me? her inner voice cried.

She felt so new, so vulnerable, like a soft, wet butterfly emerging from its cocoon. Her wings hadn't even had time to dry yet, and they were asking her to fly. Still raw from the chafing of change, she was being asked to make one more; she was now being challenged to be all that she could be. No longer could she hide behind what, for all these years, had served her so well. If she failed, if she received ridicule and shame, she could not point her accusing finger at the one who had always carried her blame. Derek would not be there this time. No, this time it was her choice, and she would have to grow enough to accept whatever consequences it would bring.

What she had experienced on Tower Hill would not go away. Her sleep of denial was at an end. She was awake at last!

"Just give me a sign!" she cried out from her awakening awareness. "I'm weak, help me decide what to do! I'm not ready for all of this! Help me, dear Lord, help me!"

It was always the same. Struggling with her fears, she would exhaust herself in the process and then, only when she felt she could endure no more, cry out for help. Peace, then, always came.

As serenity flooded her, Lexie marvelled at the stubbornness of the human soul. Over and over again, it insisted on suffering, refusing to believe peace was within its Creator's domain. Just by calling out the name of the divine, peace was given. And always it was the same. Simple whispered words would wash over her, "My peace be with you."

So simple! All that was required was the request of a pure and humble heart. Why did the human soul resist so?

Drifting off to sleep, the questions were stilled for the time being. For now, faith seemed enough, at least until the new day.

As she fell deeper into sleep, Lexie found part of her mind strangely distracted by a repetitive sound. Struggling to become more aware, she deliberately focused her attention. What was it? At first it had seemed far away as if it was coming from the apartment above. No, it seemed louder, closer. What was it? Listening intently, she recognized it as a familiar sound, one she had heard often. Think, she told herself. You've heard this many times before.

That was it! It was the sound of running water. That must be it. The tenant upstairs was taking a shower. That's all it was. Content with that explanation, she groggily tried to drift back to sleep.

But the sound was stubbornly still there, intruding upon her peace. In fact it seemed to be getting louder, persistently, annoyingly demanding her attention. It now was so loud there was no doubt it was coming from somewhere in the apartment. She hoisted herself up on her elbows and looked about the living room, but in the semi-darkness she could see nothing amiss. The shadow of the full moon cast an eerie light as it shone through the partially open blinds, but nothing else seemed changed. Getting up silently, she padded down the hall in the direction of her parents' bedroom and the bathroom. One of them was probably up using the washroom, and she wanted to make sure everything was all right.

As she passed by their room she noticed their door tightly shut. Further on down the hall, she saw the bathroom dark and empty.

"Am I going crazy? I know I hear water running somewhere. Now where is it?" She turned and headed for the living room.

As she stood beside her bed, listening, she realized it was coming from the kitchen.

Snapping on the light, she stood in the doorway, her face the same colour as its pale walls. Directly ahead of her, under the black square of the window that looked out into the night, was the lever of the single tap, still with the dishcloth draped neatly over it, pulled fully upright! Water was gushing forth!

Frozen in the doorway, she realized nothing else was changed from the way she had left the room only a short time before. There were no signs of anyone else's presence. How could there be? Anyone who had come into that room would have had to pass right by her. There was only one way in and one way out other than the window, and it was firmly shut!

"I don't believe this! This can't be happening! There has to be logical explanation! Things like this just don't happen." Lexie was now talking to herself.

The sound of the water rushing furiously into the empty sink jarred her back to reality, and she did the normal thing to do in that situation. Regardless of how unbelievable the event, her conditioning told her that a running tap should be turned off, if there was no need for the water. As she moved forward into the room to turn it off, she became aware of a presence behind her.

Startled, she turned quickly to see her mother, her face as white as her hair, standing barefoot and as incredulous as she.

"Did you do that?" she asked. "Why have you turned the tap on full blast in the middle of the night and left it running, Lexie?"

"I didn't," she answered simply. "We need to talk about this Mom. I know there's got to be a logical explanation for this. Maybe you need a plumber." After she turned off the water, she took her mother by the arm and steered her toward the living room couch.

As they sat together, Lexie explained as best she could what she had experienced. Her mother's eyes grew wide, but she said nothing. She simply got up, went to the small desk in the hall where she kept a journal she had been writing, then handed Lexie a bright orange exercise book titled, "My Channelling."

"This has some of my early sessions in it Lexie. I think there's one you may be interested to see."

With that she took back the book and flipped through it until she found the place she wanted. Curling back the page she handed the book to Lexie.

"Here," she pointed to the bottom of a page, "read that."

Underlined in red ink was a paragraph in answer to a pencilled question just above it. The question simply asked, "How am I to know if all this is true? Can you give me a sign?"

And their answer, scrawled in Mrs. Alexander's hand, leapt out at Lexie!

"You humans, why are you so difficult? We will oblige you one day with a sign, and let there be no mistake; there will be no more doubt. When the time is right, we will make our presence known. But be aware, true faith is a constant. You must know that YOU CANNOT TURN US OFF AND ON LIKE A TAP!"

Lexie looked up from the page, her hand shaking. What was she to do with this? Could there now be doubt? Surely, "they" could not be more clear!

Mother and daughter, eyes locked, shared a small smile of understanding. Two souls standing in the light, in a tiny house, on the bank of a river, flecks in time, sparks of consciousness, swirling in the vortex of all creation, like water unerringly seeking its destination, circling down a drain. Droplets side by side, they had come, following their destiny, trustingly flowing into the vast sink of humaness.

CHAPTER TWENTY-FOUR:

WHEN THE BOUGH BREAKS

೪

"When the bough breaks,
The cradle will fall
And down will come baby,
Cradle and all."

Fall of innocence
Rape of reason
For this travesty
There is no season.

What is shattered
Cannot be mended.
Prematurely exposed
Betrayed, abandoned,
Unprotected,
Bearing another's mark.
Used, blighted, spoiled
Doomed to feel
Fractured,
Broken of heart.

"Mom, can I talk to you?" Jessica's voice came from behind, startling Lexie from her reflective mood. A warm mug of tea cupped in her hands, Lexie had been sitting at her kitchen table, staring out at the soft snow shrouding their backyard. A bleak January day, Lexie felt as grey as the sky itself. During these long, dreary winter months, she never did well, for she missed the sun. It was as if its warm light on her skin nourished her. Today, she felt her mood would never end just as she felt this winter would never end. Pessimistically, she was sure if there was any light at the end of her tunnel, it surely would be that of a freight train!

Derek had been out of the house now for months, and Lexie rarely communicated with him. When they did talk, it always ended the same way with Derek becoming angry and abusive. Because of these explosive outbursts, Jessica and Jade wanted as little to do with him as possible, choosing not to spend any time with him.

Lexie's depression today had been partially precipitated by the arrival of her credit card bill. Finally free from Derek's restraints on her spending, she had provided a lavish Christmas for her daughters—one she couldn't afford. Derek had been right about something—Lexie couldn't maintain their large house and support her children by herself. Derek had not paid a cent of child support! To continue spending more than she was earning would be disastrous, and she was worried. The house had not sold at the exorbitant price Derek had insisted upon. In fact they had not had one single offer.

Lexie, surprisingly, was experiencing a growing reluctance to have the house sold as it was becoming apparent that her daughters did not want to lose their home. Clinging to it like a rock of solidarity and saneness in a world where everything else seemed to be shifting under their feet, even Jessica was now coming home from university every chance she had. Lexie was becoming convinced it would be best if they stayed on at least until Jade went away to school. Secondly, she was beginning to realize the only way she could realize a fair settlement was to buy out Derek's interest at a discounted rate in lieu of child support. She knew she would be left to finish raising and educating her daughters while spending hard-earned dollars taking her delinquent husband to court. He had said more than once that the girls were old enough to be on their own and had made it very clear he had no intention of voluntarily paying support. No, the only hope she had was that Derek would eventually need money badly enough to agree to a lump-sum settlement. Then she would be able to sell the house and free up the money she needed. He still did not have a job, but had started his own construction business, and Lexie suspected he was earning money under the table. The question that now loomed menacingly was—would she run out of money before he did?

Another daunting dilemma was how to convince Derek that what she was prepared to offer was a fair price? It seemed to Lexie that fair was a very relative term depending on whose point of view was taken. Even she herself was having difficulty deciding. She had no desire to punish Derek nor seek revenge. All she wanted was her freedom. What had she done so terribly wrong except decide she no longer wanted to live her life with him? It seemed, however, that he was going to make her pay dearly for her release.

"Mom, are you listening? Mom, I really need to talk to you before I leave." Jessica's voice interrupted Lexie's thoughts and turning her head, she focused on her daughter's young face. She didn't like the worry she saw there. Apprehension cut through Lexie like a knife. What was she going to have to deal with now? What more would she have to "fix"?

Every time her children came to her with problems, she felt pressured to make the world into a perfect place. Wasn't that what her mother had always done? Mrs. Alexander had always appeared to have the answers, always been so sure she was right, always able to find someone or something else to blame for failures leaving Lexie to feel that her family, and especially her mother, were somehow special or unique. In Lexie's eyes her mother possessed the wisdom and strength of an infallible being. She had never heard her ever admit to being wrong about anything. It was all Lexie had known, the only way she'd seen how to parent, and she struggled to be just the same. Why then did she question herself so often, deriding herself for falling short as she stood in her mother's perfect shadow?

Always seeming to be effortlessly in control, her mother had never appeared to doubt herself as Lexie so often did. Lexie was so overburdened by parenting at times, trying to do it like her mother had. Intuitively she knew she owed her daughters more than always telling them what to do and how to do it. Recognizing her role was one of giving guidance and support, allowing them to make their own mistakes and to learn from them, she still did not allow herself freedom from guilt each time they failed. Why was it that she still felt responsible for everything that ever happened to them? If they were unhappy, she felt it was her inadequacy as a mother that was the cause. Carried with her was the illusion, the belief, that if somehow she was just the perfect mother, if she did everything right, she could miraculously shield her daughters from any unhappiness. Her children would grow up in a storybook world where they would automatically live out storybook lives and live happily ever after. Lexie did not yet know the difference between being responsible to someone and being responsible for them. Not only carrying the burden of her own unhappiness, she also took on the responsibility for her children's lives. No wonder she was growing so weary of always having to rescue, fix, and provide the right answers. Now, since the separation, their needs had intensified. She was all her children had. One parent had deserted them, and she was determined she would be there for them, no matter how weary of the responsibility she was becoming.

As she sat across the kitchen table from her daughter and looked into that concerned young face, she waited for her to put into words the pain she saw etched there. Familiar fingers of ice-cold dread closed around her heart as in that moment the horror of the last few months flashed through her mind.

How could it get any worse? she wondered to herself.

Yet somehow she knew it was about to.

As she got ready for bed that night, her body going though the motions like a robot, she allowed her mind to drift back over what Jessica had confessed earlier that day. She searched for clues to understand, to make sense of the horrific information she had been given. In a state of shock, from a place of total numbness, she walked and moved, thought and spoke. Not even sure how or what she had said in response to her daughter when her story had been told, she suspected she had said and done all the right things, but had she really been connected to what was happening? She thought not. How could she? How could anyone? Her state of shock was protecting her from assimilating knowledge that could consume and destroy if taken in all at once.

Going over what had been said, searching to make sense of what she could not yet believe was true, Lexie began to pull into awareness all the forgotten remembrances, fitting them like pieces of a puzzle now horrifically falling into place.

They had talked about Jessica's bulimia. Seeing a therapist off and on, there were times Jessica had to stop as the pain of self-discovery became too intense, but always she would go back, knowing that her very survival depended on understanding the compulsion that drove her to control her body in such a self-destructive way.

It was odd, Jessica had said, that as soon as her parents had separated, the compulsion to make herself sick had immediately lessened. She felt somehow less threatened, safer, and yet she did not know why. As she had probed into her childhood, looking for clues to her compulsive behaviour, she had discovered she was no stranger to throwing up the contents of her stomach. Lexie, too, confirmed her memories. Jessica had often been sick shortly after arriving at the day care centre in the mornings. Yet within half an hour she would be fine, busily eating a snack with no apparent signs of illness. Lexie had put it down to upsets caused by being left in new surroundings. And then there had been the many nights when Lexie had been out all evening working at the Pink Cloud Lounge when she would come home to find Jessica's bed sheets piled in a soiled, vomit-filled mass in the laundry room. Derek would just say that Jessica had simply thrown up all her dinner after going to bed, yet there never seemed to be anything wrong with her when Lexie checked on her. No fever, no flu, and she would be perfectly fine the next day. It worried Lexie at the time, but since Jessica showed no other symptoms, she allowed things to slip by unexplained.

Now other memories were beginning to bubble to the surface. There was the special way Derek had always treated Jessica, as if he only had one daughter. Derek would often address his comments only to Jessica, centring her out as his favourite. Totally ignoring Jade, he would have little to say to her except to order her about, telling her to clean up her room or to do the chores around the house. Also, he often even favoured Jessica over Lexie herself, trying to enlist his daughter's support when he and Lexie were having a disagreement, taking a special interest in doing things for Jessica, being protective of her.

Lexie had noticed this special bond forming, as she thought back on it, when she had worked at the bar. Jessica had been about eight or nine at the time. Lexie knew that Derek had openly called her a slut in front of Jessica and had said that if Lexie ever left them, Jessica would have to look after him. She would be the one who would be special to him. Jessica even remembered the day she had found Lexie's wedding rings on the dresser, and slipping them on her finger had said to herself, "Now I'm married to Daddy."

Jessica had been so difficult to deal with during that time, confronting her, challenging her at every turn, and she had seemed so angry. Lexie could not imagine why; she thought she had taken great pains to keep her desire to end her marriage a secret from her children.

When they had moved to the larger house and Lexie had become so involved in her business, her relationship with Jessica had improved. Her daughter had begun to confide in her more, to trust again that she was not about to leave them all. One day, Jessica had come to her and had made a strange request. It had been with regard to Derek and the way he was behaving with her. She explained to Lexie that she did not like the way her dad played with her, getting her down on the carpet and tickling her, not letting her up even when she begged him to stop. Getting older now and beginning to develop breasts, Jessica felt uncomfortable about the way Derek was touching her she said. Lexie had informed him of what Jessica had said, and he had stopped "rough housing" as he called it, but he often brought the incident up, and he bitterly blamed Lexie for driving what he thought was a wedge between him and his daughter.

Then there was the way her children dressed that had always vaguely bothered her. She supposed a lot of it was due to either the dictates of fashion or the normal modesty of growing, developing girls, but it made her uneasy. Both of her daughters had willowy, attractive bodies and both of them hid themselves in volumes of billowing clothes. Everything had to be at least two sizes too big. When they swam in the pool, they never went without the protective covering of a T-shirt over their swim suits. Lexie would marvel at how they would insist on swimming in a wet, soggy, clinging garment often wrapping itself constrictingly around their bodies making them shiver with the cold as they stood at the side of the pool. Nothing, absolutely nothing could persuade them to be seen in only a bathing suit.

Just as she was about to slip under the bedcovers, a final nagging memory stopped her in her tracks. *Why did this particular event stick out in her mind?* she wondered. Call it intuition, that strange way of knowing things she had, but she sensed so much more had been said than just the words Derek had hurled at her that night. Understanding enough psychology to know what projection was, she had watched Derek's back as he angrily left the room, and she realized he hadn't been talking about her.

"You're sick Lexie. You're a real sicko. Some of the things you've done! A psychiatrist would have a field day with you!"

She wasn't a "sicko." She knew that, never having done anything she was truly ashamed of. She had her emotional problems, yes that was true, but a "sicko"? No, that suggested things done in secret - deep, dark deeds that feared exposure in the light of day. No, there was none of that in her past. What was Derek talking about? The thought had startled her when it came.

He's talking about himself! He has secrets and shame! How could she have been so blind?

It had not been easy for her daughter to say what she had said, squirming in her chair during the telling of it, crossing and uncrossing her legs, shifting her weight each time a remembrance would cause her body to react involuntarily with a quiver of disgust.

Jessica's body remembered even if her mind did not. It had been talking to her for a long, long time. Only now, with her father out of the house, had Jessica felt safe enough to listen and to share what it had to say. No longer able to still the persistent whisperings surfacing in her mind, yet no longer wanting to claim control of her body by throwing up its contents, she knew she had to find another way. When her mother had left her father, she, Jessica, had been absolved of her responsibility to protect, maintain, and perpetuate a sick and dying relationship at the expense of her own healing and growth. No longer could she deny that the sight of her father repulsed her, that the sight of any man's naked flesh sent ripples of sickening disgust shivering through her body. Unable to look across the dinner table at her father's slim tongue or chewing mouth for years now, involuntarily crossing her legs, she would tighten the grip of her thigh muscles protectively across her groin, every time she heard the smacking or slurping sounds of his eating. The same sounds would send panicked pangs of remembrance shooting through her genitals. Shrinking now from any form of physical touch, she was isolating herself from men, unable to sleep at night without the security of a locked bedroom door and layers of bedclothes covering her.

Recently having moved to a new apartment off campus, the first thing she had done was to change her phone number, making it very clear to everyone that her father was not to have it or her new address. Soaked with sweat, she would often awake at night to check the locks on her door, convinced her father had been trying to visit her during the night.

That night as Lexie lay down on the bed, staring absently into the blackness of the room, she felt so weary, so full of despair. How could it possibly be true? How could she have failed her daughter so? To have eaten, slept, and lived with a man for twenty-three years and not known what he was capable of, not known what ugly secrets he had to hide, she now wanted to hide. Hide in sleep. Escape into denial. Run from the ugly reality of her daughter's words. All that she possessed she would gladly give if only it could be an ugly dream.

What was different? Where was she? She seemed awake as she lifted herself from the bed to look around. She knew this place. It was so familiar, a room out of the past. Staring at the patterned paper on the walls, she then got up from the bed and walked into the hall. Why was she here? What had brought her back to the west-side bungalow of years ago?

She went looking for her children. Where were Jessica and Jade? It was the middle of the night, and they were not in their beds. She walked further down the hall, past the kitchen and toward the stairs leading to the basement. As she peered down the stairwell, she could see the flickering blue light of the television as it cast an eerie glow up the walls.

Surely her little ones could not be watching television at this hour?

She felt her way down the stairs, her feet silent on the steps as she went. Instinctively she knew she must be quiet for here she was not meant to be.

Frozen, she stood breathlessly at the bottom of the stairs. Her ears strained for the sounds she knew would come. She was not alone, that she knew. She could feel the energies of the others present in this basement room.

That voice! She knew that deep male voice so well. It droned on as if in a medicated, mindless trance.

"Yes, yes, that's so good...So good...Yes, that's right...That's what to do...That's their job. You're daddy's little wife aren't you?"

Lexie clutched at her insides. The revulsion she felt wanted to explode outward, as her stomach pushed its contents up into her throat.

Doubled over, again clutching at her abdomen, Lexie folded her arms over it to protect herself from the clawing, suffocating pain. She strained to leave her own body, to flee what it was she was about to see. As her body crumpled under her, she lurched forward sinking slowly to her knees. Her head fell backward, exposing her long white throat, her mouth slowly opening as black and wide as a cavernous cave and from the depths of her insides, as the scene formed, coming into being in front of her eyes, came one long, primal scream.

"Nooooooooo! It can't be...!"

There, there they were—moving, breathing, pulsing images before her very eyes! Then the horror of it all froze, unmoving, becoming a snapshot hanging suspended for her to view, to witness all that had gone on in that darkened room at the foot of the stairs.

She knelt before the scene in her dream, knowing in an instant imprint all that had transpired, every movement, every thought, every feeling, every energy that had left its mark in time.

There he sat in his large, black leather chair, like a king in his castle. And there she knelt before his throne, little princess, little wife, powerless and pure.

He'd said those words to her as he'd taken her small head in his hands and guided her tiny rosebud of a mouth over his swollen, erect penis. He'd moved her head in rhythm with his words. Cooing to her, his eyes narrow slits in his smiling face, his body tensed, rising up to meet her.

And as her mouth had filled with his flesh, the tears of bewilderment trickled down her small cheeks, her eyes held in a wide and frightened, unseeing stare.

Why was he doing this strange, hurtful thing? When would it stop? She could only endure.

As the thrusting continued in the flickering light of the TV screen, with her father's soft moans still in her ears, young Jessica knew there was yet another still, small presence in the room. In the dark shadows stood the outline of a tiny girl of three, stuffed animal dangling from her hand by an ear, pyjamas rumpled and face flushed with sleepiness as the other hand nervously twirled the hair by her ear. And born of compassionate love for another innocent soul, the fear of realization gripped at Jessica as through her mind flew the thought, "Jade sees this too!"

And there Lexie had stood in front of that suspended scene, like a movie played in her mind, the actors never aware of who their audience had been, leaving her to awake to the reality of her dream.

She felt pinned to the bed by the sheer weight of despair. She knew from whence her dream had come. Each image, each sound, each awareness, recorded unerringly complete in the memory of the one who had stored, all those years, stuffed and denied the hideous, hidden horrors of that night.

She had dipped into Jessica's mind, pulling from it what had been secret and stored far too long, bringing finally into the light all the secret shame of that darkened basement room.

Shivering, she lay in her bed. She pulled the covers up tightly around her for comfort and warmth, having connected with the thoughts of another had left her shaken and unsure. It had happened to her before. At times she could even hear people think. She knew she would never have proof of what she had "seen." Her daughter's memories still lay buried deep, just beginning to surface. They caused, for now, only tiny ripples on the surface.

There was to be no sleep for Lexie that night, her thoughts triggering every emotion as she paced back and forth in her room, moving through the hot flush of outrage, to horrific disgust, to quivering disbelief, and back again through despair and sorrow into a sense of personal failure. She paced. She thought. She agonized. What was she to do with this knowledge tinged as it was with the unbelievable? Who could ever accept such a thing? Could she ever even believe it herself? A thought returned to her again and again. Just like Shelley on the stair, she knew that in some way she had been there. What she had seen had been true. Tonight by some strange magic born of compassion for the flesh of her flesh, she had been transported back in time, to stand and to view, that which she needed to know.

Returning to her cold, empty bed, she slipped wearily beneath the covers, and she heard her mind whisper to her in its old familiar way, *We'll think about this tomorrow.* Working her way deeper under the covers, she turned her head toward the window to see the light of the new day dawning.

It was tomorrow, today.

CHAPTER TWENTY-FIVE:

HOME AGAIN

ॐ

Today, my soul soars liberated and free,
Heady heights reached
Spiralling upwards to sunbright sky,
Touching the inner me,
Knowing the difference between
That which was the "You"
And that which was the "Me."

Today, in my hand I took the key
Unlocking gates I myself had designed
Stepping from dungeons of deepest denial
Into rooms of vaulted light.

Today, years long in its creating,
I danced and skipped
Amid towering monuments to human will
And yet, though I value all that is concrete
And real about me still,
I came home again this day
To my child-like awe and power.
Reconnecting to the very beat and breath of life
Knowing today, yesterday and tomorrow still

Spirit is all that can be real.
Even this the Creator gives over
Bestowing the gift of free will,
Our spirits destined only to ever be
Imprisoned by none other
Than the "Me."

"I've been so low, I had to reach up to kiss a snake's ass!"

Lexie looked up from her place in the circle to see from where *that* male voice had come. Everyone was obviously enjoying this gentleman's outrageous humour and she was curious.

She was curious about a lot of things lately, it seemed, having begun a true voyage of self-discovery since leaving Derek. What her father had told her was true, nothing was ever all one person's fault. Determined to find out what part she had played in her own unhappiness all those empty years, she was equally determined she would never again make the same mistake in future relationships. Accepting that in order to find the happiness she craved, she would have to do a great deal of work on herself first, discovering just what it was she wanted and what it was that made her happy. Needing to define her own personal boundaries, she explored the behaviours she would accept and those she would not. Before she could express to anyone else how she wanted to be treated, she had to become clear about how she treated herself.

One thing she was clear about, however. She was not looking for another man in her life. After her experience with Philip, she had no desire to become obsessively enmeshed with another human being. Enjoying her freedom, she was intoxicated by the incredible sense of power that came with making her own decisions without worrying what someone else would say or do.

True, she had more challenges in her daily life than she had ever had before, but she was so filled with her own power, so alive with the energy of choice, she was shielded somewhat from the reality of the responsibilities facing her. She ached every day for the fate of her two, young daughters as she watched Jessica struggle with her memories, and Jade charge through her life as an angry teenager with a chip on her shoulder the size of a redwood tree. Faith had brought Lexie this far, and she was convinced faith would carry her through. Somehow, she had to believe that everything would fall into place. One day she and her daughters would be healed.

Rapidly running out of money, she knew Derek was standing by, waiting for her to run out of choices. Fuelled by faith, Lexie trusted that the abundant universe would move to fill her needs if not her greeds. The problem she was having was with understanding and accepting the difference between the two.

Her conflicts, her uncertainties, her feelings of suppressed rage, and her raw fear, these followed her into her meditations. In meditation the great garment of worry woven by the thoughts of her day would slip from her shoulders like an oversized cloak. As her body responded and relaxed, perhaps for the first time in her anxious day, she allowed it to drink deeply of the breath of life, the very air that surrounded her, and she would become filled with an awesome awareness. In the great scheme of things, all that concerned and frightened her was insignificant! Fear was only a parasite with no true life of its own. Without the food of thought, it withered and died.

As she moved into a place of perfect trust, she felt herself surrounded by the beings of pure light who had become known to her as the "Council of One." Drawn up into soft, white light, into a place with no limiting boundaries of time or space, Lexie became one with all that was, ebbing and flowing, married to the rhythm of life, coming to understand she was indeed connected to all that is. She was pure energy. As such she could never be destroyed, only changed, transformed. They called her, "spark of the infinite, child of God, whole and perfect in every way, perfect in her imperfection." They guided her, granted her insight into all that was unfolding around her, and above all counselled her to be patient, to trust, to believe that, like all humanity, she was more, so much more than her senses had deceived her into believing. Always came the incredible feeling of being loved and accepted just as she was. It mattered not what mistakes she had made in her life, for they said, there were no mistakes, only lessons.

Left with a sense of certainty, Lexie came to understand that all she experienced in the light was true reality; her earthly existence was simply the shadow. Cares slipped away from her, and she became filled with the incredible presence of being.

Gifted each time with a richness of internal experience far surpassing anything she had known outside of herself, it never ceased to amaze her how, leaving her meditation, she could slip so quickly, so easily, back into the darkness of fear and doubt. It should not have surprised her for exposure to the nightly news revealed to her an earthly home shrouded in a blanket of negative, fear-filled energy. Without constant vigilance the inevitable result was to be pulled into the world's darkness. Even though her heightened awareness manifested itself almost every day now, still she doubted. Lexie often sat with someone who had come to her seeking guidance. She would go into her meditative state and proceed to tell the seeker all manner of information about himself or herself—information she had no earthly way of knowing. With her eyes closed, she would "scan" their bodies, "seeing" them with her inner eye, and she could and did accurately diagnose emotional and physical problems.

Because of the accuracy of her work, a group of people formed around her who regularly sought the guidance of her Council of One. Time after time she would amaze both them and herself with the accuracy of the insights given to all who asked.

Still, she doubted herself. Her first words as she came out of her meditative state and stared into the wide, incredulous eyes of those around her were always the same, "Well, what were the hits and what were the misses?"

Always she wanted to know how correct her channelling had been. Even when she had been asked a question in a foreign language, and her answer had come back clear and accurate, she still doubted. She never questioned that our physical existence was only one form of life expressing itself, believing the universe to be unfolding according to Divine plan, but what of her part in it all? The fact that she seemed to be more awake and aware than most "normal" people still frightened and challenged her. Who was she that people would come to listen to divine wisdom channelled through her?

There was one characteristic that she possessed, however, that made any other course of action unthinkable. This characteristic and the fact that she had always known, could not escape knowing, certain things about herself led her inevitably to explore further the strange abilities she seemed to be developing. She was a teacher. She would always be a teacher. That was the first thing she knew. Another thing she knew equally well was that she had been born here with a purpose, a mission. Driven most of her life, she sought to come into alignment with that purpose. This knowledge combined with the unique characteristic that she had the unfailing, innocent trust of a child left her no other choice but to pass on what she was experiencing. Truly she believed, deep within, that her life was guided, and if she humbly remained open to the possibility, the hand of the divine could touch her life. Thus, she offered herself as a tool to be used in the shaping of the consciousness of this world, and it would never have occurred to her to resist the process. Perhaps all those years Derek had systematically chipped away at her sense of self had served a purpose. While losing her inflated sense of ego, Lexie had made room for more of herself, the true spiritual self, to enter into awareness. Ego, fearing its own death, often bolts shut the door to higher understanding. The ruler of the conscious mind, the gatekeeper that yeas and nays all that passes through, understands that to give up its power over discernment means to give up control. To give up control, the ego believes, is death.

Lexie had discovered that to be born anew there must be the death of the old self. To see with new eyes, there must be a closing of the old. Shut minds made open and trusting like those of a child, filled slates erased and written on anew, a letting go in order to receive, this was the process the ego resisted. Like a clenched fist held up in defiance, the conscious mind often fights to hang onto what it perceives as truth. How then can divine wisdom, be gifted into a hand closed so tightly? *Let go to receive!* That was the message she received over and over again. *Hold your mind and heart open like an upturned palm, ready to receive, trusting that which comes, to be truth.*

Lexie had no difficulty receiving guidance. Her difficulty was acting upon it. To those whom much is given, much is expected. That became her conflict. How was she to live and teach these beliefs when fear was always so near - fear of ridicule, fear of being wrong, fear of being seen as different or unbalanced? Still hooked into the "otherness" of her existence, she had not completely learned the dictum, "What other people think of me is none of my business!"

More work was needed before Lexie could fully believe uniqueness to be a blessing, not a curse.

Lexie bounced into the Twelve Step meeting that night. In spite of so much of the doubt in her life, there was one thing that never changed; one emotion that was always constant. She was passionately grateful for her freedom! Derek had been her greatest teacher, her greatest mirror! When she had finally been ready to let go of the critical, controlling parent within herself, then she had been able to let Derek go. By rejecting that part of herself, she had been free to reject him. Like always attracts like. Sick can only attract sick. She was learning to thank God every day for Derek's presence in her life. He had allowed her to see just how critical of herself she had been. He had now become a symbol of all that she no longer wanted to be. Letting him go had signalled her readiness to nurture and parent herself in a loving, accepting way. Gone from her inner life was the finger-shaking, never-to-be-pleased parent. Disappearing from her outer life was the finger-shaking, never-to-be-pleased husband. That new freedom put the bounce in her walk!

When she focused on her freedom, she was able to shrug off her doubts and do what she had always had a natural talent for. Whatever else could be said about Lexie, she at times had the apability to express the sheer joy of being! There was an indomitable love of life in her that, even though often buried in an avalanche of self-doubt, always struggled heroically to the surface.

Her two-pronged personality caused her, at times, to soar in a euphoric state believing everything was within her grasp and at other times, to crash in despair believing nothing to be within her reach. Long ago, she had learned to accept the cyclical nature of her self-concept.

Most meeting nights, though, she was alive with confidence. It showed in the bounce in her walk, the jaunty way she held her head, the animated way she talked and shared. Each time she told her story here, she was reminded that she had found a key to her freedom and happiness. In finally coming to her own rescue, Lexie had gained a powerful, firsthand understanding of self-empowerment. An eager disciple of this new knowledge, she was willing to share it with all who chose to listen. Gone was her shyness of only a few months before. She now spoke with the courage which came from having championed herself. Finally having claimed the frightened, insecure little girl who had lived inside her all those years, she had taken her hand and stood with her as she had defiantly said no to the abuses in her life. Now she could believe in a conquering hero. *He* had not ridden in on his charging white steed as all the myths of society had taught her. No. Instead, *she* had stood firmly, strength coming from within not without, repeating over and over again, defining as she spoke, the boundaries of the self. She had refused to back down, refused to compromise, refused to put others first, refused to be intimidated, simply stating and restating what was acceptable. That, Lexie now knew, was the true measure of individual courage. She had not run out on herself when her needs had been challenged.

Quietly, determinedly, Lexie had stood firm refusing to settle for anything less than what she required—to live with dignity. Lexie had finally internalized the ancient Greek temple inscription, coming to "Know Thyself." In doing so, she had been able to put that person fully, unashamedly out into the world. By making her needs known, without apology for them, Lexie had finally revealed who she was to the others around her. In these rooms she was learning how not to be defined by the "otherness" of existence. Her focus was now more on herself, less on others. She was defining who she was, and the resulting sense of empowerment coursing through her could make her literally glow. At times she felt as if she had swallowed sunshine. Light and energy seemed to radiate out of every pore. Her face beamed. There were days when she was alive with the energy of living! She knew she'd found a home, following like so many others with her here, the Twelve Spiritual Steps that led out of the dry desert of personal bondage into the rich, promised land of self-determination.

Those were the good days. Then there were the days when her responsibilities weighed heavily on her, and she would slip into the dark doldrums of incapacitating fear. To cope, she went persistently to her meetings, she meditated, she talked long hours with her friends, she signed on at countless workshops, she read mountains of books, she took baseball bats to innocent couches bashing at them in rage, she screamed and cried and smashed the steering wheel with her fists as she drove deserted roads, her empty car the only witness to her pain. From calm to crazy, she did whatever she felt she had to do to bring about change, to break old, self-defeating, limiting patterns of relating to her world and the people in it. She knew it was either be committed to her recovery or be committed!

And the days, the bad ones, gradually became fewer. Her worst day alone was better than her best day with Derek.

She had undertaken a quest with her first steps away from Derek, seeking a way to understand herself, searching for assurance that she would never again give her power away to a man, or to anything else, for that matter. Her searching had led her to these meeting rooms where she came one night a week to listen and share her experience, strength, and hope. This was a Twelve Step meeting, a place filled with others, who for whatever reasons, had also made people or things outside of themselves their "higher power."

It was here in the Twelve Step meetings that she realized she indeed was in the right place. Long, long ago, when she had been dating Derek, a strange, yet common phenomenon had taken place, rather like making a deal with the devil. She had sold her soul, her freedom, for protection. Handing over her power to Derek, in return, he was always to take care of her. Then she had disconnected from who she was, abandoning her own power of self-determination.

Now, she understood Derek was not evil. The true evil here, the "devil" who had seduced her was the false belief that another could be responsible for her. Lexie had forgotten the Divinity of being, that all are truly designers of their own destinies, bestowed with the Creator's gift of free will.

Derek had not deliberately set out to destroy her soul. She had perpetrated that upon herself by allowing his constant assaults upon her integrity. No, he had simply been playing out a role patterned for him by the controlling members of his family and a patriarchal society. He had believed acting tough and taking charge would ensure the love of the woman in his life, manipulating all that was around them, providing for them both. He believed that was what males did. The position of unchallenged power in his own home was the reward for his success in internalizing this warrior role. In exchange for this privileged position, he accepted that he would live without the solace of tenderness, with fear and anxiety his companions, always hypervigilant to all that occurred, responsible for providing for "his" woman, making her happy, and facing the harsh, cruel realities of a world operating according to the dictum of the "Survival of the Fittest."

Lexie, for her part of the bargain, would be spared this fear and anxiety. Whenever she felt threatened she could find refuge in the thought that Derek was strong enough and smart enough to protect her, to somehow magically fix everything. After all, he was her rescuing, avenging prince. Wasn't that his job?

As with all fairy tales, it seemed, no one had bothered to write the ending past the line, "They lived happily ever after." Lexie herself had never looked beyond marriage, defining herself instead within its limiting framework. Marriage was to be all that she was, just like the fairy tale, with the rest of her story left untold. Ignored was the gradual discontent that grew like thick, choking, brambled vines over the confining walls of her protected "castle" and her restrictive role. Believing her fate to be permanent, Lexie had accepted her role of submission. Her abandonment was so complete that she had convinced herself her that her lifeless sleep had been life itself. She had not foreseen the sleeping princess within her awakening one day on her own, the kiss of a prince unneeded.

Thus, she had waited in vain all those unhappy years for Derek to rescue her. He had been her "higher power" for most of her adult life. Always deferring to him, looking up to him, expecting guidance from him, she had assumed he had known best. Derek truly had enjoyed a god-like status in her life.

And just like the ungrateful and complaining people of God in Scripture, Lexie also had shaken her fist and blamed Derek, just as they had blamed their God when all did not go in life as it should.

Oh, how much easier that was than taking responsibility for herself! Come to think of it, she was not much different from most people she knew. All were quick to take credit for the good things in their lives whether they were directly responsible for them or not. Never, though, had she heard of anyone who had stood up before others and said, "I'm a failure, and I did it all by myself!"

Well, that's what she was learning to do in these rooms—learning to stop blaming others for the state of her life. They had told her, "You know, when you're pointing one finger of blame at someone else, there are always three pointing back at you!"

The literature she was given to read and all the wise and wonderful individuals she met shared gems of wisdom with her. She had never met such people before, at least not in such numbers. These were people who by most standards would not be considered a success by society, but who were possessed of such nobility, serenity, and deep conviction, that no matter what the world handed them, they were living their lives by their own standards. No masks here, there was no pretence. Through pain these people had learned how to become unflinchingly honest, both with themselves and with others. The price of self-deception and denial they knew for they had waded deep into that river and lived most of their lives mired in its mud, paying its price through their addictions and compulsions. Chemical dependencies, work addiction, excessive exercise, destructive eating patterns, compulsive spending, gambling, sex—you name it, the people who walked through the doors of these meetings had tried it all, done everything possible to fill that gaping sense of emptiness within that came to be known simply as "the hole in the soul."

They told their stories week after week, and Lexie would sit and listen, often shocked by the brutal honesty of what was shared, and every time, without fail, she would be touched as the individual took responsibility for his or her part in the events they described. Gone was the blaming. Gone was the concern for the social acceptability of what he had done or she had failed to do. The only criteria left was a personal code of integrity found by diligently searching deep within. These people were getting honest, with themselves and with the world, and they were healing. Their words were setting them free from their lives of bondage.

"To thine own self be true!" It was such a simple formula for happiness and a worthwhile life. *Why did it have to be so hard to figure ourselves out?* Lexie wondered. It seemed it had taken her half a lifetime.

She came each week without fail. The people she met in these rooms were her reality check. Here she could talk about what was occurring in her life, really talk, without anyone interrupting her, giving her advice, or judging her. They just listened politely to all that she had to say. When she was finished, there was no comment made about what she had said, whether right or wrong. There was only acceptance that what you had said was true for you. Occasionally, someone might call out these words of encouragement when you had finished speaking, "Keep comin' back. You're in the right place!" and the room would erupt in good-natured laughter as a sign that all understood. It had been a subtle way of pointing out that perhaps the individual sharing had strayed a bit from the fundamentals of the Twelve Steps, that perhaps he or she needed to work their programme more honestly. That was what Lexie meant when she called these meetings her reality check. Rarely did she come to her meeting and not hear something that seemed to be exactly what she needed. As she listened to others share their experiences, strengths and hopes, an understanding or awareness would slowly begin to form in her mind and the answer she sought would be there. Through reflection, Lexie brought to herself all she needed to know. In being open and receptive in mind and heart, Lexie saw time and time again how troubling questions which would have baffled and caused her great anguish before, simply melted away with the simplicity of the solution that presented itself as she sat in those rooms week after week. "Seek the truth and it shall set you free!"

There was another nugget of truth Lexie witnessed working itself out again and again during her spiritual recovery. It said simply, "When the student is ready, the teacher appears." Or even the simpler version, "You get what you need when you need it."

In the Twelve Step meeting rooms, it was accepted that this was your place to share your perception of the reality of things. As they sat together looking at and listening to one another across the circles of sharing, they all held up metaphorical mirrors for one another. They taught one another and they learned from one another at the same time. They would see themselves in another's life story and they would learn about themselves.

They would smile and nod often as Lexie talked, and she knew her story had touched them also. Many were experiencing the same reality she was. She was not alone. Others also knew that same sense of lonely detachment that had made her always feel as if she wasn't quite normal, that she was somehow inexplicably different. Others shared her feeling that they too, were somehow frauds, that if their true feelings were found out, they would no longer be lovable. Tears of others so often flowed as they listened to the pain in her story, the pain of her powerlessness, the abuse of one individual perpetrated on another!

Here she learned how to forgive herself and how to forgive Derek, realizing that the abuser is just as damaged as the victim, that Derek crossed her boundaries because he did not understand what it was to have any of his own. Abused as a child, his personal boundaries stomped across, he had only perpetuated what had been done to him. How could he understand the dignity of another when he, himself, had been allowed none?

Week after week she came, she talked, she shared, she listened, and she learned. Her support group gave her just that, support. Here she knew she could be fully, honestly who she was and be loved and accepted for that. She had never before been in such a haven of simple, worldly wisdom as those Twelve Step meeting rooms. People from all walks of life, now willing to put away all the foolish, transient things that fill so many of our hours with strife, focused instead on what they saw as truly the destination of this life journey. No more, no less than, to arrive at the end of our time, whole, perfect, precious, and free just as we had begun. Ending one's life loving and pure of heart, that was the true test of having lived well upon this earth.

Driving down a wide boulevard lined with stately homes and tall trees, Lexie found herself thinking, "Oh no. This woman is rich, and this is a Jewish area too! What can we possibly have in common?"

Her thoughts made her uneasy as Lexie prided herself on being completely accepting of others. The stir of discrimination she had felt had made her feel a quiver of shame. "No, it's not that," she rationalized to herself. "It's just that we come from two different worlds. How can she possibly help me?"

It was only because a dear friend had been urging her to see this woman for over three years that Lexie turned into the driveway and got out of her car in front of the large, sprawling house.

Having noticed the difference in her friend, watching her grow ever calmer and more peaceful about her life, Lexie, being a very practical person had decided to give counselling a try. Her motto now being, "If it works, it bears investigating. The proof is in the result."

Her finger on the bell, she stood before the big, white front door, when suddenly it opened to reveal a diminutive woman, with soft black hair, smiling red lips, and flashing white teeth. As Lexie looked into the woman's dark, smiling eyes, she wondered if she had found another home, another place where she could be free, where it would be all right to be just who she was meant to be. She stepped calmly through the door.

After the session, Lexie sat outside in her car a moment fingering the business card she had been given. *Imagine,* she thought, *me seeing a shrink! I always thought therapists were just for people who were crazy!*

She laughed at herself as she started her car. *Keep coming back,* she said to herself. *You're in the right place!*

As she left the therapist named Rose who lived on Sunflower Street, Lexie wondered about the symbolism, always one to look for significance in names and numbers. Did they hold, in some strange code, the significance of the events unfolding in her life? So many times, it seemed numbers and names had been prophetic. Wasn't it odd that her therapist's name was Rose? What a powerful symbol that flower was for her! She had always loved roses, believing they represented the bittersweet nature of life here on earth. The bloom, a metaphor for the incredible beauty and completeness of our existence, but only expressed at the end of a long stem filled with sharp thorns.

And Sunflower Street! How about that? She envisioned a whole field of giant sunflowers slowly turning, seeking the rays of the warm sun. *Hey, that's just like me. That's what I'm going to be doing each time I arrive here on this street. Growing, seeking my inner sun.*

Tears trickled down her cheek. This was going to be so hard. Growth and change could hurt so! Rose had warned her they would dip deeply into her past, dealing with all the issues of her child-hood, explaining that was where all painful issues originally came from. We just keep dragging around our emotional baggage from our childhoods, looking to play out the same scenarios again and again, convinced each time we dive into new relationships that we'll get it right. If only we do it better, the new person in our life will love us more, treat us better, and so on. Round and round we go looking to mend the brokenness of our family of origin. Until those issues are laid to rest, Rose had solemnly told her, there can be no true peace within us.

"You may be a grown woman of forty-four walking around in an adult body, but emotionally, you may be no more than three or four! You're frozen there, trapped by unresolved feelings, held prisoner by the infant within, looking at the world through the eyes of a wounded child!"

That first day, what Rose had said, Lexie found to be shocking. If it were true, it meant almost everyone needed help dealing with residue from their childhoods! Perhaps she should think about taking up a new career—in counselling!

Even though Lexie wanted to get better, she still insisted she'd had a wonderful childhood, and at that, this tiny, cultured lady, had thrown out a word with which Lexie would become very familiar!

"Bullshit!" she'd said, as Lexie's jaw dropped in total surprise. The words had been followed by a soft smile and a mischievous twinkle of the eye, but Lexie got the message. Here, too, honesty equalled healing!

"You wouldn't be the way you are if Mother and Father had been the way you describe them! Didn't you tell me just a few minutes before that your mother was controlling; that she suffered from an eating disorder after you were born, that she never held you as a young child? What about that father who sat reading his newspaper every night? Was he there for you emotionally? Did he do things with you? Spend time with you?"

Relentlessly came her questions, crumbling the walls of denial Lexie had built around her family of origin, toppling the unrealistic pedestals upon which she had placed her parents.

With the word *bullshit* still ringing in her ears, Lexie drove home sobbing. She had started the final and the most difficult phase of her healing. Sick and tired of being sick and tired, Lexie had been driven to make changes in her life. Now she was preparing to truly understand the pain that had brought them about. Like peeling the layers of an onion, she knew this process with Rose was to be the removal of the final, most delicate layers, bringing her ever closer to who she truly was.

"It's going to hurt like hell! I just know it is! It's going to get worse before it gets better! Can I do this?" she asked herself through her tears.

"The only way out is through!" The Twelve Step slogan became her answer.

Sitting this summer night in a meeting, reflecting on the path her life was taking, living one day at a time, focused on the present, attempting to no longer let those two great thieves of happiness—regret about the past, and fear of the future—rob her of her peace of mind, Lexie was diligently working her programme, outlined by the Twelve Steps of Co-Dependents Anonymous, an offshoot of Alcoholics Anonymous. It had been designed for people with dysfunctional dependency and enmeshment behaviour patterns, for as many addicts had discovered, relationship problems were almost always the root cause of their addictions. The first waves of recovering alcoholics, in their relentless search for personal truth, had over the years come to understand that recovery was so much more than putting the cork in the bottle. Their addiction had been a means of surviving the dysfunctional and emotionally-destroying relationships within their first families. As they came to understand that as addicts they continued to perpetuate these unhealthy dynamics in their future relationships, an organization evolved to help heal the alcoholic beyond the realm of just ceasing to drink. Even when free of the insanity of alcohol, the dysfunctional behaviour patterns, the aching empty feelings, had remained. It was then recognized by many that more healing work had to be done. Without the medication of addiction numbing them to their pain, they had been driven to heal their emotional issues.

Never a chemically addicted person, Lexie still shared many of the same issues which drove people to drink, use drugs, gamble, vomit, starve, and abuse themselves and others. All frightened, emotionally-immature individuals looking outside of themselves for their answers, they had handed their power over to some "-ism"—alcoholism, workaholism—it didn't matter. All addictions were the same. Only when the realization came that having control of their lives meant taking that control from the addiction and handing it over to a power greater than themselves did release from the bondage of addiction finally come.

Lexie had been addicted to Derek. It was as simple as that. She had made him her higher power, giving him the responsibility for her life and her happiness! Power traded for protection, it had worked for her for many years. She'd been able to stay child-like, never really growing up, able to blame Derek for all her woes. Sadly, the dysfunction had stunted Derek's growth as well. He was stuck as the all-powerful, always-right higher power, never free to be vulnerable or needy, never allowed to be a fully-feeling human being.

Unplugged from her unhealthy dependency, many aspects of Lexie's life now seemed to be coming together. In meditation, the Council of One had often told her that to be a fully-functioning human being, it was necessary to have all aspects of the self in balance. This balance would result in a serenity and powerful feeling of centredness. From this centre would flow all that was necessary to sustain the integrity, and thus, the peace of mind of the individual. Like the hub of a wheel, the individual would remain constant, while all her life events revolved around her. Whatever occurred would be handled with a calm sense of surety. The Council further explained that there were four areas to be aligned in order to achieve this state of balance. If any area were neglected or overemphasized, an imbalance would result. Life would become more and more of an effort, resistance would be encountered, like travelling the road of life with a wobble in your wheel!

Over and over her Council told her, "Look to be spiritually, physically, intellectually, and emotionally balanced. All these aspects of the self are to be in harmony with none overshadowing the other. Only then can true serenity be achieved."

Rose was to help her fit that last piece into place. So often her emotions sabotaged her peace of mind. The ability to love was one of her greatest strengths, but the ability to love too much had also been one of her greatest weaknesses. Balance. Always the answer was balance. Not too much, not too little. Love of the Creator, love of self, love of others, all in balance.

Intellectual balancing, what of that? thought Lexie. Like so many others in Western society, she had lived in her head most of her life, intellectualizing everything, including herself. It had been her way of escaping her feelings. Heart and mind had divorced long ago.

Perhaps my heart should sue for mental cruelty, she thought wryly, for she had certainly prided herself in her ability to rationalize, reason, and denounce as foolish the whispers of her heart.

Learning to listen to those whispers, she now stopped and asked herself, *What is this I am feeling?*

Physical balance. Now that was the only easy one. Humbled, lying helpless for months while her back had healed, she had developed a great reverence for her body. As a result she had become devoted to regular exercise and a healthy diet. Without exercise her back would go into open rebellion, stiffening up so that she could barely get out of bed. Her body had forcefully made its needs known, pain the catalyst necessitating her habits of health.

The spiritual self had led the way for all other aspects to come into alignment. Even as a very young child, Lexie could never conceive of living life on this harsh, difficult planet without the inner light of spirit whispering encouragingly to her again and again, "There is more. There is always more!"

Too bad she hadn't taken the time sooner to ask for details!

Bringing her wheel of life into balance, allowing it to turn serenely as it manifested an external beauty and harmony around an internal core of pure, indestructible, spiritual energy. That became her quest!

Feeling good about herself, better than she had in years, sitting serenely at her Twelve Step meeting, Lexie was jolted out of her reverie by another outrageous comment, and she realized with a start, that because of this man's humour, she especially enjoyed the meetings where he was present.

"Ya, I've felt a lot like a rattlesnake caught in a lawn mower this past year. Probably looked a bit like one too at times, but I've figured one thing out all these months in programme. When I feel that old sense of overwhelming FEAR coming down on me, I just remember what that word means."

He got quiet for a moment and his voice lowered in seriousness.

"Ya, it means, Face Everything And Recover."

All heads in the room nodded their silent agreement.

He cleared his throat, working uneasily to manage the emotion surfacing in him. Embodied in that statement was an admission of his own dysfunctionality, an admission of his past mistakes. Millionaire or bum, it made no difference. He knew they were all in the right place. Deeply humbled by his life of the last year, he had been forcefully shown that even his fortune was no protection from emotional pain.

But, not one to remain maudlin for long, possessing too much Irish impishness for that, his big, blue eyes twinkled, the tanned skin around them crinkling up with the hint of a smile well contained as he savoured the moment. He knew he had the group right where he wanted them. Then it came. He had given them the bitter, now he was about to deliver the sweet, for he understood one thing well. When we finally learn to laugh at ourselves, we heal!

"Yeah, you know you guys," he snorted. "FEAR doesn't stand for 'Fuck Everything And Run!'"

The room erupted in gales of appreciative, understanding laughter.

Him, again! I should have known. She had come to enjoy the big, burly blonde man's style of sharing. He didn't take himself too seriously, and she liked that. As she was changing, the people she wanted around her seemed to reflect that change. Her readiness to laugh at herself and life signalled that a new "teacher" was about to appear.

"You all understand the no cross-talk rule, I presume?" Lexie smiled at the faces surrounding her. Lexie went on, "We're here to share our experiences, strengths, and hopes and if our sharing is only 'dumping' on others we'll not grow. Cross-talking refers to commenting on what another has said. That is not our job. We're not trained therapists here, and we don't pretend to be able to solve each other's problems. In fact being focused on others and trying to fix the people in our lives is probably what got us here in the first place!"

With that, Lexie, who had volunteered to chair this small group session, smiled, looked around the circle and asked, "Who'd like to share first?"

There was an awkward silence, a clearing of throats, and then the familiar statement, "Hi, my name is Dan, and I'm a codependent committed to my recovery."

While he talked on, Lexie was aware of the simple, powerful process in which this young man, a recovering human being, was involved. The first words out of his mouth had challenged denial. Admitting his problem to himself and to others was Step One: "Admitted I was powerless over other people and that my life had become unmanageable!"

"Hi, Dan," the group had echoed back to him. "Welcome!"

And there it was! Such a simple thing, but it was exactly why these programmes worked. Two simple statements strung one after the other, and they carried such an awesome power to heal! Admission followed by acceptance. That was the key. Unconditional acceptance. Dan had not introduced himself by saying, "Hi, my name is Dan, and I'm a success in life!" No one knew or cared what Dan did, how much he earned, where he lived, what kind of car he drove, if he even owned one, whether he beat his wife, loved his kids, or went to church each Sunday. It just didn't matter! What mattered was that he was another human being struggling to make sense out of his life and because of that fact, and that fact alone, he was acceptable. Admission and acceptance. The Twelve Step programme had been so phenomenally successful, achieving results where all else had failed, because the programme recognized the incredible healing power of unconditional love. No matter who you were, or how unlovable you envisioned yourself to be, as these people witnessed the emergence of your true self, they welcomed and supported you. Not only that, they even told you to keep coming back! In the acceptance and support of these groups, all could find a new day dawning, a new beginning, hope for a better way. In learning, one day at a time, to live life as it had been intended, precious and free, these individuals who had merely survived life before, looked at the world through new eyes. As they learned to give themselves unconditional love and nurturing, they learned to give the same to others and as they changed, others in their lives either changed with them or moved out of their sphere of influence. And so where there had been anxiety, fear, mistrust, and manipulation before, the recovering addicts now found themselves surrounded with simple, calm, loving acceptance. It was a manifestation of the law of cause and effect. All that is going on outside our lives, all that surrounds us, is merely a reflection of what is going on inside. The world is our mirror; the people closest to us are our greatest teachers. Look at your life and learn about yourself.

The group ended its sharing, repeating together the words of the serenity prayer, and Lexie heard herself say the now familiar words:

God, grant me the serenity to accept the things I cannot change,
The courage to change the things I can
And the wisdom to know the difference.

As the meeting ended, the person beside Lexie shook his head and said, "Ya, that wisdom part. That's the tough one."

She smiled to herself as she stood up to leave. *Trust the universe to bring you what you need,* she thought to herself. *It's all about trust!*

As she walked back to rejoin the large group, a thought passed fleetingly through her mind. That burly, blonde man had been in her group again tonight. He'd been in the same small group as she had now for the past several weeks. She wasn't sure, but she could have sworn his number hadn't been the same as hers when they had called them out, dividing the large group up into smaller subgroups.

Hmmmmmm, she thought to herself. *Next week I'll pay more attention to what he does. I wonder…"*

"Four," she called out the next week as she sat in the large circle of the group meeting. She watched as everyone called out their numbers. When it came to her blonde man, she heard him distinctly call out, "One."

Well, he's definitely not supposed to be in my group this week. We'll see what happens.

After the coffee break when everyone was gathering in their designated small groups, there he was settling into group four's space, directly across from her. Throughout the session, he studied her carefully, listening intently to every word she said. *There's no doubt he knows a great deal about me by now,* she thought. *I've certainly held nothing back in these meetings!*

She began to look at him more closely, more aware of his presence.

After the meeting, many of them went to a local restaurant to socialize. It was here they would often network, offering advice if asked, passing on information they felt would be helpful, or seeking out a sponsor in the programme, someone they could call on for emotional support in times of need. There he was again, sitting at her table and watching her, again listening intently to all she had to say. He seemed a quiet man himself, not talking often, but when he did, he had such a marvellous way of wrapping everything that had been said in the last half hour into one little gem of humorous wisdom! A man of few words, but when he did speak, people appreciated the simple grace of what he had to say.

My god, she realized. *He's going to ask me out on a date!* She'd known even before the words had come out of his mouth!

What am I going to do about this? I can't believe I didn't see this coming sooner! Sometimes, Lexie, you are so dumb about these things, so unaware that someone could be interested in you. You figure that because you're not looking for a relationship, no one else is. Talk about egocentric thinking!

God, this is what is called Thirteen Stepping in the programme, isn't it? she thought to herself. *They warn newcomers about this. Dating someone in programme, before you're clear about your own issues, can have real pitfalls. After all, isn't that why we're all here? We were all relationship junkies, involved with others so we didn't have to be involved with ourselves! Lord, how am I going to handle this one?*

She mentally searched through all the stories, all the wisdom she had gleaned from her programme over the last few months. One comment made to her seemed to jump out at her now. Someone, she couldn't remember who, had responded to her question about the practice of "thirteen stepping" as dating was called, and they had simply said, "You can't learn about relationships in a closet! You've gotta get into one!"

Lordy, lordy! Lexie thought. *Do I want to do this? Do I want to date this man?* What she didn't realize was that she *was* asking herself what *she* wanted in this situation! That was progress!

At the same time the question came out of his mouth, the answer came into her mind.

Yes.

The logic that had helped her arrive at that answer went something like this: *He looks like a really nice man even if I don't think he's my type. I'm not particularly attracted to him so it should be a good safe place to start. I doubt that a relationship will develop, but it might be nice to go out and have some fun again.*

Driving home that night, she went over in her mind all that she had learned in the past weeks about this man. That was one thing about meeting someone in a recovery programme; there was a very good chance you were seeing the real person stripped of pretence. *One encouraging thing,* thought Lexie, *is at least men in the programme are aware they need help and are willing to change. That's better than most of the others walking around out there on the streets.* If she had to take a chance with anyone in a relationship, she felt she was at least stacking the odds in her favour by seeing someone who wasn't medicating his feelings through addictions and compulsive behaviours or being so busy running from the truth of his life that he was numbed by the novocaine of denial.

At least this guy would know better than to respond with, "I'm happy. We don't have a problem," she thought with sadness.

Awareness. That was the key. If this man was going to meetings, there was at least an awareness that the way he had been conducting his life up to this point had not worked. He had become teachable.

He came striding up to her front door that Saturday night dressed in a long, leather greatcoat to his ankles. It had a slit right up the back.

I wonder where he left his horse? Lexie chuckled to herself.

It was the latest fashion she knew, patterned as it was after the Australian outback riding coat.

I like that! she thought to herself. *A man with a sense of style and the courage to dress the way he wants to. What a change from Derek!*

Her blonde man's name was Thomas Allen Crown. He was fifty years old and the founder of a successful commercial real estate firm known as Crown Realty. He had made a fortune in the boom years of the last decade and had retired from his business leaving a manager to run it while he speculated away much of his fortune in the commodity market, his compulsion to make money taking him in search of broader horizons.

The company had been his child, his love, his passion for many years, born of his dream to carve out a niche no one else believed could be profitable. He hung tenaciously on to his dreams, even when everyone said it couldn't be done, and he'd proven them all wrong, everyone. Over the course of the next twenty years, he had gone on to make himself and all who worked for him very wealthy!

There had been a price exacted for his success. So focused on his dream that it had edged out everything else in his life, he had become obsessed with his work, with making money, and he'd allowed no time for children, a home, or for socializing and small talk. Everything he did served only one purpose—to build his fortune. If it did not, Thomas Crown did not bother with it.

As the years had gone by, he had avoided feeling the emptiness of his life, filling himself with alcohol and clouds of nicotine. Every night he stood in his office, drink in hand, cigarette always smouldering near by, and he would listen and advise, manipulate and control all those whose lives revolved around his.

Having internalized the belief that he could grow rich by helping others to do so, he became enmeshed in their lives and their problems, becoming a father to them all. His company functioned like one big codependent, dysfunctional family system and Thomas Crown felt responsible for it all!

And through it all he drank, smoked, and gambled compulsively trying to stuff his fear, his nagging sense of worthlessness, his emptiness. His marriage deteriorated before his very eyes as his wife had first one affair and then another. He did not see them as warning signs, as her way of crying out for his attention. All he saw was his hurt, the injustice done to him. Still he clung to her, telling himself he forgave her and burying his resentments in fantasies about other women. He ached to experience the conquest of other women, to avenge his hurt, yet life without his wife terrified him. For almost all of his twenty-six years of marriage, he had lived in fear of being left alone.

The day after their twenty-fifth wedding anniversary, his wife had started the process of ending their marriage. Wounded deeply by all the recognition and accolade heaped solely upon her husband for the success of the business that she had worked by his side to build, she had decided she could no longer go on with the empty shell of their life together.

Reacting to her decision, he desperately, frantically made changes in his life, flying immediately to New Mexico to spend a month in a treatment centre drying out. Coming off the alcohol and the cigarettes the day he arrived, he was introduced to the Twelve Step meeting and saw a therapist every day. When he returned home, he stood forlornly on the front step of his home only to read the note his wife had left pinned there. There was no mistaking its message; he read her words and his heart sank. There would be no second chance for Thomas Crown.

Bluntly, unfeelingly, her words had simply said: "You don't live here any more. Your clothes are packed, and in your car. You'll find them at 72 West Drive. I've rented that house in your name. That's where you live now."

The marriage thus ended, she took a million dollars in cash and assets with her. He was left with an ailing real estate company and the job of piecing together an understanding of how and why his life was now in shambles.

Reeling, he lived at recovery meetings, sometimes attending two or three a day. His daily planner was filled with appointments with therapists, health specialists, anyone he felt could help him understand and heal. So intense had his pain of rejection been that he never, ever wanted to be in that place again. Ignoring all gentle nudges to change over the many past years, he had finally received a blow that hit him right between the eyes with a not-so-gentle two-by-four. His life, at long last, had his attention.

Piecing together the details of Thomas's life, Lexie had to admit that the fact that he had been chemically addicted frightened her. But as she sat through dinner with him on their first night out together, she felt his gentleness as well as his pain as he said he did not blame anyone but himself, and he knew he had to change.

He made her laugh, really laugh, like she had not done in a very long time. His sense of self-deprecating humour surfaced often through that first date. Anyone who could laugh at himself was able to be more tolerant of others and of life in general she had discovered.

They pulled into her driveway, and Lexie's hand was on the door handle, ready to get out. She had no intention of getting involved with this man.

"I'll walk you to your door," he said, smiling at her.

"Oh, no. You don't have to do that." She was already making her move to get out.

He laughed. She turned and looked into his boyish, blue-eyed face.

"I thought if I did, I might get a kiss goodnight!"

He looked so innocent, so unassuming, so silently strong yet gentle, that she felt her resolve melting.

"Why not?" she heard herself answer flippantly.

Why not indeed! Turning to face him after she had fit her key into the lock, she saw him waiting patiently behind her. She prepared to give him a quick, friendly peck and then head into her house.

True to his word, he was every bit the gentleman, bending over her and placing a soft, gentle kiss on her lips.

No sooner had his lips left hers than she reached up, put her arms around his neck and wrapping her hands around the back of his head, pulled his face down toward hers, and placed her lips full on his. Not once, but twice more.

The only thought registering in her mind while she was busy kissing him was, "I want more of this!"

Breaking breathlessly away, she shut the door and leaned her weight full against it.

"Wow! What was that? I think I'm going to be involved whether I want to be or not!"

As she climbed the stairs to her bedroom, a recurring thought, nagging at her for weeks, pushed her to do something she had dismissed as nonsense.

Searching through her dresser drawer she found a sheaf of pink papers she had put there many years before. They contained information from a psychic reading which had been so strange, so shattering, that Lexie had been unable to destroy them. She had also hidden the papers from Derek.

As she pulled out the crumpled pieces and unfolded them, she sank down onto her bed, her eyes looking for the part she knew was there.

The old fortuneteller, looking up at her, had started and said the words right in the middle of shuffling. With a piercing, steady gaze, the cards suspended, she had said to Lexie like a bolt out of the blue, "Has anyone ever told you, you will be married more than once?"

Before Lexie had a chance to recover, she had again looked down at her cards, finished shuffling, and gone on to say. "Yes, here it is. You will be involved with a blonde man. He has a blonde woman around him, and they are involved in business together. No matter. You're going to marry him and be his business partner. I see the symbol of a Crown here and something to do with royalty or royalties."

The reading had gone on to tell of many more things, all of which had come true. It supposedly spanned a seven-year period of her life and as the years had ticked by surpassing the final year, and Lexie had remained married to Derek, she had dismissed the information as misguided. The prediction would surface occasionally in times of her unhappiness, but she always shrugged it off. The possibility of being married once more when she wasn't even free of the marriage she was in seemed so far away, so distant.

She had all but forgotten it. Until now.

Her hand trembled. Not wanting to read more into this than she should, she remembered that while the prediction itself was right, the interpretation of it often was not. But, she wondered, how many blonde men were there who could make her feel the way she had tonight?

"You get what you need when you need it." It was a well-worn meeting platitude, and it pretty much summed up Thomas Crown's role in her life.

They spent a lot of time together, and they were exactly what one another needed. Fitting together like a hand in a glove, their relationship became easy, effortless.

This is how relationships should be! Lexie thought ecstatically. *It's so easy to be with him because there's no judgement, no criticism. I'm free to be who I am and he respects me for it. I always knew being in love should be this way!*

Yes, she had to admit it. She was falling in love. But there was more, so much more that had opened up to her when Thomas Crown had walked into her life.

Watching her write her thoughts one day in the journal she kept, he started tentatively to outline his plan, a plan he had been formulating for quite some time now.

"Lexie, please don't take this the wrong way," he began. "But I've noticed two things about you that in my mind have come together as something potentially good for both of us."

Intrigued, Lexie looked up from her writing. Where was he going with this?

"You seem to write effortlessly, and you can get feelings down on paper like no one I've ever seen before. Some of the stuff about when you were a little kid, I mean, I can't believe how it makes me feel. You know, the tears well up inside of me when I read your words. It's like you understand *my* pain."

He took a deep breath. "Now here's the part I don't want you to misunderstand. Well, the fact is, I know you could use some extra money to get through this time with Derek, and I have this idea that you could write a book. A book about what it's like to grow up like we did; maybe help people understand themselves better. And if you want to, I'd be willing to help."

Lexie could only stare at him in amazement. Sure she'd always said she should write a book about her life, didn't everybody? But to actually do it, well, that was another matter entirely, never having written anything that had been published before. What made him think she could become a successful author just like that? Was he crazy or just crazy in love? Lexie knew emotion could cloud judgement, but she was intrigued. A seed had been planted.

"Do you think I could do it? Really?" she asked like a little kid, filled with amazement standing in front of a fairy godmother who'd just said, "Make a wish. Any wish!"

"Me, Alexis Alexander, an author? I just don't know. What would I say?"

"I think you already know," Tom answered quietly.

Lexie began. Awkwardly she'd sat at her computer, staring blankly into space, a cold shiver of fear running through her. It was absolutely ludicrous to think she could write a novel! She was a teacher not a writer.

"But, I know my students learn best when I use stories," she thought to herself. "Maybe if I just told my story…" Then she did what she was learning to do more and more these days—she slipped into the silence and asked for guidance.

"If this is meant to be, I know the words will come," she whispered to the wall.

And come they did, in a flood! Her inexperienced fingers flew over the keyboard attempting to capture each new thought and when at last she stopped, pages had been written. The story had a life of its own as if it had already been in her mind waiting, silently, patiently to be told.

Maybe, just maybe, she thought to herself, *I can do this.*

With each page the character grew, becoming more real. It was as if Lexie was rebirthing herself, labouring to bring forth her new life. Intense pain, no longer contained by denial, flooded her, threatening to wash from her consciousness the very reason for the process itself. Now, she found herself wanting to escape, to run from this self-appointed task. More than halfway through the writing of her story, Lexie, once again mired in despair, convinced herself she could never do what she had set out to do. Surrounded by reflections of herself, mirrors wrapped around her on all sides, Lexie sat one dreary day applying her mask of makeup, image looking at image. Suspended in a moment of time, her hand held in midair, adjusting the wisps of hair framing her face. Lexie heard the soft, familiar whisper ripple once again through her consciousness, "Why are you doing this? Is this the way it should be?"

Looking into that mirror, drawn deeper and deeper into gold-flecked eyes, she searched for an answer within herself. Looking boldly, powerfully, back at her were the eyes of the child who lived within the pages of her prose, daring her to finish!

"Coward! Let me grow! Give me life again! Take responsibility for what I became!"

Wiping too familiar tears of self-pity from her face, Lexie descended the stairs of the home Derek had left her in hoping she would sink in a sea of debt, walked into her den, and sat down with pad and pen. With hope for her future and determination to finish her past, she outlined the final chapters of her book. Chapters, she knew, which would bring her story to an end.

"If you don't shut up, I'll drive you into tomorrow! So help me God, I will, you bitch!"

Lexie could feel the flesh of Derek's knuckles as they brushed her cheek. Watching the rapid rise and fall of his chest, her eyes were transfixed, her body rigid as Derek hung menacingly over her. Leaden seconds ticked by, heavy with saving silence for to say one thing more would bring Derek's fist crashing into her face. Pinned to her chair by his menacing bulk, she knew the power to maim her was literally in his hands!

Looking beyond him, she saw Jessica, horror etched on her face. Emerging from another room of Derek's new apartment when he had raised his voice, she had now found the courage to plead for reason.

"Dad! What are you doing?! Look at yourself! It's over, Dad. Can't you just let Mom go?"

Derek's hand dropped to his side and he turned to face her, the pain of betrayal contorting his face.

Even though her father was wounded by her words, Jessica could not stop. She had to make him understand! Whatever he was, he was still her father, the only one she had, and she could not bear the thought he might hate her! The loyal, always hopeful, inner child reached out for, if no longer his love, then at the very least, his understanding.

"Dad, you've asked me why I've shut you out? Well, there it is, right there! Look at what you're doing! You can't be trusted! You only love us when we do what you want! How can I believe you when you say you love me, that you'll do anything to get me back, when I see the way you treat Mom. It's disgusting, Dad! You need help!"

With that said, she yanked his apartment door open, preparing to escape. She had taken a huge risk, and she knew what was coming next.

"Jessica, it's not how it looks. Your mother, she...she drives me to do this. She just won't listen to reason! It's her fault I get so violent. Let's go into the other room alone...Let me talk to you some more.

I can explain. Make you see my side of all this…" his words trailed off.

While he had been pleading with Jessica, Lexie had slowly raised herself out of the chair and was now quietly working her way toward the door. She too knew what was coming, and she wanted to be ready for it. The pattern was always the same.

As Jessica stood looking at her father, an expressions of contempt played across her pretty face.

"No, Dad," she said flatly. "Not this time. I'm not your little girl any more."

For a stunned moment Derek stood looking first at one and then the other. The realization slowly dawned. They were somehow different. Having stepped out of the circle of interaction, refusing to be sidetracked from the issue by his attacks on their character, they each demonstrated a new pattern of relating, and he was left standing foolishly exposed as the bully he was. Reacting in the only way he knew, he threw himself at them in a blind, explosive fit of rage, his body shaking as he spat out the words.

"Get the hell out then! Both of you! You bitches! Burn in hell! I never want to see either of you again!"

Grabbing Lexie roughly by the arm, he pulled her to the door and threw her unceremoniously into the hall. He then shoved Jessica out after her. The sound of the dead bolt sliding into place seemed his final judgement.

Trembling, they drove home in silence, both in shock, but once they arrived, Lexie said to the brave, young girl who had challenged her abusive father, "I'm going to do something I should have done a long time ago."

With that, she picked up the phone and dialled the police.

"I'll need to know everything that happened, Mrs. Gaust. Then I can advise you of your rights. I've been trained to handle just such situations as these." The handsome officer smiled at them both as he settled himself into a chair and prepared to take notes.

"He's so young!" thought Lexie to herself. "What can he possibly understand about all this? I'm so ashamed! Damn you, Derek! Why did it have to come to this? You and I fighting like little kids unable to settle our differences. Now this. Our immaturity is to be a matter of public record!"

It made her sad as she looked at the two, beautiful young faces in the room with her. What a tragedy that men and women so often made one another the enemy. Taking a deep breath, she faced the police officer, not sorry she had called him. Sad, yes. Sorry, no. Learning the difference between loving and enabling, she now understood that as long as she put herself in Derek's space, she was providing him with the opportunity to abuse her. What she and Jessica had done tonight had been very foolish, and she resolved it would never happen again. This young officer's presence signalled that Lexie was finally ready to do whatever was necessary to shield herself and her daughters from further abuse, even if it meant withdrawing herself from her own addiction to Derek and his chaos.

"Can you tell me just why you and your daughter went to visit Mr. Gaust tonight?" the officer's voice intruded upon her thoughts.

"I can answer that," Jessica's voice, clear and strong, came from across the room. "It was mainly for me. I asked Mom to go for support. You see, this is really hard for me, sir, you see, well, I have a situation with my father. Let's just say I'm in therapy because of my relationship with him. I had reached a point in my recovery where I felt I just had to confront him. I needed to have him hear what I had to say."

Jessica looked quickly at the officer, beseeching him not to press for more details, and then with her face and neck flaming, she looked quickly away.

God, this is so hard for her! thought Lexie, her mind flashing back to the quiet, sweet little girl she had been. *How could he? How could he have done such a thing to her?* Lexie's mind still reeled with the horror of it all.

Listening tonight as Jessica had confronted her father, she had felt her daughter's pain, her deep sense of sadness at his betrayal.

Derek had insisted he talk with his daughter in private, taking her into the other room when she had asked to speak to him. That was so typically his style thought Lexie. Always divide and conquer. Always play one against the other.

He needn't have bothered. Lexie could hear her daughter's angry words clearly through the thin walls of his apartment.

With each accusation Jessica had told her truth, not waiting nor caring for her father's validation. She told of her life of fear under his roof, how he had robbed her of her innocence, her safety, her sense of self. She told him of her need for support groups and therapy sessions, of the sheer panic that would descend upon her at the thought of being with a man. She spoke of the nightmares torturing her night and day. As she spoke, he listened silently, his eyes staring belligerently into hers, no warmth, compassion, or comfort there, only cold, grey eyes looking back at her. Her throat began to close in around her words, choking them off. She despised this man! From his lips, she needed to hear why!

"Why, Daddy?" The broken inner child whispered the unanswerable question.

In agony she waited as the silence descended like a wall, feeling as if she would explode outside of herself, flying into a million shattered pieces, destroyed by the secret she kept locked within. If she was to survive, she had to say the words!

"Dad, it was you wasn't it?" She whispered. "You're the reason I'm the way I am." Pausing, she looked directly into his face. "You made me do things to you, disgusting things, didn't you?" Her eyes never left his.

Her father's slid to the floor.

"How can you think that of me? You're being ridiculous," he mumbled weakly, his voice trailing off. In a heartbeat, he had changed the subject, as if her words had never been spoken. The conversation was ended; the matter closed. Derek had no desire to explore the matter further; his daughter would have to do her healing on her own.

"After that he became abusive with Mom." Jessica added.

Lexie was abruptly brought back to the present with the mention of her name.

Gently prodding them about other incidences of abuse, the officer documented them all. Then stroking his face thoughtfully, he took his time before responding. "Well, Mrs. Gaust, I'm afraid there's not a lot we can do here. Am I correct when I say that you were in Mr. Gaust's apartment and that you were there uninvited?"

"Yes. We had felt it best to just drop in on him rather than let him prepare for our arrival. Why, is that important?" Lexie asked.

"It's important because you were technically trespassing on his property. In this particular case of threatened assault, the law can do nothing to help you. However, if you had pressed charges the time he assaulted you in your own home, then we could have acted."

"Could you have arrested him then?" Lexie asked incredulously. She was having a hard time believing the law could act so swiftly to protect abused wives.

"Yes, we could have arrested him that time if you had been prepared to lay charges." The officer was very specific.

"I see," Lexie mused. Impressed and gratified at being treated with such respect, she certainly could not complain that she was not being taken seriously by the local law enforcement agency. It didn't stop there, however.

The officer looked at her with concern. "Mrs. Gaust, there is something I can do for you, however. It really bothers me to see men who think they can talk to women with their fists. I can pay your husband an official visit and give him a warning. That might frighten him into behaving himself. If he's the type of man you say he is, he probably has a fear of authority figures. I can quite accurately tell him that if he threatens you again, he will be arrested. We will also have a record of this incident on file. If he bothers you, or even so much as comes to the house, use this phone number to call the station. Ask for me or if I'm not there, just quote this file number. That way we can give you the protection you need."

With that he got up to leave and as Lexie shook his hand, she felt blessed to live in a time and place where a woman's right to live free from physical domestic violence was being protected.

Grandma only had her broom. With that thought, Lexie felt proud of all the women who had travelled the long, arduous path of restoring the dignity of being female. She also felt affection for all the caring men, who, often challenging the custom of their times, had also helped smooth the way.

The officer was true to his word, and Lexie heard nothing from Derek for months.

"What do you mean I have no claim to it?"

Lexie, in her lawyer's office with files stacked around the desk, children poking their heads through the doorway, and a secretary interrupting every five minutes to find a misplaced file, was finding what she had been told incomprehensible. On top of all of these apparent signs of incompetence and unprofessional business practice, previously ignored because Lexie had wanted to be represented by a female lawyer, she was now hearing information her lawyer had assumed Lexie already knew. It was just too much to bear!

"No, no, dear! Child support is not paid retroactively. How long have you been separated now, anyway?" her lawyer asked distractedly as she went rummaging through the pile looking for Lexie's file.

It was time for a new lawyer! Woman or no woman, the bonds of sisterhood only went so far. In Lexie's way of thinking, equal rights should demand equal competence.

Assume, assume. Lexie ran the word over and over in her head as she left the office. *You know what that word stands for don't you?* she asked herself. *Ass-u-me. Makes an ass outa u and an ass outa me!*

Yes, she knew what the word meant. She was also learning it was not what lawyers told you that you had to watch out for. It was what they didn't say that seemed to separate you from your money!

Having grown through all of these experiences, Lexie sat across from her new lawyer, a three hundred dollar an hour Queen's Counsel, and she proceeded to tell him what she wanted done. She had to take responsibility for directing the process for the lawyer's advice and knowledge could not take the place of, was not intended to take the place of, her own decision making. What would she accept and what would she not accept? This was the ultimate exercise for an individual without good personal boundaries. Perhaps, you really do get what you need when you need it.

Her new lawyer was known in legal circles as a barracuda—the one lawyers went to when they wanted their divorces.

Well, why not? thought Lexie. *I'm going swimming with a shark.*

At the beginning of their productive, if expensive relationship, a dapper, elegantly dressed, Stewart James Douglas, Queen's Counsel lawyer, extended his hand and in a very cultured British accent assured her he would attend immediately to all they had discussed.

Just how much is self-respect worth? Lexie asked herself as she descended the lofty office tower to the street below. She supposed she could roll over and play dead about this whole situation. Derek had no intention of supporting his children; that was very evident. Perhaps it would be easier and cheaper to just let it all go. That's how she'd handled so much of Derek's bad behaviour in the past. She'd just let it go.

Yes, and that nearly cost me my sanity! her mind shot back. Just where were all these thoughts coming from lately? Hardly recognizing her own thinking, it was like a different person was living in her head—one whom she was coming to love and respect! This new, stronger being believed when someone pushed unfairly, you owed it to yourself to push back! Wow! What a new concept! If for no one else but herself, she needed her day in court with Derek.

"Guilty! Guilty! Guilty! You're wrong, Mrs. Gaust. You owe your husband a living! It was your job to take care of his needs! He wasn't so bad! You just failed to live up to your duties as his wife! You just expected too much from him. You were born to suffer. You're still meant to suffer! As an inferior female, I order you to support this male emotionally and financially as long as you live!"

The wooden wall of the judge's bench loomed in front of her. The male in black robes leered over at her. She was shrinking, shrivelling inside.

No! No! No! It just couldn't be so! No judge today would rule that way, would they? Desperate to be heard, to make the judge reconsider, she pummelled her fists against the barricade in front of her.

"It's not fair! It's not fair!" she screamed. "All I wanted was my freedom!"

The rush of breath being sucked into her lungs, the roar of the blood racing past her ears, the jerk as her body catapulted her upright and back into consciousness, left her soaked with sweat, sitting in the middle of her rumpled bed, facing the fear of her nightmare. What if Derek won?

He had countersued immediately after Lexie's lawyer had filed her petition for child support. His position was that he was no longer employed and therefore could not support his childrenand also required personal support from Lexie who was working. His countersuit went on to state that because one child was over eighteen and the other rapidly approaching that age, he had no legal obligation to be financially responsible for them even though they were both still in school full time.

Lexie was well aware Derek could legally sue for support. Recent legislation had conferred the right of spousal support on men as well as women. Equality was a two-edged sword which could cut both ways. Derek also intended to claim half of her teacher's pension.

Overreacting as she often did, Lexie moved into the fear that Derek would not only deprive her of what was rightfully hers, but go on to exact more than his pound of flesh. Driven by vindictiveness, Derek had declared he would never let her go, that if he could not have her he would make her life hell.

Images of destitute divorced women, flashed through her fear-filled mind. Why had she dared to rattle Derek's cage? Why hadn't she left well enough alone? Already the legal bills were mounting.

Raised as most of her generation had been on a weekly diet of Perry Mason courtroom dramas, Lexie was startled to experience her country's legal system firsthand. Her nightmare of pleading before a judge most likely would never happen. When her case finally was presented for decision, she would not even be required to be present! She would be required to appear at a procedure called an Examination of Discovery. This phrase actually described the process quite well. Lexie and Derek, at different times, would be required to appear and make themselves available for questioning by the other party's lawyer. Examined under oath, every word would be dutifully recorded.

Taken into a small informal room, they would be allowed to drink coffee or smoke, and in the presence of the two lawyers and a secretary, would proceed to answer, honestly and directly, all questions posed to them by the opposing side's legal counsel. Her part of the procedure would probably take two hours or so she had been told.

Arriving at the large downtown office building well before the appointed time, she was nervous, but well prepared, having gone over her sworn affidavit many times. She knew Derek's lawyer would use the facts contained in it as the basis for his questions, and she had also been told he would concentrate on catching her in a lie.

Mr. Douglas had also told her to volunteer no more information than was asked for. Looking carefully at her, he'd then said he didn't feel it was required to give her the rest of his standard client speech about being pleasant and polite. That, he said, she would handle quite naturally. He had informed her the reason for politeness was not to make life easier for the lawyers but to impress upon Derek's lawyer that she was someone a judge could like. That, he said, would make it harder for him to build a convincing case against her in the event this ever did make it to court.

Lexie was absolutely amazed at the strategies behind everything. *These guys are playing chess with my future!* she thought. *What ever happened to the good old-fashioned idea that justice will prevail?*

Having taken to heart her lawyer's advice, she no longer dealt with Derek directly, and she had been relieved that she would not have to be present in the room at the same time. The memory of her husband's fist in her face was fresh enough that she had no intention of putting herself at risk again.

It was with shock then that she looked up from her seat in the waiting room to see Derek bearing down on her. She had not been warned he was being examined right before she was. She stood stunned as curt, formal introductions were made and then, as the two lawyers took a moment to speak to one another, Derek zeroed in on her.

Taking her elbow to steer her away from them, he bent down and hissed in her ear. "Can we talk, alone?" There was an uneasy tone in his voice.

Lexie turned and looked into those unflinching, steel-grey eyes.

Like an electric shock, she knew! She could read his fear. It had not gone well for him. He had been caught up in his own lies and manipulations.

But, he never gives up! thought Lexie. *He still wants to work on me, hoping to convince me to get back into line. He has to win at all costs, any way he can!*

For just a split second, she wavered. A small part of her felt sorry for this frightened man-child who could only define himself by what he could control. Perhaps she should be fair to him and hear him out. Then it struck her. Was she nuts? Nothing changes if nothing changes! This man had been abusive for over twenty-three years! When was it going to be enough?

"No. That's not possible." Without apology or excuse, she turned and walked into the examination room, anxious to begin the end.

Seated across the table was a plump, full-faced man Lexie learned was Mr. Ratting, Derek's lawyer. With her own lawyer at her side, Lexie looked over at the secretary who was in front of a keyboard with a strange cone-shaped mouth piece placed so she could dictate into it. Then while observing her husband's choice of lawyer more carefully, she wondered what she could glean from his countenance. Like attracts like she thought ruefully. If that's true, I'm in for a rough afternoon!

He was good at his job, very good. Pleasant and smiling, but all the while looking for discrepancies, he went over her statement thoroughly, asking for documents to support much of the information. Often, he would begin his line of questioning in a very relaxed, friendly way, then, when he felt her guard was down, his tone would change, and he would challenge her response. With any misstep on her part, he would have been very capable of destroying her credibility.

But she didn't lie. Not out to cheat Derek of what was rightfully his, she had no desire to destroy him financially. Any falsehoods in her statements were born of her misperceptions.

Lexie had searched her soul and had answered the best way she knew how. A terrible liar, she had no skill in or patience for negotiation. Naively, she was hoping for a simple win-win solution.

However, she could not resist one last parting critical thought. As they all stood up to leave the room and Derek's lawyer laid his briefcase on the table to snap it shut, she noticed, embossed in gold letters along its side, the initials 'Q.C.'

A Queen's Counsel lawyer! They were the cream of the crop in the legal system. So typical of Derek she thought—no money to support his children, but money for the best in lawyers.

There was nothing to do but return home and wait as it would likely be months before the next step in the process. If a settlement out of court was not possible, the two lawyers would then go forward to argue before a judge. Neither Lexie nor Derek was required to be present at that time, their cases argued solely on the basis of the testimony they had given today.

Even though she felt reasonably good about how the day had gone, she went home full of the 'what ifs' mantra of negative meditation. Lexie was so well practised that she could do it any time of day or night, while walking around, through all kinds of distractions, while someone was talking to her, while she was eating, watching a movie, or having sex.

Lexie was not alone in the practice of this type of meditation; she had noticed it was the most widely used socially acceptable means of dealing with problems. Openly everywhere, around office watercoolers, dinner tables, schoolrooms, hospitals, and highways, people indulged in its practice. But strangely enough, no one ever seemed to report on its effectiveness. Every time she used negative meditation, it took her further away from her centre of peacefulness. She wondered if other practitioners had the same negative result? In the Twelve Step programme Lexie had learned that what you focus on, you get more of. No wonder she'd had so much fear in her life! She resolved to stop what the she had come to think of as negative meditation, but what the rest of the world simply called worrying.

Habit had allowed many fears to swirl, circling, hovering around the centre of her being. Now, two times each day, she would switch gears and move forward, going within to her peaceful centre. There, in the eye of the storm, she would find calm. In these moments of quiet she would know she was doing what she needed to do. No matter what the result, the process was the purpose.

Connecting daily with an unseen power, a force gifted her with the understanding that she could survive whatever came her way.

"That which does not kill us, makes us stronger!" she would hear herself say.

Going into the silence, Lexie could feel a calmness befall her, and she would feel a presence, walking every step of this frightening journey with her, supporting her, guiding her, even carrying her when needed. Sitting in the silence, she would dialogue inside her head with this God of hers, and over the months a strange awareness took hold. All she required was already given!

In the silence, her fear-filled inner voice stilled, she begged, bargained, and pleaded no longer. Like a novice, seated in a hushed and hallowed concert hall come to witness a master perform, Lexie at last understood how to fulfil her human divinity. Finally, she did that which was destined by divine design. She listened! And in the silence, wisdom came. Words, thoughts, phrases—simple, pure, knowing. The ego's constant chatter at last stilled, it exited the stage, leaving the spotlight focused where it belonged. There, in the centre of this drama called life, flooding and filling all with its light, the still, small voice called her home to herself.

The barren, budless, boughs of the trees, buffeted by the raw, spring wind whipped to and fro in front of the large panes of glass soaring all the way to the ceiling and filling the courtroom walls. Seated at the back of the long, narrow room, directly in line with the centre point of the judge's bench, Lexie's lawyer sat nervously beside her, fingering the brightly marked and underlined transcript pages. Deep in his own thoughts, he left Lexie to observe the room and its proceedings on her own.

Entering the half-empty courtroom that day, she scanned it quickly, searching for Derek's presence, noting Mr. Ratting's head as it bobbed up in surprise at her appearance. Fully aware that her presence was not required, this day, Lexie knew, had a significance far beyond any of the outcomes it might generate.

Her presence was a statement of commitment to herself. Whatever occurred, she wanted to be a part of it, never again to passively hand over the responsibility for her life to another.

Derek, she noted, had chosen not to be present.

Sensing proceedings were about to begin, her lawyer stirred nervously beside her, clearing his throat in preparation.

Good, thought Lexie. *I'm glad he's nervous. It means he cares about doing a good job, especially now that I'm here to watch what he does.*

She had faith in her lawyer in as much as she could have faith in anyone steeped in a system she believed was less than perfect when responding to the need for justice. Educate not legislate had always been her belief. She dreamed of the day when just principles would be so internalized people would behave in harmony with them—a day when love would lead unerringly to the fulfilment of the law.

"All rise!" The rumbling sound of bodies lifting from their seats, the pounding of the gavel to bring court to order, startled Lexie from her reflections.

Here we go! she thought. Silently, comfortably, she sat trusting the process.

Listening intently as Mr. Douglas read from her husband's transcript, Lexie was shocked as disturbing facts were revealed. Her lawyer was holding nothing back.

Even though this was a civil court with no jurisdiction over criminal matters, Mr. Douglas did not hesitate for a moment to bring out—in rebuttal to Mr. Ratting's statement that because the daughters refused to see their father he was justified in his lack of financial support—the reason for that refusal. Bluntly, he stated the oldest daughter believed she had been sexually abused by the father and was now in therapy for treatment of said abuse.

Queried by the judge as to the father's reply to this accusation, Mr. Ratting read a section of transcript which said simply, "Yes, I am aware that she believes that." Nothing more was asked or volunteered on the matter.

Lexie could not help but wonder if the judge was affected by this information. She, herself, had certainly thought a lot about it lately and had discussed the matter at length with Jessica many times. Convinced Derek was guilty, she had no qualms about exposing him. Keeping his sickness secret, she believed, was more than he deserved. But, she had to respect that this horrid thing had happened to her daughter and not to her. Jessica had to be the one to decide how it would be dealt with. And Jessica, as victims often do, still carried shame about the abuse. Reluctant to bring it out into the open because she feared the reaction of others, Jessica had thus chosen not to proceed with legal action against her father. Lexie hoped for the day when Jessica would be free of shame, knowing in her heart that the child is blameless. For now, Lexie had to have faith enough in her beautiful daughter to let her travel her own path and accept as vindication enough Jessica's permission to have the abuse stated for the record during these proceedings.

"That would have been done then for the purposed of income tax evasion?" The judge was asking for clarification on a point raised by her lawyer. It seemed Mr. Douglas, in his examination of Derek's bankbooks, had discovered large sums of money passing through the accounts that Derek could not explain. None of this money appeared as income on Derek's financial statements.

So! thought Lexie. *He has been earning money all along!*

There it was. The reason she was sitting in this courtroom. Derek always put money first! She'd been unable to live with that any longer.

Mr. Douglas wrapped up his presentation and turned the courtroom floor over to Derek's lawyer, smiling at Lexie confidently as he slid into the seat beside her, well pleased with the job he had done for his client.

Lexie also felt there was very little which could be said to redeem Derek. Cleverly his lawyer, however, made a valiant effort building his case around the ages of the children and stating precedents where child support had been denied on that basis.

As the judge asked for a recess to further consider the material before rendering his decision, Lexie was fully aware that his ruling would be made solely on the basis of what the law stated each was responsible for. Impersonal and impartial, the law looked strictly at facts and figures and interpreted them in the light of legisled definitions of fairness and previous interpretations of that fairness. The judge's decision would have little to do with the perceived injustice of one person's control over another.

As everyone filed back into the courtroom after the recess, Lexie sat at the back once again, peaceful within herself. To have come this far was enough. This day in court had been about her personal growth, not about Derek or his money, and she was content to leave it at that.

"All rise!" The judge entered and took his seat.

He looks so young, she thought to herself. *How can he possibly understand all this? Maybe they're all just starting to look so young, because I'm getting older.* She chuckled inside herself, amazed at how lighthearted she felt. Did all of this—money, power, and control—really matter that much?

She looked out through the tall windows as she rose. The sun was breaking through the grey clouds, filling the courtroom with light.

"Mr. Gaust's claim for spousal support is denied. Child support for the oldest child, Jessica Alexandra Gaust is denied on the basis of age. Support for the youngest child, Jade Emily Gaust, is awarded to be paid monthly beginning immediately. Collection of said support to be made the responsibility of the court. All court costs awarded to Mrs. Gaust. A full transcript of my decision is available from the court clerk. Proceedings on this interim matter now concluded. Next case please."

That was it. She'd done exactly what she had set out to do, winning a victory in principle at least! The laws of society would make Derek do that which he was not moral enough or mature enough to do on his own. Like a petulant child who had not agreed with the way the game had been played, Derek had tried to take his toys and go home. *Well,* Lexie thought, *if love wasn't enough to make you play fair, then the law is.*

Strange, Lexie mused. *The support awarded is the exact amount Jessica's therapy costs each month!*

No longer did Lexie feel the panic of not being able to provide for her children, recognizing she must get out of their way and let them take responsibility for their own futures. Still, she chose to take the amount as a sign of divine justice. Was Derek being held accountable for the abuse of his daughter, if not in the courts of this world, then in the grand scheme of things?

Striding out of the courtroom, her head held high, she took her lawyer's hand and shook it firmly, thanking him. Then she turned from him and walked proudly to the door leading to the steps outside. She felt strong, empowered!

Heads turned as she walked by them, and she could feel the waves of energy emanating from her. Every part of her felt alive, filled with the power of life. She'd done it! She'd stood up to her fears, faced them, conquered them! She'd gone into battle and she'd won, at long last, rescuing herself! In this moment, there was nothing she feared to face!

Striding toward the door that led to the outside world, her face beaming, her hand outstretched, she reached for its brass handle.

"Let me," came a male voice beside her.

Lexie beamed as he swung the door wide for her.

"It must be my lucky day!" she said, the smile still in her voice.

"No," he said, thoughtfully appraising all she was. "You just live right."

She paused a moment to take in this strange reply, and then answered on her way through the door, "Now I do. Now I do."

The refrain continued to whisper happily in her heart as she stepped out into the April sunshine.

Standing for a moment to catch her breath, Lexie stared up at the tall, sky-filling buildings surrounding her. She could feel dwarfed by them or uplifted by them, whichever she chose, for they represented the powerful potential of the human spirit to soar above all earthly limitations. Today, Lexie was soaring!

Joyously, purposefully she shot her arms up into the air again and again, doing a crazy victory dance. She had to move, to express this energy flowing through her. From her insides came an incredible word filled with power! The force of it threw her head back as it tumbled from her throat. Her face skyward, her feet gleefully skipped over one another.

"Yes! Yes! YES!" she chanted. "Yes, to life and all that it is!"

A taxicab pulled up to the curb in front of her. Its door swung open. "Can I take you home, Miss?" the driver asked.

"Yes, at last you can."

"It's two years, two years. Tomorrow it will be two years ago I asked for my freedom."

Lexie was sitting in the same backyard, looking at the same swimming pool with the afternoon sun sparkling on its waters. The roses in her garden were in full, glorious bloom, the sun was again on her face, and she had again said the words.

A week before, Jessica had careened off the road on her way home from work, barely escaping from the wrecked car with her life. For well over a year there had been no contact with Derek. Was it the realization that he had come close to never having the opportunity to speak to his daughter again that prompted him to pick up the telephone that day? Lexie did not know, and she did not care. In her mind, Derek had chosen his own path.

As she hung up the phone, she thanked God for two things. Her daughter had survived, and Derek was at last willing to let go.

Abusive and angry, he had hung up on her three separate times. Still finding it difficult to accept he could not control her through intimidation, he cursed and he swore, but he finally accepted her terms.

In a flat, expressionless tone he had at last said the words she wanted to hear. Through it all she had remained calm, unmovable, a broken record stating the same conditions over and over again. Refusing to be drawn into his accusations, she did not challenge his perception of the truth. She would only say in response, "I'm sorry you feel that way, but here is what I am prepared to do. Here is what I can accept."

Simply stating and restating her position, she did not waver.

The words finally came. "I'll accept your offer to settle, Lexie."

It was a fair offer. She had been told so by the many professionals whose advice she had sought. It was also the same offer she had made years ago and for which she had been thrown out of Derek's apartment!

As much as she loved her own daughter, Lexie did not believe it had been Jessica's narrow brush with death that had caused Derek's change of heart. No, it was something much simpler than that. Derek was running out of money. His own lies had tripped him up. The court collection agency was closing in on him, threatening to seize his assets.

Surveying the beauty of the backyard, Lexie had placed the phone gently, thoughtfully back in its cradle. It would be hard to leave all of this, but it was a symbol of a way of life she no longer embraced, and she knew the house had to be sold.

"A perfect piece of fruit, rotten at its core."

She remembered how she had felt that day two years before. She had all the material things, the appearance of success that should have been so gratifying, but Lexie had felt a bitter hollowness, a void never to be filled. Everything had been built around the wrong relationship! Power had been handed over without a whimper, the marriage alive, but the bride dead!

Lexie smiled in remembrance. *The relationship I should have built was with myself! I should have been my own centre. Well,* she laughed out loud at the irony of the thought, *now the marriage is dead, but the bride lives!*

In the stillness of the moment, she sat fully aware of her thoughts, her feelings, fully present in this moment of her life.

Pulsing with the serene joy and acceptance of being all that she was, she was thinking about her life, today!

EPILOGUE

꒒

Casandra Hart's mother, after intensive therapy at the age of sixty, discovered she had been a victim of childhood sexual abuse. At the tender age of three, bewildered, she had stood at the foot of her parents' bed trying to express to her mother what her father had done to her only moments before.

Years of self-destructive addictive behaviour led Ms. Hart's mother to therapy, where she found the courage to seek validation from her siblings. One after another, they confirmed they too had suffered a similar fate at the hands of a controlling, rage-aholic father, both feared and paradoxically adored.

The author, her life thus shaped by the sexual abuse and subsequent addiction of a parent, is still on her journey of self-discovery. Leaving teaching to write, pursue her ministry, speak at Twelve Step meetings, and lead self-empowerment seminars, she is passionately committed to helping her fellow "travellers." As she uses her gift of channelled insights, her experiences in the service of others have only deepened her belief in something "more."

She writes because she believes that "True freedom is liberating someone by telling your story."

ABOUT THE AUTHOR

༉

Casandra Hart, teacher, author, nondenominational minister, and seminar leader now resides happily in Toronto, Canada. With two grown daughters, she is also a very proud grandmother.

After ending a twenty-three-year verbally and physically abusive marriage, she was determined never again to experience that type of pain and shame. Finding herself attending twelve-step meetings for recovering codependents (modeled after the spiritually based recovery program of Alcoholics Anonymous), she became aware, through a systematic and honest self-examination, that she had indeed been addicted to toxic relationships.

As part of the healing process, it was suggested she do a "fourth step"—a fearless and searching moral inventory of her life.

Her book, *The Sovereign Soul: A Story of Personal Power*, is the result of that step.

Whether you received *The Sovereign Soul: A Story of Personal Power* as a gift, borrowed it from a friend, or purchased it yourself, here at Sovereign Soul Seminars, we're glad you read it!

If you are interested in sharing your response with the author, would like information about her speaking engagements, or would like to invite her to speak at an event you are hosting, please address all correspondence to:

Sovereign Soul Seminars,
20 Harding Blvd. W., Suite 901,
Richmond Hill, Ont.
CANADA
L4C 9S4
e-mail casandrahart@rogers.com
or visit her website at
www.hart2heart.ca

Printed in the United States
66041LVS00003B/61-171

9 781600 344640